TOKYO STATION

Also by Martin Cruz Smith

MARTIN CRUZ SMITH

TOKYO STATION

MACMILLAN

First published 2002 by Simon and Schuster, Inc., New York

First published in Great Britain 2002 by Macmillan
an imprint of Pan Macmillan Ltd
Pan Macmillan, 20 New Wharf Road, London N1 9RR
Oxford and Basingstoke
Associated companies throughout the world
panmacmillan.com

ISBN 1 405 00116 X HB
ISBN 0 333 90692 6 PB

Copyright © Titanic Productions 2002

The right of Martin Cruz Smith to be identified as the
author of this work has been asserted by him in accordance
with the Copyright, Designs and Patents Act 1988.

The permissions on page vi constitute an extension of
this copyright page.

3 5 7 9 8 6 4 2

A CIP catalogue record for this book is available from
the British Library.

Printed and bound in Great Britain by
Mackays of Chatham plc, Chatham, Kent

For Em

ACKNOWLEDGMENTS

IT IS ALWAYS AMAZING how generously people offer their time, encouragement and expertise to a writer they have never met before. For the writer, they are the bridge that mysteriously appears as he crosses an abyss.

In America, I am indebted to Mary Culnane and Joe Morganti, Serge Petroff and Hiro Sato, Irwin Scheiner and Cecil Uyehara. Kathryn Sprague, Nell and Nelson Branco and Luisa Cruz Smith read various versions of the book. Ann Lamott shared the letters written home by her grandfather, a missionary in prewar Japan. Knox Berger shared the notes he made on a fire raid over Tokyo. David Rosenthal rolled the dice with Harry.

In Japan, I was aided and informed by Toshio Kanamura, Misao Maeda, Peter O'Connor, Armin Rump and Allen West, Andrew and Mariko Obermeier. Takashi Utagawa chased facts, maps and charcoal-powered taxis. David Satterwhite and Clifford Clarke described the unique experience of growing up as a Southern Baptist in Japan.

Finally, Jish Martin read manuscript, translated material and corrected mistakes almost as fast as I produced them.

And Ted Van Doorn took it on himself to literally lead me through another world.

TOKYO STATION

Letter from Tokyo

JAPAN APPEARS CALM AT BRINK OF WAR
British Protest "Defeatist Speech" by American

By Al DeGeorge
Special to <u>The Christian Science Monitor</u>

TOKYO, DEC. 5—While last-minute negotiations to avert war between
the United States and Japan approached their deadline in Washington,
the average citizen of Tokyo basked in unusually pleasant December
weather. This month is traditionally given to New Year's preparations
and 1941 is no exception. Residents are sprucing up their houses,
restuffing quilts and setting out new tatamis, the grass mats that
cover the floor of every Japanese home. When Tokyoites meet, they dis-
cuss not matters of state but how, despite food rationing, to secure the
oranges and lobsters that no New Year's celebration would be complete
without. Even decorative pine boughs are in short supply, since the
American embargo on oil has put most civilian trucks on blocks. One
way or another, residents find ingenious solutions to problems caused
by the embargo's sweeping ban on everything from steel and rubber to
aviation fuel. In the case of oil, most taxis now run on charcoal
burned by a stove in the trunk. Cars may not have the old oomph, but
passengers in Tokyo have learned to be patient.

In a country where the emperor is worshiped, there is no doubt about
Japan's position in the negotiations, that Japan has fairly won China
and deserves to have the embargo lifted. The American position, that
Japan must withdraw its troops first, is considered hypocritical or mis-
guided. Secretary of State Cordell Hull and Secretary of War Henry
Stimson are regarded here as unfriendly, but the Japanese people have
great faith in President Franklin Roosevelt as a more sympathetic ear.
A Ginza noodle vendor gave his appraisal of the high-level stalemate:
"It is the same with all negotiations. At the last moment, resolution!"

In fact, one of the most anticipated events is the release of the
censor's list of new films from Hollywood. There is no embargo on American movies. They fill the theaters, and stars like Bette Davis and Cary

-1-

Grant grace the covers of fan magazines here. The older generation may sit still for Kabuki, but the younger set is wild for the silver screen.

The only frayed nerves visible showed in a speech delivered today at the Chrysanthemum Club, the meeting place for Tokyo's banking and industrial elite. American businessman Harry Niles declared that Japan had just as much right to interfere in China as America did to "send the marines into Mexico or Cuba." Niles described the American embargo as an effort to "starve the hardworking people of Japan." He also attacked Great Britain for "sucking the life's blood of half the world and calling it a Christian duty."

British Embassy First Secretary Sir Arnold Beechum said that Niles's words were "out-and-out defeatist. The French and the Danes fell through the treasonous activities of collaborationists just like Niles. We are seriously considering a protest to the American embassy over the activities of their national." The American embassy refused to comment, although one official suggested that Niles had stood outside embassy control for a long time. The official, who preferred anonymity, said the club's choice of Niles as its speaker was telling. "It's a strong suggestion of Japanese impatience with the talks in Washington, an ominous indication, I'm afraid."

Otherwise, the city went about its business in its usual brisk fashion, squirreling away treats for the New Year, perhaps lighting an extra stick of incense to pray with, but apparently confident that no final rupture will break Japan's amiable relationship with the United States.

CABLE TRANSMISSION
DENIED

MUST BE TRANSLATED INTO JAPANESE FOR CABLE TRANSMISSION

1922

1

FIVE SAMURAI crept forward with a scuffle of sandals, eyes lit like opals by a late setting sun. A bloody haze flooded the alley, tinting street banners red, soaking drab wooden shops and houses in a crimson wash.

The story was tragic, true, profoundly satisfying. Lord Asano had been taunted by the unscrupulous Lord Kira into drawing a sword in the shogun's presence, an act punishable by death. He was beheaded, his estate confiscated and his retainers dispersed as ronin, wandering samurai with neither home nor allegiance. Although the evil Kira went unpunished, he watched the samurai, especially their captain, Oishi, for the slightest sign that they plotted revenge. And when, after two years, Kira's vigilance finally relaxed, on a snowy December night, Oishi gathered the forty-six other ronin he trusted most, scaled the walls of Kira's palace, hacked the guards to pieces, hauled Kira himself from his hiding place and cut off his head, which they carried to the grave of their dead Lord Asano.

Gen, the strongest and fastest boy, played Oishi, his leadership marked by the aviator's goggles he set high on his head. Hajime, second in command, had a face round as a pie pan and wore a baseball catcher's quilted vest as his suit of armor. Tetsu wrapped muslin around his waist, the style of a criminal in training. The Kaga twins,

Taro and Jiro, were rotund boys in raveled sweaters. Both were ready to eat nails for Gen if he asked. Each of the five boys swung a bamboo rod for a sword, and each was deadly serious.

Gen motioned Hajime to look around the ragpicker's cart, Tetsu to search among the sacks stacked outside the rice shop, the twins to block any escape from a side alley of brothels and inns. Prostitutes watched from their latticed windows. It was summer, the peak of a warm afternoon, with neither clouds nor customers in sight, shabbiness plain, the city's poor clapboard houses huddled like a hundred thousand boats battered and driven by storm from the bay to founder along rivers, canals and filthy sluices, here and there a glint of gilded shrines, at all levels laundry rigged on poles, and everywhere the scurrying of children like rats on a deck.

"Kira!" Gen called out. "Lord Kira, we know you're here!"

A whore with a face painted white as plaster hissed at Tetsu and nodded through her bars to a pile of empty sake tubs at the alley's end. Gen approached with wide-apart legs, his bamboo sword held high over his head with both hands. As he brought it down, the tubs thumped like drums. His second stroke was a thrust. The tubs rolled away and Harry squirmed out, his ear pouring blood.

Tetsu jabbed at Harry. The twins joined in until Harry swung his own rod and drove them back. Harry wore two layers of woolen sweaters, shorts and sneakers. He could take a blow or two.

"Submit, submit," Tetsu screamed, whipping up his courage and raining down blows that Harry had no problem deflecting. Gen swung his pole like a baseball bat across Harry's leg, dropping him to one knee. The twins synchronized their blows on Harry's sword until he threw a tub at their heads and bolted by Tetsu.

"The gaijin," Hajime shouted. "The gaijin is getting away."

This always happened. No one wanted to be the vile Lord Kira. Harry was Kira because he was a gaijin, a foreigner, not Japanese at all. As soon as the hunt began in earnest, the fact that he was a gaijin was reason enough for the chase. Harry's hair was as closely cropped as the other boys'. He went to school with them, dressed and moved exactly like them. Didn't matter.

Down the street, a storyteller in a dirty jacket had gathered smaller kids around his paper slide show of the Golden Bat, champion of justice, a grotesque hero who wore a skull mask, white tights and a scarlet cloak. Harry slipped between them and the cart of an orange-ice vendor.

"It's going for the wagon," Hajime said. A gaijin was always "it."

Harry ducked around the ragpicker's teetering wagon and between the legs of the wagon's swaybacked horse, tipping a sack at the rice shop and pausing only long enough to whack Tetsu's shin. The twins weren't fast, but they understood commands, and Gen ordered them to block the doorway to a peep show called the Museum of Curiosities. Hajime threw his rod like a spear to catch Harry in the back. Harry stumbled and felt a hot, damp stab of blood.

"Submit, submit!" Tetsu hopped on one leg because the muslin had started unwrapping from his stomach from the effort of the chase.

"Got it!" Hajime tripped Harry, sending him rolling over the ground and through an open door into the dark yeasty interior of a bar. A workman drinking beer at the counter stood, measured his boot and kicked Harry back out.

The action had drawn the twins from the peep-show door, and Harry raced for it. The peep show itself was a gallery of muted lights, "mermaids" that were papier-mâché monsters stitched to fish and "exotic nudes" that were plaster statues. Harry backed up the stairs past the peep-show entrance, where constricted space meant he faced only one attacker at a time. The twins squeezed forward, falling over each other to reach Harry. Gen took their place, goggles over his eyes to show he meant business. Harry took a stiff jab in the stomach, another on his knee, gave a short chop on Gen's shoulder in return but knew that, step by step, he was losing ground, and the stairway ended on the second floor at a door with a sign that said No ENTRANCE. THIS DOOR IS LOCKED AT ALL TIMES.

Blood ran down Harry's neck and inside his sweater. At school their one-armed military instructor, Sergeant Sato, gave all the boys bayonet practice with bamboo poles. He would march them onto the baseball diamond dressed in padded vests and wicker helmets to train them in thrust and parry. Gen excelled in attack. Since Harry, the only gaijin in school, was always chosen as a target, he had become adept at self-defense.

7

Hajime launched his spear again. Its tip raked the crown of Harry's head and bounced off the door. Gen broke Harry's pole with one stroke and, with another, hit Harry's shoulder so hard his arm went numb. Pressed against the door, Harry tried to defend himself with the halves of the pole, but the blows came faster, while Gen demanded over and over, "Submit! Submit!"

Magically, the door opened. Harry rolled backward over a pile of shoes and sandals and found himself on a reed mat looking up at a gaunt man in a black suit and French beret and a circle of women in short satin skirts and cardboard crowns. Cigarettes dangled from expressions of surprise. The air was thick with smoke, talcum, the fumes of mosquito coils and the heavily perfumed sweat of chorus girls.

The man carried an ivory cigarette holder in fingers painted red, blue and black. He tipped his chair to count Gen, Hajime, Tetsu and the Kaga twins gathered at the top of the stairs. "Hey, what are you trying to do, kill him? And five against one? What kind of fair fight is that?"

"We were just playing," Gen said.

"The poor boy is covered with blood." One of the women knelt to lift Harry's head and wiped his face with a wet cloth. He noticed that she had painted her eyebrows as perfect half-moons.

"He's not even Japanese," Hajime said over Gen's shoulder.

The woman reacted with such shock that Harry was afraid she would drop him like a spider. "Look at that, he's right."

"It's the missionary boy," another woman said. "He's always running through the street with this gang."

A man in a straw boater heaved into view. "Well"—he laughed—"it looks like the gang has turned on him."

"We were only playing," Harry said.

"He defends them?" the man in the beret said. "That's loyalty for you."

"It speaks Japanese?" Someone pressed forward to observe Harry more carefully.

"It speaks a little," Gen said.

The woman with the cloth said, "Well, your victim isn't going any-place until he stops bleeding."

Harry's head stung, but he didn't find it unbearable to be in the gentle hands of a chorus girl with half-moon eyes, bare white shoulders and a paper crown, or to have his shoes removed by another chorus girl as if he were a soldier honorably wounded and carried from a field of battle. He took in the narrow room of vanity mirrors, screens, costumes glittering on racks, the photographs of movie stars pinned to the walls. The floor mats were covered with peanut shells and orange rinds, paper fortunes and cigarette butts.

"Achilles stays here." The man in the beret smiled as if he had read Harry's mind. "The rest of you can scram. This is a theater. Can't you see you're in a women's changing room? This is a private area."

"You're here," Gen said.

"That's different," the man with the boater said. "He's an artist, and I'm a manager. Go ahead, get out of here."

"We'll be waiting outside," Hajime threatened. From farther down the stairs, the twins rattled their poles with menace.

Harry looked up at the woman with the cloth. "What is your name?"

"Oharu."

"Oharu, can my friend stay, too?" Harry pointed to Gen.

"That's what you call a friend?" Oharu asked.

"See, that's Japanese spirit, what we call Yamato spirit," the artist said. "Loyal to the bitter, irrational end."

"But he's not Japanese," the manager said.

"Japanese is as Japanese does." The artist laughed through yellowed teeth.

"Can he stay?" Harry asked.

Oharu shrugged. "Okay. Your friend can wait to take you home. But only him, no one else."

"Forget him," Hajime said into Gen's ear. "We'll get him later."

Gen wavered on the threshold. He pulled the goggles from his eyes as if seeing for the first time the women amid their cushions and mirrors, the packs of gold-tipped Westminster cigarettes, tissues and powder puffs, the sardonic men angled in their chairs under a blue cloud of cigarette smoke and mosquito coils stirred languidly by an overhead fan. Gen looked back at the stairway of boys, then handed his bamboo

8192

pole to Hajime, slipped off his clogs to step inside and closed the door behind him.

"How is it you speak Japanese?" the artist asked Harry.

"I go to school."

"Japanese school?"

"Yes."

"And bow every day to the emperor's portrait?"

"Yes."

"Extraordinary. Where are your parents?"

"They're missionaries, they're traveling."

"Saving Japanese souls?"

"I guess so."

"Remarkable. Well, fair is fair. We will try to do something for your soul while you are here."

Harry's position as the center of attention was short-lived. A music hall might offer thirty comic skits and musical numbers and as many dancers and singers. Performers shuttled in and out, admitting a brief gasp of orchestra music before the door to the stage slammed shut again. Costume changes from, say, Little Bo Peep to a sailor suit were done on the run, Bo Peep's hoop skirts tossed in all directions for the wardrobe mistress to retrieve. Three or four women shared a single mirror. While Oharu removed Harry's sweaters to wipe blood from his chest, he watched a dancer hardly older than himself slip behind a screen to strip and pull on a ballerina's tutu. In the mirror he could see all of her.

Harry's experience with women was mixed, because his mother was on the road so often as partner to his father's ministry. Since Harry had been a sickly child, he had stayed in Tokyo with his nurse, who knew no better than to treat him like a Japanese. So he had grown up in a world of indulgent warmth and mixed baths, a Japanese boy who pretended to be an American son when his parents visited. But still a boy who had only speculated about the painted faces that stared from the windows of the brothels a few blocks from his home. There was something ancient and still and hooded about the whores in their kimonos. Now he was surrounded by an entirely different kind of woman, casually undressed and full of modern life, and in the space of a few minutes he had fallen in love first with Oharu and her half-moon brows and powdered shoulders, and then with the ballerina. If pain was the price of a sight like this, he could bear it. Sitting up, with the blood wiped off, he was small and skinny with a collection of welts and scratches, but his features were almost as uniform and his eyes nearly as dark as a Japanese boy's.

The artist offered Gen and Harry cigarettes.

"You shouldn't do that," Oharu said. "They don't smoke."

"Don't be silly, these are Tokyo boys, not farm boys from your rice paddy. Besides, cigarettes cut the pain."

"All the same, when the gaijin feels better, they have to go. I have work to do," the manager announced, although Harry hadn't seen him budge. "Anyway, it's too crowded in here. Hot, too."

"Damn." The artist felt his jacket pockets. "Now I'm out of fags."

Harry thought for a second. "What kind of cigarettes? We can get them for you. If you're thirsty, we can get beer, too."

"You'll just take the money and run," the manager said.

"I'll stay. Gen can go."

Gen had been dignified and watchful. He gave Harry a narrow look that asked when he had started giving orders.

"Next time," Harry said, "I'll go and Gen can stay."

It was a matter of adapting to the situation, and Harry's point of view had altered in the last ten minutes. A new reality had revealed itself, with more possibilities in this second-floor music-hall changing room than he'd ever imagined. Much better than playing samurai.

"It would be nice for the girls if we had someone willing to run for drinks and cigarettes," Oharu said. "Instead of men who just sit around and make comments about our legs."

The manager was unconvinced. He picked his collar from the sweat on his neck and gave Harry a closer scrutiny. "Your father really is a missionary?"

"Yes."

"Well, missionaries don't smoke or drink. So how would you even know where to go?"

Harry could have told the manager about his uncle Orin, a missionary who had come from Louisville to Tokyo's pleasure quarter and fallen from grace like a high diver hitting the water. Instead, Harry lit his cigarette and released an O of smoke. It rose and unraveled in the fan.

"For free?" the manager asked.

"Yes."

"Both of you?"

Harry looked over to Gen, who still held back, sensitive about the prerogatives of leadership. The door to the stage flew open for a change of acts, singers dressed in graduation gowns rushing out as ballet dancers poured in. The ballerina Harry had seen before didn't even bother with the privacy of a screen to strip to her skin, towel herself off and pull on a majorette costume with a rising sun on the front. To Harry, her change of costumes suggested a wide range of talents and many facets of personality. Gen had been watching, too.

"Yes," said Gen. "I'm with him."

"You should be. Look at him, a minute ago he was about to lose his head, and now he's in Oharu's lap. That is a lucky boy."

Was it only luck, Harry wondered? The way the fight had unfolded, the stumbling upstairs into the theater's roost, encountering Oharu and the artist, the transition of him and Gen from would-be samurai to men of the world all had a dreamlike quality, as if he had stepped through a looking glass to see a subtly altered, more defined image from the other side.

Otherwise, nothing changed. The following day he and Gen were at school again. They marched onto the baseball field in the afternoon and had the usual bayonet drill with Sergeant Sato. Harry put on his padded vest and wicker helmet so that, one after the other, Jiro and Taro, Tetsu and Hajime could take turns pummeling the gaijin. Gen beat Harry into the ground more viciously than ever.

At the end of the drill, the sergeant asked what their ambition in life was and, to a boy, they shouted. "To die for the emperor!"

No one shouted more fervently than Harry.

1941

2

HARRY AND MICHIKO were dancing barefoot to the Artie Shaw version of "Begin the Beguine," the Latin sap taken out of the music and replaced by jungle drums.

There was room to dance because Harry didn't own much, he wasn't a collector of Oriental knickknacks—netsuke or swords—like a lot of expatriates in Tokyo. Only a low table, oil heater, gramophone and records, armoire for Western clothes and a wall hanging of Fuji. An oval mirror reflected the red of a neon sign outside.

An erotic zone for the Japanese was the nape of the neck. Harry slipped behind Michiko and put his lips to the bump at the top of her spine, between her shoulder blades, and ran a finger up to the dark V where her hair began, black and sleek, cut short to show off the delicate ivory whorl of her ears. She was skinny and her breasts were small, but her very smoothness was sensual. At the base of her neck where it pulsed were three pinpoint moles, like drops of ink on rice paper. Michiko took his hand and slid it down her stomach while he shifted behind her. When a Japanese said yes and meant it, the word "Hai!" came directly from the chest. It was the way she said "Harry" over and over. In Japanese prints, the courtesan bit a sash to keep from crying out in passion. Not Michiko. Sex with Michiko was like mating with a cat; Harry was surprised sometimes afterward that his ear wasn't notched. But she did possess him, she claimed all of him with a backward glance.

How old was she, twenty? He was thirty, old enough to know that her heart-shaped face was offered as innocently as the ace of spades. And if Saint Peter asked him at the Pearly Gates, "Why did you do it?" Harry admitted that the only honest answer would be "Because it fit." Before lovers leaped into the red-hot mouth of a volcano, did they pause to reconsider? When two addicts decided to share the same ball of opium, did they ask, "Is this a good idea?" His sole defense was that no one fit him like Michiko, and each time was different.

"Harry," she said, "did I tell you that you were the first man I kissed? I saw kissing in Western movies. I never did it."

"Do you like it?"

"Not really," she said and bit his lip, and he let go.

"Jesus, what is this about?"

"You're leaving me, aren't you, Harry. I can tell."

"Christ." It was amazing how women could turn it off, Harry thought. Like a golden faucet. He felt his lip. "Damn it, Michiko. You could leave scars."

"I wish."

Michiko plumped herself down on a tatami and pulled on white socks with split toes. As if those were enough wardrobe in themselves, she sat cross-legged, not knees forward like a woman should, and took a cigarette and her own matches. She was the only Japanese woman he knew who made love naked. Polite Japanese women pitched their voices high when talking to men. Michiko talked to men, women, dogs all the same.

"I can't leave. There are no ships going to sea, there haven't been for weeks."

"You could fly."

"If I could get to Hong Kong or Manila, I could catch the Clipper, but I can't get to Hong Kong or Manila. They won't even let me leave Tokyo."

"You go all the time to see your Western women."

"That's different."

"Tell me, are they fat German fraus or Englishwomen with faces like horses? It's the Englishwoman you're always calling, that cow."

"A horse or a cow, which is it?"

She sucked on her cigarette hard enough to light her eyes. "Westerners smell of butter. Rancid butter. The only good thing I can say for you, Harry, is that for an American, you don't smell so bad."

"There's a lovely compliment." Harry pulled on pants for dignity's sake and fumbled for cigarettes. Michiko had a physical horror of Western women, their color, size, everything. They did seem a little gross next to the fineness of her hands, the sharpness of her brows, the inky curls at the base of her white stomach. But, call it a breadth of taste, he liked Western women, too. "Michiko, I hate to remind you, but we're not married."

"I don't want to be married to you."

"Good." She was an independent free-love Communist, after all, and he was grateful for any dry rock he could stand on when talking to her. "So what the hell are you talking about?"

She had the kind of gaze that penetrated the dark. Harry sensed there was some sort of silent conversation going on, a test of wills that he was losing. Michiko was complicated. She might be Japanese, but she was from Osaka, and Osaka women didn't mince words or back down. She was a doctrinaire Red who kept stacks of *Vogue* under a Shinto shrine in a corner of the room. She was a feminist and, at the same time, was a great admirer of a Tokyo woman who, denied her lover's attention, had famously strangled him and sliced off his privates to carry close to her heart. What frightened Harry was that he knew Michiko regarded a double suicide of lovers as a happy ending, but she'd be willing to settle for a murder-suicide if need be. It seemed to him that the safest possible course was to deny they were lovers at all.

"You're never jealous, are you, Harry?"

"How do I answer a question like that? Should I be?"

"Yes. You should be sick with it. That's love."

"No," Harry said, "that's nuts."

"Maybe you just wanted a Japanese girl?"

17

"I think I could have found an easier one."

Some Americans did take up with Japanese women for the exoticism. Harry, though, had been raised in Japan. A corn-fed girl from Kansas was stranger to him.

Michiko's long look continued, as if she were sending out small invisible scouts to test his defenses.

"The Western woman, is she married? If she's here, she must be married."

"I had no idea when I found you on the street and took you in like a wet stray that you were going to be so suspicious."

Suspicion was in season. Harry moved to the side of the window to look down on the street, at the flow of figures in dark winter kimonos. The evening was balmy for December. The warble of a street vendor's flute floated up, and at the corner a customer in a black suit shoveled noodles from a box into his mouth. In front of a teahouse at the other end of the block, a taller man nibbled a bun. Plainclothesmen had always watched missionaries, too. It was as if he'd inherited a pair of shadows.

"I saw them," Michiko said. "Are you in trouble?"

"No. Harry Niles is the safest man in Japan."

"You've done nothing wrong?"

"Right or wrong doesn't matter." He remembered his father, a Bible thumper with never a doubt in his righteousness. Harry's confidence was in his unrighteousness, his ability to dodge the consequences.

"So, are you going to leave?" Michiko asked. She took a long draw on her cigarette and rearranged her limbs, leaning back on her hands, legs forward, ankles crossed. He could just make out her eyes, the dark caps of her breasts. "You can tell me. I'm used to men who disappoint."

"What about the men in the Party, your local Lenins?"

"The men in the Party talked all day about the oppression of the working class, but every night they headed to the brothels. You know why I chose you, Harry? Because with an American, I had no expectations. I couldn't be disappointed."

Harry didn't know quite what she meant. The big problem with

Michiko was that she acknowledged no rational position, only emotion in the extreme, whereas Harry regarded himself as pure reason.

"Do you want us to burn down, Harry?"

It took him a moment to notice his cigarette carried an ash an inch long. People who lived on straw mats had a ready supply of ashtrays. The one he picked up was ceramic and said PACIFIC FLEET OFFICERS CLUB—PEARL HARBOR, HAWAII around a gilded anchor. Hawaii sounded good. Sunday would be the pre-Christmas party at Pearl, the same as at all U.S. Navy officers clubs around the world.

"Know what?" Harry said. "We should have a party. We're too tense, everyone is. We'll have a few friends over. A couple of the old reporters, artists, movie people."

"That's like the club every night."

"Okay, Michiko, what would make you happy? I'm not going anywhere, I promise. The entire Japanese Empire has marshaled its forces to keep me here. I'm blocked by land and sea and air. Even if I went to the States, what would I be, what would I do? My talent is speaking more Japanese than most Americans, and more English than most Japanese. Big deal. And I know how to buy yen and sell a movie and read a corporate ledger."

"Harry, you're a con man."

"I'm a philosopher. My philosophy is, give the people what they want."

"Do you give women what they want?"

Michiko was capable of retroactive jealousy. She had nothing in common with the mousy Japanese wife or mincing geisha. Harry slipped behind her and picked his words as carefully as a man choosing what could be a necktie or a rope. "I try."

"With all women?"

"No, but with interesting women I try hard. You are interesting."

"Other women?"

"Boring."

"Western women?"

He slid a hand around her. "The worst."

"How?"

"Too big, too busty, too blond. Just awful."

She took a deep drag, and her cigarette flared. "I should burn you every time you lie. They're really awful?"

"Unbearable."

"There won't be a war?"

"Not with the United States. Just war talk."

"You won't leave?"

"No, I'll be right here. Here and here and here." He put his lips to the beauty marks on her back. *"And do the things I really might."*

"So you're staying?"

"As long as you want. *I'm telling you true.* . . " He dug his fingers in her hair, soft and thick as water.

"You swear?"

He whispered, *"If I could be with you."*

"Okay, okay, Harry." Michiko let her head loll in his hand. She stubbed out her cigarette and pulled off her socks. "You win."

THE HAPPY PARIS had originally been a tearoom. Harry had transformed it with saloon tables, a bar stocked with Scotch instead of sake and a red neon sign of the Eiffel Tower that sizzled over the door. Half the clientele were foreign correspondents who had been blithely assigned by the AP, UPI or Reuters without a word of Japanese. Some were mere children sent directly from the Missouri School of Journalism. Harry took mercy on them as if he were their pastor and they were his flock, translating for them the gospel of Domei, the Japanese news agency. The other regulars were Japanese reporters, who parked motorcycles outside the club for a quick getaway in case war broke out, and Japanese businessmen who had traveled the world, liked American music and knew one Dorsey brother from the other. The closer war seemed, the more people packed the Happy Paris and all of Tokyo's bars and theaters, peep shows and brothels.

They didn't come for geishas. Geishas were a luxury reserved for financial big shots and the military elite. But if it was a rare man who could afford a geisha, a couple of yen could buy even a poor man the attentions of a café waitress. Waitresses came in all varieties, sweet or acid, shy or sharp, wrapped in kimonos or little more than a skirt and garter.

Many came for Michiko. Michiko was the Record Girl for the Happy Paris. Her task was simply to stand in a sequined jacket by a Capehart jukebox as tall as she was and, at her own mysterious whim, push the buttons for music—"Begin the Beguine" followed by Basie followed by Peggy Lee. Seventy-eights changed in slow motion from tone arm to turntable under an illuminated canopy of milk-blue glass, and dropped down the spindle with an audible sigh. Michiko did virtually nothing. The waitresses, Kimi and Haruko, circulated in short tricolor skirts. Haruko patterned herself from her hair to her toes on Michiko, but her legs were sausages in contrast to Michiko's in their silky hose. While Haruko and Kimi had actually been geishas and could simper and giggle with the best, Michiko cut customers dead. She played only records of her choice, a balance of swing and blues, closing her eyes and swaying so subtly to a song that she sometimes seemed asleep. The year before, there had been a fan magazine devoted to her—"The Sultry Queen of Jazz: Her Music, Her Hobbies, Her Weaknesses!"—totally fabricated, of course, with some snapshots. What made Michiko stand out most, Harry thought, was that even in the middle of a crowded club, with a dozen tables and booths full of voices, food and drinks shuttling back and forth on trays, she could have been alone. Michiko maintained a lack of self-consciousness that, added to a complete lack of morality, lent her a feline independence. She replaced "My Heart Stood Still" with "Any Old Time," Shaw's clarinet made lush with a saxophone reed.

Harry turned away to deal with Willie and DeGeorge. Al DeGeorge was the correspondent of *The Christian Science Monitor* and as stir-crazy as a zoo bear. Willie Staub was a young German businessman headed home from China via Japan and looked like an innocent among thieves.

DeGeorge was saying, "Harry runs a pool on when war will start between America and Japan, Tokyo time. Say there's even military action. The Philippines are on our side of the dateline, Hawaii's a day behind, doesn't matter, has to be Tokyo time. There's got to be at least ten thousand yen in there now. Of course, the house—that's Harry—

takes five percent. Harry would take five percent on the apocalypse. Today's the fifth. Hell, Willie, you've still got most of December. I got Christmas Day."

"You're a sentimentalist," said Harry.

"The only problem," DeGeorge said, "is that if we're still here when the war begins, we're fucked. No way out." He directed a baleful gaze at Harry. "Rumor is, they're going to get Nippon Air flying again. Put on a show with champagne, cute air hostesses and photographers, and fly some foreign bigwigs to Hong Kong as if everything is absolutely normal. My question is, who gets on that plane?" He turned to Willie. "The embassy sent special-delivery letters telling all Americans to leave. But no, we waited to see what Harry would do. We figured the boat Harry takes, that's the last boat out. Now all the boats are gone and we're down to a single plane."

"I don't know anything about this," Willie said. "I just got here."

"The Nazis must have told you to stay away from Harry."

"I am a Nazi."

"Willie *thinks* he's a Nazi," Harry told DeGeorge. "Anyway, don't you have a job to do? Didn't you tell me that the first man who calls the war can pick up a Pulitzer?"

"There's no point in staying if I can't do my job. No one will be interviewed by an American. I can't even get them on the telephone because the Japs say all calls have to be in Japanese. Who speaks Japanese?"

Willie told Harry, "My embassy said you were engaged in sharp practices and I should stay away from you."

"Good advice," said Harry.

"But they don't want me, either. I told them about my China report."

"What report?" DeGeorge asked.

Harry said, "Willie was factory manager for Deutsche-Fon in China. He saw a lot."

DeGeorge lowered his voice. "Jap atrocities? Rape of Nanking?"

"Exactly," Willie said.

"Old news."

"Not in Berlin. Germans should know these things."

"It was just one of those things . . . " Michiko hugged herself as if holding someone tight, her face conveying a private reverie that men in the Happy Paris yearned to join. The noise level was high because the Japanese loved to drink and got drunk fast and flirted with the waitresses even as they craved Michiko. Kimi batted her eyes at Willie, who had the golden looks of Gary Cooper and displayed a wounded Cooperish look when people disappointed him.

"I don't think the German people are interested in atrocities," Harry said. "There's been a lot going on there that you haven't heard about in the hinterlands of Asia."

"But Germany is winning the war."

"Maybe. You should probably keep your nose clean and stay away from me."

"You're the only person I know in Tokyo. Also I had to show you something." Willie pulled a folded newspaper from his jacket, but Harry was distracted by a customer who grabbed Haruko and planted her on his lap while she squirmed like a satin worm. This wasn't a rare occurrence; she had many admirers.

Harry joined them. "Haruko, go wait on tables. Matsu, let her go."

"He's just playful," Haruko said.

"He's drunk."

"That, too."

Matsu released her and let his head roll sloppily. He had an artistic beard and wore a viewfinder around his neck, in case anyone forgot his calling.

"It was just one of those nights," Matsu sang along.

"You're pissed."

Matsu inhaled deeply and broke into a grin. "Yesss, I think so. I hope so. Harry, do you remember *Watching Cherry Blossoms Fall*?"

"A sensitive film."

"My film, thank you. Do you think, afterward, that people will remember that film when they think of the director Matsu?"

"After what?"

Matsu lifted the viewfinder to his eye and scanned the room. "This is beautiful. Not Paris, I'm sorry, but still beautiful. Because the only time you'll know the soul of another man is when he's drunk. And a man can tell things to a waitress that he will never tell his wife. This is a happy place."

"That's very profound. How is the new film?"

"Just starting."

"A love story?"

"No lovers. Many planes."

"You're still with Toho Studios?"

"No." Matsu laughed, and somewhere in the laugh was a moan. "Not anymore."

Harry finally grasped the other man's despair. "They called you up."

"I will serve the emperor." Matsu tucked in his chin.

"What are you going to do in the army? You're a moviemaker."

"I'll still be making films. I'm going in the morning, but I wanted to see Michiko one more time. That is the image I want to carry with me, the unattainable Michiko. Unless you think perhaps I can attain her."

"You can't afford her."

"But I'm rich," Matsu said. "Tonight I'm rich." From an envelope he pulled a stack of crisp, light green bills that said JAPANESE GOVERN-MENT in English. Matsu stuffed the bills back into the envelope. "For my new assignment. There will be many planes, many tanks. No cherry blossoms."

"*A trip to the moon on gossamer wings . . .* " Michiko mouthed the words as if each rested momentarily on her lips. Not that she understood English.

Harry returned to his table. "Sorry. A conversation about the arts."

"This is what I have to show you." Willie unfolded a newspaper to a picture of soldiers in winter coats raising their rifles as they walked down the gangway of a transport ship. He passed it to Harry. "I saw it at the German embassy today. I can't read it, but I know you can."

The photo caption read, "WELCOME HOME. Hero Returns from China to Well-Deserved Honors." Although the page was smudged—newspapers hadn't had decent paper stock for years—Harry saw that the man on the ramp was a colonel with the deep-set eyes of a fasting monk. A long sword in a utilitarian sheath hung from his belt.

"Ishigami. How about that?"

"That's what I thought," Willie said.

"Who is it?" DeGeorge asked.

"A long-lost friend," Harry said. "I ought to read the newspapers more thoroughly."

DeGeorge asked Harry, "What day is left in the pool for Willie?"

"The eighth. That's Monday. War in three days is cutting it a little close."

"I don't bet," Willie said.

"A social bet," said DeGeorge. "Could happen."

Harry shook his head. "Ninety new American films have just arrived. *Too Hot to Handle, Tarzan Escapes, One Hundred Men and a Girl*. Who on earth would go to war when there's entertainment like that?"

"What do you do here, Harry?" Willie asked.

DeGeorge said, "Ostensibly, he's a movie rep. He does something else, I've just never been able to figure out what the fuck it is. Is it true, Harry, you're actually giving a speech at the Chrysanthemum Club tomorrow? You, at the Chrysanthemum Club?"

"I'm virtually respectable."

Willie returned to the picture in the newspaper. "Can Ishigami find you?"

"You did," Harry said. He didn't want to look at the picture, as if the image might sense his attention and look up from the page.

"*If we'd thought a bit, of the end of it . . .* " Michiko whispered with the song. Sometimes she seemed to know every nuance of the lyrics, Harry thought, sometimes she might have been repeating nonsense. He couldn't tell anymore.

"So, really and truly, Harry, is it going up?" DeGeorge asked.

"What?"

"The big balloon. War. Everyone's reading about last-minute negotiations in Washington. What do I tell the readers of *The Christian Science Monitor* and *Reader's Digest* and *The Saturday Evening Post* while they drink their warm Postum and listen to *Amos 'n Andy* and *Fibber McGee*, what do I tell Mr. and Mrs. America about the glorious Japanese Empire?"

"Tell them that the Japanese have only the purest of intentions. As exemplified by their actions in China, right, Willie?"

Willie kept his mouth shut.

"Weren't you in China?" DeGeorge asked Harry.

"Not for long."

"What are you going to do?" Willie asked Harry.

"I don't know. No good deed goes unpunished, right?"

"You must leave Japan."

"How? Americans can't even leave town. Maybe Ishigami just wants to say hello." Harry tried to hoist a smile for Willie's sake. "Maybe this whole war scare will just blow over."

"You think so?" asked Willie.

Not a chance, Harry thought. He had performed one decent act in his life, and something so out of character was bound to catch up. Michiko followed Artie Shaw with Benny Goodman, clarinets for the ages. Goodman was the complete musician: he could cover registers high and low. In comparison, Shaw was all flash, living at the higher register, poised for a crash. Harry figured he was more like Shaw. When he looked at the picture of Ishigami, he was back in Nanking all over again. Ten Chinese prisoners knelt in the light of torches, hands tied behind their backs. A corporal ladled water from a bucket over Ishigami's sword. Ishigami took a practice swing and left a shining fan of water in the air.

Kimi shook Harry's shoulder to get his attention. "There's a soldier at the door."

The blood left Harry's face as he rose from his chair, expecting the worst, but it was only a sergeant with a gun, shouting, "Come out, Lord Kira, wherever you are!"

3

HARRY MOTIONED MICHIKO to play a new record while he steered the drunk out onto the street and took the gun away. It was a Baby Nambu, Luger-styled like a full-size Nambu pistol but easier to hide. The sergeant's balance was none too steady. He had fallen or walked into a lamppost; his nose was bloody, and when he sneezed, he sprayed blood off his mustache. Harry was to some degree relieved to get away from DeGeorge's constant probing and step into the jostling of the street outside, a weekend crowd out for entertainment and prurient interest, off to cafés or after women. A geisha with a face as white as porcelain slipped into an elegant willow house across the street. A stilt walker advertised Ebisu beer. Men in kimonos wore squashed fedoras; nothing in Japan was so disregarded as a hat brim. University students paraded in filthy uniforms and caps. Pickpockets warmed their hands at carts selling sweet potatoes. Harry tucked the gun into his belt.

"I'll find you a taxi, Sergeant," Harry said. "No charge."

"Harry! Harry, it's me!" The soldier tried to pull his tunic straight. "It's me, Hajime!"

"Hajime?"

"S'me. Harry, such a long time. Old friends, yes?" Hajime said, although Harry didn't remember him as a friend. More the schoolmate most likely to be reborn as vermin. The eyeglasses and mustache were new, but behind them was the same round face. Harry remembered how, as a boy, Hajime had been the most relentless of tormentors, the first to set on Harry, the last to leave off. "Buy me a drink?"

"I'll find you a ride." Harry peeled Hajime's hand off his sleeve.

"Wait, wait." Hajime backpedaled, undid the buttons of his pants and pissed in a gutter as passersby jumped aside. The Japanese were the cleanest people on earth, but they made extraordinary allowances for drunks. A man could kiss his boss or piss in the street as long he was deemed under the influence. The nosebleed started again.

Harry gave him a handkerchief. "Keep it and button yourself up."

Head back, handkerchief pressed against his nose, Hajime staggered under the neon sign. The Eiffel Tower sizzled like a rocket; everyone near it wore a red glow.

"This is your own club, I hear. 'Happy Palace.' "

"Paris."

"Something like that. Just one drink, Harry. Meet your new friends."

"Would you like to piss on their shoes or bleed on them?"

"I need to have a good time, Harry. I'm shipping out tomorrow. That's why I was celebrating."

"By yourself?"

Hajime leaned on him. "There's no one, Harry. No wife, no family. Friends are worthless shits. But we had great times, Harry. 'Forty-seven Ronin,' that was us. A little rough, but no harm meant, Harry. How long has it been? Lord Kira, that was you."

"I remember." Harry directed Hajime toward the corner. There would be taxis at the theaters.

"China. I've been to China, Harry. I could tell you stories."

"I bet you could." Harry knew that a real friend would inquire into Hajime's military career, but war stories didn't appeal to Harry. With the Japanese spy mania, it was unwise for a Westerner to ask a soldier anything: where he'd been stationed, where he was going, doing what.

"Americans don't go to war, do they? So you're safe."

"I hope so."

"I want to see your famous club, celebrate there."

"I'm going to do you a bigger favor. I'm going to put you in a taxi."

Hajime tried to wrestle free. "Now you're rich, you're too good for your old friends. Let's see your club."

"No."

"Then promise me something." Hajime stopped struggling and lowered his voice. "Promise to see me off tomorrow, Harry? Sixteen hundred, Tokyo Station."

"You can find someone else."

"You, Harry. Just to have someone there. Promise?"

Hajime wore a smirk, but maybe that was his sole expression, Harry thought. Like one size fits all. "You'll get in a taxi if I do?"

"Yes."

"Okay. Tokyo Station, four o'clock." There were other things to do on a Sunday afternoon. Bidding Hajime a fond adieu wasn't high on Harry's list.

"You'll be there?" Hajime asked.

"Scout's honor."

Harry stopped a taxi, stuffed Hajime into the backseat and gave the driver two yen, which would cover the meter to anywhere in the city and clean a bloody seat. As the car moved off, Hajime stuck his head out the window. His eyeglasses were bright with theater lights, but there was something hidden behind Hajime's expression, some nasty surprise tucked under his mustache or kept up his sleeve.

"Tokyo Station, Harry."

Harry gave the taxi a halfhearted wave. The car had disappeared in the crowd when Harry remembered the gun still in his belt. He kicked himself. A gun might be useful if Ishigami caught up with him, but Harry didn't want to shoot anyone. It was against the law to possess a handgun, and his first instinct was to ditch it. The trouble was that a soldier who lost a weapon entrusted to him by the emperor could face a firing squad, which was a little stiff even for someone as unpleasant as Hajime. Now Harry really would have to see him again just to return it.

In the meantime, there was plenty to do. Harry's part of Tokyo was Asakusa, and its theater row was lit with side-by-side marquees like

Broadway. Life-size posters of samurai stood between cardboard cutouts of Clark Gable and Mickey Mouse. A customer could see Gable, go next door to a samurai film and end up at a newsreel theater to follow warplanes in action over China. Tall banners animated by the evening breeze invited the passerby to music halls like the Fuji and the International. The Folies, where Oharu used to dance, had been closed on charges of frivolity, but the Tokiwaza Theater still offered all-female swordplay, and Kabuki had special devotees, prostitutes tattooed with the faces of their favorite actors. Fortune-tellers in tents with gnostic symbols read palms, faces, feet, bumps on the head. Food stalls sold sake and shochu, sweet-potato vodka poured into a glass set in a little bowl until both glass and bowl brimmed over. Asakusa brimmed over. It was set between the pleasure quarter's thousand licensed women and the elegant willow houses of the geishas and was called the Floating World in part for its evanescent, irrepressible quality. It was also called the Nightless City. Harry watched police with short sabers stroll by. The rest of Tokyo hewed to wartime regulations about brothels closing by ten and willow houses by eleven. But there was always action in Asakusa, which was too bizarre, too full of life to quell.

Warmed by shochu, Harry found a pay phone and made a call. A woman answered.

"Are you alone?" Harry asked.

"Not exactly."

"How about tomorrow? Matsuya's roof at two."

"I'm sorry, this is a bad connection."

A man came on the line. "Beechum here."

"The lady of the house?" Harry switched to the querulous voice of an old woman uncertain about her *l*'s and *r*'s.

"What?"

"The lady of the house, please?"

"Busy. Do you have any idea what time it is?"

"She want to learn geisha dance, to play shamisen, to pour tea. I tell her she has to be Japanese to be geisha. Not Japanese, very difficult."

"My wife has no interest in being a geisha girl."

"Flower arranging is possible. Or prepare sukiyaki. Or maybe squid."

"Are you quite mad?"

The man hung up. Too bad, Harry thought, though the course of adultery ne'er did run smooth. He considered wandering over to the Rheingold, a German version of the Happy. The Rheingold served Berlin pancakes with Holsten beer. The waitresses wore dirndls and were renamed Bertha and Brunhilda, gruesome enough; but worse, their jukebox played only waltz and schmaltz. Harry decided he couldn't tolerate that. Still, the night was young. There was a hearts game at the Imperial Hotel, expats killing time with pissant pots. Better games were on river barges. Where the river Sumida lazed along Asakusa, boat after boat hosted games of dice. Merchants, brothel madams, famous actors bet serious money, and because the boats were run by yakuza instead of amateurs, the games were honest. Sometimes it was better to join a game midway, when you were fresh and the other players stale, for as the Good Book said, *The last shall be first, and the first last: for many be called, but few chosen.*

Heading for the river, Harry took a shortcut through a jigsaw puzzle of dark streets without names. Cars could pass through some streets, only bikes through others, and in some alleys the pedestrians squeezed between walls that nearly touched. Harry was at home, though. These were the escape routes he grew up in. From a chestnut cart, Harry bought a bag of nuts that were hot and charred, the skin split open and the meat as sweet as candy. Oharu came to mind. Harry remembered, as a kid, bringing her chestnuts wrapped in a cloth. "My hero," Oharu would say and kiss his cheek. He saw more sparks down the street and thought that another chestnut cart lay ahead until he heard the singsong Klaxon of a fire engine.

The fire was down a side street at a tailor's shop; Harry knew the place, which was near the garage where he kept his car. He had often seen the tailor and his wife, a grandmother, a girl and her younger brother eating dinner in the room behind, the tailor's eye on the open shop door and any possible trade that might be lured by his window display of the cheapest cotton, rayon and sufu. The house was old, built of wood frame with a bamboo front, the typical tinderbox Japanese lived in. The fire was already in full throat, an oven roar accompanied by exploding glass and the excited whoosh of paper screens. The crowd inched close, in awe of how a hovel's straw, books, bedding, needles and thread could transcend themselves into such a beautiful tower of flame, the sort of fireworks that spread, rose and blossomed a second time into a glowing maelstrom. The way Eskimos had words for different kinds of snow, the Japanese had words for fire: deliberate, accidental, initial flame, approaching blaze, invading, spreading, overwhelming fire. Harry found himself next to the tailor, who was explaining through his tears and with many apologies how the girl had left her homework on a space heater. The paper had caught fire and fallen and lit a mat, then a screen and scraps of rayon that lit as fast as candlewicks. Sufu was worse. It was a new wartime material, ersatz cloth made of wood fibers, basically cellulose that disintegrated after three or four washings but burned like hell. One minute, the tailor said, one minute the family was out of the room, and then it was too late. Harry saw the wife and children, everyone painted orange and black in the fire's glow. Two Red Cross workers bore off the grandmother on a litter. Air-raid drills were all the fashion. Well, this was more like the real thing.

A pumper arrived with a company of firemen. In helmets of lacquered leather with paneled neck protectors they looked like samurai in armor launching a siege. They hosed one another until their jackets of heavy cotton were soaked. One man climbed with a hose to the top of a tall ladder that was supported by nothing but the strong arms of his companions. Other firemen swung stout poles with metal scythes to tear down not only the burning house but also the tattoo shop and eel grill on either side. No one protested, not in a city where sparks swarmed over the rooftops like visible contagion and a hundred thousand could die in a single blaze. A second wall peeled off, revealing a tailor's dummy trapped by flames. Screens burned from the center, stairs step by step. Hell, Harry thought, why not just build the whole damn thing of matches? Smoke swirled like cannon fire, and all the windows of the street lit, as if each house yearned to join in. The fire-men regrouped, their jackets steaming. Firemen had a special incentive in leveling whole neighborhoods, since their second occupation was construction. What they tore down, they rebuilt. Not a bad racket, it seemed to Harry. However, there was more than money in such a drama of smoke and flames. It sometimes struck him that there was in the Japanese a majestic perversity that made them build for fire, leaving open the chance that at any time they could be wiped from the map just so they could start from scratch again.

But the tailor was defeated. He sank to the ground, a man who would hang himself if he had a rafter and a rope, his eyes dazed by the light that was consuming his life's possessions, as if he had been displaced from his home by a visiting dragon. He looked vaguely in the direction of the ambulance siren and returned his stupefied gaze to his daughter, the girl who had left her homework on the heater. She was a plump girl who looked like she wished she were already dead. He lifted his eyes to his wife, who looked to Harry like a wrung-out rag, beyond tears. It wasn't just their shop and home, it was their neighbors' homes and shops, too, which involved the idiocy of honor and face. As a third house collapsed the tailor sucked air through his teeth and seemed to draw in his eyes to avoid the unbearable sight.

Harry opened his billfold and found a hundred-yen note. And another hundred-yen note, which cleaned him out. He pressed the money into the wife's hand.

The tailor's boy ran toward the fire, not directly in but obliquely around the firemen. A sack he had been holding had slipped from his hands, spilling small boxes. The boy bent forward as he ran, and Harry saw that he was chasing beetles perhaps two inches long. Every boy kept pet beetles at some point, kept and fed and pampered them. The beetles scuttled nimbly ahead, a miniature menagerie flying in short bursts, not so much drawn to the flames as confused by the fiery heat and glow. Even after a fireman seized the boy by the scruff of his neck and dragged him away from the flames, he struggled to break free. Harry followed the beetles through puddles of water and picked up the insects one by one, depositing them in his jacket pockets. The beetles were black beauties, some equipped with antlers, some with horns. Four had disappeared underfoot into the crowd, but Harry was satisfied that he had rounded up the majority, and when he delivered them, the boy identified each by name as he replaced them in their boxes.

From the peak of a ladder, a fireman swung his pole like an executioner's ax and the house next door came down, front punched in, sides sliding together, a house of cards in a city of cards. Glutted, the fire took on a rosy glow that made Harry feel thoroughly baked. He noticed that his pants and sleeves were wet and smudged. He finally noticed by a reflection of the fire in sequined lapels that Michiko was in the crowd, watching him instead of the flames.

HARRY STANK SO MUCH of smoke that he went straight up to the apartment while Michiko closed the club. He undressed and soaped thoroughly at a bucket, sucked in his balls and sank into a tub of water so hot the steam was suffocating. When he was settled against the velvety wood, he lit a cigarette and let his head rest against the rim. A bath for Harry was both ritual and amniotic fluid. It was his context, the sea he swam in. His missionary parents had been too busy wearing out shoe leather on the byways of Japan to enjoy salubrious moments in a bath, but Harry had been brought up on his nurse's back. That was how Japanese learned how to behave, bowing whenever their mother—or nurse—bowed. Who had washed him but his nurse? And what followed the washing? A bath veiled in steam, where Harry was as Japanese as the next man.

Through the steam, he noticed Michiko enter the narrow bathroom with Hajime's gun. She aimed it at Harry. "Did you call her?"

"Who?"

"You know who."

"Ah, this is one of those circular conversations."

"*Her.*" The gun bobbed for emphasis.

"She couldn't talk. Her husband was there."

A Japanese face could be flat as paper, slits carved for the eyes and mouth. Michiko showed no emotion at all. "If we were married, you could have a mistress, I wouldn't care. But I am your mistress. I could kill you and then me."

She aimed at his head, his heart, his head. It was distracting. Also, he was too old for this. Suicide was for the young.

"Have you ever fired a gun before?" Harry asked. It was amazing what he didn't know about Michiko.

"No."

"I'll bet you a hundred yen you can empty that gun at this range and not hit me."

"Your life is worth that little? A hundred yen?"

"Eight shots, Michiko. You're not going to get better odds than that."

"I could do it so easily."

"Keep your elbows flexed. You know, it's moments like these that make me wonder what marriage with you would actually be like. Michiko, if you're not going to shoot me, could you get me a drink?"

"So irritating. Why do you have a gun?"

"An old friend came by."

"And left you this?"

"I'll give it back tomorrow." He pointed to the water. "Michiko, I do believe there's room for you."

"Harry, we know from experience there is not. Why are you giving a speech to bankers tomorrow?"

"Why not? I'm a respectable businessman."

"Respectable? Have you ever looked at yourself, Harry?"

"Well, you're not exactly the girl next door, either. Okay, I'm going to see bankers in the morning to screw them out of some money. I'm going to be charming and well rested. That means that right now I will enjoy a soak and a cigarette. Unless you are going to shoot me, of course."

"You're leaving, aren't you?"

"I explained before that I can't."

"But you always have an angle." The Nambu had a dart-shaped sight. Harry waited for it to waver. Not a millimeter. "Who is this?" Michiko asked.

Harry wafted steam aside and saw that in her other hand, Michiko held the newspaper picture of Ishigami. "Where did you get that?"

"Your German friend. Who is it?"

"An officer we knew in China. I guess he's back."

"Yes. He came to the club tonight after you left."

As the news sank in, the bath seemed warmer.

"Tonight?"

"Yes."

"Exactly what happened?" Harry asked.

"He went to the bar and asked for you. Kondo said he didn't know where you were. The colonel asked where you lived, and Kondo said he didn't know that, either. They talked a little."

That was okay, Harry thought. The bartender had four sons in the military. Ishigami wouldn't hurt Kondo. "Did he talk to anyone else?"

"The German."

"Willie? What did Willie say?"

"He doesn't speak Japanese. The colonel saw this picture on the table and was amused."

Ishigami amused? That didn't sound pretty.

"Was he in uniform?"

"Yes."

"Did he threaten anyone?"

"No."

Harry was relieved at that. Sometimes soldiers busted up cafés out of patriotic fervor. Harry paid for protection from that sort of agitation, and whether he was leaving town or not, he disliked being out good money.

"As soon as he was gone, I came looking for you."

That was pure Michiko, Harry thought. She saw no contradiction in holding a gun on him while expressing concern for his safety.

"Then nothing really happened, right?"

Her eyes narrowed, and Harry waited. He could tell she was mustering an attack on a new front. "If there's a war, what will you do?"

"There won't be a war."

"If there is."

"There won't be."

"If."

A man stands on a rock in a river, and sooner or later he slips. Harry regretted his words even as they left his mouth: "I'll tell you what I'm not going to do. I'm not going to be a sucker, a fall guy, the chump left holding the bag."

She lowered the gun.

"Ah. That's all I need to know."

"Michiko, don't take that the wrong way. That doesn't mean I'm skipping—"

But she disappeared from the doorway.

The news that Ishigami hadn't forgotten was unnerving. Harry had blithely assumed that no one would survive four years of leading bayonet charges on the China front, yet here he was at the Happy Paris. Ishigami, Ishigami, Ishigami. Sounded like the sweep of legs through high grass. It was like walking down through a misty valley and seeing a white kimono far behind but gaining.

Of course Harry was skipping town. Any sane person would. People expected war back in June, and now they were in December, each day like a drop of water trying to fall. The way he saw it, the Westerners trapped in Tokyo were there for a reason. They could have gotten out earlier, but they were grown-ups who had made decisions to stick by their Japanese investments or their Japanese wives. Missionaries wanted to scoop a few more souls. DeGeorge wanted one more Pulitzer. If they were counting on Harry to be their weather vane, forget it. Three more days and there would be no Harry Niles in Tokyo or its vicinity. That was the purpose of his talk at the Chrysanthemum Club, not just to massage an audience of bankers but to earn a million-dollar ticket out of Tokyo. It was a matter of playing his cards in the right order at the right time. He didn't like the news that Ishigami was in uniform, which probably included a sidearm and sword, but he remembered what the poet said: "I went into my bath a pessimist and came out an optimist." All he had to do was dodge the colonel for two days, and then it was clear sailing.

Wrapped in a light kimono, Harry wandered with his glass into the living room, which was dark, bedding spread on the floor. Michiko was tucked under the quilt, the gun in her hand. He felt like he was defanging her by easing the gun from her fingers. She stirred, moving her head in dreamy motion.

He had literally run into her when they met, Harry at the wheel of his car, Michiko bloody from a crackdown on the last Reds in Tokyo, a police sweep that scattered the comrades over rooftops and down alleys. Harry had pulled Michiko into the car and driven off, the first in a series of impulsive decisions he regretted, such as taking her home, patching her head, letting her stay the night. She left in the morning and returned a week later, her hair hacked short, with a pack containing a prayer wheel and the works of Marx and Engels. She stayed another night and another and never left Harry's for good; that was two years ago. If he'd left her on the street, if he'd given her over to the police, if he hadn't fed her the morning after he'd rescued her. That was probably the worst mistake of all, the fatal bowl of miso. If he'd just returned her silence when she left instead of asking whether she liked Western music. Gratitude was always a dicey issue in Japan; the very word *arigato* meant both "thank you" and "you have placed a sickening obligation on me." When she returned, she presented him with an Ellington record. What was interesting was that it was one of the few Ellington albums he didn't own, which suggested the possibility that in the middle of the night, her head bandaged, she had searched his apartment while he slept. Besides admitting she was a Red, she told him nothing about her past. Never did. Harry had seen others like her, tough girls from the mills who organized unions in spite of the owners and police, who got their education from night school rather than Tokyo Women's College and read *Red Flag* instead of *Housewife's Friend*. Men, when they went to prison for radical activities, got religion and dedicated their confessions to the emperor. Women like Michiko hanged themselves in their cells rather than give their keepers an inch of satisfaction. Harry had gotten her into the chorus line at the Folies, but she was too argumentative for management, so when the war scare chased his American musicians from the Happy Paris to Hawaii, he replaced them by making her the enigmatic and, apart from lyrics, silent Record Girl.

He heard a scraping outside. The club's neon sign was off, but in the haze of the streetlamp Harry saw the discreet gate of the willow house directly across from the Happy Paris. A willow house was an establishment where geishas entertained. Harry was no fan of geisha parties, but he occasionally hung out in a back room across the street just to escape DeGeorge, if nothing else. A cart with metal-rimmed wheels went by, the nocturnal visit of the night-soil man visiting homes without plumbing, gathering what kept the rice fields fertile, the cycle of life at its most basic. The cart moved aside to let pass a van with the crossed poles and looped wires of a radio direction finder on the roof. The van sifted the air for illegal transmissions the way a boat night-trolled for squid. Or, Harry speculated, if the van was from the Thought Police, perhaps they were trying to sift dangerous ideas out of the air. They typically liked to raid suspects around three in the morning, but this time they seemed to be just passing through. The surveillance usually annoyed Harry, but with Ishigami on the prowl, the added security was welcome. Anyway, in one week, two at the most, Harry would be in the States. He saw himself driving down Wilshire, having that first martini at the Mexican place around the corner from Paramount where they stuffed the olives with chili peppers. He could taste it.

When Harry left the window and approached the bed again, he saw that Michiko had moved the quilt aside in her sleep. The looseness of an underkimono made her limbs ghostly thin, half submerged in silk. Wouldn't it be a relief to be with an American girl, a big blonde built for a convertible? He knelt and, with no more pressure than the weight of the air, ran his fingertips around the base of her thumb and up her arm to the warmth and soft hair in the hollow under her arm, then along her collarbone to the line of her cheek as if committing to memory her shape and smoothness, a calligrapher writing in the dark.

4

THE THEATER'S DRESSING ROOM was an entry to a new world for young Harry Niles. He and Gen ran errands for singers, dancers, musicians, comedians and magicians, fetching cigarettes, beer by the case, cough syrup for the codeine. Vitamin B was the rage. Soon Oharu would let no one but Harry give her injections. She twisted in her chair, offering her soft, smooth bottom.

Harry's guide to this new Japan was the artist Kato. With his French beret, color-stained fingers and silver-headed walking stick, Kato cut a consumptive, sophisticated figure. Looking back, Harry realized that Kato must have been only in his twenties at the time, but he was the first person Harry met who had actually been to France and seemed to know about the world. Harry's father, the pastor Roger Niles, knew about heaven and hell but not so much about the here and now. In turn, Kato took an interest in Harry the way a man might adopt a monkey. The idea that a gaijin could speak like a Japanese, eat like a Japanese and shoplift cigarettes like a born thief entertained Kato on a philosophical level, and the fact that Harry was a missionary's son amused him enormously.

Harry lived for Saturdays between shows when he, Kato and Oharu walked around Asakusa like the royalty of a raffish kingdom. Asakusa stood for pleasure, for theaters, music halls, ballrooms, tea-rooms, licensed and unlicensed women. Everyone could afford *something* in Asakusa. And everyone, of course, admired Oharu in her pill-box hat, white gloves and long French dress that slithered over her like a snake. She had a dancer's athletic body. Silk hugged her legs and slid across her body while she looked blandly out from under her painted brows.

Sometimes they would step outside Asakusa to a French patisserie in the Ginza to devour éclairs or visit the Tokyo Station Hotel, which was built into one of the station's domes. The hotel had an elevator and a plush lobby with velvet chairs, but its greatest attraction was a wrought-iron balcony that ran around the inside of the dome below a crown of plaster eagles. Harry stood on one side of the balcony, Oharu on the other, and her merest whisper would bend around the dome to his ear as if she perched on his shoulder. Once they went to Hibiya Park for a concert of *modan jazu,* modern jazz. American Negroes played a brassy, speeded-up music before an audience both stupefied and curious. When the band left the stage, people reached with a total lack of self-consciousness to touch the skin of the musicians as if their color might rub off. There was a sense at the time of change and exhilaration. Japan had been on the winning side of the Great War. Fortunes were being made. The future was at hand, nowhere nearer than in Japan, the new great nation, and especially in Tokyo, the seat of the Son of Heaven. If anyone in this center of industry noticed Harry, they saw a pale, unusually round-eyed Japanese schoolboy with a typically shaved head, ratty sweater, knickers and clogs.

Kato noticed. "We have a real discovery, Oharu. He's like an urchin out of Dickens, and he's right here in the middle of Tokyo. He has a guardian who's always drunk, so Harry gets the money orders and pays the bills. I've heard him on the telephone. Do you ever wonder how a boy his age buys sake? Harry calls the sake shop and, in the voice of a Japanese woman, says a boy, a gaijin, no less, will be by to pay and pick up the sake. That's when Harry doesn't out-and-out steal it. We may be rearing a monster, Oharu, you and I. I suspect so. I think our Harry has all the morals of a young wolf. The real question for me is, is he a monster with sensitivity. I can't waste my time with someone who has no eye for color."

On hot days, Kato, Harry and Oharu stayed in Asakusa and went to the movies. Asakusa boasted more theaters per square foot than anywhere else on earth. The three friends sat in the dark, eating dried fish with beer and watching Buster Keaton take pratfalls on the screen while, in the back of the theater, a fan blew cool air from a block of ice.

At all foreign films a Movie Man sat onstage to translate the dialogue titles and what the audience was seeing. "Now Buster is running after the train. Now the train has turned around, oh, now the train is after him. Puff, puff, puff! Puff, puff, puff! He calls out to Mary, 'Save me! Save me!' Mary calls, 'Run, Buster, run!' "

"Have you noticed," Kato would inquire loudly of all the nearby viewers, "that, according to the Movie Man, the heroine in American movies is always called Mary. Is this likely? Don't they have any other names in America? Why is the villain always named Robert?"

"Kato is an expert on villainy," Oharu said to Harry. "He says an artist has to try every vice."

"In Paris we drank green absinthe and smoked hashish," Kato said. "It was the happiest time of my life."

Three rows ahead was the dancer Harry had seen his first day backstage at the music hall, the girl who changed with such naked cool from ballerina to majorette. Despite the dark he saw every detail, the wavy perm of her hair, a hat that was not much more than a feather, the shadow of her neck, her ear like a curled finger beckoning him, although she had never spoken to him other than to send him for cigarettes.

Kato followed Harry's attention. "You like little Chizuko? Too bad, it looks like she already has an admirer."

The admirer was an army officer. Harry immediately cast for explanations: father, uncle, family friend.

"Chizuko's not for you," Oharu whispered.

"Chizuko could be perfect for him," Kato said. "A playmate his own age, inventive, full of energy."

"Leave him alone," Oharu said.

"I'm sure something can be arranged," said Kato. Oharu pinched his arm.

Afterward they took in the theater of the streets. Kato taught Harry to appreciate the storyteller with his slide show and never-changing tales, the candy maker who turned and tugged rice dough into cats and mice, the publicity bands who banged through the alleys with saxophones, drums and spinning umbrellas to sell soap, seltzer, cigarettes. The twenties were a loud, bright time of modern girls—*mogas*—who worked at new telephone exchanges, sold French perfumes in department stores, punched tickets on buses. Fashion was war. On one corner, a corps of Salvation Army uniformed like majorettes would shake tambourines and sing "Rock of Ages" while, from the next corner, the Buddhist Salvation Army in saffron robes tried to drown them out with bells and chants. No one knew how the next social advance would take place. In a Ginza department-store fire, salesgirls burned to death rather than leap down to nets and embarrass themselves. Immediately a law passed requiring salesgirls to wear panties, and two thousand years of fashion changed. There was, as Kato pointed out, nothing more beautiful than a kimono. A woman in a hand-painted kimono and obi was wrapped in a work of art. Western fashion was drab by comparison, but as color leached out of modern clothes, it spread into billboards and movie posters, matchboxes and postcards, race cars and airplane banners. And, of course, each word, each character in every sign or delivery boy's jacket was a picture. Every street was a flood of images.

Kato lived in the Ginza above a bookstore in rooms that he said were very French, very *art nouveau*. Harry didn't know what France or nouveau was like, but he didn't doubt it was exactly like this. Armchairs seemed wrapped in vines. Sconces were glass flowers on stems of brass. Even the teapot looked alive enough to hop from the brazier. French posters of ballet and cancan dancers had places of honor on the walls. Japanese prints of a young woman teasing a cat, and a geisha offering her shoulder to a tattoo needle, were strewn on a table.

Kato said, "Hokusai and Yoshitoshi, all the great Japanese artists, were inspirations for Degas and Toulouse-Lautrec. Modern art is Japanese art through French eyes."

The lecture was wasted on Harry. He much preferred the simple lines and secret messages of the Japanese prints. How the girl innocently batting with the cat revealed the provocative nape of her neck cowled in red. How the geisha bit into a cloth to stifle pain the same way lovers stifled cries of ecstasy.

"Do you paint here, too?" Harry asked. He saw no easel, paints or canvas.

"Open your eyes."

Harry noticed how Kato had positioned himself by the poster of a French cabaret, a line of cancan dancers with blue faces and red hair. In a corner, however, was the Japanese calligraphy of Kato's name. The poster was an imitation.

"You did that?"

"Good, you aren't totally blind. There's hope for you yet, Harry. You help me deliver the prints on the table and we'll meet Oharu and go to a Chinese restaurant. She loves Chinese food."

Harry didn't meet Kato's customers. It was a warm day in May, and he was happy to go along and wait outside while the artist took prints, boxed and loosely wrapped in silk cloth, around town. The last delivery was to the museum in Ueno Park. Ueno Park was famous for its hills of cherry trees, although the flowers had passed and the branches, dark as patent leather, were going to green. What Harry liked about the park were its drunken rickshaw men, street magicians, beggars and "sparrows," prostitutes who carried a ready rolled-up mat. Kato seemed to know each fire-eater, mendicant and whore.

This day, however, the usual transients had disappeared, the park was empty, sparrows flown. In a city of crowds, Ueno Park was mysteriously quiet until Harry saw red flags march over the hill, so many that the cherry trees seemed to toss in waves of red. These were followed by ranks of men wearing red bandanas tied around their heads and carrying signs that read RICE IS THE PEOPLE'S PROPERTY, a surprise to Harry, who had been taught at school that all the rice in Japan was the emperor's. Some marchers were university students, but most were life-hardened workers holding their strong fists high. As they marched, their song spread across the landscape of the park: *"Arise ye workers from your slumbers / Arise ye prisoners of want . . . "*

" 'The Internationale,' " Kato said. "It's May Day. They're Communists."

It was thrilling, the unity of voices, the forward motion of history that swept up Kato and Harry. Flags seemed to set the park on fire as the phalanx swung down a wide flight of steps to the street, where a row of police waited. Like the bank of a river, the blue line of uniforms redirected the course of the march, containing it along a high stone wall. Demonstrators ran ahead to outflank the police, but they were checked by the arrival of flatbed trucks bearing men in black head-bands, with shirtsleeves rolled back from tattooed arms. Newspapers always identified groups like this as patriotic citizens; their tattoos revealed them as yakuza, initiated members of the underworld, but criminals could be patriotic, too. All Harry knew was that it was like watching a painting of a battle come to life, in place of warring samu-rai the modern armies of the streets. Demonstrators raced, waving and snapping their flags. Men in black headbands jumped off the trucks, shouted, swung ax handles. As the two forces collided, individuals turned to indistinct forms grappling with each other. A red vanguard plunged through the black ranks, and Harry felt the flags surge, bear-ing away all opposition. Red paint splattered the trucks.

Kato clutched his package. His eyes lit up. "We'll see some action now."

As the battle became more equal, fighting became more vicious. What the thugs in black headbands lacked in group discipline, they made up for in back-alley experience. Anyone who fell was stomped before he rose, but Harry saw how oblivious to danger Kato was, and the sense of invulnerability was catching. Besides, Harry was proud to be part of any event that entertained Kato so much.

Just when Harry was sure the red flags would carry the day, horses with blue riders moved down the park steps. Mounted police carrying bamboo rods. It was wonderful, he thought, to hear the sound of hooves on stone, the muffled breathing of the horses like the Battle of Sekigahara, when Ieyasu, the founder of Tokugawa rule, crushed his enemies. It was a scene with everything except flights of arrows and the smoke of matchlocks. As marchers noticed the closing trap, confu-sion spread. They tried to organize a stand around their banners, but the impact of the horses was too much. Black headbands waded in with their shafts. Flags swayed. Toppled. One moment Harry stayed upright amid contending men, the next he was sucked under a truck like a swimmer out at sea. Between tires he saw Kato go down, walking stick and package wrested from his hands. Harry didn't see Kato's adversary, only the walking stick as it broke over Kato's head. On his elbows, Harry crawled to the package and covered it with his body. He hadn't kept track which prints had been delivered. The one he shielded could have been the girl with the cat, the strolling girl, the geisha with the tattoo artist. On the ground he recalled each one completely, the embossing of their golden kimonos, the shadowed pink around their eyes, their tremulous lips as if they were alive and asking for protection.

Once the issue was decided, the rout was swift. Demonstrators scattered, bearing the wounded they could carry. Those that didn't escape were dragged onto trucks for further beating at a less public venue, or pushed into vans by police. In a matter of minutes the street was cleared, except for strewn shoes and banners and bloody shirts. Kato staggered and giggled as if drunk on survival. A dark stripe of blood ran from his beret.

Harry looked up. "I saved the picture."

"The print?" Kato rocked on his heels. "Harry, there are hundreds of prints, every print is a copy. You risked your life for nothing, which proves you have true Yamato spirit." With his own blood, using a finger as a brush, Kato put a mark on Harry's forehead. "Because you have proved yourself a true son of Yamato, I declare you, I baptize you, Japanese."

It was, as far as Harry was concerned, true glory.

5

B Y FIVE IN THE MORNING Harry was shaved and out the door,
leaving Michiko asleep.

Asakusa had the hollow sound and desultory look of an
empty stage. Marquees that had pulsed with electric light were dark
canopies. A couple of workmen engaged in hanging a loudspeaker
from a streetlamp. A pair of geishas staggered home, face-white
almost luminous in the morning twilight, their elaborate coifs lurching with every step. Holding hands, the women maneuvered around
paving stones strewn with fish bones, toothpicks, lists of auspicious
numbers and a pack of scrofulous dogs tugging a squid in opposite
directions. One geisha hiccuped good morning to Harry, who was on
his way to the car.

Harry often dressed in a casual kimono, but for breakfast at the
Chrysanthemum Club, he wore a single-breasted suit because the club
members, those captains of Japanese trade and finance, were expecting a true-blue American. He carried Hajime's gun in a box wrapped in
a furoshiki, the same sort of cloth he used to wrap Kato's prints in.
Harry was virtually at the garage when his sleeve was tugged by a boy
in a sailor sweater. The boy was joined by a small woman who executed a bow of such respect that Harry was thrown into confusion
until he smelled the smoke on her and realized he had reached the

corner where the tailor's shop had burned the night before. Where the shop had stood was a near void. A girl with a lantern sifted through the rubble of roof tiles and iron pans and the blackened body of a sewing machine. Harry saw no other indication that a family had inhabited the spot, not a sandal, photograph, workbench, bolt of cloth, not even a thimble. Nothing was left of the neighboring tattoo and eel shops, either. The entire corner of the block had been reduced to a wet black smudge.

In whispers, the tailor's wife apologized to Harry for the inconvenience of the fire. Thanks to his generosity, they would be able to find a new shop and to help the people next door. All the time she talked, the boy tugged at Harry's jacket.

This was the sort of conversation Harry hated. First, he was on the move. He had things to do. Second, this woman's house had burned down, and she was thanking him for a few lousy yen, money that he had been on the way to gamble with. He looked around as if a magic exit sign might start flashing. To change the subject, he asked about the grandmother he had seen going off in an ambulance.

"She is much better, thank you. Thank you very much for asking. Grandmother also thanks you for your help. She also apologizes."

"It was nothing, please."

"One thing," she said and hesitated.

"Yes?"

Harry wasn't sure in the poor light, but he thought her face flushed. "My husband does not know about your help. He would not understand."

About accepting money from a gaijin? Everyone knew that the entire point of the campaign in China was to free Asia of Western entanglements. Every patriotic man took this cause as his personal mission. Women were a little more intelligent.

"Ah," Harry said.

"Very difficult." She lowered her head.

"Well."

"I am so sorry."

"I understand." But there was no mention of giving the money back, and Harry had to smile. "I'm sure you're doing the right thing. I leave it all in your hands."

"You are too kind." Her relief was so naked that Harry was embarrassed all over again. "I will say a prayer for you."

"Then we're even."

The boy kept tugging on Harry's jacket pocket and saying "For you" until Harry pulled free.

TEN THOUSAND CUTTLEFISH, dried on lines, rattled in the dawn. A year before, the Tokyo fish market had been rich in red salmon, eels in silver coils, crabs the size of monsters, rockfish, monkfish, needlefish laid like cutlery on beds of ice and massive blue-skinned tuna. No more, not since marine gasoline was reserved for the navy. The fishing fleet had gone back to oars and sails, plying the coast instead of deeper water, and the general nature of the catch had changed to mounds of shellfish, clams and oysters, mussels and cockles, as if the boats had gone for stones instead of fish. Regular gas was as tight. The week before, Harry had seen farmers pushing a truck heaped with sweet potatoes. It seemed to him that in its effort to lead the world, the entire country had gone in reverse.

He found Taro aboard his boat. It wasn't hard. Taro had been big even as a boy, as one of the faithful ronin who had hunted Harry down, and he was huge as a man, a sumo with a high forehead, topknot and tent-size kimono. An open firebox lit the fishing boat's simple lines: the low gunwales, single oarlock, seining pole at the stern.

"Tanks are drained," Taro said.

"What do you care?" Harry asked.

"You can run a taxi on charcoal, you can't run a boat." The boat had no wheelhouse, only a canvas shelter that Taro stooped under to trim lines and nets. "If my father could see this. Remember the time you came out with us and a shark got on board?"

"We jumped then."

"We jumped high. Now they want us to go out and catch shark for shoe leather. Shoe leather! I won't do it, Harry, not on my father's boat."

Harry hadn't heard Taro be so filial before. He also hadn't heard what was so urgent that Taro had to see him this early in the day. It was the same way sumos wrestled. Before the actual grappling, there might be ten minutes of glaring and stomping around the ring. Taro sat by the firebox, lit a cigarette and took a flask of sake from a tin pan on top of the box. He poured the sake into two cups that looked like doll china in his hands.

Harry squatted and tried to keep his pant cuffs clean. "It's a little early."

"Not for me," Taro mumbled. "A good fisherman would be bringing in his catch by now. Fish, not shoe leather. Kampai!"

"Kampai!" Harry threw the cup back. The last thing he wanted was to match drinks with a sumo. Sumos trained on sake. It was a breach of their etiquette to turn down a drink. Also, there was something particularly abject about Taro this morning, like an ox on its knees.

"The fishing is pretty bad?" Harry asked.

Taro poured another. "The fish are there. Fish are everywhere, but it's too far without gas. Even the bays are open."

"All the bays?"

"That's what they say."

"Every bay?"

"Yes."

"Hitokappu Bay?"

"Wide open."

"Banzai!" Harry said. Hitokappu was where the Combined Fleet had gathered in November and then barely stirred for lack of fuel. If the warships left there but hadn't appeared at any other bay in Japan, Harry wondered where an entire fleet had gone.

Taro tipped forward and became solemn. "Harry, remember Jiro?"

"Your brother? How could I forget?" Taro and Jiro were huge twins told apart by their names, meaning "firstborn" and "second."

"He made your life miserable."

"Not all the time," Harry said. "We had some fun."

"Picking pockets?"

"Yeah. Jiro was large like you. He did the bumping and I did the dipping."

"He always had money when he was with you." Taro fell silent, then said, "Jiro only helped pick pockets because the boat came to me. I was the older twin. If he'd been first, he would have been Taro and I would have been Jiro. That makes you think." He squinted into the firebox. "You know what they say about twins. The parents must have been . . . you know . . . too much."

True, Harry thought. Let a couple have twins and the neighborhood acted as if the parents were randy as dogs.

"Everyone sniggered except you, Harry. Everyone. That's why he went bad, I'm convinced."

"He was a little rough around the edges."

"The police gave him a choice, the army or jail."

"He always wanted to fight. He got his chance."

"Harry, can I ask you for a favor?"

"It depends."

"That's always your answer, isn't it?"

"It depends."

Taro felt in his sleeve and came up with a telegram. He smoothed it out against his chest and gave it to Harry, who read it by the light of the fire. The telegram offered congratulations from the army and informed the recipient when the remains of Lance Corporal Kaga Jiro would arrive at Tokyo Station.

"Christ. It's this afternoon."

"It's the first we heard that he was even hurt."

"That's tough, okay."

"Go with me, Harry?"

"I can't go with you. I'm not family."

"Mother is too weak, it would kill her to go. I just can't face Jiro alone."

"A gaijin picking up Jiro? How is that going to look?"

Taro put the cup aside, swept the deck with a paw and knelt until he'd reached a deep kowtow. No one had ever given Harry a kowtow before, least of all a sumo. The circles Harry ran in, he'd hardly ever seen one kowtow, and now two big bows in a morning, how strange was that? Not to mention the pistol in his car.

"Get up," Harry said.

53

From his facedown position, Taro's whisper was muffled. "At least meet me afterward, Harry. I can't face him alone, not yet."

"No. Now get up." Harry tugged at Taro's sleeve.

Taro was deadweight. "Harry, please."

"It's a bad idea. You're going to lie there all day?"

"Harry . . ."

Jesus Christ, Harry thought. The stupid brothers had hated each other from the day they were born, fifteen minutes apart, as Taro said.

"Shit," Harry said in English. "That means yes."

"Thank you, Harry." Taro sat up, instantly relieved, and refilled Harry's cup. "Thank you, Harry, much better."

"At the ballroom."

"The ballroom."

They drank and admired the lightening sky. A boat slipped by, a shadow at the stern working the single oar. Harry, looking for small talk, said, "Let's hope there won't be many more heroes after Jiro. Who knows, maybe Japan will pull out of China."

Taro asked, "Do you know how to catch an octopus? It's the only interesting thing I learned from fishing."

"You know, I've never tried."

"You trick him. An octopus is so smart and shy, and he spends all his time in his cave. Hooks don't work. Nets catch on the rocks. But the octopus is greedy, and he loves the color red. You tie a red rag around a pole and wave that rag down in the water, right outside the octopus's cave, and he can't resist. Out comes one tentacle at a time until he's completely wrapped around that pole. You just lift him out, because he wants his red rag, and at the cost of his own life, he won't let go. That's Japan with China. We won't let go."

SATURDAY WAS A WORKDAY. Traffic drove on the left side of the street, mainly taxis and trams, some rickshaws running doctors to the hospital around a stationary line of army trucks, four-by-two Toyotas that were really Chevrolets in disguise. Harry's own car was a low-slung Datsun built at Ford's old plant in Yokohama. Ford and GM had both had what were called "screwdriver assembly plants" until the Japanese learned enough about mass production and booted them out. Few private cars were on the road, and most of them were powered by a charcoal furnace attached to the back in a system that was ingenious but virtually powerless; uphill, passengers pushed. Harry ran on black-market gas. He figured the day he drove a car powered by charcoal was the day he cashed in his chips.

On the passenger seat was the pistol. On the car radio, Japan Broadcasting offered its usual morning fare, an exercise program of jumping jacks. "One, two! One, two! One, two!" Workmen were hanging loudspeakers from lampposts so that the general population could benefit from the same instructions. "One, two! One, two!" Tokyo was on the move.

In fits and starts. Harry had given himself an hour to get to the Chrysanthemum Club, but convoys of army trucks brought all other traffic to a halt until police rerouted everyone miles around the far side of the palace. A rag-wagon horse expired outside the Diet building, then a bike transporting a six-foot stack of noodle trays went down in front of Harry's car, and by the time he reached even the center of the city, he was forty minutes late. Usually he was entertained by Tokyo Station, the mixed bag of commuters in three-piece suits and farmers in cone-shaped hats of straw. He always enjoyed the secretly triumphant way salesgirls and switchboard operators twitched to work in their long tight skirts and little French hats. Today, however, everyone just seemed in Harry's way. Yet he discovered that, at a certain level, he didn't give a damn. Here he was at the acme of his business career, invited to dine with the Rockefellers and Carnegies of Japan, while Ishigami tracked him down like a crazed assassin. Not to mention Michiko's suspicions. He needed a ship, he needed a train, he needed a plane and here he was riding the eight ball. And part of him couldn't care less. It was the part that he didn't see often. Occasionally it looked out of the mirror and asked, What's the point of this game?

Behind the domes of Tokyo Station rose an eight-story imitation of Wall Street, a row of gray financial temples, the great banks of Japan. They stood side by side, the Ionic columns of Mitsubishi, Corinthian columns of Mitsui, tomblike doors of Sumitomo, all leading to the marble stairs and double brass doors of the Chrysanthemum Club with their famous crest of a Fuji mum within a ring. Harry tucked the Datsun behind a row of uniformed chauffeurs in Cadillacs and Packards. He might be almost an hour late, but he took the stairs one at a time, aware of the study he was receiving from bodyguards grouped on the stairs. They were retired detectives and off-duty police, chewing toothpicks or smoking cigarettes. Although the rate of political assassination had slowed, the army had made it clear it would eliminate anyone it suspected of less than white-hot patriotism, and if the atmosphere in Asakusa was frivolous, the air around the palace seemed weighted with dread and expectation. It had taken nothing less than the threat of war for the club to open its doors to Harry Niles, but once in, he found himself guided by a sort of butler dressed like a royal chamberlain. At the sixth floor, Harry was directed from the elevator to a door that was ajar to the sound of murmuring. Too late, he regretted the sake with Taro.

The worst thing was to look like a schoolboy late for class. Harry forced himself to slowly enter a dining room of a few hundred diners who fell silent at the sight of him. Palpable opprobrium and curiosity took aim, but Harry made a ninety-degree bow of apology and moved toward a head table where a conspicuously empty chair awaited him. Only when he had seated himself, made more apologies and drawn himself up to the table did he dare take in the room itself, its panels of precious woods, black persimmon and pale Yaku cedar, the blaze of chandeliers, the ornamental fires in the fireplaces at each end. The Chrysanthemum Club was *the* club of international trade, and it was, to some degree, an imitation of a London gentlemen's club, yet unmistakably Japanese. Chrysanthemums stood in crystal vases, staff in swallow-tailed suits shuffled softly around with coffee and green tea, always bowing when they passed a larger than life-size oil portrait of the club's royal sponsor, the emperor himself, a stooped, scholarly man regarding a globe with great intensity.

The diners had fallen on the last of their kippers and eggs. There were close to three hundred guests, Harry thought, not a bad muster considering how many foreigners had fled Tokyo. The Americans were an embassy attaché, a couple of Rotarians, a pair of forlorn managers from Standard Oil of New York and National City Bank, and Al

DeGeorge, who never missed a free meal. The British side was led by First Secretary Arnold Beechum, a beefy sportsman with small eyes stuck on a dome of freckles. A blockade-runner must have come in, because the Germans were well represented. Naval officers in roguishly handsome sweaters and dress blues shared a table with beaming executives from Siemens and I. G. Farben who were already anticipating a vigorous postwar economy. Willie Staub had been seated at a second table with Ambassador Ott, who had looked sick since the recent arrest of his best friend as a Russian spy, and Meisinger, a Gestapo colonel with thinning hair and greasy jowls. Meisinger's nickname was "The Butcher of Warsaw." Willie appeared distressed, though how anyone could be unhappy schmoozing with the Butcher of Warsaw, Harry couldn't imagine. Sharing a table, the Italians and Vichy French appeared locked in mutual Mediterranean contempt. Other Europeans and tame Chinese were scattered around the room, but most of Harry's audience consisted of Japanese executives sweaty around the collar because they were misunderstood. Misunderstood at home by an army just as happy to gun down capitalists as Communists and misunderstood abroad by their former friends and trading partners. Hence the breakfast address by Harry Niles.

Harry felt like a burglar allowed to work with the lights on. He didn't mind missing the eggs and toast; he preferred the unsullied chrysanthemum motif of the plate, the same design woven into the linen, engraved on water glasses, etched in silverware. His breakfast buddies at the head table were directors from IHI Engineering and NYK Shipping, the president of Nippon Air, an elderly chairman from the Yasuda Bank, all stiff as a row of bamboo sticks. On Harry's left was the last empty chair, on his right a young vice president from Yoshitaki Lines so scared of Harry that he spilled his coffee. Members rose to make announcements; the club's language was English as a nod to its international bent. Someone from the back of the room reported with regret the cancelation of a joint lunch with the American Club.

Harry was fine until the last chair was taken by a small man whose elegant pin-striped suit was contradicted by his cropped white hair, dark face and thick hands toughened with brine. It was Yoshitaki himself. Mitsubishi and Sumitomo had begun as samurai. Starting as a poor seaman, Yoshitaki had opened the Pacific for Japan shipping fifty years before by re-outfitting side-wheelers sold for scrap and facing down Chinese pirates and British gunboats. Now he was one of the wealthiest men in Japan and one of the best informed. If he didn't know exactly where the Combined Fleet was, he certainly knew in what direction it sailed. He had eyes that seemed set on a far horizon or deep into another man's soul, and he offered an expression of contempt so polite that Harry felt like a rotting fish.

Yoshitaki asked his vice president, "Do you observe the wall panels?"

"The wood is beautiful."

"Without imperfection. Such trees must be pruned for two hundred years or more," Yoshitaki said. "They must be diligently pruned and cleansed of alien infection. Allowing an alien infestation, a canker or a worm, is the greatest mistake a forester can make."

Fuck you, too, Harry thought. As he reached for the water, he noticed the two directors abruptly sit up, their eyes wide. On Harry's jacket sleeve was a large black beetle. Harry felt in his pocket and found a perforated cardboard box, wood shavings and string. The tailor's son had slipped him a beetle. That was why the boy had said, "For you."

It was a jet-black rhinoceros beetle with a sweeping upcurved horn. The beetle stepped from the sleeve to the table, shuffled its wing covers and started climbing a starched white napkin. One by one, the other guests at the head table focused on its progress, on Harry, back on the beetle. There weren't many places in the world, he thought, where dropping big insects on the table was socially acceptable, and the Chrysanthemum Club probably wasn't one of them. He felt Yoshitaki's amusement in particular.

The beetle was a robust Minotaur, with no ill effects from the fire that Harry could see. While another report from the back of the room droned on, the beast conquered the napkin and went from guest to guest examining the silverware, chinning itself on the plates as the diners drew back. Finally, as if confused by freedom, the beetle wandered back within reach of Harry, who scooped up the insect gently, let it have a little exercise from hand to hand, placed it in the box with shavings and tied the box shut tight.

"Do you have any more surprises?" Yoshitaki asked.

"I hope not."

"What a disappointment."

Harry became aware that he was being introduced. The "well-known Western businessman, keen observer of the international scene and longtime friend of Japan," that was him. He stood to a round of spotty applause. "Like raising Lazarus," his father used to say about a stiff congregation. But the old man could do it, and if his father was good with a sermon, Harry had perfected the anti-sermon. He put Michiko and Ishigami out of his mind. He walked around the table, made eye contact with Beechum, DeGeorge, Ott, a Mitsui director here, a Datsun manager there, and let the moment draw until the last cough was extinguished.

When Harry had complete silence, he began. "Americans ask me, What does Japan want? Does Japan seek to rule the Asian mainland? Does Japan have a dream of world domination? The answer is of course not. On the other hand, Japan has real needs and real aims. What Japan wants is peace in a world of stability and prosperity. A world divided into three economic spheres with three natural leaders, Germany in Europe, America in the Western Hemisphere and Japan in Asia. The old order is falling. Like any collapsing building, the faster its ruins are swept up and carted away, the safer and better for everyone. The day when the white man ruled in Asia is over. Dying empires must give way to vigorous new ones."

Harry detected a satisfied Japanese intake of breath, a susurrous pleasure that filled the room. Admittedly, in normal times the association was addressed by Nobel Prize academics, visiting business magnates or international publishers from *Fortune* or *Time*, not a moving picture rep. These were not normal times, however. The clever part of having someone like Harry talk was that he could say all those things that no well-brought-up Japanese would say to a Westerner. Harry could be disowned or discredited, but he'd say what he knew the Japanese wished they could.

"Japan has been patient. In the Great War, Japan was the staunch ally of Great Britain and the United States and secured the Pacific for its friends. For which service, all Japan asked was respect. Did Japan receive it? No. Instead, Britain and America did their best to lock the Japanese navy into an inferior status. Britain ended its friendship treaty with Japan, and the United States enacted racist immigration laws meant to insult the Japanese people. Japan had offered its hand in goodwill. In return it was slapped in the face."

Harry picked out guests he recognized.

"Slapped." He looked toward Beechum. "Japan has never understood this lack of sympathy from England. The Japanese ask, Why was it proper for one island nation to fatten on the lifeblood of peoples around the world and not proper for another nation to help its close neighbors develop a modern economy? Why is it a Christian duty for England to enslave Africa, India, Burma and Malaysia and not right for Japan to lead the peoples of Asia toward prosperity and independence? Take Hong Kong, for example. The truth is that England has no more legal claim on Hong Kong than Japan has on Scotland or Wales. It has no right, only might, which is why England boasts about the naval guns it has placed in Singapore. England claims to be keeping the peace, when in fact it is ruling the roost with eighteen-inch guns. Or desperately trying to." The British table traded dark glances. Well, this was probably one of the few speeches in Japan they understood, Harry thought; the British community in Tokyo was famous for its ignorance of Japanese.

By then Harry had moved briskly on to Roy Hooper, the American attaché, a man with all the misplaced faith and optimism of a missionary. "Japan also asks its American friends, Why is a 'Monroe Doctrine' reason enough for you to declare an entire hemisphere your own private concern? What gives you the right to rush marines into Mexico or Cuba or the Panama Canal? Who gave you the right to seize Hawaii, thousands of miles away from the American mainland? How is it you can claim the right for all these invasions, but let Japan respond to provocations from a neighbor or help the people of Manchukuo liberate themselves from centuries of ignorance and exploitation and Japan is pilloried for so-called aggression and driven from the League of Nations? Why? Because there is one law for white men and another law for Japanese."

Delivering this sort of speech was like grilling steak, Harry thought. You did one side, then the other. The main thing was to keep the coals hot.

"Nowhere is this lack of honesty or fairness more clear than in China. England says it is only protecting the rights of the Chinese. Is that so? Is this the same China that England conquered with repeating rifles, the same Chinese it slaughtered in Peking? The China that Britain enslaved to opium? The China that all of Europe carved up into colonies? The China of a very few rich and hundreds of millions wearing rags and surviving on scraps from the European table?" When Beechum's pinkness darkened to red, Harry returned to Hooper. "Then there are the protests from America. America is different, America doesn't want an empire, it only wants markets. America claims no properties in China, all it wants is free trade, an Open Door for export and import, a level playing field for innocent commercial interests. Which means different things in different places. In China it means that the banks of New York can buy Chinese war bonds and subsidize year after year of conflict and misery. In China it means a market for the cotton mills of South Carolina and Alabama. But in the United States it means a closed market to Japanese cotton, not to mention Japanese silk. Again, one law for the white man, another law for the Japanese."

Hooper smiled sorrowfully and shook his head. His father had indeed been a missionary, and Hooper Jr. had banged a drum for the Salvation Army in the streets of Tokyo only to be attacked by the Buddhist Salvation Army, which young Harry had joined for the fights. Harry went on to list the resources and materials held back or embargoed from Japan by the United States and Britain: rubber, scrap iron, steel, aluminum, magnesium, copper, brass, zinc, nickel, tin, lead, wolfram, airplane parts and, foremost, oil. All in an attempt to starve the hardworking people of an island with no natural resources. Even in rice. The British held back jute so the Japanese couldn't bag their own rice! As he rattled off statistics, Harry did sneak a sympathetic look at a pair of businessmen from Standard Oil and National City, marooned in Tokyo as first Washington froze Japanese assets and then Japan froze American. Whenever the two visited the Happy Paris, Harry stood them their first round of drinks.

"Japan may be the most beautiful and serene of nations, but it has virtually no natural resources. Its economy is based entirely on hard work and discipline. Facing a hostile encirclement by America, the British Empire and their allies in the Dutch East Indies, what choice does Japan have but to search for raw materials in its own natural sphere of Asia? Not to exploit its neighbors but to bring them the modernization, education, industry and medicine the West never did. That's why when fellow Americans ask me what the Japanese want, I tell them that Japan wants justice and peace. I tell them that Japan wants Asia for Asians, and that it's about time."

Mission accomplished. The British and Americans sat silent and aghast while the Japanese broke into the most sincere applause Harry had ever received. After he finished and the meeting was declared over, a banker from Yasuda purred like an old cat. "A very interesting talk, very forceful but not necessarily inaccurate."

"Not totally inaccurate, I hope," Harry said. "Just a few thoughts that I wanted to share."

Others at the table, however, hung back to gauge Yoshitaki's reaction. The silence grew while the shipping magnate studied Harry up and down. Yoshitaki was so dark his eyebrows looked singed, and his concentration was so complete that he and Harry might have been the only two men in the hall.

"I must tell you, Mr. Niles, that I was opposed to having you speak here today. I was not opposed to the speech itself so much as opposed to you. I did not, in fact, hear anything I did not expect you to say. I simply felt that your very presence degraded the prestige of the Chrysanthemum Club. I felt you would say anything to advance yourself. You are a marginal creature, like a crab that feeds neither in the water nor on land but in the rocks between. And even after hearing you today, I find that all of that is still true. But I would have to admit, I can no longer say that in no way are you Japanese."

Harry knew enough to be silent.

Yoshitaki said, "At the beginning of my career, I was at sea for years at a time, sometimes alone on virtual wrecks, no room for a dog or a cat, but I kept a beetle in a jar. One beetle for four years. Two ships went down under me, and I swam away with that jar each time. A good friend."

"Did it have a name?" Harry asked.

"Napoleon."

"A world conqueror of a beetle."

"I liked to think so. And the name of your beetle?"

"Oishi," Harry came up with.

"The faithful samurai? Very good."

Those few words were enough. The sight of a legend like Yoshitaki conversing with Harry Niles in such a familiar manner had an immediate effect. As soon as Yoshitaki departed, other members queued to add their thanks for such an incisive, sympathetic analysis. Bankers who would have crossed the street to avoid him the day before proffered their business cards. Harry bowed, read each card with grave attention, placed it in a lacquered card case, bowed again, mumbling as humbly as possible.

The president of Nippon Air oozed tact and satisfaction, like a maître d' leading a favored customer to the best table in the house. "As you know, on Monday, Nippon Air is reinstituting international flights to Hong Kong. We think this will help establish a sense of normality and confidence in the region. There will be press and photographers. Just an overnight at the Matsubara Hotel in Hong Kong and then a return. A number of your compatriots are asking to be on that flight, but you can appreciate how important it is that our foreign passengers be truly reliable friends of Japan."

"I certainly do." "Reliable" meant that the son of a bitch was smart enough to praise Japan on the way to Hong Kong and dumb enough to come back.

"I think you have alleviated any concerns about your reliability this morning."

"Thank you." Harry added a bow and held his breath.

"So," the president of Nippon Air let his words fall to a whisper of snowflakes, "you might be able to make yourself available on Monday? Haneda Field at noon. We will be flying a new DC-3. No tickets necessary. I, personally, will put you on the passenger list. Does this please you?"

"It pleases me to have earned your trust." Gone like a greased weasel, Harry thought.

Only when Mr. Nippon Air was done did other guests approach.

"How does it feel," Beechum asked, "to be the most despised white man in Asia?"

"Pretty good this morning, thanks."

"Your 'fellow Americans'? I doubt you've been to America for a year in your entire life. A cute performance. That ought to buy the Happy Paris another month's protection. You're the sort that in England we would drag through the streets behind a horse."

"Is that the England of bad food and good canings?"

The smell of Beechum's bay rum was more intense the warmer he grew. Harry had never seen the man with so much spit and personality before. "You think your friends look so good against coolies. Just watch when the little yellow Johnnies go up against the guns in Singapore."

" 'Yellow Johnnies'? That doesn't sound like diplomatic language to me."

Beechum said, "I for one hope they do give it a go. This entire circus will be over in a week, and then where will you be?"

"The next circus, I suppose."

"Not when we're done with you. Because there will come a day," Beechum promised. "There will come a day."

Willie motioned that he would wait outside, but Meisinger, the Gestapo chief, shook Harry's hand and went right to the point. "You didn't mention Jews."

"Didn't I?"

"So-called refugees. You haven't noticed them?"

"You know the truth? The truth is that in Japan, all Westerners look pretty much alike."

"Impossible," Meisinger said.

"Stick around."

Well, that was probably not appreciated, Harry thought, but if you even pretended to be friendly to someone like Meisinger, you ended up with the Butcher of Warsaw singing the Horst Wessel song in the Happy Paris. Harry didn't think he was willing to suffer that, and he knew Michiko wouldn't.

"They've got a little list, Harry," Hooper said as Meisinger marched away. The American attaché was a gangly, brush-cut man with a bow tie and an empathetic smile. "A speech for the Japanese? Are you totally nuts?"

"Who's got a list?"

"Everyone's got a list, Russians, British, Germans. We have a list. Not to mention the Japanese. You've made enemies everywhere."

"Just throwing light on the international scene."

"Fuel on the fire. Harry, what's going to happen is going to happen. You and I can't affect anything at this point, and unless you have some way of disappearing magically from the scene, I suggest you pull your head in. You're still doing asset searches for the Japanese?"

"I might look through a dusty ledger or two."

"It's called colluding with the enemy."

"Hoop, we're not at war yet."

"I hate that nickname. Anyway, if things do blow up in your face and you find yourself running for your life, I'm supposed to tell you not to come to the American embassy."

"Have I ever gone to the embassy?"

"So you know. They don't consider you American."

"Hoop, I always knew that."

Harry was feeling good, feeling great. Once again, his luck had come through. Who would have thought a beetle was the way to Yoshitaki's heart? But had he transgressed in his speech? Had he crossed a certain unforgivable line? Didn't matter, Harry was walking on air. By the time he made it to the street, Willie was waiting with DeGeorge, whose taxi wasn't going anywhere soon. The driver poured fresh charcoal into the top of the furnace and cranked a fan.

"Like riding a fucking hibachi," DeGeorge said.

"I wish the readers of *The Christian Science Monitor* could hear the language of their illustrious reporter," Harry said.

"Last-minute plea for peace, my ass."

" 'Japan's Business Leaders Friendly to America,' I think that's your headline right there."

"A goddamn apology for war. It's happening, isn't it? I saw you talking to the head of Nippon Air. Any word about the plane to Hong Kong?"

"Why would he tell me?"

"I don't know." DeGeorge turned to Willie. "All I know is that Harry is Mr. Connected and Protected. One day we're going to look around and Harry will be down the rabbit hole, and that'll be one day too fucking late for the rest of us."

"I never know if you use 'fucking' as an adverb or an adjective," Harry said. "I guess that's why you're the Pulitzer Prize winner and I'm not."

"Fuck you. I'm going to meet Beechum. Get the British embassy's reaction to this defeatist bullshit." DeGeorge gave his taxi a final glance and turned back to Harry. "Give me a ride?"

EARLY DECEMBER could produce days like this, spells of crystalline sunlight and the smell of citrus, smudged this winter by charcoal smoke. Willie sat in front with Harry and rolled down his window as they headed west along the turgid, pea-green moat that wrapped around the imperial castle. All traffic in the center of the city had to go around the palace. No street ran through it, subway under it or air route over it, and no nearby building could even be built high enough to look down on the divine presence, so the city revolved around a powerful absence, a flat green mountain, a hole, the idea of a hidden, undisturbed, jewel-like virtue. Even the castle presented a trick of perspective, the enormous, closely fitted stones made so low by the angle and length of the walls that imperial guards standing at the base, their rifles in white parade socks, looked like toy figures. All that was visible over the walls of the palace itself was a hint of curved eaves and tiled roofs behind a red tracery of maples. The moat was famous for its golden carp. As a boy, Harry would pay ten sen for a paper scoop at a goldfish tank and try to capture as many fish as possible before the paper fell apart, believing this established some sort of connection between himself and the Son of Heaven.

They passed a bus that had slowed so riders could remove their hats and bow in the direction of the emperor.

Willie said, "In spite of China, this seems quite wonderful to me. Serene, as you said."

"Serene?" DeGeorge had a laugh like the scrape of a shovel. "Hey, they assassinated three prime ministers in sixteen years. Murder, incorporated, doesn't have a record like the Japs, so 'serene' may not be the right word. Things are going to pop, the only question is when. The man who names the day just walks in and picks up that Pulitzer, right, Harry?"

"Could be."

"They're holding last-ditch negotiations in Washington that are going nowhere." DeGeorge leaned forward to Willie's ear. "Napoleon's army ran on its stomach, armies today run on their gas tanks. April a year ago, the Japs bought three times their usual amount of oil from the States. Roosevelt made a big show of cutting the Japs off of East Coast oil and sending it to England. Didn't matter, the Japs just bought all the oil on the West Coast. And aviation fuel? As much as we could sell. Not to mention steel and scrap iron. The Jap navy is built out of old Fords and Frigidaires. All the time, of course, FDR was starting to build three times as many tanks and battleships. Then, this July, we cut them off, no oil, no rubber, no steel, no nothing. There comes a certain point when the Japs are as strong as they're going to get, and every day from then on they're weaker. That's when the shooting starts. I figure we're there just about now."

Harry stopped the car at the stone pillars and wrought-iron gates of what looked like a pocket version of Buckingham Palace, right down to a lion and unicorn in the center of the pediment. The Embassy of His Britannic Majesty had hedges and potted froufrou around the courtyard, where some staff had changed to cricket whites to toss a ball back and forth. Now, there was a stiff upper lip, playing fields of Eton and all that stuff, Harry thought.

DeGeorge swung out of the car and leaned in the window on Harry's side. "I'd ask you in, Harry, but I don't think you'd get past the door. I mean, the Japs have a point, everyone has a point. But I'm like you, I have newspapers to sell."

"So you're going to write that Beechum says I'm the lowest form of life on earth?"

"Nothing personal. I know you understand. What I'm worried about is Michiko. She reads something like this and she'll cut my balls off."

"Michiko is not a faithful reader of the *Monitor.*" Harry put the Datsun in gear. "She doesn't even know you're a reporter, she just thinks you'd paint your ass and screw apes for free sherry."

"Well, fuck you, Harry," DeGeorge shouted as the car drove off. "Just fuck you."

"The Brits love it when you scream obscenities on their driveway," Harry said to Willie. "They'll ask DeGeorge back again and again." He noticed that Willie still seemed unsettled, although they had just visited such a lovely embassy, and on the opposite side of the boulevard, the imperial moat continued along a landscape of maples russet and orange. "Sorry. I told you last night it probably wasn't such a good idea for you to be seen with me."

"I understand."

"It's not that I don't enjoy seeing you, and I'm grateful for the warning about Ishigami, but I'm on kind of a schedule. Anyway, all good Germans should be getting out as fast as they can."

"It's not as simple as that."

"What's the problem? Short of money? Something personal?" Harry waited while Willie cleared his throat, then again: once too often. "Don't tell me it's a woman."

"It is a woman."

"Don't tell me it's a Chinese woman, you're not that stupid. You know better. Willie, I will take silence as confession." Harry glanced over. "Oh, boy."

"It's not what you think."

"So far, I'm guessing pretty good. I thought you had a haus and hausfrau back in Berlin."

"Dresden."

"Good old Dresden, where they serve that beer and salted herring you've pined for for so long. Don't complicate things, Willie. If you're out of China and you're alive, you're ahead of the game."

"She's a teacher."

"She could be Madame Curie for all the good that's going to do either of you. She's waiting for word from you? She's safe in Shanghai? Hong Kong? I can get money to her if that's the problem. You just get yourself back to Germany while you can."

"I brought her with me."

"That's not the answer I hoped for. She has a transit visa?"

"No."

"Then how did you bring her? She would have to be family. Willie, Willie, tell me you didn't do it."

"We're married."

Harry found his flask. "And the little dirndl back in Dresden?"

"She remarried a year ago. She got tired of waiting."

"Apparently so did you." Good Scotch was wasted on the headache Harry was developing. He had to get something to eat. "Willie, if you wanted a woman, you could have bought one in Shanghai for five dollars, ten dollars for a Russian. Want to be a saint about it? When you leave the country, you throw in a bonus hundred and you've earned your clean good-bye."

"It's not like that. She is a teacher. Harry, there are times I could kill you myself."

"Ishigami's got the corner on that. You're going to take the new Mrs. Staub to Germany? I know you're a fervent Nazi, but have you ever actually read *Mein Kampf*?"

"Of course I have. I have read all the führer's works."

"Did you happen to read the part about Asians being subhuman, or were you stuck with the special Asian edition of the book?"

"I don't remember any derogatory reference to Asians." Willie accepted the flask. He had that disappointed look again, Harry thought, the wounded Lohengrin.

"I'm just saying it's possible that your bride may be a little uncomfortable residing among the master race."

Willie said, "I came to you for advice because you also have such a relationship and it seems successful."

"What relationship?"

"You and Michiko."

"Michiko?"

"You seem to be together."

Like two people with drawn knives, Harry thought. "In a sense. But our relationship is based on something more solid than love. It's based on business, on the Happy Paris. She draws a crowd, I make money, I pay her."

"It looks like much more than that."

"That's because you're a romantic. You see things through rose-colored glasses. You think I live with Madame Butterfly and that the führer is a Boy Scout leader."

"You seem to have a high opinion of the Japanese. I heard your speech. Today you said many good things about the Japanese people."

"They're not people," Harry said, "they're customers. Big difference."

The palace grounds finally passed behind them, succeeded by an avenue of restaurants and souvenir shops that sold the military flag of a rising sun with sixteen rays. Over the trees to the left stood the crossbeams of an enormous torii gate.

"I'd like you to meet Iris," Willie said.

"The Chinese schoolmistress Iris? No, thanks. The nicer she is, the less I want to meet her."

"We're staying at the Imperial Hotel. Colonel Meisinger says they have a good British tea there in the afternoon. Perhaps we could get together today. With Iris, that is, not Meisinger."

"I'm a little busy." If nothing else, Harry had an appointment in Yokohama on a project for the navy. "Were you listening to DeGeorge? There could be a war here before the end of the year."

"Or maybe not. The British seem to think the Japanese will back down."

"Beechum told you that?"

"He didn't have to, I can see for myself. I know you think I am naive, but I was a plant manager in China for five years, and I understand industry. When I see cars and trucks running on charcoal, I know Japan is in no condition to wage war against a country with such a huge industrial base as the United States. The Japanese must understand that."

"Sounds logical."

"I hope so."

Harry decided he had the time to pull over. "You need to see something else."

The two got out of the car, and Harry led Willie on foot across the road and through a screen of evergreens toward the torii gate they had glimpsed before. No proportions were simpler than the two upright and two horizontal beams, especially those of a giant gate covered in a dull glow of bronze. Around the gate, yellow ginkgo leaves drifted to the ground. On the far side gleamed the gilded eaves of a large shrine, its interior obscured by a white banner with the royal sixteen-petal chrysanthemum design draped above the stairs. The banner breathed like a sail in a light breeze. White doves swooped in and out.

"The Yasukuni Shrine," Harry said.

"What religion is this?"

"This is Japan. This is the heart. A friend and I used to pick pockets on the subway, then we'd come here and he'd dump his share in the offering box. One day we talked about what we were going to do when we grew up. I was going to be rich. He said what he wanted was to become a soldier so he could die for the emperor. And he got his wish. If you're captured or surrender, you're worse than dead, and you shame your family: but if you die fighting, you become a kind of a god, and this is your shrine, along with all the other loyal Japanese who died for their emperors. Since the fighting in China started, there are a hundred thousand new gods here. It used to be fun. There were wrestlers, jugglers, puppets, snake charmers."

"It still seems popular."

"Oh, it's that."

The shrine provided worship and entertainment. Farm couples reverently arrived in their best clothes and clogs to pray for dead sons, but the path was lined with stalls selling love charms, toy tanks, peanuts, waffles, paper cutouts of cranes, chrysanthemums, yin and yang. Students in uniforms and girls in sailor blouses snaked through the crowd. Soldiers hardly older than schoolboys gorged on sweet potatoes hot from a grill. What caught Willie's eye were women circulating with white sashes.

"Why is there so much excitement about sashes?"

"Thousand-stitch belts. You get one red stitch each from a thousand women. A soldier who wears one thinks he's invulnerable, despite all evidence to the contrary. Pilots wear them, which saves a hundred pounds in armor plating."

"Your friend had such a belt?"

"A big belt. His brother was a sumo." Harry stopped at a stone basin, scooped the cold water to his lips and dropped coins into the alms box for a joss stick that he lit and planted in the brazier's sand, pausing to let smoke envelop him. He clapped his hands, lowered his head and maintained a bow. When he straightened up, he asked Willie, "Would you want to fight people like this?"

Harry became aware of a dozen army officers in field uniforms with handguns and full-size samurai swords who had focused on him. Bodyguards, China vets with dark faces and narrow eyes. Usually this sort of scrutiny didn't bother him, but just the reminder that Ishigami was in Tokyo made Harry feel the impulse to flee. Finally, the officers shifted their gaze and scanned the throng. Guarding whom? Children on their fathers' shoulders were the first to point to a figure emerging from under the shrine's billowing sheet. He wore white gloves and army drab, had three stars on his collar and carried his cap in his hands. A row of priests in white miters escorted him, but he had the stride of a man who knew the address of the gods perfectly well by himself.

"General Tojo," Harry whispered.

"The prime minister?" Willie asked.

"Prime minister *and* minister of war, a tough parley to beat. He pays his respects most days. Well, he sent a lot of heroes here, he should show up."

With his bowed legs, shaved head, mustache and spectacles, Tojo fit the bill of a cartoon Japanese. Harry remembered him from the geisha houses in Asakusa as a loudmouth with a big cigar. In fact, what always struck Harry was how un-Japanese Tojo was. Most Japanese strove so hard for modesty they could be virtually inarticulate, while the general had a paranoid's talent for public ranting. On the other hand, his paranoia was well deserved. There were army officers ready to shoot Tojo because they thought he wasn't warlike enough. No wonder he had bodyguards.

"A bad sign he's here?" Willie asked.

"No, it's normal. A bad sign would be Tojo playing Santa, that would be scary."

"Do you think he was praying for peace?"

Harry gave the question consideration. "I think he was praying for oil."

6

I T WAS HARD to save a nation of sixty million souls. The Japanese let in few missionaries, including only twenty Southern Baptists, and those with the proviso that they accommodate the state by proving useful as teachers or doctors. They lived in Western houses, ate Western food, learned just enough Japanese to limp through a hymn. They performed good deeds and played bridge and waited for mail from home. All year they looked forward to summer, to well-earned vacations in the cool of the mountains, backgammon on the lawn, rowing on highland lakes, and over time the fiery evangelism they had brought to Japan seemed more and more like some out-moded, slightly ridiculous apparel.

Not Roger and Harriet Niles. To them, evangelism was the pure and ardent task of preaching the Word of God. That was their calling, the reason they had come halfway around the world, and they refused to dilute their time by spending it in a classroom or vaccinating the poor. People derided them as "railroad preachers." They traveled the country from Kagoshima in the south to snowbound Hokkaido, and any-time Roger could corner a group on a ferry or train, he would bring out his Bible and Harriet would translate his message in her halting Japanese. They even moved Harry and his uncle Orin from the safe embrace of the Methodists' compound to the rough streets of Asakusa to be more authentic and closer to the population they were trying to reach.

Still, for all their sacrifices, preaching to the Japanese was like trying to cleave water. The Japanese would smile, bow and say anything to move a gaijin along. Or would accept Jesus as a mere backup to Buddha. The truth was that for all their efforts, while Christian missions gathered converts by the millions in China and Korea, missions in Japan were a failure. Not just Baptists, all missions. It was for Roger, however, a personal failure, a crown of thorns sharp with mockery. He and Harriet would return to Tokyo exhausted only to see Orin wasted by drink, and their son Harry a sort of amphibian, neither honest nor stupid, neither adult nor innocent, neither American nor Japanese.

Harry found his parents' visits like sharing quarters with the hounds of hell. It was embarrassingly clear when the family attended services how little of Harry the congregation had seen. Harry had the Bible down, though. The wild-eyed revelations of Saint John the Divine were Scripture Harry had memorized as an insurance policy for whenever his father examined him about the condition of his soul or the imminence of Judgment Day. All the same, Harry's every word and move were followed by eyes quick to catch any deviation from a norm that was alien to him. He didn't remind Roger and Harriet of themselves. He preferred sandals to shoes, samurai to cowboys, raw fish to red meat. Harry didn't bring home tow-haired friends to play with; he didn't bring friends at all, because he wasn't going to expose his parents to a gang that included the unwashed Kaga twins or a criminal-in-training like Tetsu. So Roger and Harriet were only too happy to accept an invitation to Fourth of July celebrations at the American embassy. The entire American community would be there. It would be like going home.

Came the Glorious Fourth, and the embassy garden was decorated with bunting and paper lanterns in red, white and blue. On the terraces, Japanese staff in kimonos with American-eagle crests set out tables of tea sandwiches, deviled eggs, cucumber salad, sweet pickles, angel food cake and lemonade. Adults followed a path edged in azaleas to join a champagne reception in the ambassador's residence, a white clapboard house and porch that could have been found in Ohio. Outside, children were entertained by blindman's buff and potato-sack races across the lawn.

"This is actually American territory, Harry," Harriet said.

"We're in Japan."

"Yes," Roger Niles said, "but legally an embassy is the territory of the country of the ambassador. The American ambassador runs things here."

"The emperor rules all Japan."

"Not here," Roger said.

Harriet said, "You're in America just as if you were standing at the Washington Monument. And look, American kids."

Harry was miserable. All the other American children in Tokyo went to the American School. He didn't know them and he didn't want to know them. Dressed in a new suit and oxfords, he felt as if he were in disguise. Also, it was embarrassing to see how pleased his mother was to visit the embassy. She believed that the special events in life were like a sachet in a suitcase, it sweetened the clothes and didn't make the luggage one bit heavier. Besides, after a year of traveling among strangers, it was a relief for her to be patriotic, to be an American among Americans. She squinted up to admire how the Stars and Stripes basked in the rays of descending sun. There were supposed to be fireworks in the evening and skits performed by the kids. What Harry was going to do, he wouldn't say.

Except for Episcopalians, who were practically Catholic anyway, missionaries abstained from champagne and stayed outside by the lemonade. Baptist families joined a circle of Synod of Christ, Dutch Reformed and Methodists.

Roger Niles took the opportunity to ask the group, "You know what makes me sick?"

There was an uneasy pause. Niles had a reputation for zeal.

"What makes you sick, dear?" Harriet asked.

"The holier-than-thou act the China missions always pull. As if we were in league with the devil just because our call is in Japan."

"True," a Methodist minister named Hooper allowed. "We get it, too."

"Well, I wouldn't trade today for anything in China," Harriet said. "What about you, Harry?"

"China is old and backward. Japan can help China back on its feet." Harry had learned that at school.

"America can help China back on its feet," Hooper said softly.

"Sometimes I think what Harry needs is a trip back home," Roger said. "Would you like that, Harry, a good, long visit back home?"

"I am home." Harry didn't know much about Louisville, but he doubted that it measured up to Tokyo.

"Your real home," Harriet said.

"Our folks have never seen Harry," Roger told the others. "Harry, you have a lot of cousins you don't even know."

Harry had seen snapshots of them. The boys, slouching, buttoned to the neck, were always arrayed in ascending height before signs like RED MAN'S GORGE and STONEWALL JACKSON'S PLACE OF BIRTH. The girls had round eyes and dull, stringy hair just like the girls at the embassy.

A line of elderly Japanese guests cut through to reach the refreshments. Roger Niles said, "Look, they don't even beg your pardon. Typical."

Because they know you can't speak Japanese, Harry thought, surprised by his own scorn. He'd heard his parents try.

"Maybe Harry needs to get out there and mix," Hooper suggested. "My son would be happy to introduce him to the other boys."

What Harry had planned to do was go along the river with Gen and catch fireflies they could sell to geisha houses at ten sen apiece for firefly lamps. It had rained in the morning, and a clear night after wet weather made fireflies rise so thick that a good catcher could fill a paper sack, both hands and his mouth with captive flies. Instead, a shorter boy in a baseball cap was leading him to a game of tug-of-war being refereed by two embassy clerks.

The boy gave Harry a skeptical examination. "My name is Roy, but my friends call me Hoop. What's your name?"

"Oishi," Harry said.

"Oishi? That doesn't sound American."

"Who said it was?" Still, Harry was amazed. "You never heard of the Forty-seven Ronin?"

"No. I'm going to recite 'Casey at the Bat' for entertainment. What are you going to do?"

"I'm going to disappear."

The clerks each had fat cheeks and shiny, lubricated hair. They arranged tug-of-war teams on either side of the embassy's reflecting pool, smaller boys to the middle of the rope, larger boys at the ends. When one side had the advantage, the other side was dragged into the water. Almost immediately Roy Hooper lost his baseball cap in the pool, and Harry's oxfords were soaked. By his third time in the water, Harry saw by the smirks on their faces that the larger boys on each side were having fun pulling and giving way by turns, staying dry while boys in front got drenched. The same poorly concealed smile spread through the clerks, a collusion of the strong against the weak. Harry found the cap, filled it with scummy water, marched to the last on the rope, a robust boy in a Hawaiian shirt with a patch of beard on his chin, and stuffed the cap over his head. The boy hit Harry so hard he collapsed like an accordion, but he hung on to the boy's arm and dragged him to the ground. When the boy got on top, Harry head-butted him and bit his nose.

"Fight fair!" The clerks pulled the two up.

The bigger boy swung at Harry who ducked under the punch, grabbed him by the shirt and threw him down to the ground. It was what Harry had trained to do at school for years.

"Dirty fighter, are you?" someone said as Harry was pulled off again, but he broke free and ran for the trees and azaleas that screened the lawn from the street. The clerks got a late jump, and by the time they reached the trees, Harry was halfway up a pine and out of their sight. Their footsteps tramped around the needles.

"A missionary kid, can you believe that?"

"Almost bit his nose off, Jesus!"

"Probably went over the wall, the little son of a bitch."

Roger Niles's voice joined in. "Do you know where my son went?"

"No, sir. But it's getting dark and he could be anywhere now."

"Harry? Harry?"

"I wouldn't worry, sir. An American boy in Tokyo, where's he going to go?"

"Harry?"

"Got to go set up the fireworks, sir."

"Kind of a wild boy there, sir."

Two pairs of footsteps retreated. Roger Niles tramped back and forth calling Harry's name for another minute before he left. Harry heard one more set of steps slip between the trees, then his mother's voice. "Harry, I know we don't see you as much as we would like, but I do feel you are a special child, that you are protected like Moses was protected even in a frail cradle of reeds. That an angel watches over you and that you may seem a prince of Egypt when you are truly something even better. Could you come out now, Harry, wherever you are? For the love of your mother, could you do that, Harry?"

But Harry noticed that one branch of the tree he was in reached over the embassy wall to the garden next door, a rich man's garden banked with willows and maples, fountains of artfully worn stones and, over a pool, a haze of flickering yellow-green lights. As soon as his mother was gone, Harry climbed out on the branch and dropped into the garden.

The back of the house was a long balcony of summer screens made of threaded reeds, none lit from within that Harry could see. He slid a panel open and automatically slipped off his wet shoes before moving onto the mats of a richly spare room with a painted scroll hanging by a cedar post. Red lacquered sake cups seemed to float on a low table as black as ink.

"What are you doing here?"

Harry jumped, but it was only Roy Hooper at the open panel. Harry was surprised but turned the question around. "What are *you* doing here?"

"Following you."

"Then take off your shoes."

Harry moved from room to room. The owner had to be very rich judging by the screens of gold leaf and shelves of fine china that glowed in the shadows. Harry rummaged until he found a large glass jar with a perforated lid in the kitchen and black cotton cloth in a linen drawer.

"Are you stealing?" Roy Hooper asked.

"Don't be stupid. Just taking what I need."

By the time they returned to the garden, they heard the machine-gun report of firecrackers from the embassy and saw the occasional rocket zip high enough to be seen above the wall, followed by home-sick renditions of "Take Me Out to the Ballgame" and "Down by the Old Mill Stream." Meanwhile, Harry and Roy Hooper caught fireflies.

Around the pond were maples, dwarf pines and pillows of moss where fireflies swarmed in luminescent clouds. The darker the evening grew, the easier they were to see. Fireflies spread like a pulsating carpet over the damp grass, congregated under a drooping mulberry, spangled the water. Roy Hooper would hold the jar while Harry caught a firefly with both hands and gently blew it through the mouth of the jar. Brooms were another good way to carry fireflies, and a broom could look like a jeweled fan but wouldn't serve for this instance. Caught, fireflies flashed brighter in distress. Crushed, they emitted a burning green. In half an hour the glass jar was a glowing ball of captives, at least ten yen's worth at a geisha house, and Harry wrapped it in the black cloth to carry back over the wall.

The entertainment had just concluded when Harry and Roy Hooper returned. A couple hundred guests were still gathered on the lawn in the red, white and blue illumination of lanterns. The diplomatic corps sat in chairs that had begun to settle and list in the soft turf. Babies slept in their fathers' arms. A whiff of sulfur hung in the air.

"The prodigal sons," announced the clerk functioning as master of ceremonies. "Too bad they missed out on all the fun."

"They had sparklers," Harriet told Harry. "You know how you love sparklers."

"What have you got there?" Roger Niles asked. In the dark, despite its black cover, a faint halo surrounded the jar.

"Nothing."

"It's something worth making fools of us," his father said. "Let's see."

"Let's all see," the clerk picked up.

Roy Hooper's knees went soft as he felt the clamp of his father's hand.

"I'm disappointed in you," Reverend Hooper hissed.

"Or I'll send you home to Louisville," Roger told Harry under his breath. "I swear it."

"It's for the entertainment," Harry said.

"The entertainment is over," Roger said.

The clerk said, "One more act, that's fine with us. Isn't that fine, folks? This is a very different boy here. I bet he's got real different entertainment."

There was scattered applause in general, a snigger from the boy with a bandage on his nose. It was getting late. Most people wanted to go home. The ambassador yawned and fell into an expression of such boredom he could have been watching from the moon.

"Turn off the lamps," said Harry. "Just for a minute?"

When the lanterns went dark, there was a reflexive whimper from the younger children. Harry unscrewed the lid, and the jar underlit his face.

"It's a surprise," he said.

Harry put his mouth to the jar. As he raised his head, a light rose from his lips, flashed and took wing. He took another breath from the jar and blew a green tracer bullet in the eye of a clerk, a deeper breath and poured a glowing machine-gun fusillade at the guests. Dipped into the jar to feed himself and blew until his fingers and lips were smeared with green fire. The ambassador tried to brush the luminescence off his sleeves, spreading it instead. Children squirmed from their parents, screamed and ran into the dark. For a brief moment before Roger Niles seized him, Harry ruled, marching with the roar of fireflies.

7

HARRY DROVE for half an hour under a dazzling sun from Tokyo to Yokohama Bay only to find waiting for him the familiar shadows of Shozo and Go, the same plainclothes police that had watched his apartment at night. In the daylight Sergeant Shozo had a droll smile belied by heavy knuckles hanging from his sleeve. Corporal Go was young, with the zeal of a guard dog pulling on a chain. They were with the accountant from Long Beach Oil.

Long Beach shared a black-stained dock with Standard Oil of New York and Rising Sun, which sounded Japanese but was actually Royal Dutch-Shell. Long Beach wasn't much more than a small warehouse of corrugated steel, while Standard and Rising Sun fronted the water with miles of pipeline and acres of ten-thousand-barrel tanks. Didn't matter. In the most important regard they were no different, because no American or Dutch company, big or small, had delivered oil to Japan since July, six months before.

"Please." The accountant unlocked the warehouse door.

"I'm so curious," Shozo told Harry. "All this time I have heard about your special connections to the navy. Now we'll find out."

It was winter inside. Harry could see his breath by the clerkish light of green-shaded lamps that hung over a glassed-in office area. Rolltop desks crowded between file cabinets, chalkboards with lists of ships and ports, framed prices and schedules that showed the delivery of Venezuela crude at fourteen cents a barrel. Everything was spick-and-span, as if the American managers might return at any second, probably tidier without them. Harry stopped at a poster of the tanker *Tampico* with her ports of call—Galveston, Long Beach, Yokohama—a route that was history now. A snapshot tacked next to it showed a group of men around a racehorse. The rest of the warehouse held a truck loaded with ships' stores of canned foods gathering dust. Tucked around the truck were the wide-mouthed hoses that were usually laid straight on a dock, each hose dedicated to a different product: marine gas, dirty diesel, sweet crude and sour. Harry felt like the Big Bad Wolf asked into a house of straw.

The accountant's name was Kawamura. He was about sixty years of age, with a long neck and more hair in his ears than on his head. Harry knew the type, the salaryman who was first to the office, last to leave, whose identity was his work and whose sole delight was a binge at New Year's. He was Harry's target, but Harry had not expected the participation of Shozo and Go. Kawamura trembled and kept his eyes down, the decision of a man who didn't know which way to look.

Sergeant Shozo showed Harry a fountain pen. "Waterman, from my wife. I want to document this case. You have made my life and the life of Corporal Go so interesting."

Harry preferred to be ignored. The Special Higher Police countered espionage, but they were also called Thought Police, responsible for detecting deviant ideas. Harry was riddled with deviant ideas. Like, how the hell had Shozo and Go heard about this meeting? How had they found Kawamura?

Shozo opened a notebook. " 'Son of missionaries, born in Tokyo, grew up wild in Asakusa. Catching cats for shamisen skins. Running errands for prostitutes and dancers.' I would have traded places with you in a minute. When my mother took me by the pleasure quarters, the girls would always tease me from their windows, and my mother would almost pull my arm out of its socket."

"You must have been pulling the other way."

"Very hard." Shozo flipped a page. "Your parents had no idea what you were doing?"

"They could cover more ground without me. I stayed in Tokyo with an uncle who was drinking himself to death. I spoke Japanese. I sent the telegrams and collected the money for him. It was simpler that way."

"You would have made a great criminal. Don't you think so, Corporal?"

Go waved a pudgy fist at Harry. "All foreign correspondents are spies! All foreign reporters are spies! All foreigners are spies!"

Harry said, "No foreign resident has proven his usefulness to the Japanese government more than I have."

"That's what I was telling the corporal," Shozo said. "On the face of it, no American has been more useful to Japan. For example, Japan has an unfortunate shortage of oil. For a time you had a company to create petroleum?"

"Synthetic petroleum."

Shozo consulted his notes. "From pine sap. You persuaded Japanese banks during a time of national emergency to invest in pine sap?"

"That was one of a variety of approaches."

"When people talk about you and oil, they whisper about a magic show. What would that magic show be?"

"I have no idea."

"No idea?"

"None."

"You also proposed getting motor oil from sardines."

"It's theoretically possible."

"You have no scientific background?"

"Just business."

"Making money. Better than cat skins, too. What is the saying, what is it they say in English? It's very fitting."

"There's more than one way to skin a cat."

"Yes!" Shozo's mouth turned down into a smile. "That's what they say. 'More than one way to skin a cat'! That's what you are, a cat skinner, an American cat skinner."

Shozo's voice was drowned by a reverberation that shook the walls, a rolling thunder that rose to full throttle and abruptly quit, leaving expectancy and silence until a man in a leather coat and goggles slapped open the door. With a dispatch bag over his shoulder, a broad, confident face and thick hair sculpted by the wind, he was an image off a war-bonds poster. He pulled off gloves and goggles as he entered. Gen always arrived as if he'd just returned from the front, and sometimes he had, because he was more than an aviator, he was in Naval Operations. He bowed to Shozo and Go, winked at Harry. If he was surprised by the presence of the Special Higher Police, he didn't show it.

"Sorry to keep you waiting," Gen said. "It's been a busy day."

"You seem to know Harry Niles," Shozo said.

"Oh, I know Harry." Gen shrugged his coat off of navy blues. The sight of a lieutenant's stripes on the sleeve prompted Kawamura to give Gen an additional ninety-degree bow.

"I'm in the dark," Shozo said. "I am told that Mr. Niles performs valuable services, but I can't imagine what they are."

"You'll see." From his dispatch bag Gen took a legal-size book of faded maroon that he laid on the desk and opened. "The ledger of Long Beach Oil. Fascinating reading."

The entries were in India ink for English and blue for Japanese. As Kawamura stared down at the pages, he sweated despite the warehouse chill.

Gen explained to Shozo, "Kawamura is the accountant of Long Beach Oil. He finds himself in an unusual and uncomfortable position because Long Beach assets have been frozen by the Japanese government in retaliation for the freezing of Japanese assets and properties in the United States. The American managers of the company have gone back to the United States, leaving Kawamura, their senior Japanese employee, in a caretaker position, and he has carried out his duty to his employer faithfully."

"And faithfully to the emperor," Kawamura interjected.

"Of course." Gen grinned at Harry.

As kids, Gen and Harry used to strut around Asakusa in dark

glasses like hoods. One day they were getting their fortunes told in the temple when they heard a nasal buzzing overhead, looked up and saw a biplane come in low to waggle its wings over Buddha. Gen took off his dark glasses. The plane came by again, a silvery vision towing a sign that said EBISU BEER. It made Harry thirsty, but it changed Gen's life. Determined to fly, he became a model student who headed to the Naval Academy and aviation, then the University of California at Berkeley, studying English. Gen actually put more time in at American schools than Harry, and at Berkeley, he had picked up a little American sis-boom-bah, which fitted him for the navy general staff. The army's model was Germany, but navy comers tended to admire the British and the States and adopted a tradition of white gloves and ballroom manners. Somehow Gen Yoshimura had found the money to cover the costs that nagged at a student and officer. Harry thought there must have been some scrimping. With his poor-boy ambition and American style, Gen was a perfect amalgam.

"Let's assume," Gen told Kawamura, "that your employers were anxious as to how exactly the freeze of assets would be carried out here—whether there would be appropriation of their property, damage or misuse. By now they should be reassured that the Emergency Board for the Protection of Foreign Commercial Interests has the well-being of Long Beach Oil in mind. The freeze is an unhappy but temporary measure. It is a system that only works, however, when everyone cooperates, as most American companies have done."

"Yes." Kawamura tried to ignore Harry, as if not acknowledging a wolf would make it go away.

"But," Gen said, "there have been exceptions. Unfortunately, some American companies have created Japanese subsidiaries in which they attempt to hide assets. In other cases, American companies underreport their assets or their activity. The more critical the commodity, the greater chance of inaccurate reporting. Yo-yos, for example, have been accurately accounted for. Oil has not."

"I still don't understand," Kawamura said.

"Let's take an example," Harry said. "According to your own ledger, the tanker *Sister Jane* left California for Japan on May first with ten thousand barrels of oil. On May fifteenth, the *Sister Jane* arrived here and delivered one thousand barrels. It left the States with more oil than it delivered, ten times as much."

Kawamura finally exploded. "What is an American doing here? Is he an expert on trade?"

Harry said, "I'm an expert on cooking the books. It's the last item in the ledger. Read it."

Kawamura put on spectacles to read the page. "Ah, well, this is all a misunderstanding, a simple error. The first number was written as ten thousand but later corrected to one thousand. One thousand barrels left Long Beach, one thousand arrived here. You can see there is even the initial P for Pomeroy, our branch manager, to show his correction. There was no attempt to disguise anything. I would never have allowed it."

"I remember Pomeroy," Harry said. "Lived right next to the race-track. Pomeroy went home?"

"He is gone, yes."

"To Long Beach?" Gen asked.

"Los Angeles."

"He treated you well?" Harry asked.

"Always."

"It's quite an honor to be left in charge?" Gen asked.

"He trusts me, I think," Kawamura said.

"He should," Harry said. "You are obviously a stout defender of Long Beach Oil. But why the mistake? Why did a full ten thousand gallons of oil have to be corrected to a mere one thousand?"

"I don't know. I am embarrassed that there should be even the sug-gestion of a discrepancy. I can assure you, however, that when a ship arrives, we measure the quantity of oil in each tank on the ship before it is pumped, and again at the storage tanks after."

"How do they measure the oil on the ship?" Shozo asked.

"Tape and plumb bob," Harry said.

"Japan depends on oil," Gen said. "Japanese soldiers are giving their lives every day for oil."

Harry said, "It's hardly worth taking one thousand barrels across the Pacific. Did the *Sister Jane* stop on the way?"

"Only Hawaii," Kawamura said.

"Hawaii?" Gen asked.

"There was a problem with a sick seaman, as I remember. The ship was only in dock two nights."

"Tough luck for the seaman," said Harry. "But maybe a stroke of good luck for the rest of the crew. Honolulu has a lot of hot spots. Do you think the captain gave the crew two days' liberty?"

"I wouldn't know."

"Do you think maybe he pumped out nine thousand gallons of oil when the crew wasn't around?" asked Gen.

"No."

Harry said, "I'm just wondering why someone thought the *Sister Jane* left Long Beach with a lot of oil and ended up here with very little."

"No one was cheated. Whether it was one thousand or ten thousand, that was what we sold, no more, no less." Kawamura looked to Shozo for support, but the policeman's expression was grim. Go had started to giggle, which even Harry found unnerving. "I'm sure Pomeroy would have a good explanation if he were here."

"But he's not here and you are," Harry said. "I looked through the entire ledger, and in the twelve months before the freeze on deliveries, there were three other corrections for shortages of deliveries, totaling another thirty-six thousand barrels of oil that Japan desperately needed. You'll find the 'corrections' on pages five, eleven and fifteen, a little smudged but definitely altered." Kawamura flipped from page to page. This was like hunting rabbit, Harry thought. You didn't chase rabbits, you lit a fire and they came to you if you showed them a safe way out. "Who actually had possession of this ledger, you or Pomeroy?"

"Pomeroy."

Gen asked, "Who wrote down the number of barrels leaving Long Beach and arriving here?"

"Pomeroy." Kawamura looked ready to pull his head in his collar if he could.

"You didn't actually run the books on oil at all, did you?" Harry said. "That was the manager's job. After all, you're a financial man, not an oilman. What you were really in charge of was the branch budget, the payroll, dock fees, accounts payable. It must have been confusing to suddenly have to deal with customs, immigration, bills of lading. I doubt you ever would have noticed these barrel amounts."

"I didn't."

"But thirty-six thousand barrels and nine thousand, that is forty-five thousand barrels of oil," Shozo said. "Where did it go?"

"Good question," Harry said. "I personally think that Kawamura here is an honest Japanese employee duped by the American manager Pomeroy, who is probably at the racetrack at Santa Anita even as we speak."

Gen asked Shozo to take Kawamura outside.

"Let me." Go gathered the accountant.

"Just a dupe," Harry reminded the corporal.

"No Japanese should be duped," Go shouted back as he dragged Kawamura through the door. "All Americans are spies!"

On his way out, Shozo said to Harry, "I take it back. You would have made a good policeman, too."

The instant the door shut behind the sergeant, Gen slapped the desk. "God, that was fun." He dropped into a chair and put his feet up. Sometimes Gen's slovenliness struck Harry as virtually American. "I remember, as a kid, watching you do the change-from-a-hundred-yen-note scam, wondering how you always walked away with more money than you started."

"It's just how you count, forward or back. How did Shozo and Go know about this meeting?"

"I told them. It was for your protection. They were going to pick you up, so I had to show them how valuable you were."

"You could have warned me."

"No time. Everything's happening so fast."

"Like what?"

"Life." Gen leaned forward to spear a cigarette from Harry. "Did I ever tell you how I got in with the C in C?" The commander in chief of the Combined Fleet was Admiral Yamamoto. Naval personnel reverently called him the C in C.

"No."

"It was thanks to you. I was in the mess with some other officers, and suddenly the C in C himself was at the hatch asking whether anyone played poker. You know how it is with junior officers, one wrong answer can ruin a career. Guys played bridge, but no one was going to admit they gambled. Without even thinking, I said yes. He almost grabbed me by the neck to get me out of there, then I had to race to stay up with him to the senior mess, where there was a poker game of admirals and commanders, the C in C's inner circle. One had to go, and they needed a fourth. It's not much of a game without at least four players. The C in C gave me half of his own chips and said two things. First, that he didn't trust any man who wasn't willing to gamble. Second, that there was no point in playing except for money. That's what you always say, too."

"God's truth. So, how did you do?"

"Won a little. The C in C asked where I learned to play poker like that. I said Cal. He learned at Harvard. Anyway, from then on, whenever they needed a fourth, they called on me."

"Cal and Harvard? Wow, were you in the same fraternity? Both smoke briar pipes?"

"Come on, Harry."

"In other words, you gave me no credit for teaching you the most valuable thing you ever learned."

"Harry, you're the ace I keep up my sleeve."

"Shozo asked about the Magic Show."

"Oh, he did? What did you say?"

"That I didn't know what he was talking about. That's what I always say."

"Good. First the police know about it, then the army knows about it, then we're all in the drink." Gen pulled a folder tied with a red ribbon from the dispatch bag to signal a change in subject. He undid the ribbon and opened to a loose page that he stared at as if it were half in code: "This is the new total. With shortages of two hundred thousand gallons of oil from Petromar, and two hundred and forty thousand from Manzanita Oil added to Long Beach, altogether four hundred eighty-five thousand barrels of oil seem to have been diverted from Japan to Hawaii. There are enough tanks at Pearl Harbor to hold about four million gallons. We estimate they are already full. Where are they putting the extra oil that you have found? And if you found some, there is probably much more. There must be other tanks in Hawaii, and the only information we have on where they are is your story about an American contractor you met in Shanghai who claimed to have put reinforced tanks in a valley behind Waikiki."

"He was drunk. We were in a bar. He could have made it up."

"Why that story, though?"

"Gen, it's all stories. Books were altered, so what? Books are always altered, and mistakes are always made. The same with Manzanita and Petromar. It's fun to run Kawamura in circles, but we can't prove anything. Let me ask you this, have your people ever found those mysterious tanks? Why stick them in a valley? When did they build railroad tracks or oil pipes or access roads? The man was drunk. We were at the Olympic Bar in Shanghai, longest bar in the world, ten languages going at the same time, with two Russian girls who didn't understand a word, so I don't even know why he was boasting. You've been to the Olympic, it's a mob scene. I didn't get his name or his company, and he didn't draw a map on the back of a cocktail coaster. It's all smoke, Gen."

"It's four hundred and eighty-five thousand gallons, Harry. At least."

"I suppose it's a lot of oil. But it's just a story, that's all."

"If you could remember anything else. What he looked like?"

"He was fat and loud and drunk."

"Anything else?"

"What I know, you know. The only way to prove it is to fly over every valley in Oahu. Until then it's a rumor, a glass of fog. Why believe it at all?"

Gen released a smile with Pepsodent dazzle. "Because of the Magic Show. You nailed someone who had everyone else fooled."

"All I said was I saw a magician in China. I could have been wrong."

"You weren't. And the place you met him was the Olympic Bar in Shanghai, the same place you met this contractor. So we can't ignore anything you say happened there."

"Has this been good for your career? Get you more attention from the C in C?"

"It hasn't hurt." Gen was still smiling. "And I take care of you in return."

"Well, that's what I want to talk about." Harry mashed one cigarette and tapped out another. "You know what's more important to me than spies?"

"What?"

"My neck."

It took Gen a second. "What are you talking about?"

"Ishigami's back from China. I don't mind going over the company books from Long Beach Oil or Manzanita, you name it, anything to help an empire in need. Now I need some help. You do remember Ishigami?"

Gen's smile went flat. "The name is familiar. He's been in China, right?"

"Most of all, Nanking. His picture was in the paper yesterday. I'm surprised you missed it."

Gen put the ledger and folder back together and returned them to the dispatch bag. "Nanking was four years ago. You'll have to remind me what you were doing there. Or should I say, the scam?"

"For the Japanese government, looking for river tankers, trying to find them before they were scuttled. I was along in case there were any Americans on board. I might have liberated a car or two."

"You just never give it a rest, do you, Harry? You can't pull that around Ishigami."

"Well, he holds a grudge, and now he's after me. Call him off."

Gen threw on his leather coat, slipped the dispatch bag over his shoulder, pulled on his gloves. "He's in the army. The army and navy don't even talk to each other. The army spies on me. They spy on the C in C. Anyway, I understand they brought Ishigami back to do propaganda. After all, he is a hero."

"He's homicidal."

"Right now everybody's tense. We'll all be pulling together soon enough."

"That old team spirit?"

"You got it. In the meantime, our job is to protect the C in C from the crazies."

Harry followed Gen out the door to a Harley the size of a pony with a teardrop tank and low-slung fenders. There was something about the way Gen swung onto the bike, how he kicked the starter and twisted the throttle so that the bike ached to race away, that disquieted Harry.

"The C in C is a good gambler," Harry had to shout over the sound.

"Better than you, Harry. He broke the bank at Monte Carlo. They say he could have been a professional gambler. He really considered it."

Harry had heard the same stories. "Roulette is a tough game, okay. You don't play other players, you play the house, and the house odds are inexorably against you. You know about odds?"

"I know the odds." Gen slipped his goggles over his eyes. The glass spread his eyes like a mask.

"Do you? America outproduces Japan in oil by seven hundred to one. How do you like those odds?"

"That's why it's important to get all the oil we can."

"Really? Do you think a few extra drops of oil in Hawaii make any difference?"

"Every drop makes a difference."

Harry reached and turned the throttle down.

"No. Listen to me. What makes a difference is Standard Oil and Royal Shell. What makes a difference is a fountain, a flood of oil. Japan used to get ninety percent of its oil from America, sixty percent from Standard and Shell alone. That's five million gallons a year. Japan hasn't gotten one drop from Shell or America since June. Most of the oil in Japan goes to the navy, and the navy doesn't have enough oil to complete an exercise at sea. Don't ask how I know these things, you know they're true. Cut off oil and everything will come to a stop. I would guess six months. If Japan goes to war, it has to win by then. The odds? Fifty to one. Worse than Monte Carlo. I know how Naval Operations works. A lot of the planning is done by junior officers like you. Tell them the damn odds." No deal. Gen could have been a statue on a horse. "I'm only saying, let them know the odds. If there's a war, it won't be won with blood and sweat, it'll be won by the side that has the oil, that's all." Still no reaction from Gen. "Okay, try this. Aviation fuel is eighty-nine octane, which the United States has an endless supply of. Japan doesn't, so it designs the Zero, a wonderful fighter, to fly on piss. American planes will fly faster and farther not because of the pilots but because of the fuel. It won't be a matter of courage or skill, it will just be better fuel." Gen might have been stone. Not a word had penetrated.

"The difference is spirit and men," Gen said.

"Right. By the way, remember Jiro from our gang in Asakusa, how much he wanted to die for the emperor? He made it. He's in heaven now. I lit a stick for him today."

"If he died for the emperor, I am happy for him."

No American sis-boom-bah now, Harry thought. Just pure Japanese.

Gen milked the throttle again and seemed to regard his old friend from a great distance. "I'll do what I can about Ishigami. You know, Harry, Nippon Air came to me about putting you on the plane to Hong Kong. I backed you up. You shouldn't be spreading defeatist propaganda."

"Just numbers, Gen, forget I mentioned them. I appreciate everything you did to get me on the plane."

"When is it taking off?"

"Monday the eighth."

"Two days. Okay, I'll see about Ishigami. You stay out of trouble."

Gen put the Harley into gear. His hair snapped back as the bike surged and chased its noise along the dock. Across the bay under Yokohama's verdant bluff, Harry saw ships offloading the wealth of empire: bales of cotton from China, bags of rice from Thailand, sugar and sweet tropical fruits from semitropical Formosa and, from Manchuria—now the Japanese creation of Manchukuo—iron ore and lumber. A German blockade-runner, a gray freighter with a tarp over a forward gun, stood off by itself. The ships of Yoshitaki Lines were everywhere, there wasn't enough waterfront to go around. Sampans and barges swarmed to other freighters anchored out, the barges loaded until they shipped water. Through the sheer physical effort of a single oarsman, a sampan could move a half-ton of goods. Along the Bund, stevedores in straw hats and padded jackets swung on hooks, clambered up nets and trotted with handcarts between railway cars, men in motion everywhere. The scene put Harry in mind of a drunk bingeing on his last full bottle. But the days when Yokohama swallowed a full measure of sweet Maracaibo crude or clean American diesel the color of honey, those days were gone.

ON THE WAY back to Tokyo, Harry drove by Haneda Field. In the far distance was a white tower and hangars. Harry was tempted to visit Nippon operations and see the plane they were flying to Hong Kong, a DC-3 with a full bar and sleeper seats, but he quelled the urge when soldiers appeared along the edge of the road, and decided it wouldn't do for a gaijin to show too much interest in an airport. On the other side of the road, however, were ballplayers on a field. It was a small field with grassy slopes for bleachers and a little scoreboard beside a bottle-shaped sign for Asahi beer, but Harry recognized the team's gray flannel uniforms with black and orange piping even from his car, and he rolled up to a clubhouse of cinder blocks painted green. The ticket window was shut. Harry walked through the turnstiles to the batting screen and joined a couple of reporters who were arguing over who was paid more money, Bob Feller or Satchel Paige. Feller was the biggest star in American baseball, but Paige sneaked around that fact by playing both the Negro league and winter ball.

The Tokyo Giants were taking advantage of the warm weather to hold an off-season workout. Not just for rookies; Harry spotted the home-run slugger Kawakami and the pitcher Sawamura, who once struck out Ruth, Foxx and Gehrig in a row. Japanese were fanatical about practice. Pitchers threw hundreds of pitches a day, which was probably why their arms wore out so soon. Especially with breaking pitches, a Japanese specialty. Every few minutes a fighter plane would pass overhead, towing its shadow across the diamond and up over the slope to the airfield across the road. Otherwise the scene was immaculately normal. One coach hit grounders to the infield, another lofted fly balls toward players stationed in front of the beer sign, pitchers lobbed the ball back and forth on the sidelines. Sawamura had lost two seasons to active duty in China and was resurrecting what had been the league's best fastball. With each pitch, the catcher's mitt produced a satisfying pop.

Harry was a Giants fan, and no one on the team ever had to pay for a drink at the Happy Paris. He liked practice almost as much as games. He found a meditative calm in the repetition of the infielders as they broke for the ball, fielded the good hop, set their feet and fired to first. They refused to backhand grounders or dive for liners, but otherwise they were as good as Americans. Also, they played honorable baseball: they would never slide with their spikes high to break up a double play or throw a knockdown pitch. During the season every game had an epic dimension; when the Giants lost, there was mourning throughout Tokyo, and an error on the field demanded an apology from a shamefaced player to his entire team. After games, writers raced back to the office on motorcycles to file their stories. Even at a winter workout like this, when Kawakami, "The King of Batting," walked to the plate with his famous red bat—fashioned from a sacred tree in a secret forest—the writers studied every swing as if he were a great actor onstage. When he knocked a ball over the scoreboard, they oohed and aahed like children. The Japanese were crazy for home runs.

One of the Giants ran off the field, leaving Sawamura no one to throw to, so he motioned Harry to pick up a loose glove. The pitcher had such a smooth motion and the ball came with such easy velocity that Harry's hand stung with every catch, but he was damned if he was going to let it get by him or be distracted by a line of bombers coming out of the sun, practicing an approach in close formation. As the planes passed overhead, the gunners in their bubbles seemed near enough to shout to.

When Harry's arm warmed, the ball went back and forth with more energy. A game of catch was a conversation in which nothing in particular need be said. Motion was all, motion and the elongation of time. Activity around the field—grounders, fly balls, the pitchers' easygoing throws—took on the steady nature of a metronome. At the batting cage, Kawakami took a cut. The ball rose and hung, spotlit by the sun, as a fighter that had just taken off from Haneda came over the clubhouse. For a moment the ball and plane merged. Then the fighter passed, trailing a shadow that leaped the outfield fence. And the ball came down into a glove and the fielder threw it cleanly, on one hop, to home.

8

A FTER THE BATTLE at Ueno Park, Kato took Harry into his confidence more and more, allowing him into his studio and paying him to deliver finished work. Harry liked the studio for its sophisticated jumble of Greek statues, samurai armor, urns stuffed with props like umbrellas, swords and peacock feathers. Artfully out-of-focus photographs of French haystacks and cathedrals covered the walls, plaster casts of feet and hands weighted the cloths that covered works in progress. Whether his models posed in kimonos or without, Kato always wore a studio coat and beret because, as he said, "Professional decorum is never so essential as with a naked woman."

Western art was for himself. For money, Kato produced purely Japanese woodblock prints. It was a transformation to Harry. Kato was no longer an imitation Frenchman fussing over a palette, he was a master who could capture the contours of a model with a seemingly continuous line of ink. The model herself was no longer a sallow, short-limbed version of a Parisian prostitute but a delicate courtesan wrapped in a silk kimono. Better yet for a boy like Harry, the process was a puzzle to be disassembled and put back together. Kato's sketch went to a carver who sent back a close-grained cherry-wood keyblock and as many as ten other blocks carved for separate colors. Sometimes Kato sent the blocks to a printer, sometimes he did the printing himself. He printed one color a day, from light to dark—clamshell for white, red lead for tan, turmeric for yellow, redbud for pink, safflower for red, cochineal for crimson, dayflower for blue, lampblack for ebony—on soft mulberry paper. Kimonos were always a challenge, with their patterns of peacock eyes, russet leaves, cherry blossoms, peonies. The subtlest color of all, however, was skin, painted with the lightest pink to flatten the fibers of the paper. Layer by layer the colors coalesced into an image, the slattern into an innocent beauty, a swirl of lampblack for a teapot's steam, a dusting of mica to suggest the night. Harry enjoyed the misdirection. Great artists like Hokusai or Kuniyoshi could each print a series called *Thirty-six Views of Mount Fuji*, which were not pictures of Fuji but of life in Tokyo, of courtesans or fishermen or peddlers stumbling up a hill with a small, hazy Fuji floating serenely in the background.

Harry arrived once when Kato had gone for medicine and left the door unlocked. Harry was inside alone, stealing a smoke, when an ember fell from the cigarette and burned a drop cloth. He had to move a plaster cast to refold the cloth and hide the incriminating hole and, in doing so, uncovered a work in progress that he had not seen before: a courtesan in an elegant black-and-blue-striped kimono, her hair knotted and embellished with a tall white comb. What was different about this print was that she was in the pleated leather back of a large car, leaning to one side with a cigarette to accept a light from a male hand holding a lit match. The more Harry looked, the more he saw the artistry in the two sources of light, the match's small ball of fire and the moon through the rear window of the car. How her twisted position revealed the line of her neck. How loose strands of hair and the kimono's rumpled surface indicated a recent intimacy. What surprised him most was that the woman was Oharu.

Oharu was Harry's best friend at the theater, his older sister and secret love. Harry had seen her only in chic skirts and French hats. He moved another cast to pull more of the drop cloth off. A second, almost finished print was of Oharu at a cherry-blossom party, wrapped in a maiden's pink kimono and seated on a quilt covered with fallen pink and white blossoms. It would have been a portrait of innocence itself, except for the fact that the quilt was planted with bottles of sake and beer. Oharu slumped to the side, her eyes slitted with drink, a ukulele forgotten in her hands. Golden bees crawled over the blossoms, bottles, Oharu's hair. A third print was so dark it took Harry a moment to understand it was a ballroom flecked by the reflections from a mirror ball on dancing couples, black figures on a blue floor, the only one identifiable, Oharu, in a red kimono waiting by the slanted light of a half-open door.

By now Harry couldn't stop. He uncovered a stack of prints, a catalog of copulation, on every page a samurai or monk inserting his monstrously swollen erection into a woman experiencing such transport that her eyelids were closed and her teeth bit into cloth as if to stifle any outcry, while, under a kimono's disarray, her legs splayed, the gaping bush lay exposed and her toes curled in ecstasy. The main thing so far as Harry was concerned was that the prints were antiques, not of Oharu.

"Interested?" Kato asked.

Harry hadn't heard the artist return. There was no point in trying to hide the prints. "What are they?"

"Treasures. Instruction for a bride, entertainment for an old man, a charm a samurai would be proud to carry in his helmet. Now items of shame, victims of Western morality. You know, Harry, Westerners know so little about and seem to take so little pleasure in sex, it's a wonder they propagate at all. Your father, of course, is the worst."

"Why him?"

"Because he is a missionary and a missionary is a murderer, only he murders the soul. And he is smug about it. If it were up to your father, Japan would have no Shinto, no Buddha, no Son of Heaven and no sex. What would be left?"

"What about the pictures of Oharu? I like those."

"You do? One moment you're a snoop, the next you're a connoisseur."

"Could I buy one?"

"Buy?" Kato put the medicine down to cough, slowly open his cigarette case and regauge the conversation. "That's different. I should treat you with more respect. These portraits of Oharu are not for any

ordinary print run. They are one-of-a-kind, special collector's edi-
tions."

"I'll pay over time."

"It might take your lifetime. I don't know of any missionary boy,
even you, Harry, who can afford that. Which one were you thinking
of?"

Harry scanned Oharu in the car, the cherry blossoms, the ballroom.
"The ballroom."

"Ah, very telling, because she seems to be waiting, doesn't she,
hoping to dance. The room is so dark you might even be in it. You'd
wait for the right dance, of course. She's a little tall for you now, but in
the fantasy she's perfect, her ear to your cheek. That's the charm, you
know, of the ballroom dancer or café waitress. Not sex but conversation. Japanese men don't talk to their wives. The most normal relationship they have is with their favorite waitress. How would you get
that kind of money, Harry?"

Harry was truculent, devoid of ideas. "Some way."

"That covers a lot of ground, all of it dishonest. I'll have to think
about that before you start robbing people in the streets. But, as an
artist, I've never been more flattered."

Harry was good with a knife and glue, and Kato found work for
him after school at the Museum of Curiosities, helping the proprietor
patch its half-human monsters. Harry especially liked the mermaids
with their long horsehair and lacquered skin of papier-mâché,
hideous fangs and sunken eyes, like the remains of a nightmare
washed up on a beach. Harry earned more money when Kato
entrusted him with the carving of censors' seals for certain reproduc-
tions, fakes. Kato taught him how to trace old seals on translucent
paper, transfer the paper to balsa and carve an exact copy that would
add the stamp of authenticity.

"Who knows?" Kato said. "You may be an artist yet."

"I can't draw."

"But you have a steady hand. Do you suppose that comes from
picking pockets?"

"I'm not doing that so much anymore."

"Go ahead. Artists steal all the time, that's why taste is so important."

One thing preyed on Harry's mind. "You're not going to hold it against me that my father is a missionary?"

"No. I've taken my revenge on him."

"What kind?" Harry wondered how Kato could ever reach a zealot like Roger Niles.

"Ah, Harry, you're revenge enough."

9

A TEA CART WITH scones and cream, strudel and napoleons rattled around the lobby of the Imperial Hotel. The Imperial had been the safe haven of well-heeled tourists, especially Americans who were amplified, on-the-road versions of themselves, busy with backslaps and laughs that had boomed up to the lobby's timbers. The Imperial had been designed by Frank Lloyd Wright, who piled brick and lava rock in a grandiose style suggestive of a Mayan temple. Harry thought the hotel, with its vaulting shadows and wintry drafts, was a proper set for *Dracula*. Still, it was sad to see the tea cart make its circuit around the lobby like a trolley car in an empty city.

Also, Harry owed the Imperial. He'd come back to Japan for a public relations job that fizzled and left him high and dry, with not even enough money for return passage, until the American All-Stars came to town. Babe Ruth, Lou Gehrig and Lefty O'Doul led a tour by the world's greatest ballplayers and their wives. Naturally, they stayed at the Imperial. Harry was stalking the lobby for a tourist who might need a knowledgeable guide when a receptionist came up all aflutter. Harry expected the heave-ho. Instead, the receptionist bowed and asked if he would please proceed to the pool garden. When Harry got there, he found an official welcome that was falling apart. On one side of the garden were the Japanese in formal cutaways and kimonos with stacks of boxes, on the other side was a straggling line of the All-Stars in baseball uniforms and their wives in furs. In the middle was a movie camera with an operator who spoke no English, which was just as well because every time his assistant tried to push Mrs. Ruth within camera range, she told him to keep his mitts off. The Babe had had a little brandy in his breakfast coffee and tried to nudge O'Doul into the water. When the Babe's wife told him to stop acting like an ape, the Babe gave her a playful pop on the shoulder. Meanwhile, the Japanese hosts grew smaller, their eyes wider. The girls in kimonos inched back, ready to run. One of the wives, a marcelled blonde in a fox stole, yawned and spat a wad of gum into the pool, setting off a tussle among the goldfish.

Harry figured this was a classic case of nothing to lose. He stepped forward and announced in English, on behalf of the hotel, how honored the Imperial was by the presence of the All-Stars and their lovely wives, and responded in Japanese, on behalf of the players, how impressed they were by the warm hospitality of the famous Imperial Hotel. He spoke rapidly, no seam between English and Japanese, respectfully but with animation, easing each side toward the middle of the garden, directing the cameraman to start filming, interpreting speeches back and forth, signaling the Japanese girls it was safe to distribute gifts, a happi coat for each player and towels for their wives.

"Do I look wet?" Mrs. Ruth asked Mrs. Gehrig.

The Babe got in the mood, posed in his happi coat and pushed a dimple into his cheek. Before leaving the garden for the ballpark, he lit a huge Havana and asked Harry, "Kid, you want to make some change? My stepdaughter's along. She's cute and she likes to trip the light fantastic. Just keep your hand off her ass or I will feed you to the fucking goldfish."

"Sounds good," said Harry. He stuck with the All-Stars for the rest of their tour and, by the end, had been hired by the movie company to do promotion, which was the kind of work he had done in the States. From then on he felt a debt of gratitude to both the Babe and the Imperial.

Now he picked up a paper from the hotel newsstand for any word of Ishigami. Nothing. Found an article about the Giants' midwinter practice and dedication to victory. Returned to the front page and read that the Germans had as good as taken Moscow, as they had for weeks. In America, Charles Lindbergh declared that there was "no danger to this country from without." Tensions in Washington had eased, negotiations were back on track. Roosevelt was more conciliatory. According to *Ripley's Believe It or Not*, most chimps were left-handed. All the stories sounded equally likely to Harry.

The bar was virtually empty. The only occupants Harry saw at first were German officers from the blockade-runner. It was a long run from Bordeaux, evading British cruisers or the torpedo of a submarine, twenty thousand miles not to fire a shot but to carry precious rubber to Germany, and there was something exhausted about the men and the way they sank into their schnapps. Of course, the Imperial was lucky to have them. Aside from troopships, international travel had come to a halt. Tokyo's World Fair and Olympic Games had been canceled, luxury liners called home, embassy dependents ordered out. In the far corner Harry found Willie Staub with DeGeorge and Lady Beechum.

"Harry." Alice Beechum offered her hand for a kiss. She was pink as a petit four offering a taste. Pink as a Gainsborough portrait, pinker than pink with an exuberant mass of ginger hair. On the Tokyo stage, actresses who played Europeans wore ginger wigs. Alice's blue eyes and ginger hair were her very own, and Harry also remembered breasts with the tang of Chanel.

"Lady Alice. I saw your husband this morning."

"Yes. He was so worked up when he got home, he was ready to strangle puppies. He told me he gave you quite the rocket. He was very proud. Then he went off to toss medicine balls or something with his pals."

"You're not a popular man at the British embassy, Harry," DeGeorge said.

"I'll slit my throat."

"Get in line."

Willie was sipping tea, but for everyone else at the table "tea" meant martinis or Mount Fujis, gin with a peak of frothed egg white. Harry wondered, would this be his social circle for the duration if he missed the plane? The expats of the Imperial bar? DeGeorge, who dripped acid like a wreck leaking oil?

Willie asked, "What would they do to you? You'd be enemy aliens, but there are conventions about this sort of thing. They wouldn't put you in jail."

"Or make us learn Japanese," DeGeorge said. "I'd rather be behind bars."

"This conversation is absolutely sparkling," Alice Beechum told Harry. "But I was wondering, how is that little Michiko of yours?"

"Speaking of . . ." Willie said.

Harry's heart sank when he followed Willie's eyes to a young Chinese woman making her way toward the table. She wore a silk cheongsam with a pattern of peonies, her hair was twisted into a chignon set off by an ivory comb and her eyes were bright with hope. Harry had to say that she was a little chubby, a bad sign since it suggested that she was real and Willie truly loved her. She was, in short, a disastrous complication for a man who should be traveling light. The problem was that Germans were such romantics. Not as romantic as Japanese; the Japanese *preferred* sad endings and suicide. But what Willie needed after China was a *Wanderjahr* on a beach somewhere, or searching the desert for philosophy, anything but dragging some poor Chinese girl to Nazi Germany.

"Iris is a teacher," Willie said after introductions. "We're hoping she'll be able to continue doing that in Germany."

"I suppose that would be up to the local *Gauleiter* or *Gruppenführer,*" Harry said.

"Yes."

"Have you tried the Mount Fuji?" DeGeorge asked Iris. "It was invented here."

"Inventing alcoholic drinks is a major pastime of the expatriate community," Harry said to her. "Where did you teach?"

"At a missionary school," she said.

"Iris's father is a Methodist minister," Willie said. "Her mother went to Wesleyan College in the United States, and her oldest brother is a graduate of Yale."

"Well, your English sounds better than mine," Harry said. Even the cupped echoes of Iris's Chinese intonation were charming.

"What university did you attend, Harry?" Willie asked.

"Bible college."

"But you chose not to become a missionary?" Iris said.

"I did publicity for Paramount and Universal. Pretty much the same thing. Are you enjoying the hotel?"

"It doesn't seem Japanese," Iris said.

"Not at all. Like Valhalla with Oriental lamps. But the emperor is a major shareholder, and that makes it Japanese enough."

"Earthquake-proof," DeGeorge added. "That's all this tourist needs to know."

"How is Michiko?" Willie tried to steer the conversation.

"Yes," Alice said, "we all want to know. Is Michiko doing a little flower arranging or is she whisking tea?"

"There's a gal who could whisk the balls off a bulldog," DeGeorge said.

"According to Willie, she has musical interests," Iris said.

"Contemporary music," Harry said.

"Iris plays the piano," Willie said. "Mozart, Bach."

"Michiko plays the record player. Basie, Beiderbecke."

"That calls for another round." DeGeorge summoned the waiter.

"Is there any news on the negotiations in Washington?" Willie asked.

"The U.S. wants Japan out of China. Japan wants to stay. It's the old story of the monkey and the cookie jar. He can't get his hand out without letting the cookie go, so he doesn't get the cookie or his hand. Now, Harry may have a different version, he's the number one defender of the Japanese."

"I just think there were lots of hands already in that cookie jar. British, Russian and American."

"You know what I hear, Harry? The Japs are selling the Chinese cigarettes laced with opium."

"Well, the British once fought a war in China to sell opium. The Japanese are great admirers of the British."

"He really is incorrigible," Alice Beechum said.

"You never thought of being a missionary?" Iris asked.

"Maybe I should," Harry said. "It's a good racket. Missionaries stole Hawaii."

"Not everybody sees it that way," DeGeorge said.

"Because they read *Time*, published by the son of a China missionary. The American people are fed stories about Chiang Kai-shek as though he's Washington at Valley Forge. The most sanctimonious lobby in the United States is China missionaries, and if we have a war, it will be due in good part to them."

"You really have no sense of morality at all, do you, Harry?" DeGeorge said.

Iris bowed like a flower in the wind and changed the subject. "Michiko sounds very interesting. I so look forward to meeting her."

"That depends on how long you're going to be here, I suppose. Willie?"

"Perhaps for a while. The embassy is slow about giving us our papers."

"Willie has his papers, but the embassy is holding back mine," Iris said. "They say he should go, and I would follow."

Willie said, "They'll never give her papers once I go."

"What's their reason for stalling?"

"They claim that the background of any foreign applicant must be investigated for unhealthy political involvement. That's natural, I understand. But there are no investigative German agencies in China, and it seems any such investigation would have to be carried out by Japanese authorities. Although Germany and Japan are allies, there seems to be a lack of cooperation."

"Imagine that."

"That's why we're turning to you, Harry. You have influence with the Japanese. I saw this morning at the Chrysanthemum Club how you swayed them. They might approve Iris for you. Then, if they sent an approval to the German embassy, something would happen. Otherwise, they may force me to go alone."

"Why does Harry have influence with the Japanese, that's what I want to know," DeGeorge said.

Harry took the deep breath of a surgeon reluctant to cut. "Willie, your embassy gave you good advice. Get Iris someplace like Macao, then you go home to Germany and wait. According to the führer, the war will be over in a week or two."

"What if it's not?"

"Yes," Alice Beechum said. "What if, for some unlikely reason, it's not?"

"A year or two. True love can wait."

Willie's cheeks turned red. "Anything can happen. Harry, you have to help."

"I didn't get her into this. You could have had the honeymoon without the preacher. You could have had your fun and said good-bye. You could have left Iris in China with enough money to buy her safety."

"I am not a prostitute." Tears sprang down Iris's face.

"Money is not just for prostitutes," Harry said. "The Bible says, 'For where your treasure is, there will your heart be also.' The Portuguese are a kind and worldly people, and they're neutral. Portuguese Macao is probably the safest place on earth."

"Harry Niles, marital adviser. Willie, let me explain," Alice said. "If we were in England, Harry would help my marriage by being my co-respondent, the 'other man.' We'd arrange compromising photos in bed. He'd be perfect because his reputation can't get any blacker. He is the bar other villains measure themselves by."

Harry said, "Aren't you supposed to be at a meeting of 'British Housewives Against the Huns'?"

"I'm kind of curious," DeGeorge said and hunched closer to Willie. "Why would you even ask Harry Niles to help? When did Harry Niles lift a finger for his fellow man?"

Willie looked away.

"Seriously," DeGeorge said, "how could you ask Harry?"

"In China . . ." Iris began.

"I don't know," Willie said.

"Hey, I'm a reporter," DeGeorge said. "I smell something here, Willie. You knew Harry in China. 'Fess up."

"Willie," Harry said. They'd agreed not to talk about this.

"I heard Harry got in a tight spot in China," DeGeorge said. "Was it stealing cars, or a scam like his pine-tree gasoline?"

"Don't do it," Harry told Willie.

"No, they think I'm a fool for asking you to help. I'll tell them why."

DeGeorge sat forward to share the joke. The martinis arrived, and Harry sank with one into his chair. Sometime or other he had to get some food.

Willie said, "I was manager of Deutsche-Fon in Nanking. We handled the telephone exchange and electrical power. By December it was clear that the Japanese army would attack because Nanking was the capital, and once it surrendered, everyone assumed that the war would be over. But the Chinese resisted more than was expected, and even when the city fell, the army wouldn't surrender, which infuriated the Japanese, and they began executing people. They shot men in the back of the head or bayoneted them or beheaded them or drowned them individually and in groups. I have heard estimates of ten thousand to a hundred thousand dead. I personally would say many more. I had hundreds of Chinese employees I was responsible for, them and their families. I was not alone. There were twenty other Westerners left in Nanking, mainly German businessmen and American missionaries, and we created an international safety zone to protect Chinese whose homes had burned. I was elected head of the committee, a position I accepted because I was also head of the Nazi Party in Nanking and had to set a moral tone.

"The zone was only a few square kilometers, but soon we had three hundred thousand Chinese under our protection. Though, as I said, there were only twenty of us, so the protection was not very good. Every day the Japanese would come to take away women to rape. Some we saved, some we did not. The Japanese came for men to kill. They roped them together a hundred at a time. Some we saved, most we did not. Or they robbed them. The Japanese took jade, gold, rugs, watches, wooden spoons. Attacked safes with guns, grenades, acetylene torches. If they took a woman away to search, we knew we would never see her again. We saved who we could.

"We had to feed all these poor people. We transported bags of rice in my car, the roof of which I covered with a white sheet with a red cross, so that we wouldn't be fired on, because cars were always being commandeered and the drivers killed. Every time we went for rice, someone would run from a house to tell us his wife or his daughter was being raped inside, would we help? I had a Nazi armband. With that as my authority, I stopped some incidents, but I was not always successful. One time when I was failing, our driver, one of the Americans, a new face, got out with me. Since he had a stethoscope, I assumed he was a doctor. He brushed a line of soldiers aside, pushed up the girl's skirt, proceeded to examine her and spoke to the soldiers in Japanese. Apparently he convinced them the girl had a venereal disease. That was Harry. I don't know where he got the stethoscope, I think he stole it. From then on, Harry was my driver."

Harry studied the ceiling's Gothic gloom, the crosspieces of concrete and lava rock. All they lacked were bats.

Willie went on, "Sometimes Harry and I would patrol in the car and load it with girls. Harry altered documents from the Japanese command so they seemed to give him the authority to prevent the spread of infection among the troops, which meant removing the women from their rapists. For added authority, he wore one of my armbands to pretend he was German, too.

"It wasn't only women. We had a truck. Harry and I would load it with men taken from hiding and put on a top layer of the dead bodies in case we were stopped, which we often were. Harry would produce papers ordering us to remove bodies around the zone to prevent cholera or typhoid. He was excellent at creating official papers. The killing went on for weeks. When new Japanese recruits arrived, they were drilled in the use of the bayonet with live Chinese, to accustom them to blood. One officer, a Lieutenant Ishigami, became a kind of legend for beheading a hundred Chinese."

"End of the story," Harry said. "Willie, you've said enough."

"Except that Ishigami came to the Happy Paris last night after you left."

"Enough."

Willie slid back in his chair. "Very well. Anyway, that's part of what happened in Nanking and why I am perhaps not such a fool to think

that Harry, the Harry Niles I knew in China, might possibly help us
here."

The table was quiet. Finally DeGeorge said, "Harry with a swastika
on his arm? I can picture that."

"No. Harry was heroic."

"Maybe. You don't speak any Japanese, you don't really know
what actually transpired, you know only what Harry told you. But
Harry in a Nazi armband, that I can believe."

"I'll call some people about Iris," Harry said.

"I would be forever grateful." Willie jumped up to shake Harry's
hand. "At the War Ministry? Someone from the military police would
be best. High up?"

"Well, people with influence."

"Thank you," Iris said. "You are just as Willie described."

"Willie has a hell of an imagination." Harry stood to leave. "Nice to
meet you. Only, no more fairy tales."

"You can't stay?" Willie said.

"I'm off, too, to Matsuya's for the necessities, soap, Scotch, cigarettes," Alice said.

"Lady Beechum thinks there may be a war in a day or two," said
DeGeorge.

Harry said, "Your husband says, 'The little yellow Johnnies don't
have the nerve.' "

"There you are." She lifted a smile to Harry. "It's men like Arnold
who have put the British Empire where it is today."

AN ENTIRELY DIFFERENT Hajime was at Tokyo Station. Gone was last
night's maudlin drunk and in his place was a sober Hajime in khaki,
field cap and cape. The railroad platform was crowded with recruits,
parents, friends, little brothers waving flags, sisters delivering thousand-stitch belts with all their protective powers. Some men were
shipping out for the second time, but most were boys clumsy in their
helmets and field packs with bedrolls and entrenching tools. Banners
hung vertically from lamp poles announced, ONE HUNDRED MILLION
ADVANCING LIKE A WALL OF FLAME!, the sort of wish some travelers

could do without, Harry thought. A brass band produced a rendition of "My Old Kentucky Home" that shook dust from the station's spidery skylights.

Hajime regarded the confusion with a veteran's detachment. "Thanks for coming, Harry," he said. "All you need is one friend to see you off, right?"

"I guess so." Harry probably would not have come at all if it hadn't been for Hajime's gun. Harry gave it to him still boxed and wrapped as if handing over a farewell gift. Since its loss was punishable by death, Harry expected a little gratitude. Instead, Hajime demanded a smoke. Harry gave him a pack, and Hajime lit up with ostentatious ease.

"Thanks. Remember the days when we used to run around Asakusa? We ruled the roost, Harry. You and me and Gen, we ruled the roost."

Hajime had done well by the army, however. Here he was in a crisply ironed uniform with a sergeant major's tabs, a waxed and bristling mustache and thick spectacles that magnified his self-importance, no sign of the falling down drunk who had pissed on the street outside the Happy Paris the night before. He was still loathsome, but he had no family or friends, and Harry supposed that, after all, someone ought to see the son of a bitch off. It didn't seem to matter to anyone on the platform that Harry wasn't Japanese. In this crowd, with its blur of emotion, he seemed to blend in well enough.

"These kids think they've been through boot camp," Hajime said. "Wait until I get my hands on them. Do you know why a soldier will charge a machine gun across an open field?"

"Why?"

"Because he's more afraid of me."

Which was true enough. Harry had heard plenty of stories about recruits considered too short or tall or slow or quick who had been beaten until their noses were split, teeth lost, eardrums burst. Supposedly it was a psychological approach, to create a rage that could be turned on the enemy. Rage and fear plus devotion to the emperor. Harry was always amazed how the army could take so many young scholars, gentle poets, honest farm boys and fishermen's sons and turn them into killers. It took the hard work of men like Hajime.

"Well, I can see why you're so eager to get back to China. Ever afraid of a bullet from your own men?"

"I never turn my back on them."

The train was late. The crowd shifted to fill the platform without falling onto the tracks. Fathers sucked in their chins with pride while women seemed more ambivalent about sending off sons who looked young enough to be trading baseball cards. A man in a bowler asked Harry, "Would you be so kind?" and handed him a camera, a little spring-bellows Pearlette. Harry took a picture of the man with a young recruit who had a bright red face from ceremonial farewell cups of sake and a thousand-stitch belt tied like a scarf around his neck, a son who was obviously the measure of his father's love.

"Remember 'Forty-seven Ronin'?" Hajime said. "Remember how we let you in even though you weren't Japanese?"

"I think you needed someone to chase."

"We had a great gang. Then you and Gen started hanging around the theater and dumped the rest of us."

"We grew up."

"What was the name of that dancer you were so crazy about? Oharu? That was terrible about her."

"What's the point, Hajime?"

"The point is, I know how much you wanted to be Japanese, and now you see you're not."

"What are you talking about?"

"This. This army is only for real Japanese, that is why it is unstoppable. This is a pure army. No pretend Japanese here. You think you know everything, you always thought you were so clever. Soon enough there won't be a white man left in Asia, and that includes you."

Hajime's voice rose with the approach of a locomotive drawing a train decked in red and white bunting. Flags flew on the engine's steam domes and boiler front. Recruits who had already been gathered from other stations leaned out coach windows to shout over the explosion of air brakes, squeal of rails and renewed fervor of the band, which welcomed them with a popular song.

Bullets, tanks and bayonets
Bivouac with grass for a pillow.
My father, appearing in a dream,
Encourages me to die and come home.

"Hold this." Hajime handed back the gun while he cleaned the lenses of his glasses. There was a rush to board because the train was running late. This was a city where people were physically packed into subways and onto buses. Harry let families shoulder by to the steps for leave-taking, mothers and fathers bowing to their soldier-sons with much trembling but no crying. Hajime set the glasses on his face and took a step backward up to the railroad car.

"Don't forget this." Harry stretched out an arm with the package.

"From me to you," Hajime said. A smirk crept across his face as if this was a moment he had waited years for, a payback for ancient debts. The locomotive let off a snort of steam, aching to roll; Japanese engines were thoroughbreds, black and slim. At once, the press of bodies, enthusiasm and noise carried Hajime all the way up the steps of a coach that was rocking from the motion of soldiers finding seats.

"It's yours," Harry shouted.

The tide of embarkation, boys aching to leave good-byes behind, pushed Hajime into the car. "Too late," he said, or something like that, his words overwhelmed by the noise of the band. The press grew greater, and the next time Harry saw Hajime was at an open window where families passed up last-second remembrances and boxes of food. Hajime pulled aside his cape to open his holster flap and show Harry another pistol, a full-size Nambu, already nestled there.

"Good luck, Harry," Hajime mouthed through the window.

The train shuddered and began to slide along the platform. Harry tried to push forward to Hajime, but the wall of bodies and banners and flags was too dense to breach. The fervent waving of hands prevented Harry from even following Hajime's coach by sight. The boys were going, hurtling toward destiny with lives that weighed less than a feather, with the bulletproof prayers of their loved ones, to open a whole new dawn for Asia. With such purity of spirit, how could they fail?

10

AIJIN WERE FREAKS, and Harry's parents were the biggest freaks of all. The pair of them preaching the gospel on a street corner was almost mortally embarrassing to Harry. First was the presumption of preaching at all before being asked. Second was his father's total inability to speak Japanese. Third was his mother's partial Japanese. Fourth was the fact that she spoke not women's but men's Japanese, full of bluster no decent woman would use. Fifth was the way she stood beside her husband instead of behind him. Sixth was their mysterious ignorance about how much and to whom to bow. Seventh was their loudness. Eighth was their clumsiness. Ninth was their color. Tenth was their size. Those were the Ten Sins of Gaijin, and every day Roger and Harriet Niles were guilty of each one. And if there was any contradiction between Harry's condemnation of them and his own black reputation, it escaped him. Sundays were the worst. A Baptist church had no stained glass or popish carvings, only pews leading up to the choir organ and pastor's pulpit and, in between, the satin curtain that veiled the baptismal well. The order of service was call to worship, Scripture, prayer and sermon leading to the testimonials of believers. Thus was the hand of Jesus made visible, His intervention and the redemption of a sinner followed by hymns translated and sung in Japanese in triumphant dissonant satisfaction.

Or the service would include baptism, when the veil of purple satin was drawn aside for an immersion into water that cleansed the soul, a drama that, when he was in town, Roger Niles conducted with the theatrical vigor of the original John the Baptist. The entire congregation would lean forward and hold its breath, all transfixed except for two figures in the front row, Harry and his uncle Orin, who both smelled of mint, his uncle to cover the reek of whiskey, Harry to hide a taste for cigarettes. He would rather have been strolling with Kato and Oharu, taking in fresh air on the Rokku or, better yet, sharing a smoke in a movie house.

Oddly enough, Harry actually liked the painting of the river Jordan above the well. The artist had depicted Jesus in white robes and John in a lion skin, wading into azure water with the spirit descending from heaven in the form of a dove. Cedars and date palms fringed the riverbanks, and around the entire scene was a string of pearls. Harry found the scene calming, not the baptism itself but the slowly flowing river.

Kyoto had a river like that. The summer after Harry had met Kato, he and his parents had gone down to the old capital, which had a Baptist hospital and church. While the congregation attacked the hymns, Harry slipped out and wandered behind the church. There the river lay, brown-green water with torpid folds and ripples under a yellow haze. A branch trailed like an idle hand in the water. On a twig, two dragonflies touched tails of gold. Harry sat at the base of the tree to dig cigarettes from his shirt.

"Share?"

Harry looked up at an American girl, a couple of years younger, with tangled curly hair and a dusty sundress. She was plain, with a square jaw and broad teeth, but she had the most dazzling eyes Harry had ever seen, like the glass heel of a Coca-Cola bottle crushed into crystals. He lit her a cigarette just to see what she would do. She let out a sensual exhale and leaned against the tree.

"I know who you are. You're Harry Niles, the wild boy. Everyone says your parents don't have a real church."

"You sure know a lot."

"They even send you to a Japanese school."

"Why not? I don't want to be a snob. Anyway, my dad preaches in church when he's in Tokyo. If you don't like it, play somewhere else."

She squatted next to him. Her shoes were cracked, and her elbows were scabby, but Harry recognized self-possession when he was next to it.

"I know why you're here," she said.

Harry didn't know. It was just a trip to Kyoto, although the decision had come out of the blue. He shrugged. "Church business." Sundays were always full of church business, fund and oversight committees, temperance leagues and spirit rallies. Sunday could be boring in infinite ways.

"The trial," she said.

"A trial?"

"They call it a mission meeting, but it's a trial, my dad says."

"Someone stole the offering?" If there was something worth stealing, Harry wanted to know.

"Not really stealing," she said.

"What?"

"Currency rates."

That beat Harry. He frowned because he didn't like looking stupid. "What's that?"

"It's not illegal," she said. She took a stick and scratched into the ground. "If you turn in dollars for Chinese yuan at this rate in Shanghai, then trade yuan for Japanese yen, and then come home and trade yen back to dollars, you can double your money."

"That's legal?"

"Um-hum."

Harry stared at the numbers as if glimpsing an entire new alphabet. She wiped them out with her hand.

"Why'd you do that?"

"Missionaries aren't supposed to trade money. Even if it's for mission work or food for people. So they're going to have a trial."

She glanced across the river, and on the far bank, Harry saw a man walking alone with his head down among a shadowy copse of willows.

"Where's your mom?"

"Dead. Of pneumonia."

"So what are you going to do?"

"I think they'll send us back to Florida. I'd just as soon stay."

"Ever been?" Harry hadn't been to the States yet.

"Yeah. All they say is 'Say something in Japanese.' They couldn't find Japan on a map. They think you're stuck up because they're so stupid."

"You have a pretty high opinion of yourself."

She shrugged. They sat quietly for a while and watched the slow passage of the stream. Harry felt her brilliant eyes light on him and dart away.

"Can you swim?" she asked.

"Sure." He was a good swimmer, which was fairly un-Japanese. The Japanese liked going to the beach and splashing in the waves as a group, but going for a swim was regarded as virtually antisocial.

She said, "If I stayed in Japan, I'd be a pearl diver. Ever see pearl divers?"

"Pictures." They were bare-breasted girls who wore goggles.

"Here." She took his hand and put a pearl in it. The pearl was milky blue, with a hole drilled in it. Harry guessed it had probably fallen off a strand. He could see her diving under a pew for it.

"What am I going to do with one pearl?"

"Do you want more? I can get more."

Her eyes were so intense that Harry said, "No, one's plenty."

"Put it in your pocket."

After he did so, she took his hand and slipped it under her dress and up her thigh, which was so skinny he felt the bone. She had no chest, no shape at all, but her eyes were so intense, so many blues and greens at one time, that Harry couldn't take his hand away until a voice came over the water. "Abby? Abigail?" The man on the far bank was waving. She let Harry's hand slide out and whispered, "I have to go."

"Abby?" Harry said.

"Yes?" She swung her focus back to him.

"Double the money? Really?"

"Yes."

"That's great. Thanks."

She stood, stepped on her cigarette and hesitated on the verge of something inexpressible.

"Hope your dad does okay," Harry said.

She nodded. After she was gone, darting along the trees that fringed the river, her gaze still seemed to hover over Harry.

Harry lost the pearl almost immediately. He learned later that the church reprimanded Abby's father but allowed him to remain. Harry heard the following year that Abby got pneumonia and died in Japan, just like her mother.

11

GONDOLA SWUNG on a cable above the rooftop garden of the Matsuya department store. Sheathed in aluminum, streamlined and shining, the gondola looked like a spaceship from the future. The interior was more down-to-earth, with leather straps and wicker seats, but Harry and Alice Beechum had the craft to themselves and, from its porthole windows, a view of the Ginza's wide avenues, willow trees, French cafés. The gondola floated eight stories above trolleys, noodle wagons, the buzz of motorcycles racing to different newspapers. Farther off were waves of blue roof tiles and the green ridge of the imperial palace; to the south, rising over charcoal smoke, the white cone of Fuji.

The rooftop garden offered the foot-weary shopper an amusement park high in the air. Spider monkeys flew from tree to tree within a huge wire mesh enclosure. Cages displayed macaws, peccaries, raccoons. Children pedaled cars around a track while their mothers contemplated bonsai gardens. The latest attraction was a tank of water fifty feet in diameter holding model warships of the Japanese and American navies. Boys gathered around naval cadets who manipulated radio controls that sent the two fleets around the tank, the Japanese chasing the American, the Rising Sun after the Stars and Stripes. Battleships the size of sharks led aircraft carriers, cruisers and destroyers, their screws churning up swells. Out of tinny loudspeakers poured a navy anthem: *"Across the sea, a corpse floating in water / Across the mountains, a corpse in grass."* The Japanese ships began firing, each salvo of guns signaled by red lights in their barrels and black smoke spewing from the Americans in retreat.

Harry said, "You know, there's hardly anything as satisfying as a rigged fight. An honest fight is just a brawl, a rigged fight is theater."

"You always have the most individual opinions." Alice sat back in her riding suit of green tweed, her head resting on the golden pillow of her hair. Maybe it was the English complexion that made tweed sensual, Harry thought. He couldn't help but think of stiff woolen fibers pricking her delicate skin, her map of light freckles and the fine down on her arms and the nape of her neck. She was saying, "I did my best to blacken your reputation after you left the Imperial, but you have to stop your friend Willie from telling any more tales about Nanking."

"He got carried away."

"He's going to get you killed with those stories. The Japanese have a different version of their victory in Nanking. Willie tells me that you're also being stalked by a man with a sword, a Colonel Ishigami."

"I can handle Ishigami."

"Oh, well, then nothing to worry about. Do you remember the wonderful stage direction from Shakespeare, 'Exit, pursued by a bear'? You seem to have any number of bears. So, tell me what happened. Quick, did you get on the plane?"

Harry grinned. From a furoshiki, he lifted out two glasses and a split of champagne that he'd picked up in the Matsuya food emporium.

"I didn't just get on the plane. After this morning's little talk, my friend from Nippon Air will personally tuck me into my seat." He thumbed off the cork and caught the foam as it rose. Opening champagne in such close quarters was chancy, but for some occasions sake would not do. "I'm going to sit right next to you, Alice. We will wave good-bye to Tokyo together. I may even teach you poker on the way."

"Harry, you're the worst man I ever met."

"Even I blush. Cheers," Harry said as if laying down a winning hand. "Nippon Air to Hong Kong on Monday the eighth. BOAC out of

Hong Kong to catch the Clipper in Manila, then Midway, Hawaii and California, in that order. Happy?"

"Ecstatic."

"Sounds like smooth sailing to me."

Alice shielded her eyes to watch a salesclerk down on the roof demonstrate a yo-yo. The yo-yo spun in place to Walk the Dog and snapped into orbit for Around the World. She asked, "What does Madame Butterfly think of you going?"

"Michiko? I'm telling her tonight. I have to give her a chance to make other arrangements. I'll set her up financially."

"Do you think that will make her happy?"

Harry thought that "happy" was not a word that really related to Michiko. "Happy" was fatuous, like a helium balloon. Michiko carried the threat of a larger pop. "I'll explain things to her. I'll say it's time to go. I'll wear armor plate."

"That would probably be wise." As the cable lurched, a thud came from within the furoshiki at Harry's feet. "Did I speak too soon?"

Harry spread the cloth and lifted the lid of the cigar box so that Alice could see the pistol inside.

"That's lovely. Harry, you're aware that it's illegal to own a hand-gun?"

"I got stuck with it. It's an army pistol. A Baby Nambu."

"Why would a soldier leave his gun with you?"

"It was a setup, he had his own."

"If it was a setup, he'll tell the police. Leave the gun with me. I have some degree of immunity, and once I get home, I'll throw it in with Beechum's collection. He has elephant guns, African spears, the lot."

"No, but I'd appreciate it if you took the box." He tucked the pistol into the back of his belt and tried to settle in his seat.

"Comfortable?" Alice asked.

"Been more."

"What are you going to do with it? This is not Chicago, people don't carry guns. You're not thinking of using it on Ishigami, are you?"

"A foreigner shoot a war hero? That would be an interesting form of suicide." He spied a soldier and a girl sharing cotton candy. Public displays of affection were frowned on, but exceptions were made for boys who were shipping out. "You know, this rooftop used to be *the* place for suicides. You should have been here. Lovers lined up to hold hands and jump two at a time. It caused some anxiety about shopping in the neighborhood. You came for a cute chapeau and ended up planted in the sidewalk by a pair of star-crossed lovers. The silver lining is, since the war, suicides are down."

"Has Michiko ever suggested a double jump?"

"Well, she's romantic that way."

"Wasn't there an American reporter last year who died after he fell from the first story of a police station? The police said he jumped."

"He probably didn't have many options."

"Whereas you only have to hide a gun from police who are already following you."

"I'll get rid of it, don't worry." A gondola swung by in the opposite direction. Two little girls in red kimonos bowed from the passing car while Alice studied Harry as if from a distance rather than knee-to-knee.

"Harry, we had fun, didn't we?"

"Lots of fun." It was true. Alice was fun, and there was no danger with her of being murdered out of jealousy or pique. A man could sink with Alice under the billowing waves of her soft mattress and down-filled quilt with the assurance that he would come up alive. She was brilliant with the Japanese language, loved the way the "flute" found its way to the "precious pearl" and positions like "Cat and Mouse in One Hole." Her sheets were so scented with Chanel it was like nesting in a rose. The only problem was that Michiko could detect Chanel from a block away. "And we'll have more fun. Have you told Beechum?"

"Good Lord, no. He thinks I'm going for a lark and be back in a day. My brother owns a coffee plantation in Kenya. The whites there lead a life of stupid dissipation. You and I could go there, and no one would know the difference."

"Pull a Duke of Windsor? You'd marry a common American?"

"I don't propose to make an honest man out of you, no one could do that. I am only suggesting that there are people who disapprove of you. People at your own embassy. They could make things uncomfortable for you if you return home."

"People have always disapproved of me. When people approve of me, you have my permission to shoot me in the head. I am not escaping here to hang out at a water hole in Africa. I want to show you Hollywood, Monterey, Big Sur."

The gondola dipped by the monkey enclosure, where residents basked on branches. Nonetheless, Alice shivered. Harry noticed when she gave him back her empty glass how red her knuckles were. The tip of her nose was also red, which made her more endearing. She said, "Every day my maid searches the rubbish bin for incriminating evidence about me. She's very sweet. She asked if I could leave something, anything she could give the police. I try to help her and stuff the bin with crossword puzzles. The police seem to find them extremely promising."

"You won't have any trouble keeping them happy." Harry had seen her finish the crossword puzzle of *The Times* as quickly as she could write. She did crossword puzzles in four languages. Most of the day, she was a brainless thing who spent her life at the Ginza's shops and smart cafés, but every morning she spent in the code room of the British embassy. Even Beechum didn't know. Her husband thought she had volunteered as a coffee lady, which he thought a damn good sign.

"The Thought Police are after you, Harry. They aren't going to stop you from taking off?"

"We're working together. I'm thinking good thoughts now."

"You told them about the Magic Show?"

"Not that."

Her rosy cheeks drained of color. "You didn't take them to Yokohama. Tell me you didn't take them there."

"They showed up. Maybe that will satisfy them I'm doing my part for the war effort."

"What part is that?"

"Everyone contributes in their own fashion. You're a genius. I'm a businessman, kind of."

"You're a gambler."

"So is Yamamoto. He knows that no navy can go to war without a source of oil, and the closest source to Japan is Dutch Sumatra, thousands of miles away. Sinking the American Pacific fleet isn't enough, because Roosevelt can move ships at full speed from the Atlantic. They'll refuel at Pearl and start sinking the emperor's sloppy little tankers. But if the Japanese knock out all the oil at Pearl first, that changes everything. It wouldn't be hard. All you need is a Zero with a fifty-caliber gun to blow those tanks to kingdom come. Then the nearest fuel to Pearl Harbor is California, thousands of miles away. Every new drop would have to be brought by American tankers, which are in short supply because they're fueling England and getting sunk on the North Atlantic route. The fleet at Pearl is replaceable. Wiping out the oil tanks would buy Japan one year, maybe two."

"This is insane." Alice closed her eyes. "First the gun, now this."

"So all I'm doing is adding an element of caution."

"You're still altering company ledgers?"

"A little. It's not like the books were locked up, not adequately. No one gets hurt, because the American managers the Japanese might blame are back in the States and out of reach. It's a harmless ploy, if you will, to create the possibility in the Japanese mind that oil was delivered in a secretive manner to tanks they haven't located. You know how meticulous and paranoid the Japanese are. This is the sort of thing that drives them crazy. They can't be so sure an attack will actually locate and wipe out all the oil reserves in Hawaii. Yamamoto understands odds. If he doesn't think he can nail both the fleet and the oil, he won't touch Pearl. No Pearl, no war."

"What happens when the Special Higher Police and the Japanese navy discover that you deluded them?"

"They won't find that out unless they fly over every valley on Oahu. Anyway, the fact is, I have discouraged them about this piece of information. I tell them over and over how phony it sounds to me. The more I deny it, the more they believe. That's when you know a sucker is hooked, when you can't chase him away."

"Is that it, they've swallowed the bait so deep? Then why get on the plane?"

"It's a stupid gambler who doesn't hedge his bet. Besides, you'll be on it."

"Harry, I despair."

"Well, it's worth a try."

The porthole opened on pivots. Harry found cigarettes and lit one for her, too.

"Have you let Butterfly in on your little game?" Alice asked.

"No, she wouldn't turn me in, but she might kill me."

"You don't find anything the least pathological about your relationship with her?"

Harry considered. "I'd say it keeps me sharp."

"No doubt." She looked down as a store clerk blew a cornet to announce a sale of balsa-and-paper gliders that hung like mayflies from a pole. "May I tell you something? I have been in and out of the embassy code room for two years now. We have sent London a steady stream of information that, I am now convinced, is flushed immediately into the Thames. We speak to the deaf. Yesterday we received a cable asking whether German pilots were flying for the Japanese. London doesn't think the Japanese can fly planes. It's a matter of eyesight, they say, and thick glasses. The Japanese are as bad; they don't think Americans can fight. Harry, no amount of information, accurate or inaccurate, makes any difference now. What makes you suddenly want to be a hero? It's perverse."

He delivered what he thought was his most ingratiating smile. "Alice, I'm not going to be a hero. It's not my style. Besides, heroes get caught, that's what makes them so heroic. I don't get caught."

"Harry, everyone gets caught."

"How about you?"

"I'm a diplomat's wife. Once war starts, we'll simply be exchanged for Japanese diplomats."

" 'Once'? That's an interesting choice of word." Harry took her hand and traced the lines of her palm as if they held a secret. "Lady Alice, is there something in the air? Do you know something I don't?"

"I know when to quit. Harry, I hate it when you look at me like that. Sometimes you are very Japanese."

"Is that so?"

"I think I finally have you figured out. I have your code, Harry. You're like a crossword puzzle where every tenth word the answer is in Japanese. Maybe that explains Michiko."

"Maybe."

"And it wouldn't matter if I did know something you didn't. There's nothing we can do about it now."

"Who cares? We'll be oiling each other in a cabana at the Beverly Hills Hotel. It's not a safari, but it has its charms. Why are you smiling?"

"Harry, it's a fantasy. You and I were not meant to be with anyone. It's sheer incompatibility that keeps us together."

"We'll give it a shot."

"Realistically, how long do you think we would last?"

"I give us six months."

"Beechum will cut me off, I won't have a penny."

"Three months."

"Will you drink heavily and beat me?"

"Like a gong."

"Like a church bell, an American would say."

"Backing out?"

"No. I would like you to do me a favor, however, and help your friend Willie before you go."

"Willie and Iris? I already said I would. What do you care?"

"I like Willie's stories. If you're going to help him, do it fast."

The gondola descended over the ice-cream stand and pedal-car track and a volley of exuberant cheers from the schoolboys watching the battle in the tank. If the naval engagement was ever in doubt, its outcome now was clear. The Japanese fleet plowed at full speed through the water, guns glowing from the fire of their shells, while the American fleet waddled in disorder, stacks pouring charcoal smoke that signified hits in the engine room. Some American warships were so enveloped by smoke that they seemed to be sinking. The scene suggested wholesale horror and confusion, men diving from the decks and trying to outswim burning oil or the suction of a great ship going under and overcrowded lifeboats circled by sharks. As Harry and Alice emerged from the gondola, he didn't notice anyone in the crowd watching them. Everyone was too captivated by the battle in the tank. The excitement was so overwhelming that some boys couldn't stand still. They ran with their arms out like torpedo planes or raised imaginary periscopes. The loudspeaker sang, *"Across the sea, water-soaked corpses, we shall die by the side of our lord."* The children chanted, "Banzai! Banzai! Banzai!"

ALTHOUGH HARRY WANTED to ditch the gun, he assumed he was being followed. Just to see, he detoured through an arcade specializing in pets. The passageway rang with a mixed chorus of canaries, lovebirds, cockatoos and a nightingale that trilled from a shrouded cage. Kittens, their tails bobbed to prevent them from turning into goblins, mewed in a fruit box. A weasel slunk round and round in a basket. There was only one beetle dealer, with a lean wintertime stock.

"What you want is a stag beetle." The dealer kept his hands in steady motion so that the beetle, a two-inch monster with antlers, walked from the back of one hand to the other. "There is no better investment in insects. A rhinoceros beetle like yours will drop dead after a single mating. What kind of champion is that? A stag beetle fattens off passion. No? Wait, I have more." He indicated a cage with a six-inch mantis, a green stiletto. "Do you enjoy the educational sight of a wife eating her husband's head? No?"

Harry didn't enjoy that or the sight of two plainclothes police squatting by the fruit box to tease the kittens. Two cops on foot and probably two waiting in a car near his. Forget subtlety.

"Do you have trouble sleeping? Maybe you like the bucolic sound of crickets? I have crickets that are genuine songsters. No, you're not a country boy. You're Tokyo-bred, like me." The beetle dealer kept the treadmill of his hands going while he looked Harry up and down. "Then it comes to this. If sports are your interest and you want your money back tenfold, a stag is your best bet."

Harry bet on horses, not beetles, not since he was a kid. However, he bought a bamboo beetle cage with a bed of wood flakes. He was trying to leave town, and what did he have now, Harry thought. First a gun. Now a beetle. Terrific.

WHEN WESTERN DANCING was declared unpatriotic, a storage company run by yakuza took over the Asakusa Ballroom and covered its parquet floor with stacks of scenery and flats from the surrounding music halls and theaters. The yakuza specialized in the business of theatrical storage because it was a good excuse for men to hang around doing nothing. The ballroom had also become a refuge for the ne'er-do-wells of wartime society, out-of-work dance instructors practicing to the raspy tango of a gramophone, horseplayers with time on their hands since the racetracks were closed. A midday card game was going when Harry arrived. Taro sat holding a box of his brother's ashes, and although the sumo filled a pair of chairs and was dressed in yards of rich kimono, he looked undone and deflated.

"All I can think of is my brother," he told Harry.

"Have you eaten?"

"I couldn't."

"Jiro would like you to eat. I think Jiro would like me to eat, too."

A boy was attending the cardplayers. Harry sent him for noodles from the kitchen next door. The cardplayers kept an eye on Taro and the box. Gamblers were superstitious. Not reverent but easily spooked. They didn't like anything written in red, because red was the color of call-up notices from the army. They hated the color white because it suggested death, and here Taro had brought a white box with THE REMAINS OF KAGA JIRO written in brushstrokes down the side. A short man in a wasp-waisted suit arrived in a rush as if he'd been summoned. The cardplayers called him over, and seconds later he moved with bouncy strides toward Harry and Taro.

"Tetsu." Harry gave his old friend a bow.

Tetsu had done well. Providentially too short for the five-foot requirement of the army, he had fulfilled his youthful aspiration to become a yakuza and ran the ballroom game. Not that it was so difficult. The games were raided by police in the same desultory spirit that licensed prostitutes were supposed to study ethics once a week.

"Harry, Taro, good to see you both. Let's go get something to eat. You like Chinese?"

"The food's coming," Harry said.

"Jiro." Taro indicated the wooden box.

Tetsu said, "I'm sorry. I mean, you must be so proud. Jiro's ashes? Oh." He bowed to the box. "All the same, we should go somewhere else. Harry, you understand. It's Agawa, the old guy. He says the box is disturbing. He says he can't even count his cards."

Harry looked over at a player with a gristly neck.

Taro sighed. "Let's go."

"Wait. Agawa can play with a tango at his back, but he can't play when the ashes of a hero are carried in?" Harry did not like to see the deceased slighted or a grieving brother, a sumo no less, diminished. "Hey, Agawa, do you know what tomorrow is?"

"I'm playing a hand, as you can see."

"What's tomorrow?"

"Sunday, as any fool knows." Agawa shared a grin with his friends.

"The date?"

"December seventh."

"A big day," Harry said. "Maybe the biggest day in history."

Agawa went on arranging the cards in his hand. "How is that?"

"Awhile back, a bishop figured out through a careful examination of the Bible that Noah's flood began on December seventh, 2347 B.C. That's two thousand three hundred and forty-seven years before the birth of Christ. Tomorrow is the anniversary. In fact, it's the uh . . ."

When Harry started counting on his fingers, Agawa said, "The four thousand two hundred and eighty-eighth anniversary."

"That's right. Agawa-san, you have the quickest mind here. It sounds like you count just fine."

Agawa put his cards down. "The entire thing is ridiculous. There was no Noah's flood, not in Japan. The whole thing is a fairy tale."

"Isn't it amazing what people believe?" Harry said. "Fairy tales and superstitions, demons and ghosts. You're a rational man, Agawa-san, and you wouldn't mind that our friend Taro brought the ashes of his brother, do you? Thanks."

Agawa grunted, which Harry took as not necessarily yes or no but at least not violent objection. Harry suspected that two Japanese didn't need words at all, they could communicate perfectly well with grunts, grimaces, winces, frowns, inhales, exhales, eyes cast down and to the side, brows furrowed with concern or gathered in anger, not to even mention bows.

Tetsu was pleased. Like a traditional yakuza, he hated confrontation. He played with a cigarette lighter, which drew respectful attention to the fact that he missed the little finger of his left hand, had cut it off, actually, to atone for some shame he had brought on his boss. People didn't know or care what the shame was. Sincere atonement was all. He said, "That was smooth, Harry."

With the tension broken, the cardplayers came over to commiserate with Taro, acknowledging the white box with that inexpressible combination of pride and regret people felt for those who had sacrificed themselves for the emperor. At the same time they sized up Taro, all but squeezing his arms, because they were sumo fans. Betting on the semi-sacred sport of sumo was illegal except for members of sumo fan clubs, who were expected to be devotees wagering token sums. Naturally, everyone in the ballroom—including Harry—was a member of one sumo fan club or another, and during a tournament, they bet fortunes. It helped that sumo was eminently fixable, particularly now. Food was rationed even at sumo stables, and lower-ranked wrestlers had to survive on the scraps that top-ranked sumos left. Harry had seen young sumos famished after a morning's workout, wandering the food stalls for handouts, as sad a sight as hippos browsing in a riverbed gone dry.

Goro joined them. He was elegantly dressed, a pickpocket who had married well and no longer dipped but couldn't resist bad company. He prodded Tetsu. "Show them the latest."

Tetsu pulled off his jacket and tie and dropped his shirt off his shoulders. His upper body, from his neck to his waist, was continuous tattoos, on his chest a Siberian tiger stepping into a pool defended by an octopus and on his back the image of a smiling Buddha, eyes closed, hands prayerfully together, ignoring monsters and dragons that swarmed on all sides. To Harry, Tetsu looked baptized not in water but in ink. When they were boys, Harry was the one who had accompanied Tetsu to his first tattoo session, performed by a drunk on a bench in Ueno Park with bamboo slivers instead of steel needles. Tetsu twisted now and pointed to his new addition, a goblin creeping around his kidney. The inks were sharp and fresh, the skin puffy and Tetsu's face betrayed a sweat of tattoo fever.

Harry said, "That's got to make an impression in the public baths."

"And women." Goro spoke like an expert. "Of a certain kind."

"What do you think old Kato would have thought?" Tetsu asked Harry.

"He would have said you were a walking masterpiece."

"Yeah? It's good to see you and Taro. And Jiro, of course." Tetsu pulled on his shirt. "We're most of the old gang, four out of six, right? Then there's Hajime, good riddance, and Gen, way up in the navy."

Taro climbed out of his funk when the noodles arrived. You had to water a plant and feed a sumo, it was as simple as that, Harry thought. Taro again became a mountain of dignity delicately scented by the wax that stiffened his topknot. As he relaxed, the cardplayers pumped him for information about other sumos. Had this one lost a fingernail? Had that one jammed a toe? The dance instructors dropped the needle on a fresh record and traded places. They moved in silhouette, tangling and untangling their legs. Harry remembered that the first time Oharu had sneaked him into the ballroom, an imitation Rudy Vallee was singing through a megaphone. A dance cost three yen, and men bought a strip of tickets before they were admitted past a velvet rope to a floor where two hundred couples milled under the hypnotic spell of a mirror ball trying out the fox-trot, the waltz, the Bruce. Women in Western gowns sat demurely along the wall while men walked back and forth to exercise their scrutiny. Oharu led Harry up to an empty mezzanine, which had a view of the bandstand and an engineer in a cockpit over the entrance, alternating colored lights and the mirror ball. Reflections raced across the floor. Harry felt them flit across his face. He also noticed that few of the men actually knew how to dance.

"It's just to hold a woman," Oharu whispered. "She may be the only woman he'll ever hold."

"Except a whore," Harry pointed out.

"Well, this is nicer. The girls are only paid by the number of tickets they turn in, so they have to be pleasing."

"How come we're the only ones up here?"

"The management closed it off. They don't want the customers sitting, they want them dancing and buying more tickets. Besides, too many things can happen in the dark."

"Like what?"

"Things. Sometimes a man forces himself on a woman."

"If anyone tried that on you, I'd stop him."

"I know you would."

She had only to brush her lips gently against his cheek and he burned.

TETSU WAS EXPLAINING to Taro and the cardplayers that a small sumo had a natural advantage. "Smaller men have more spirit. It's concentrated."

While Tetsu was in an expansive mood, Harry drew him aside and raised the subject of Iris's travel clearance. The problem was purely bureaucratic, as Harry described it, something that could be resolved in a minute by a phone call to the Foreign Ministry from a respected patriotic group like, say, National Purity. National Purity put patriotism into action, assassinating liberals and moderates, trimming and changing the nature of political discourse. National Purity touched high and low. The same superpatriots who were honored guests at the imperial palace used yakuza to extract protection money from businesses large and small. Harry kept the Happy Paris open not by doing anything as crass as handing money to a bagman, but with generous donations at the shrine of National Purity.

Harry said, "This time I want to meet our patriotic friend at National Purity in person so that I can explain the situation and ask his advice. Then he will make a call to the ministry. Very simple. This is for a German ally, after all. But I want you to go with me, so that when I vouch for the German, you can vouch for me."

"I don't know, Harry."

"There'll be a donation to your favorite shrine, too."

"Oh."

Harry set the time. He considered mentioning the gun. However, now that he'd brought up Iris, he didn't want to queer the deal. A gun was a red flag; yakuza themselves rarely used guns, and for a civilian to unload one suggested major complications. Why would Hajime go to such trouble to foist a gun on him unless it had been involved in at least a triple homicide? Harry couldn't forget Hajime smirking through the train window, letting his own gun peek from its holster.

Agawa walked over from the card game. He nodded toward the box next to Taro. "Is everything in there? I know someone who got a box that was empty."

"Empty?" Taro was alarmed.

"Just saying. It was a shock to the family."

"That would kill my mother." Taro picked up the box tentatively. The box was wisteria wood sanded to a satin finish and tied with a white sash. He had carried it to the ballroom but hadn't tested its heft before.

Agawa said, "There should be an official album of the unit Jiro fought in, along with photos of the emperor, the imperial standard, regimental banner and commanding officers, plus personal snapshots, a map and description of the circumstances in which he died and clippings of his fingernails and hair. And the ashes and pulverized bone, of course, in a stoppered container or a sack."

"It sounds as if everything is in there." Taro tipped the box one way and then the other.

"Better be sure," Agawa said.

"I'm not ready for this, Harry," Taro said. "I'm not prepared."

"You'll have to open it at home," Agawa said.

Taro set the box on his lap and fumbled with the sash, his big fingers turned to rubber. He lifted the lid as if opening a tomb.

"Everything there?" Agawa asked.

Taro reached in and delicately sorted through the contents. "The album. The album and a little sack for ashes, but the sack is empty." His face went as white as the box. "That's all."

"That's outrageous," Agawa said. "You should make a protest."

"You don't want to make a protest," Harry said. "Let's go."

"This is going to kill your mother," Agawa said.

"We're going." Harry put the lid back on and helped Taro to his feet.

While Tetsu carried the box, Harry got Taro to the ballroom foyer and set him on a chair, which he sagged over on both sides. Harry sent Tetsu back to keep anyone from following.

The chair trembled under Taro's weight. He said, "I took the boat away from Jiro, and now I lost his ashes. I should have looked out for him. He was my little brother."

"By fifteen minutes. He probably kicked you out, he was that sort of person."

Taro hung his head. "Now to lose his ashes."

"You didn't lose Jiro's ashes."

"My mother will think so. She'll tell everyone I deliberately lost them."

"You didn't."

This was a perfect example, Harry thought, of how a tiny woman could make a sumo tread in fear. He looked around at the foyer's dirty carpet, cloakroom alcove, clouded ashtrays, broken abacus and a cold potbellied stove. Harry opened the box and took out the empty sack.

"What are you doing, Harry?"

"Making things right."

Before Taro could move, Harry opened the stove trap and, with the shuttle, transferred ash. One scoop half filled the bag. Harry drew the drawstring tight, deposited the sack in the box, wiped his fingers on his pants and knelt a little to bring his eyes directly to Taro's.

"Now you have the ashes. Now your mother will have peace of mind. You will have peace of mind, too, because you will know that you have done everything possible to make her happy and allow her to pray for him. You have lost him, and now he is found. A good shepherd rejoices more in the one lost sheep he has found than in the hundred that never strayed."

"You think so?"

"I'm sure of it." Harry retied the sash and looped it over Taro's head for carrying.

"I could kill Agawa. It's good he asked, though."

"Funny how things work out."

"How can I thank you?"

"Now that you mention it, I'm presenting a donation to the head of National Purity, who is a famous sumo fan. Why don't you come and set a patriotic tone?" He gave Taro the time and place. "I'll be counting on you."

"Sure, Harry. I'm sorry, I fell apart there for a minute."

"No harm done. Ready?"

Taro rose to his feet, a full-size sumo again. They got out on the street, and with every step, he was steadier and more impressive, shoulders squared, expression solemn. Once on the Rokku, he and Harry parted ways. Watching Taro stride through the crowd, Harry felt not so much the pride of the good shepherd as he did the satisfaction of a butcher who managed at all times to keep his thumb on the scale.

12

IT WAS ON an evening in April that Gen introduced Harry to the Magic Show. They had met at a new John Wayne movie and afterward strolled like cowboys in a marquee glow. Most naval officers were shorn like sheep, but Gen had managed to hang on to his hair, and in his panama hat, he exuded a style and confidence that made Harry want to hang back and applaud. Gen's only problem was that he looked more like an actor playing a hero than a real hero. He had been assigned to Operations, and while another officer on the rise might have severed relations with as dubious a character as Harry, it wasn't in Gen to be careful. Their relationship was too old, too strong, too complicated. Trust and distrust seesawed between them. Gen knew Harry too well, and that went both ways.

Gen consulted his watch from time to time, which meant nothing to Harry until they returned to the Happy Paris and Gen suggested the willow house across the street instead. Through the window slats of the Paris, Harry saw Michiko lean on the jukebox, waiting for him, mouthing some whispery song in a wreath of smoke. At the willow house, a lantern winked a more discreet welcome within an open gate.

"You're kidding," Harry said. "You're drunk."

"No." And he wasn't, Harry realized. Gen was sober. "I have a friend inside. You'd enjoy him."

"At a geisha party?"

"No geishas. He wants to play cards."

"There are games all over town."

"He's very private. You'd enjoy him. Just meet him, and if you're not interested, you can leave. Five minutes, Harry."

From the willow-house gate, a path of stones led across a lawn of moss to an entryway of polished cedar. Sure enough, Harry and Gen had barely left their shoes when, from behind paper panels slid shut, they heard the unmistakable sound of parties in progress: drunken toasts, the stumbling over musical pillows (a version of musical chairs) and the puns and feeble double entendres that passed for jokes. Rich drunks and simpering dolls, that was a geisha party so far as Harry was concerned. The cultural aspect fit into a thimble. The level of entertainment was prehistoric. One girl might sing like a lark, and the next one's major talent might be tying a cherry stem with her tongue. The proprietor, hunchbacked from bowing, always greeted a customer at the front door. For once he was absent.

Gen led Harry to the room farthest from the street, traditionally the best and quietest accommodation. It was a room Harry sometimes escaped to from the Paris; in turn, he gave geishas a ride home when they were too tipsy to walk. A round window looked out on a softly illuminated garden of bonsai and ferns. A standing screen was decorated with gilded carp swimming across blue silk. There were no geishas now, however, only a short man in a threadbare kimono shuffling cards. He had a deeply lined, tanned and compact body, as if any more weight was baggage. His gray hair was shaved to the nub, and he was missing the middle and index fingers of his left hand. He didn't rise to greet Harry or pretend to bow but seemed amiable and informal enough.

"I hear you play," he told Harry.

"Deal them."

The man dealt the cards facedown for five-card stud, and they played one on one with a one-yen ante just to make it interesting. The man was good; he had discipline, card memory, a sense of the changing odds, a natural poker face and, most important, an amused detachment that allowed him to take the loss or win of a hand as just deserts. It took until two in the morning for Harry to clean him out.

"You see, this is what I mean," the man told Gen as Harry raked in the final pot. "You can start by putting in just one yen or one ship or one soldier and still lose everything if you don't know when to leave the table. Leaving the table is not something Japanese are very good at." He held up his hands for Harry. "Sometimes you even have to leave fingers on the table. I lost two fingers when my own gun blew up. But the geishas here are very nice. The usual charge for a manicure from a geisha is one yen. For me, just eighty sen."

"Who were you shooting at?"

"Russians. It was war, it was perfectly legal."

The songs and laughs from other rooms had died and disappeared. Quiet descended on the willow house. Gen had watched the entire poker game without saying a word or even stirring except to empty an ashtray or fetch tea. Everything the older man did, Gen followed with the attention and respect of an altar boy. "I am a terrible customer for geishas," the man said. "I don't drink, and I don't have much to spend, but the geishas humor me nonetheless. I find the back room here restful." He rubbed his head with embarrassment. "I tried to go home tonight, the first time I've been home in months, and I was locked out. My wife had taken the children on vacation, I suppose. So I came here with my loose change and some cards to make my fortune. Unfortunately, I ran into you, and now I have nothing at all."

"I warned you," Gen said.

"You were right. I will listen to my junior officers in the future." The man returned to Harry. "Where did I go wrong?"

"Nowhere special. You just didn't have enough money, so you let me buy two pots, and then you had to be too aggressive. Then the losses snowballed."

"That's so true! You know, there were times when I seriously thought of leaving the sea and becoming a full-time gambler. Not cards. Roulette. I had a very encouraging experience once at Monte Carlo. Also I like dice."

"We could try that." Harry fished a pair from his jacket.

"Oh, I don't I think I should play with someone who carries dice just in case."

"I extend credit."

"Even more dangerous. Lieutenant, your friend is as good as advertised." The man rubbed his hands together. "Excellent!"

From his corner, Gen beamed with pride.

"Do you have a system?" the man asked Harry.

"No, I let the other man have a system, and I try to figure it out."

"You bet on anything?"

"Cards, cars, dogs, horses, pigeons, about anything."

"The lieutenant told me about the car race at Tamagawa."

Tamagawa was a track on the way to Yokohama.

"They have good races," Harry said. "Bentleys, Bugattis, Mercedeses."

"Is it true that you entered a car with an airplane engine?"

"A Curtis thirteen-cylinder engine."

"It stayed on the ground?"

"Barely, but it won."

"That's what matters. I wish I could have seen that."

Gen said, "Some of the other competitors were upset."

"Too bad," the man said. "The losing side is always upset." He returned to Harry. "But you are also a businessman with an interest in oil."

"I help the government develop sources of oil," Harry said.

"From . . . ? "

"Shale, mostly, but also looking at alternative sources."

"What does that mean?"

There was something about the man that suggested bullshit wouldn't do. "Pine trees."

The man grinned in wonder. "As a boy, I understand, you sold cat skins. I suppose you will be squeezing them for oil, too."

"Let's say Japan doesn't have the usual sources of oil."

"You don't have to tell me." The man's smile folded. "I used to drink, a little. Then I encountered the most sobering sight in my life. It was a Texas oil field. Oil rigs as far as you could see in any direction. One Texas oil field that outproduced all of Japan. I visited assembly lines in Detroit and skyscrapers in New York City, but the last thing I see when I close my eyes at night is that oil field. Whenever I mention oil, the army says not to worry because we Japanese have Yamato spirit. Yamato spirit, Yamato spirit, that's all the army knows. They say Japan is so different, so superior, we will necessarily win. You know, I have seen the cherry trees in Washington, and they are just as beautiful. The army talks about the incomparable Japanese character. Well, you can tell a lot about character and intelligence by how a man approaches a woman. A Japanese goes up to a woman and demands, 'Give me a lay.' Even a prostitute would say no. An American shows up with flowers and presents and gets what he wants. So much for moral superiority, and so much for results. The army can have Yamato spirit, give me oil."

The man spoke with such intensity that it took Harry a moment to find the air to answer. "I can't get you Texas."

"No, I understand, but it seems to me that you have exactly the sort of skeptical eye and varied experience we need for a certain situation. You are unique. The lieutenant was right, you are just the man."

Harry didn't know how flattered to be. "For what?"

"Do you do card tricks?"

"I just play cards, I'm not a magician."

"You know magicians?"

"Dozens. Magicians with doves, rabbits, scarves, saws, feats of mental telepathy, whatever you want."

"Are you free tomorrow night?"

"For a magic show?"

The man developed a smile. "That's the problem, we don't know quite what it is. It's magic or a miracle. I'm hoping you will tell us."

A NAVY CAR with an anchor insignia picked Harry up at the Paris the following night. Gen was inside behind window curtains. He wore navy blues, and his easygoing manner of the previous evening was replaced by a somber mood.

"Where's our friend with the cards?" Harry asked.

"He'll be there. No names," Gen warned Harry.

"Whatever you say."

It didn't matter. Harry knew the player's name. Anyone who read a newspaper or saw newsreels knew the dour face and blunt manner of the commander in chief of the Combined Fleet. Although no names had been exchanged, Harry had recognized Yamamoto as soon as the admiral shuffled the deck of cards with the famous eight fingers instead of ten. Harry also understood that the meeting had been engineered for invisibility, at midnight in the back room of a willow house with no witnesses but the loyal acolyte Gen. Could Harry claim that he had even been introduced to Yamamoto? No. That was okay. A lot of people didn't want to be associated with Harry.

Gen said, "This is a very sensitive situation."

"You mean your career is on the line. Magic or miracle, what is that supposed to mean? The Great Man has looked me over and approved, but I'm still kept in the dark. Give me a clue."

"You have to see it to believe it."

"That's a good clue. Are we talking about the resurrection? Water to wine? A burning bush?"

"On a par."

"On a par? Wow. Like parting the sea and just marching where you want to go?"

"Sort of. This is very big, but . . ." Gen lowered his voice. "But there is also a risk of embarrassment."

"Losing face?"

"Not face. Enormous, disastrous embarrassment."

That sounded intriguing to Harry, but Gen shook his head to indicate the end of the conversation. South of the palace, the driver swung into an alley behind the Navy Ministry and stopped. Gen studied the shadows, then rushed Harry out of the car and down a flight of stairs as if delivering a prostitute. Inside, they followed a trail of dusty lights through a tunnel of steam and water pipes to a door that admitted them to a basement hall of office doors. Harry wondered who would be working at one in the morning. Someone was, judging by the sound of voices and haze of light down the hall. Gen went almost on tiptoe and, when they were nearly on top of the voices, slipped Harry though a door into what was more a tight space than a proper room, a catchall crammed with scales, sterilizing trays, bedpans. At eye level was an inset pane of glass.

Gen whispered, "On the other side, it's a mirror. This used to be a medical clinic where we examined pilots. Sometimes that demanded discreet observation."

Harry observed a room dominated by a metal table supporting a tank of water about eight feet wide and four feet high, a good-size aquarium that contained, instead of sand and fish, six bottles of blue glass. Each bottle was sealed and connected via an overhead electrical line to a battery big enough for a submarine. It had to be like moving a piano to get it in. V-shaped wands wrapped in copper wire stood around the tank, and over it hung a copper sphere. A small but impressive audience had been gathered: four navy officers, no grade less than a commander, and two unhappy civilians. Harry noticed a couple of petty officers with pistols standing at the door. He also saw Yamamoto, with so many rings around his sleeves they looked as if he had dipped his cuffs in gold. The uniform seemed to weigh on him, and his attention, like everyone else's, was anxiously focused on a gaunt man in a white lab coat jotting numbers from a bank of gauges individually wired to the copper wands. Welder's goggles hung around everyone's neck. By Harry's watch, five minutes elapsed before the man in the lab coat raised his head and declared. "Progress, definite progress."

"Progress in what?" Harry asked Gen. "What is he doing?"

Gen couldn't get the words out right away. "He's making oil."

"What do you mean?"

"He's turning water into oil."

Harry actually took a step back. He wasn't dazzled by much, but this was blinding. "Water into oil?"

"You can smile, but I've seen him do it."

"I don't think even God tried that. Water and wine, yes; oil, no. You realize it's impossible."

"Opinion is divided," Gen granted. "The program is secret."

"I bet. What's the researcher's name?"

"Ito. Dr. Ito."

While Ito adjusted controls, Gen explained what the doctor had explained to him, that the table of the elements was neither fixed nor limited and that through "electric remapping," their atomic bonds could be broken and recombined. Ito was in the middle of mapping the transitional states of elements and, in recognition of the national need, had diverted his talents and discoveries toward the transformation of water into oil. From their faces, Harry saw who in the room bought it. At least one civilian was visibly suppressing professional outrage, but there were hopefuls and believers among the navy. And it wasn't a bad show. Ito was dramatically thin, with lank hair overhanging a pale forehead and eyes hollow from lack of sleep. His coat was dirty, his hands filthy; everything about him spelled genius. He worked on the run in rubber overshoes, resetting dials, repositioning the copper wands, stopping only to cough in a tubercular way. In a hoarse voice, he said, "Perhaps that's all for tonight."

Yamamoto said, "Doctor, would you please try one more time? It's so important."

Ito seemed to gather inner strength. "One more."

He pulled on rubber gauntlets as he moved to an oversize switch. At his lead, everyone in the room pulled on goggles with smoked lenses, and Ito seemed to wait until the entire room had stopped breathing. Harry thought that only an audience brought up on Kabuki's overheated posing would swallow Ito for a minute.

"Take your positions."

There was a general shuffling onto a rubber mat. Before Harry figured out what that was about, Ito slapped the switch handle down and the tank water turned a vivid blue. As Ito turned up the voltage, white bolts of electricity ran up the two arms of the wands, flickered back and forth, joined hands from wand to wand, then arced the tank and shot up to the overhead sphere so that tank and table were domed by an electrical jellyfish that sizzled and popped and smelled of singed wool. Gen and Harry threw up their arms to shade their eyes from light that flooded the cubicle they were in. Ito cranked a transformer, and the protoplasm threatened to spread tentacles and float from the table. It was a view of the forces of the universe, an electrical cauldron, a glimpse of Creation itself. Waves rolled on an oscilloscope screen. Ito circled the tank with a small neon tube that lit, faded, glowed again. His long hair stood on end and twisted and wrestled first toward one wand and then the other. Electricity lapped like fire up his arms, yet Ito moved with the assurance of a sorcerer. When he threw the switch off, Harry felt half blinded. Those who had been in the room with the tank looked as shaken as survivors of a lightning bolt.

"Not bad," Harry said. "Electrical arcs, sparks, everything but a hunchback running around with a bucket of brains."

Yamamoto stepped off the mat and approached the tank. He laid on his hands, minus the two fingers he'd lost pursuing Russians. Yamamoto again ready to risk all. As if his touch were a signal, a bottle stirred. It leaned, lifted clear and steadily rose to the surface, where Ito caught it, snipped its wire and set it by a rack of test tubes. Of course, Ito didn't unstop the bottle himself.

"Professor Mishima, you are such an eminent scientist. Would you do me the honor?"

The smaller, rounder civilian huffed. "This is ridiculous, this is not science."

"Please," Yamamoto said.

Mishima broke the wax seal with a penknife and poured the contents into a tube, reserving a last drop to roll around his fingertip and taste.

"What is it?" Ito asked as if they were the closest of colleagues.

The professor wiped his mouth. "Oil."

"What was in the bottle originally?"

"Water."

"Your conclusion?" Yamamoto asked.

"It's preposterous. You cannot change water to oil with a little lightning, or else the oceans would be oil."

Ito was unperturbed. "That is salt water. This is very different water."

"You cannot defy the laws of nature."

"We are rewriting the laws of nature."

"Impossible . . ." The professor tried, but he had lost, trumped by a card from his own hand.

"Perhaps this is the Yamato spirit we have heard so much about," Yamamoto said. "But, Dr. Ito, only one bottle out of six seems to have changed."

"Yes, we need more research."

The doctor went out of Harry's range of vision for a minute and returned with a new bottle of water. With great scruple, he turned his back while a vice admiral wrote on a cork. Then Ito took the cork back, immediately stopped the bottle and lit a sealing candle, the flame a tiny footlight to his face while he turned the bottle to catch the dropping wax.

"We need production," Yamamoto said.

"First research."

"With a deadline," the admiral insisted.

Ito excused himself to cough, and Harry saw the spots of red bloom in the doctor's handkerchief. Ito was sickly enough to begin with, and all at once he seemed exhausted, as if the lightning had been drawn from his own being. A chair was found for him to sit on, while coughs racked his body. Yamamoto was forced to relent, but he raised his eyes directly toward the glass that Harry watched through.

"What do you think?" asked Gen.

"Wonderful," Harry said. "Lightning bolts, levitation, transmigration. I loved it."

Gen brought diagrams to the Happy Paris at noon the following day. Michiko sorted records and watched sullenly, like a cat jealous of attention.

"You and Harry went with geishas again last night?" she asked Gen.

"I told you," Harry said. "The first was a card game."

"And last night?"

"A con." Harry spread the plans across a table. "No, more than that, it's the most beautiful con I've ever seen. This is the mother lode, this is magic."

"That's all you're going to say?" Michiko asked.

"My lips are sealed."

"I'm going out, Harry. I'm going to go spend all your money and then find a better lover."

"Hope he has a dick that rings like a bell."

"I'm not coming back."

"Have fun."

Gen shuddered as the door slammed behind her. "Kind of tough."

"No Shirley Temple," Harry said. "Have you slept?"

"I had coffee." True enough, the officers of the Japanese navy started each day with coffee and scrambled eggs. Harry's sympathy dried up.

Besides the diagrams, Gen had had the water and oil tested. The water was two parts hydrogen, one part oxygen, and the oil was the equivalent of Rising Sun crude.

"Imagine if we could produce that," Gen said. "If we could get past the experimental stage. There were six bottles. Five bottles failed to change."

"Failure is important. Adds mystery and stalls for time. The navy might want to move to production, but production would entail real amounts of oil and a staff of genuine technicians. No, a con is much happier with endless, expensive research. How much is this costing the navy now?"

"With gold water filters and electrical gear, ten thousand yen a week."

"That's worth stringing out. And anytime the navy presses for results, Ito can play Camille and start to cough to death. If I were you, I would have the doctor's handkerchief searched for a little vial of red liquid."

"You're sure this is a hoax? He's fooling real scientists."

"Well, I've been to the Universal back lot, and it looks like the doctor bought half of Frankenstein's lab. The wands are called Jacob's ladders, and the sphere is a Van de Graaff generator, wonderful for effects. The electricity is all static, perfectly harmless as long as you aren't grounded. You better tell me more about Ito."

Ito had been born in Kyoto, but his family moved first to Malaya and then London, where he claimed to have studied chemistry and physics at university level and done research with British Petroleum.

Who could say? Records from England were unavailable, burned by the Luftwaffe. Ito had recently returned to his homeland to study in solitude at Cape Sata, the southern tip of Japan. There, on a cliff overlooking the restless sea, he had achieved insight into the very nature of atomic structure. Man could split the atom. New elements were being created all the time. Water and oil were different states of electrons in flux. Rather than take the slow, cautious route of academic publication, he offered his services directly to the nation. And the navy ate it up. How could they not? Harry thought. With a reliable source of oil, they could rule the Pacific. Without oil, the Combined Fleet would sooner or later sit in port, steel hulks covered in gull shit.

"There are plenty of magicians in Asakusa. I'll ask around," Harry said.

"No. This is secret, we're not even supposed to mention his name."

"Then let me ask about the trick. I won't mention oil."

Gen laid his arm across the table. "No, these are for you alone. No one else can see anything."

Harry knew that meant that no one else should know he was involved with a navy project.

"Just you," Gen insisted. "You think Ito is not a real scientist?"

"I think I've seen him. It was years ago, at the Olympic Bar in Shanghai. I just noticed him out of the corner of my eye. He was working the tables. He was a close-up artist, card tricks, disappearing coins, and he was bald and dressed like a monk and looked completely different."

"That's it? Someone you barely noticed in a bar years ago? Who looked different?"

"And the cough and the bloody handkerchief when the British grabbed him for lifting wallets."

"Well, I think we have to be more exact than that."

Gen had listed the preparations of the experiment: the elaborate filling of the bottles with water, how witnesses marked the corks with private words or numbers that Ito didn't even see before he inserted electrical wire, sealed the cork with molten wax and set the bottle in the tank of water. Gen had listed each of Ito's steps: safety procedures of the goggles and mat, positioning of the copper wands and dialing in voltage at each to "orchestrate the electrical field."

"Does the transformation usually take one jolt?" Harry asked.

"No, it might take days before it takes effect, but once the bottles are in the tank, they can't be touched. In fact, you'd be electrocuted if you tried. Besides, guards are in the examining room around the clock."

"Why blue bottles?" They looked like medicine bottles to Harry.

"Ito says they filter harmful rays."

"But you can't see whether the contents are oil or water."

"Yes, you can. That's when the bottle rises."

"Well, there's your answer."

"You don't believe any of it?"

"Neither do you, or you wouldn't have brought me in. Yamamoto can't be fooled, not really."

"But—"

"I know." Harry had to smile. "It's like the old joke. A woman brings her husband to the psychiatrist. She says, 'Doctor, my husband is crazy. He thinks he's a chicken.' The psychiatrist says, 'Leave him with me, I'll cure him in a week.' She says, 'But we need the eggs.' That's the navy. You know this is crazy, but you need the oil."

It occurred to Harry that Yamamoto had an especially good chance of coming out of the affair looking like a fruitcake. Since he was the sanest man in the navy, and the strongest opponent to war, the army would seize on anything to discredit him. Harry was not surprised that he'd had no more direct contact with the admiral. That was the beauty of using a gaijin; he could always be disavowed.

Gen had diagrammed the room like elevations. Along the east wall were medical cabinets, carboys of water, anatomical charts. North: cabinets, scale, door and transom, table of rubber boots, gloves and smoked goggles, eye chart and optical equipment. West: crutches, copper coils, VD chart, sink, instructions for winding cloth around the midriff to counteract the G-force of a tight turn. South: wheelchairs, cabinets, the observation mirror, more carboys and a row of bottles.

"But imagine," Gen said. "Imagine if we could transform water into oil. Nothing could stop us, Harry. We could be a force for good, for progress."

"Gen, not that it makes any difference to me, but I've seen progress. I've seen mounds of progress. I've seen the streets run with progress, I've seen progress shoved into pits and stacked to the sky and burned like logs. Progress is overrated."

"But you'll help?"

"What are friends for?"

Gen laid his head on a table and closed his eyes while Harry looked at the diagrams. With cons, the simplest answer was best, you didn't have to go to Harvard to know that. Harry discounted Ito's elaborate procedure of marking and sealing corks as hokum. As for the electric lights and bangs? A hell of a show. All that really mattered was the apparent change of water to oil in six blue bottles in a tank of water. Oil was lighter than water, which was why a bottle floated when its contents were supposedly transformed by Ito's bolts of lightning. But a fine string could raise a bottle, and the change of contents could have taken place anytime. And not even six had to rise, all the con needed was one bottle to maintain excitement because this was an audience who wanted, in spite of its intelligence, to believe what a magician showed them. Houdini once made an elephant disappear in Madison Square Garden. He showed the crowd the elephant standing face out, then drew the curtain, and when he reopened it, the elephant was gone. All Houdini had done was stand the elephant sideways behind a drop of black velvet. As simple as that, because people wanted to believe.

There were other possibilities. The steadfast guards might be bribed. The irate Professor Mishima might have been a shill. That got complicated, however, and Harry focused more and more on Dr. Ito's lab coat as the most likely source of the "blood" the doctor coughed up at will and as a blind for a last-minute switch. Between the fireworks and smoked goggles and his voluminous lab coat, Ito could switch a case of beer.

At four in the afternoon, Harry woke Gen. Kondo had started setting up the bar, briskly wiping glasses. From outside came the street calls of sake vendors and fortune-tellers.

"You can't cheat an honest man."

Gen sat up and rubbed his eyes. "What are you talking about?"

"You can't cheat an honest man. Do you know what that means, college boy?"

"Yes," Gen said.

"No, you don't. It means an honest man can afford to be objective, he doesn't care one way or the other, so he's hard to fool. A mark, on the other hand, wants something for nothing. He wants the pea under the shell, his share of a lost wallet, a tip on a horse, oil for water. His objectivity is already blown, he's bought in. And because the game itself is dishonest, he can't go crying to the police when he's cheated of what he hoped to steal. Or to God because you can't change water into aviator fuel. Have you got some dress whites?"

THAT NIGHT, Harry alone slipped behind the observation mirror as Gen joined the band of witnesses. The group was entirely navy, which Harry took as a sign that scientific quibbles were on the verge of being totally ignored. With Yamamoto present, there was enough gold braid in the room for a bellpull. Only one officer was in dress whites, and that was Gen. All eyes, of course, were on Dr. Ito and the six blue bottles in the water tank.

The emaciated doctor looked as if he had spent the day under a mushroom. He did cast a spell. Officers who generally believed only in six-inch armor hung on every word. Harry concentrated on what Ito did: the restless stride around the tank, the long hands and deft fingers, the flapping laboratory coat. Everyone had pulled on dark goggles, and Ito was moving toward the switch when Gen begged to borrow his lab coat. "I'm concerned about sparks that might burn my jacket. It's the only one I own. Would you mind very much?"

The senior officers were appalled, all but Yamamoto, who looked impartially curious.

Ito hesitated. He had the ability to write amazement on his face. "You need my lab coat?"

"Yes." That was what Harry had told Gen to say.

"In that case." Ito shrugged off the coat and handed it to Gen, then continued in shirtsleeves and threw the switch.

Luminous lines of energy filled the room, pulsing back and forth from wand to sphere over the blue bed of the water tank and the dark blue bottles that trembled within. As Ito modulated the voltage, the lines spread like a hypnotic sea of rolling waves, like the view, perhaps, from Sata, where he had first glimpsed the fluid forces of nature. When he shut off the power, one bottle had already risen to the surface. Ito scooped out the bottle and elected Gen to break the seal, verify the mark on the cork and identify the contents. Gen's face burned with shame down to his white collar.

"It's oil."

"You're positive?"

"Yes, Doctor."

"Then may I have my coat?" As he pulled the coat on, Ito fell against the tank and began coughing up blood. He waved his hand like a swimmer going under. "No more experiments this week. I cannot proceed with such suspicion, the strain is too much."

The C in C averted his eyes from the disgrace of his lieutenant.

AT THREE in the morning, Harry and Gen got back to the Happy Paris to salute the end of Gen's career. Harry brought a bottle of Scotch from the bar while Gen smoked a cigarette as if he were chewing on a nail.

"Sorry, Gen. I guess it wasn't the lab coat."

"Wasn't the coat? Wasn't the *coat*? Harry, you've ruined me. I can't face those officers tomorrow."

"Technically speaking, tomorrow is today. Banzai!" Harry raised his glass.

"Banzai!" Gen threw the drink back. "One commander said I had embarrassed the entire navy. He suggested a letter of resignation."

"You were doing what Yamamoto asked you to do."

"No. I was doing what you told me to do. How could you be so sure about the coat?"

"It seemed logical. I figured, forget the light show, he's just switching bottles."

"We mark the cork. It's the same cork when we put the bottle into the water and when we pull it out, so it's the same bottle. Now what?"

"I don't know, I'm not a scientist. Maybe he's really doing it."

"Water to oil?"

"What do I know? Scientists are doing all sorts of stuff, synthetic this and that. I guess you have a real Einstein on your hands."

"A Japanese Einstein." Gen laughed. "And I'll go down in history as a fool."

"You and me."

"Harry, you won't go down in history at all. How could you say take away his lab coat? You gambled, and I'm the one who paid. If I were a samurai, I'd kill myself. No, I'd kill you first. If I had a gun, I'd shoot you right now."

"Water to oil. One of the pivotal moments in science, like the first electric bulb, that's exciting."

"And now you say he's really doing it."

"It looks that way. He puts water in a bottle and takes oil out."

"I know, I was there."

Now that Harry thought about it, he himself wasn't, not for everything. Ito had moved out of Harry's vision to fill the bottle. "He didn't use the sink tap. Where did he get the water?"

"He siphoned it."

"Why? A sink is easier." Harry remembered the diagrams of the room and the big glass carboys of water. "That's a lot of effort when a sink is right there. It's distilled water? Filtered water?"

"It's from Fuji. The water in the carboys is from a sacred spring on Mount Fuji, it's the only water Ito will use."

"Sacred water?"

"Yes."

Harry took a deep breath and raised his arms. "Praise the Lord! I feel my heart leap and the veils part. I hate to admit it, but I was starting to doubt myself. I'm sane again. Oh, it's a scam, definitely a scam."

"How?"

"I don't know. I have no idea. Ito is a better magician than I am. I do know that for con games, holy water is the best kind. Now maybe you'll let me talk to other magicians."

"I can't, Harry. You were my shot."

In his rumpled whites, Gen looked like a laundry bag. He was the football hero stopped on the one-yard line, the movie star who'd lost his script, the aviator out of gas. He was no longer in the game, in the picture or in the air, and he couldn't understand why. Handsome had gotten him only so far, which wasn't far enough. Harry had seen it before, this capacity of Gen's to lose all confidence, implode and go inert.

"Harry?" Michiko came in the door with Haruko. Both were in chic new outfits, hats and shoes, Haruko's, Harry suspected, a copy of Michiko's. "We were at Haruko's for a day and a half, waiting for you to come looking for me."

"And I was going to, as soon as Gen and I were done. I was very worried."

Seeing Gen low raised Michiko's spirits; she generally treated him as a usurper of Harry's interest, and he treated her the same. She showed Harry a small blue pharmacy bottle of laudanum from her purse. "I have enough here that I will never have to think about you again."

Harry didn't take the threat seriously. Michiko was more the hand-grenade type. "Haruko's was the first place I was going to look."

"You could have called."

"I should have. I've been thinking about you. I really have been. Missed you." He turned the jukebox on low. The plastic canopy took on a pearly hue. An arm laid a disc on the turntable, and a needle slipped into a groove while Harry's hand slid into the small of Michiko's back. *Blue moon, you saw me standing alone / Without a dream in my heart / Without a love of my own.* She was one of the few Japanese girls who knew how to dance, knew that sinuous was better than stiff and that the hips should be involved just so. He touched a certain point between two vertebrae, and her head settled on his shoulder. "You look agonizingly beautiful, you really do." Her right hand rested in his left, bottle and all, his thumb on the underside of her wrist.

When Haruko tried to get Gen to dance, he brushed her hand from his shoulder.

"Gen is feeling a little low." Harry said.

"Gen is always low," murmured Michiko.

Haruko said to Gen, "Maybe I can cheer you up. You can call me sometime. I have a phone."

"Imagine that, her own phone. Haruko has an admirer at the telephone exchange," Harry told Gen. "But she's nuts about you, always has been."

"What would cheer you up?" Haruko asked.

Gen said, "I'm just not in the mood."

"When is he?" asked Michiko. "Gen, when are you in the mood? Are you ever in the mood, Gen?"

"Don't pick on him." Harry said.

"But I want to pick on him. What kind of lover are you, Gen?"

"Not your kind."

"Definitely not, I'd say. Absolutely not."

"Ssh." Harry put his finger to Michiko's lips and took up her hand again. *You knew just what I was there for / You heard me saying a prayer for / Someone I really could care for.*

He felt how cool and delicate her fingers were around the bottle and how nubby the surface of the bottle was. They took another turn around the jukebox, but Harry's mind was already moving in a different direction.

"What now, Harry?" Michiko asked.

Harry had the pharmacy bottle. He set it beside the bottle of Scotch in front of Gen, so smartly that Haruko jumped.

"What do you see?" Harry asked.

Gen wrested his glare from Michiko and refocused. "Two bottles."

"High-class Johnnie Walker bottle. Cheap blue bottle."

"Yes."

"Wake up, what's the difference?"

"Smooth and clear. Blue and crude."

Blue glass recycled from old sake bottles, Harry thought. Glass removed too fast from the blowpipe, a fact that could save Gen's skin, to say nothing of his commission and fancy dress whites. "What makes it crude?"

"Bubbles."

"Say it again, Lieutenant."

Gen sat back. His chin and shoulders rose. "Bubbles."

• • •

BUBBLES WERE the answer.

While there were no experiments, Gen had draftsmen secretly draw all four sides of each blue bottle in the water tank and in the examining room, taking care to pinpoint every bubble in the glass, a pattern that was each bottle's "fingerprint." At the next Magic Show, Dr. Ito transformed not one but two bottles of water into oil. However, when the sketches were compared, it was plain that, while the specially marked stoppers might be the same, the bottles containing oil were not—by the evidence of their own "prints"—the bottles of water originally placed in the tank. At which point, the guards confessed to being bribed for turning a blind eye and tried to shoot themselves with their own handguns. Gen got the credit for exposing the subterfuge, and Ito went off with the police.

The main thing was that Harry had learned how paranoid and crazy the navy was on the subject of oil. By December, eight months later, when he altered shipping ledgers in Yokohama and created a tank farm in Hawaii out of thin air, he figured the navy had only itself to blame.

13

OHARU WAS A perfect model, because her expression was as blank as paper. Kato would turn out a woodblock print of her posed by a teapot and brazier, an elegant kimono with a snow-circle pattern wrapped tight around her middle and loose at the neck, her hair piled in three tiers and pierced by a gilded comb and tortoiseshell pin. The first impression the print gave was of a woman lost in thought. The viewer noticed the striped shadows cast by the bars of a prostitute's window. Steam spilling from the pot, suggestive of opportunities missed. In her sleeve, Oharu's hand crushing an empty pack of Golden Bats. Only then would the viewer see by the context—not as in a single picture but almost as in the repeated images of a film—a woman whose pride had chased away her clients and now, at day's end, the sun sinking into a red haze over the licensed quarter, had no prospects or cigarettes left when regrets were all too late.

Or not. The evening offered other patrons. The next print was of Oharu in a boat, surrounded by a constellation of fireflies that lit the water's surface. She wore a fishnet-pattern kimono, and her hair was slightly disheveled, her mouth slack and tipsy. All that could be seen of the man she was with was a sleeve of army green. The sleeve of her kimono trailed as she stared at a reflection of the moon. In the faintly glimmering lights, she seemed to melt into the water, and the moon that floated in it could have been her own pale face. It was, the young Harry thought, the face of a woman who had surrendered everything.

But no, that was the next print. The model was not Oharu but Chizuko, the small dancer Harry had seen changing into a ballerina's tutu on his first visit to backstage. Her hair, cut short as a schoolgirl's, cupped her broad face. Kato had depicted her standing in the snow, dressed in a red, slightly soiled kimono, barefoot in stilted clogs, a paper peony in her hair and a rolled tatami mat slung across her back. The mat was the trademark of a "sparrow," a prostitute with the coarsest sort of clientele. Although she was younger than Oharu, Chizuko's eyes returned the viewer's gaze with blunt directness. Her cheeks and her feet were flushed from the cold, and despite the snowflakes that swirled around her, Harry could feel her heat.

"You take them too seriously," Kato said. He and Harry were wrapping up the prints amid the drop cloths, paints and easels of his studio. "They're only pictures. Oharu attracts one sort of customer and Chizuko another, they have different appeals. The customer tells me what he wants to see, and that's what I give him. A good lesson for you, Harry, give the customer what he wants."

"But the print of Chizuko isn't like the others. There's only one copy. You ordered the printer to smash the blocks."

"That's my agreement with the customer. It's a very private issue. That's why it's important that you exercise discretion when you deliver it. You understand discretion, don't you, Harry?"

On this particular run, Gen went along. At his insistence, they stopped at a teahouse so he could see the prints. He had been as infatuated with Chizuko as Harry was with Oharu, and the image of her as the lowest form of prostitute had the same impact it had for Harry.

Harry explained, "It's just a picture, Kato says. It doesn't mean anything."

Gen wanted to tear the print in half but settled for watching Harry deliver it to a ground-floor apartment with pots of bamboo at the entryway. The door was opened by a tall, handsome man wearing a boater, white shirt and slacks as if about to go rowing in spite of the cold weather. He took delivery without a word, but Harry recognized him as the army officer who had been with Chizuko to the movie house.

"Did he invite you in?" Kato asked when Harry returned.

"No."

"Good. If he ever does ask you in, think up some excuse."

"Why?"

"Because I don't think you'd do, Harry." Kato stepped back from his painting, a view of the Seine, to glance at Harry. "You're not beautiful enough."

Harry's interest was piqued. From the occasional word dropped by Kato or Chizuko, Harry learned the customer was a rich idler, an army officer, a noble, a self-made man. Kato tended to denigrate while Chizuko embellished. Whichever, the customer ordered an unusual number of prints. A tank rolling through shell bursts. Fabled swordsmen dicing up bandits, tigers, whales. Others more macabre: a treetop swarm of winged monkeys. A woman crucifying her lover in the dark of a cave. A demon suspending a pregnant woman upside down the better to remove her liver.

Kato put more and more trust in Harry. He could send Harry to the printer to bring back a fan print, mirror print or indigo, secure in the knowledge that Harry would select the right one. Besides, on rainy winter days or during Tokyo's humid summer, it was much easier to have the boy run errands while Kato devoted his time to copies of Degas, Renoir, Monet. Kato produced his imitations for himself, not for sale. Harry would return to see Kato squeezing tubes of oil paints, glossy worms of cadmium yellow, ocher and carnelian that he daubed onto the canvas. Harry was a boy off the street, how could he tell the artist that his Japanese prints had grace and life and definition and that his French art was mud and that French flowers looked like frosting? In the meanest Japanese portrait was the dignity of a straw hat, umbrella, kimono. In comparison, French nudes looked stripped and awkward, with thick hams of pink and green. Also, French artists always seemed to be slumming. In Japanese prints, prostitutes were appreciated like royalty and heroes were made from actors, wastrels and gamblers.

Kato paused in midstroke. He was painting a blue cathedral. Blue speckled his hands, shoes, beret.

"Do you plan to be a missionary, Harry?"

"No."

"If you stay in Japan, you should think about becoming a professional gambler. It suits your personality, and the Japanese are almost as fond of gamblers as they are of samurai. I'll get you some dice."

"I have dice."

"See, you're halfway there. Tell me about your parents. Why the American compulsion to make everyone else like them? And their Japanese? They don't understand that Japanese is spoken best when it's not spoken at all. You understand, Harry, because you are a thief, and thieves are good observers. You'll never be Japanese, but I would bet that in a dark room you could fool anyone."

It was true. On sultry August evenings, Harry would go walking with Oharu between shows and entertain her by imitating vendors, beating an empty sake tub like a drum and calling in a high-pitched, nasal voice, "Clogs mended, clogs mended!" or blowing a toy bugle and singing, "Tofu! Soft-as-a-baby's-bottom tofu!" Up and down the street, housewives appeared at their doors with money in their hands. Oharu covered her laugh with her hand until she and Harry turned the corner to the theaters of the Rokku, their dominion, their part of Asakusa. Posters of the latest Hollywood epics lined the way, but what Harry liked most was the reflection in the poster case of him and Oharu strolling by, her sinuous skirt against a background of mincing kimonos, her half-moon eyebrows blandly taking in the world, her hand on Harry's arm as if they were the Rokku's crème de la crème. Fantasies of how he might become Oharu's paramour and protector flitted through Harry's mind all the time. If he could make her laugh, he could make her love him. If he rescued her from some sort of danger, then she would look at him in a whole new light. But she was fearless and needed rescuing from no one, and he understood that part of his attraction for Oharu was that she couldn't take him seriously.

Kato had given Harry a print to deliver when Oharu asked him to see a matinee of a Chaplin film with her. Gen knew the address and took the print in Harry's stead. The film was hilarious, Charlie in a department store, running down the up escalator and up the down escalator while the Movie Man sat before the screen and delivered a thoroughly superfluous "Up, up, up! Down, down, down!" Oharu rested her hand lightly on Harry's, and throughout the film, he stole glances at it and debated whether to turn his hand and hold hers or put his lips to the pale column of her throat. He did neither. Decorum was strictly maintained in movie houses. Where aisles were lit, ushers were required to wear underpants, and houselights were never dim enough to encourage physical intimacies in the audience. What stopped Harry, however, wasn't rules but fear. He was contemptuous of cowards and didn't understand the paralysis that came over him around Oharu. He could tease and joke with her, but anything serious caught in his throat.

It wasn't until Oharu left to change for her own show at the Folies that Harry realized Gen had not returned to the movie as they'd agreed. Hours had passed. By virtue of his height and looks, Gen usually stood out, but Harry didn't find him on the Rokku, in Asakusa Park or on the temple grounds. He visited Gen's house, the card game at the aquarium, their favorite café. Gen wasn't anywhere. Kato had expected Harry to deliver the print, and Harry had never let him down before.

Finally Harry took a tram across town to the customer's address, the same place he had delivered the print of Chizuko, a wooden row house that had been taken over and consolidated by someone with money. The customer answered Harry's knock wearing an airy summer kimono. He was in his mid-twenties, broad-shouldered with muscular calves, built all of a piece like a bear. Handsome was too pretty a word. Domineering with black-rimmed gray eyes under heavy brows, a man with the gravitational pull of a larger planet.

His attention wandered down to Harry. "You're Gen's friend. You've been here before."

"Yes. I am so sorry to bother you, excuse me, but would you do me the favor of telling me when Gen left?"

The customer scanned the street once more before he gestured for Harry to remove his shoes and enter. Harry followed to what were

very much man's quarters, a room dominated by a sea captain's desk
and Persian rug. Any middle-class house had a European room, but
this seemed to be the real thing. A boar's head was mounted by a
selection of Kato's demon prints, a satin bed of medals and an officer's
tunic with a shoulder torn off and stained a rust color. The dial of a
radio glowed in the corner, although the music, a lied, was turned to a
whisper. On the opposite wall were Kato's battlefield prints and a ladder of European sabers and Japanese swords. A Westminster clock
ticked on the mantel. Oriental pillows were strewn around a low
Moorish table set with cognac and dates. Gen lay on a pillow on his
side, his eyes swimming but with a curious pride that played around
his lips.

The customer sank into an armchair. He said, "Gen is interested in
the military life. I was telling him all about it."

In Japanese, the brushstrokes of a single character could define a
writer's class and education. The casually rich room, the few words
from the customer, their intonation at once formal and negligent, suggested the royal Peers' School, university, travel abroad. In an army
officer's case, that would have been Berlin.

"We're wasting your time," Harry said and hoped Gen would get to
his feet.

"Not a bit. Gen has a great deal of promise."

"He delivered the print?"

The customer gave thought to his answer. "Yes, he delivered the
print, and we fell into conversation. You're not Japanese at all, are
you?"

"No, sir."

"Ah." He bestowed a smile on Gen, who lit as if a lamp had been
turned his way. The customer stretched out his bare feet and considered Harry. The smell of fresh sweat hung in the air, along with a
leathery scent of cigars. In one corner, a dummy in a kendo mask and
armor held a wooden stave. Harry noticed murky photographs of
equestrian events, an engraved trophy for something, a gilded citation
in German and a side table holding a vase with a single white chrysanthemum. The customer seemed to have accomplished a great deal for
his young age. There was a restlessness about him that suggested a coil

under pressure. What Harry could see of the rest of the apartment was a thoroughly Japanese arrangement of screens and mats, but this European parlor had the personal shadows of a lair. The customer suddenly heaved himself out of his chair and asked Harry, "What do you know about swords?"

"The sword is the soul of the samurai."

"Quite right. And the samurai is the sword of the emperor. Try this. One hand." The customer lifted from its mount not a Japanese sword but a Western saber with blood channels and a rounded guard. With only one hand, Harry could barely hold its weight. "Meant for horse-back, really. The rider impales a man on foot, and the force of the horse's charge throws the victim over the rider's shoulder. Very mechanical. It even feels like a piece of machinery, doesn't it?"

"Yes." In Harry's hands, the saber felt like a giant wrench.

"I will give the Germans this. When they fence, they hack at each other until they're bloody, they don't back down. The scars are most impressive."

"But they don't perform seppuku, do they?" Gen said.

"No, it is strictly Japanese to take one's life by cutting the stomach open. It's an honor that has unfortunately become degraded. Today someone barely pricks his stomach before a friend cuts off his head."

"Have you ever seen it?" Gen asked.

The customer didn't answer directly. "Even the beheading is sloppy. You have to cut *through* the neck, not at it. It helps to shout."

I'll bet, thought Harry.

"You take kendo at school?" the customer asked.

"Yes," said Harry.

"Who is the best swordsman?"

"Gen."

"I'm not surprised. He is a model of youth."

"Harry is usually a target," Gen said.

"A target, if he's brave, can learn more than anyone else," the customer said. His breath was sweet from cognac. He ran his hand from Harry's shoulder blades to the base of his spine. "Stronger than you look. Now try this." He took the saber from Harry and replaced it with a samurai sword. The blade was narrow and tapered, its length marked by a wavy temper line between the steel of the edge and a darker, softer iron core. Although it was longer than the saber, and its grip was stripped to show the maker's signature stamped into the bare tang, the sword was a two-handed weapon that Harry held comfortably. Even still, it seemed in motion. "A blade of the Bizen school, the edge as sharp as a razor. The first so-called reform of Japan after the West forced its way in was to forbid samurai from carrying their swords. Thousands of swords were melted down to make bookends, souls turned into knickknacks and souvenirs. Hold it lightly, as lightly as you should hold your life." The customer squared Harry's shoulders and hips, hands like a sculptor's molding clay. When Harry twitched the man's hand off, he took Harry by the head and aimed his attention to the sword. "Do you know how a blade is made so fine and so hard? The metal is beaten and folded and beaten a hundred times, and then a hundred times more, and then another hundred, the same way a man is made into a soldier. That is why a Japanese soldier can march in his sleep, can stand at attention while the ice forms on his face. The sword is worn with its blade up so that the act of drawing becomes the act of attack. The curve of the blade puts the sword as it's drawn at the most efficient angle to strike an enemy. Every parry carries within it a thrust. That is the Yamato spirit. Hold the sword straight out. You take bayonet, too?"

"We drill at school," Gen said. "We train on Harry."

The customer asked Harry, "They train on you, yet you're still here? You have the quality of durability, if nothing else. Perhaps you have the makings of a soldier after all. But I saw you once in a movie house. You seemed more interested in women."

"He's in love with Oharu," Gen said.

"Is that true?" the customer asked Harry. "Are you in love with a woman?"

Harry felt the color in his cheeks betray him. Held straight out, the sword trembled.

"It's one thing to have a woman," the customer said. "It's another to be in love with a woman. To love a weaker person, what does that do for you? To mix inferior steel in a sword, does that make the sword weaker or stronger? Weaker . . . or . . . stronger?" He pulled back his sleeve and placed the inside of his wrist under the sword. Harry tried to hold the sword up, if not still, but his shoulders ached; the blade grew heavier and began to dip. Gen got to his knees to see. The blade's edge just touched the customer's skin, and a drop of blood circled his wrist. He didn't flinch. He said, "True love can only exist between equals."

As Harry let the blade fall, the customer neatly slipped his hand out of the way, took the sword and stepped back for more room. Sword at the perpendicular, he took a position of balance, knees slightly bent, looking right, left, making a complete turn, the blade slicing down, then on a horizontal arc, his kimono swirling around marble-smooth, muscular legs in the sort of dancelike move Harry had seen on the Kabuki stage and in samurai films, but never before with such a sense of ease and genuine menace, of an animal casually indulging in the briefest display of its claws. Harry knew in that instant the difference between being inside and outside the cage of a bear. The customer finished with a snap of the sword called "the flipping off of blood," slipped the blade under his arm as if sheathing it and bowed to Harry.

"Excuse me, that was impolite. Worse, it was melodramatic."

"No, it was wonderful," Gen said. "It was the real thing."

"Not yet," the customer said, "but in time we will see the real thing. It is unavoidable."

"He's with the Kwantung army," Gen told Harry. "That means Manchuria. They'll see action there."

"We should be going," Harry said. "Let's go, Gen."

Gen said, "It would be rude to leave."

The customer replaced the sword on the wall. He drew Gen up by the hand. "No, your friend is right, and there are more important things I'm supposed to be doing than entertaining every urchin who comes off the street."

"Can I come again?"

"Perhaps you'll deliver another print."

"You've been very kind." Harry tugged Gen toward the door.

Gen moved stiffly, reluctantly slipping his feet into his geta. The customer seemed to dismiss the two boys without as much as a nod, but as they stepped over the threshold, he told them to wait, went to the vase and bestowed on Gen the single chrysanthemum. Gen accepted the flower as if it were a sword itself, and although his thick black hair fell forward when he bowed, Harry saw a violet blush of pleasure spread across his cheeks.

HARRY FOUND KATO at the Folies, in the balcony with the manager watching a final act called "Amusing Violin." The manager wore a greasy boater and snickered through an overbite stained from cigarettes and tea. He and Harry had never gotten along since the day Harry first stumbled into the dressing room. Onstage, a comic musician playing "The Flight of the Bumblebee" was afflicted with a rubbery bow and ridiculously overlong European tails that flopped around his feet. His bow caught in the strings, flew offstage like an arrow and was retrieved by Oharu in a skimpy one-piece and net stockings. She handed the sagging bow to the comedian. As he watched her stride away, his bow stiffened. The manager laughed in and out like a donkey.

Kato said to Harry, "I hear you let Gen deliver the print to the customer. I told you that only you should take it."

"Nothing happened. He seemed to like Gen more than me."

"Why not? Gen is a far more attractive boy than you. You are a mongrel, and Gen is the ideal."

Flustered by Oharu, the comedian reached into his violin case and brought out a fan to cool himself. Not enough. He brought out an electric fan with a long cord and asked a musician in the orchestra pit to plug it in. The comedian directed its breeze up and down his body and along the bow.

"Tell me exactly what happened," Kato said.

Harry recounted the scene at the customer's house. Meanwhile, onstage, the comedian started "The Bumblebee" again but noticed a piece of paper drifting by and, in the midst of playing, speared it with his bow. It was sticky paper. It stuck to his bow, his shoe, his hand, finally to his forehead, and he played while blowing the paper up from his eyes. The audience around Harry laughed so hard they stuffed handkerchiefs into their mouths.

"This is great stuff," the manager said.

Kato said, "He gave Gen a white chrysanthemum?"

"A gift."

"And the customer, Harry. Tell me again, did he introduce himself?"

"No."

"Then I will tell you. His name is Ishigami. Lieutenant Ishigami is a rising man in the army. He is the natural son of a royal prince, no one is quite sure who, so he has the protection of the court and a stipend from the imperial household. He could have gone into banking or writing poetry, instead he chose the army. He joined the Kwantung army so that he would be sure to come under fire from bandits or Russians or Chinese, and he acquitted himself so well that admirers call him a virtual samurai. So you might ask why he is here in Tokyo. Because, Harry, Ishigami is in disgrace. A board of inquiry is looking into the accusation that he is one of a circle of junior army officers agitating against the civilian government. Ishigami says his allegiance is to the emperor, not to politicians. This has made him even more popular with the army, and with patriotic groups in general, but while the board of inquiry meets, he is forced to lie low and waste his time with the likes of you and me and, apparently, your friend Gen. That's why I wanted to send you. Ishigami wouldn't touch you. You're not his type."

"What do you mean?"

The manager leaned over. "He means that a white chrysanthemum isn't just a flower. It represents a boy's tight little asshole. You didn't know that, Harry? So I guess you don't know everything after all. There is a certain kind of samurai, and there always has been. Don't take it seriously, it's just sex."

The bow flew offstage again. Again Oharu retrieved it and peeled the paper from the comedian's forehead. She had a languid way of strolling off forever. Harry felt a proprietary claim on those legs, those long flanks to which he had administered so many vitamin shots. The comic lectured his stiffening bow, but the bow tried to follow her, dragging him across the stage.

Harry was angry and confused. "Not Gen."

"Why not?" the manager said. "Gen is a poor boy. Ishigami is a hero. His attention is worth seeking. All Gen has to offer is his beauty. If it means pulling down his pants, why not?"

"Gen's not that way."

"What way?" Kato said. "Up, down? Right, left? How would you know?" For the first time, Kato turned his eyes to Harry, who could see what a foul humor he was in. "You shouldn't have let Gen take the package, Harry. You should have done as I told you."

"I didn't think it would make any difference."

"Obviously it did."

"I always made the deliveries. Gen wanted a turn."

"Gen would do anything you do. He admires you. He also resents you. You are the stray dog that won favor, which I think made Gen all the more susceptible to attention from Ishigami. Gen has changed now, thanks to you. Not that part of Gen wasn't that way. In the end, it's all a matter of taste, and who are we to be judges, right, Harry? Well, I suppose we all admire you, you're the best example of a survivor we've ever seen. That first day when they chased you up the stairway to the dressing room, I said to myself, Here is a fish that could live in a tree if it had to. I got very fond of you. I got too close."

"What do you mean?"

Kato went back to watching the show. "I don't think I'll be using you anymore, Harry, that was a mistake. You should spend more time with your family. Won't you be going back to America soon?"

"I've never been there."

"Well, you should get ready."

Apart from movies and music, America didn't interest Harry. In Tokyo he ran his own life, and he suspected that once in the States, he would be supervised to the point of suffocation by his parents, church people, aunts and uncles and ignorant cousins. Tokyo was the world's center of color, beauty, life. What was Kentucky? He had seen films with hillbillies sitting around cracker barrels, boots up, aiming tobacco juice at spittoons. Was that him? How many times had he looked into a mirror and hoped to find himself magically given a new body of smooth skin, straight black hair and properly narrowed eyes? It almost had to happen.

"I'll make up for it," Harry said. "I'll deliver everything myself."

"Not anymore, Harry. Don't come around."

Harry tried to catch a tease in Kato's eye. "You're kidding."

Kato ignored him.

Harry tried a different tone of voice. "I'm sorry about Gen. I shouldn't have let him take it."

"Too late."

"I could lay off for a while."

"Stay away for good. I'm bored with you, Harry. You are no longer amusing."

Harry lost his breath from the swiftness of his demotion from Kato's favorite pet and confidant to . . . nothing, as if on a whim the artist had erased him from a picture.

Kato added, "No backstage visits, either. Stay away from Oharu."

"Oharu and I—"

"Oharu is no longer a friend of yours. Stay away from her."

The manager leaned across Kato to twist the knife himself. "No backstage, no girls. In fact, forget the whole theater. I'll have you tossed out the next time I see you in here."

"You can't stop me," Harry said.

"See," the manager said. "A Japanese boy would have been genuinely contrite."

"East is East and West is West, Harry," Kato said. "You were a guest, and now it's time for you to go."

The manager tugged on Kato's sleeve. "Oh, this is the finale I wanted you to see."

Kato smiled as Oharu returned with a large bee she attached to the tip of the comedian's bow. The bee buzzed menacingly. The comedian tried to shake off the bee one moment and fence with it the next while, all the time, incredibly, he went on playing, coattails wrapped around him in his passion, faster and faster and faster until he dropped to the stage like a dead man and the bow dropped from fatigue.

"Wait," the manager said.

Oharu returned with a sun flag she placed in the comedian's hand, and at once he was revived and on his feet. The curtains opened, and the entire cast of the revue—actors, chorus girls, acrobats, ventriloquists and magicians—stepped forward for a final bow, each one waving a flag. Behind them rose a battleship, an elaborate prop with triple-barreled guns and a flying bridge with more chorus girls and lines trimmed in pennants. Gun barrels boomed. Smoke rings shot from the muzzles and floated toward the balcony.

Kato turned on the manager. "When did you put this in the show? What does this militaristic garbage have to do with the music hall?"

"It's not military, it's patriotic."

"It's supreme stupidity. You're playing to the worst instincts in people."

The manager shrugged. "People love it."

Harry hadn't cried for years—with dry eyes he had survived bruises, the absence of parents, the death of pets—but now his eyes stung. Through a blur, he watched a smoke ring float by out of reach.

14

ARRY TOOK A river bus, intending to drop the gun in the water somewhere between downtown and Asakusa. The boat was narrow and the cabin crowded with shaggy students, a straw-hat brigade of young salarymen, a go hustler with his board, housewives with mesh bags of winter melon, children carrying smaller children. Harry braved the evening chill and rode in the forward open area, alone except for a businessman reading a newspaper by the lamp on the bow and a boy rolling a toy tank that sprayed sparks on the deck.

The night sky was a deep blue edged by the softest light of any major city in the world, light that escaped from paper windows and sliding doors or was the tear-shaped light of streetlamps along the banks of the Sumida. At this distance from the Ginza, there were no office buildings to blot out the view, only occasional spikes of neon like the Ebisu Beer tower or the giant illuminated clock of Ueno Station, otherwise only a steady churn behind the backs of obscure one- and two-story houses. Half-seen figures wrung clothes on balconies that overhung the water. A muted glow of patched windows gave way to a bright corner with a streetlamp, neighborhood pump, the calls of children around a street musician, which in turn gave way to the next stretch of blind windows, music swallowed as quickly as it had emerged. The only river traffic was other river buses or barges that eased in and out of canals. Harry intended to tell Michiko tonight. He'd garb his betrayal with small decencies, like leaving her the apartment and the income from the Happy Paris. That was what she was cut out for, anyway, a tough little mama-san. It was a better deal for her, she'd have to see that. He slipped his hand through the rail and let his fingers trail in icy water. He was reaching for the gun when a passenger came out of the cabin, apologized to the boy for trespassing on the battleground of the toy tank and sat next to Harry. It was Sergeant Shozo of the Special Higher Police with a briefcase, the picture of a man headed home from a hard day's work.

"I thought it was you," he told Harry. "I was just saying to myself that looked like Harry Niles, and it's you. But you have a car, why are you going by boat?"

"It's a change."

"Yes, I know what you mean. I always enjoy the river." He settled into a contemplative pose while Harry tucked the gun more out of sight. "But how are you getting back to your car?"

"Boat, I suppose. Maybe swim."

"If you flew, I wouldn't be surprised." Shozo produced a broad smile. He leaned against the rail to take in the opposite embankment, a dark ridge edged in branches. "Cherry trees. I brought my son here last year when they were in bloom. We had just seen *Tarzan*. All he wanted to do was climb the trees. Eight years old." Shozo shook his head.

"Did you like the movie?" Harry asked.

"Very much. A little racist but highly entertaining. Do you agree?"

"Terrific movie. Big boy in leather skivvies. Upper-class girl. They meet cute in the jungle, build a house in the trees and adopt a chimp. It's got everything."

"When you put it that way, yes. What I found interesting about Tarzan was his desire first to be an ape and then the recognition that he is different, setting off great psychological tension, it seems to me. What are your thoughts?"

"I'm sure Tarzan was torn."

"How was it for you when you returned to your home in the United States?"

"Well, it wasn't my home. My home was here."

"Yes. That must have been difficult."

"People adjust."

Shozo nodded sympathetically. "I'm curious. When you went back, what struck you most?"

Harry thought about it. "Dirty floors."

"Fascinating."

"Sour tea."

"Yes?"

"Dullness." No banners, no color, no design.

"I want to get this down." The sergeant opened his briefcase to take out a notebook. He unscrewed the cap of his fountain pen. "I was wondering, what did you do on your return?"

"Is this an official interrogation?"

"No, I don't think so. Do you?"

Harry did not like the trend of the conversation. Shozo was proving to have an easygoing slyness that would have served well in a card game.

A tugboat pushed by towing a coal barge. A man sitting on the coal waved the orange arc of a cigarette.

Harry finally said, "A little schooling. I was remiss on my American history and the war between the states. A short spell in Bible college and then I was on my own. Pumped gas in Kentucky, set up beach chairs in Florida, water-skied."

"Odds and ends. Mostly gambling?"

"Gambling was more steady."

Shozo smiled as if sharing the adventure. "Then you headed for California? For a young man like you, a free spirit, that must have been a logical destination." He flipped a couple of pages. "Hollywood."

"Lifeguard, pool boy, record rep. Selling records and sheet music to music stores, getting the music played on radio."

"But still mainly gambling?"

"Gambling was a way to meet people. Being a record rep, I met mostly cowboys with guitars. A lot of movie people play cards. Losing money helps them relax. I played my way into a job at Paramount in promotion."

"You didn't have any higher education in business?"

"No one in the movies has a higher education in anything. Education is the last thing you want."

"Three years at Paramount?"

"Three years of taking ingenues and wonder dogs to opening nights. Then I got an offer from another studio to open a branch here. I flew the Clipper to Manila and took the first boat from there. By the time I landed at Yokohama, the studio had folded and the job was gone."

"But you stayed," Shozo said.

"I found employment."

"You've done well." The sergeant reflected. "I find fulfillment in my own work. Not the counterespionage, that's largely mechanical. Detection and apprehension, any police can do that. What makes the work of the Special Higher Police—"

"The Thought Police."

"Thought Police, yes, is that we deal in a realm apart from ordinary crimes. We anticipate crimes. Say a man is mentally ill or Communist, isn't it better to catch him before he physically harms anyone else? Some people are not even aware of the dangerous ideas they carry. They are like innocent bearers of typhoid. Shouldn't they be isolated for the general health?"

"Then you cure them?"

"Yes and no. A gaijin is as riddled with deviant ideas as a dog with ticks. He isn't worth the time. Japanese are, by nature, healthier. We sit with them, talk with them, listen patiently to them. You know the saying that each man has a book? I believe that each man has a confession. It's a purgative process, a cleansing. I don't know why women tend to be more incorrigible, but every man has written a confession that is heartbreaking in its sincerity. I was wondering where you would fall in that range. If you were Japanese enough to be worth the effort."

Moths spun around the lamp and landed on the businessman's

newspaper. He read, shook the paper, read. Harry's eye was caught by an ad with a sleek black train muscling its way through the night: THE ASIA EXPRESS: TOUR MANCHUKUO IN COMFORT. Right now it sounded like a good idea to Harry.

Shozo asked, "What was the Magic Show? It comes up when your name is mentioned, but no one seems to know what it was."

"I don't know, either."

"Something to do with the navy?"

"I wouldn't know."

"The navy and magic, what would that be?"

"Sorry, I can't help you."

Shozo nodded. "You keep beetles, I understand."

"Yes." Oishi, the samurai beetle, was in Harry's car.

"As a boy, I used to keep lizards. My favorites were the chameleons. It fascinated me how a chameleon could be so gray on a rock or green on a branch that it was practically invisible. Sometimes I'll be following you on the street, and I lose you because you blend in so well. Then I remembered how easy it was to see the chameleons if I only changed their background. I was considering a different background for you. Have you ever been to jail?"

"Not seriously." Harry caught the shift to a new level.

"A Japanese jail is serious. Tell me why I shouldn't put you in."

"Well, to start with, I haven't broken any laws."

Shozo smiled in an indulgent way. "Harry, you break laws all the time. Even if you didn't, in Japan there are also crimes of thought or intent."

"I'm an American citizen, my thoughts don't have to be pure."

"If all else fails, there's paragraph eight."

"You're kidding."

"Paragraph eight of the National Defense Act. Giving political or economic information to foreign agents brings a penalty of ten years in jail."

"What information, what agents?"

"You know Tokyo too well. You know the sad situation of Japanese oil. You talk to diplomats and foreign correspondents. Some of them are certainly spies. You know members of the navy general staff."

"Is that what this is? Giving the navy a black eye by arresting me?"

"Tell me about the Magic Show."

"I don't know what it is."

"See, you don't cooperate at all, not sincerely. I had decided after our visit to the dock in Yokohama that, considering how much you knew, it would simply be wiser to put you in a cell and forget about you. Frankly, I don't think your embassy would raise much of a protest."

Harry caught a hesitation. "But . . ."

"But today you surprised me. Generally everything you do is for profit, everything has an angle. Today, however, you went to Tokyo Station to see an ordinary army man, a sergeant, board his train. I can't think of any advantage you gained by seeing him off. So I decided to treat you as a Japanese and give you one more opportunity to cooperate."

"He was an old friend."

"Apparently."

The tone of the engine changed as the river bus slowed and swung toward the strung lights of a dock. Harry scanned the waiting faces for the eager grin of Corporal Go. The corporal wasn't there.

Harry asked, "How is the accountant from Long Beach Oil?"

Shozo closed his briefcase. "Kawamura? We still have a few questions for him. Now he claims that he and the American manager are innocent, that someone must have altered the books recently. Can you believe that? What we have discovered is that for any Japanese with the simplest training in calligraphy, the forgery of a Western handwriting is child's play."

"Then I suppose you should look for a Japanese."

"Maybe so. Some kind of Japanese."

The businessman with the newspaper took the boy by the hand and slipped by to join the line forming in the cabin. He had left his newspaper on the bench, and Shozo pointed to a front-page photo of the special December Kabuki performance when actors performed without makeup. Their real faces looked sketched and unfinished compared to the richness of their kimonos and wigs.

Shozo said, "How interesting it would be to see the real Harry Niles."

Harry was working on a rejoinder when the boat touched and tied up. Shozo joined the line and, along with every other passenger but Harry, made a quick hop-step onto the dock, where he turned to wave a friendly good-bye. In a second he was gone, replaced by boarding passengers.

It was unclear to Harry when Shozo intended to carry through with his threat of arrest. The various police agencies were like different companies, competing one minute and cooperating the next. Shozo could trade Harry to the army for advantages down the line. The navy could protect him as long as he was on the outside. In prison, though, nothing but bad things happened.

In the meantime, there was still the gun to be disposed of. Harry had the open area of the boat to himself, until the last second when a young policeman in smart brass buttons and billed cap claimed the seat opposite. He opened a book and squeezed by the bow lamp, lifting his eyes from time to time to fix Harry with a glittering hostility. Whether Shozo had ordered the policeman on board or not, it wasn't a situation conducive to the drowning of a gun. Harry picked up the newspaper the businessman had left on the bench.

Rains in Okinawa. Photos of people in boats, pigs on roofs, a sake merchant wading through a shop knee-deep in water as empty tubs floated by.

Fashion news. Women were bringing in their outmoded Western dresses to exchange for useful coveralls made from wood fiber. A picture showed one woman admiring herself in a mirror as she added a flower to her hair.

Sports. Sumo visited army camps to express their support for men in uniform. Joe Louis pummeled a white opponent.

The policeman's eyes darted up from his book at every move Harry made. Harry turned to a page of photographs headlined CHINA WELCOMES JAPAN. In Canton, Japanese troops were welcomed by singers and dancers to a floating restaurant. At a junction of Shanghai boulevards, a single Japanese traffic officer maintained good order for thousands of Chinese. On a country lane, Japanese troops handed out candies and received flowers in return. At the Nanking city wall, Chinese boys goose-stepped and waved the flag of the rising sun. The page turned a tint of pink, and Harry looked up at an approaching bridge where a convoy of trucks was crossing with the sound of striving, underpowered diesels. Their headlights were dark, but the way was washed in red by signal lamps beamed through red filters. The policeman at the bow paid no attention. Harry wondered why a convoy would move at night, although the usual answer was sheer military stupidity. The bridge was a red haze: red soldiers looked down from red trucks. Flatbed Toyotas carried red caissons and light tanks that looked like red teapots. Red horses trotted by, and then more troops, until the boat slipped beneath into a cave of reverberating black. Perhaps it was the bow lamp's reflection on the piers or the trucks overhead, but Harry found himself back at the Nanking city wall and not in dry newsprint but in the full bloom of a summer night.

Kerosene-soaked torches ringed ten Chinese kneeling on the ground, their hands bound but no blindfolds. They had been walked for some distance, tranquilized by helplessness, eyes cast down, expressions slack. Two were obviously soldiers caught trying to escape in the general exodus from the city; they had succeeded in obtaining civilian clothes but not in erasing telltale rifle calluses from their hands. A third was a shop clerk in an apron speckled with blood from his nose. Another was an old man with a twitching mole. The fifth, Harry guessed, was a lawyer in a torn pin-striped suit; he looked like a busted mattress. Next, a coolie who was little more than a starved frame in a loincloth, then a man in a long nightshirt, as if he had been roused from bed, and a fat man—a merchant or a pawnbroker—with almost no neck. Finally, a man with eyes and mouth pressed shut, already braced for the blade; and a boy, maybe thirteen, who stank with fear. Over all ten of them lay an ocher dust daubed with blood. Perhaps a hundred soldiers gathered as ad hoc witnesses, and another fifty with more torches stood on the wall. It was the blaze on the rampart that had drawn Harry and Willie. The city was a landscape of ruin and fire, and it was sometimes difficult to tell whether violence was past, present or imminent, but Harry and Willie had long since lost their sense of personal safety. There was no personal safety, there was only bluff. Willie was a good leader because he demonstrated moral assurance on a Wagnerian scale. All the same, when he and Harry drove toward the wall, soldiers made way with smirks of disdain. The Japanese had contempt for the international safety zone to begin with, and one of the open secrets of the war was that the Chinese enemy had German advisers—in fact, German, Russian *and* American advisers—helping them resist the Japanese. A swastika on a truck could be a safeguard one moment and a target the next, especially at night. As the truck nosed its way closer to the scene, the soldiers on the wall whipped their torches all the faster. When Harry braked to a stop, a sergeant jumped on the truck's running board and shouted in his face, "Ten heads in ten strokes in under a minute! See for yourself!" As Harry and Willie got out, the soldiers eagerly pushed them forward, making them derisively honored guests. In the middle of the turmoil, a man gathered himself with the intensity of a sumo scattering salt around a ring, and Harry recognized Ishigami at once, by motion as much as looks. Ishigami had stripped to a white loincloth that accented the darkness of his face and hands and the alabaster smoothness of his body. Close up, he had sturdy legs, a long torso banded with muscle, wide shoulders and forearms thickened by hours of fencing and tiger-striped with scars. His hair was long, tied in a bun. A tub of water stood by for him to wash with when he was done and a fresh uniform for him to wear, but at the moment his mind was on his sword, and he rubbed the blade with oil of cloves that lent his hands a sharp-sweet scent. The lieutenant's orderly was a young corporal with doelike features, long hands and wrists, lips full of anxiety. Harry wondered whether the corporal had ever seen combat, or had Ishigami protected him from harm? The orderly murmured something to Ishigami, enough for Harry to catch a country boy's soft *zu-zu* accent. Ishigami glanced up, but Harry doubted there was any chance the lieutenant would connect Harry with the boy he had been fourteen years before. Ishigami wiped the blade clean, the sword weightless in his hands. Harry believed that Ishigami could probably take ten heads in ten seconds if he just waded in, but the lieutenant was a man of ritual. He positioned the orderly at his back with a bucket and ladle, practiced his approach from back to front so the kneeling men would hear only his progress. Satisfied, Ishigami returned to his starting point and took a balanced pose, breathing regulated, chin tucked in. A sergeant stepped forward with a pocket watch. Ishigami lifted his sword perpendicular to his shoulders, a silvery baton calling an orchestra to silence, all but the drone of flies. The sergeant with the watch raised his arm. There was a little respectful, preliminary coughing. The Chinese were motionless, leaning submissively, tilted toward their fate. Why no blindfolds? Harry wondered. For some reason, a white chrysanthemum came to mind. Harry took in Ishigami, the orderly, the sergeant with the stopwatch and the crowding circle in a more professional way, as if he had joined a game in progress and had maybe a second to find the chump, the weak link. He dug into his jacket and came out with a wad of money that he flourished next to a torch. "A hundred yen, a hundred yen each," Harry declared, "to Lieutenant Ishigami and his orderly, and ten yen to every soldier present if the lieutenant can take ten heads in under thirty seconds. Or let the surviving Chinese go." It was an offer that Ishigami, alone, would have despised, but the sight of the money and the sound of the offer had already inspired a cheer that spread to the heights of the wall. Here was an American crazy enough to practically burn his money. How at that point could a hero deny such a windfall to so many comrades? "Money," Harry told Ishigami, "makes things more interesting." Ishigami seemed interrupted at the top of a dive. He looked at Harry to determine if he was real or apparition. "Disappoint a lot of people," Harry said. Ishigami's eyes shone, taking in the ring of torches and enthusiastic soldiers. "Done?" Harry asked. Ishigami seemed to decide that it didn't matter what Harry was. He nodded. Done. As he raised the sword again, cords of muscle played across his chest. His hands rotated in to the top of the grip to deliver the power of his palms through the blade. Thirty seconds. The first Chinese was the most difficult one, the merchant with the fat, sweaty neck. How many bolts of silk or tins of tea or bars of soap had passed across his shop counter? How many pipes of tobacco or plates of crispy duck enjoyed? How many women lain with, lied to, regretted? No matter, it all came to this, a balmy night in the Asian Co-Prosperity Sphere when the most he could hope for was a clean cut rather than a hatchet job. Behind the man's left shoulder, Ishigami seemed absolutely balanced, sword motionless, his eyes focused an inch above the collar. The lieutenant's hand began to drop, and already the merchant's head was on the ground, separated from the body, which, still upright, jetted blood. A general expulsion of breath went round, an expression of awe as if each soldier had felt a phantom impact of the decapitation. Ishigami flicked blood off and held out the sword so that the orderly could ladle water on the blade, one side and then the other, to wash off bone and gristle. With three steps, Ishigami set himself behind one of the soldiers caught escaping, a man who knew enough to stretch his neck. Ishigami took his head off as if removing a sausage end; it dropped neatly between the dead man's knees like a bowl to catch the blood. Two heads in four seconds; Ishigami was doing well. The orderly, however, moved stiffly. The light of the torches was shifting and uncertain. A hundred yen was a staggering amount. When Ishigami held out his sword to rinse, the orderly missed and had to scoop water on the blade a second time. Worse, he failed to make way for the back-swing, which plucked the ear off the side of his head and threw the lieutenant's timing off. Ishigami only scalped the next man and had to swing a second time. When he held out his sword for water, it took him valuable seconds to realize that his orderly was too busy searching the ground for his ear to mind the ladle. It was a distraction. Ishigami looked at Harry. More precious seconds passed. Ishigami went back to work. He severed the head of the old man, mole and all. The coolie's head flew into the air like a hat tossed at graduation, and then Harry called out, "Time!" Five Chinese—deserter, clerk, lawyer, man in his nightshirt, boy—were still alive. Behind them spread soaked earth, soaked bodies, dusty heads, insect spirals, Ishigami bloody to his waist, sweaty with clots of blood, strands of hair loose from his exertions, the long arc of the sword bright red. The survivors seemed the last to realize they were alive. Harry and Willie had to lift them to their feet and drag as much as guide them toward the truck. When soldiers blocked the way, Ishigami ordered them to step aside. A wager was a wager. The last to be saved was the boy, who cried, shit and pissed, every sphincter open as Harry threw him over the tailgate. "Don't look back." Harry told Willie as they got in front. "This is loss of face, great loss, so just look ahead." Ishigami called after Harry, "How do you know my name?" Harry played deaf. "Who are you?" Ishigami shouted again. Harry ignored him, put the truck in gear and eased away from the soldiers until he dared glance in his rearview mirror and saw Ishigami turn, press the orderly to his knees and push down his head. All this Harry remembered not in sequence but as a single spherical moment, a special lens to see through . . .

The river bus approached its dock. Somehow twenty minutes had passed in a second. As the boat slowed to a muffled impact, people in the cabin gathered their packages and children and rose from their seats. Harry knew he couldn't stay on for a third ride; the policeman already gestured with his book for Harry to rise and join the other passengers disembarking. When he pushed Harry, the gun almost dropped from Harry's belt. Instead, the policeman's book fell on the deck, open to a print of two lovers, the woman's legs elevated to display the nest of her sex and the darkened, swollen length of his. The boat rocked gently. The bow lamp swung from side to side. The policeman snatched up the book and shouted, "This is art."

As if Harry were a man to disagree.

15

KATO HAD AFFECTIONATELY called Harry his "ape," his "imp," his "fearless boy"; he couldn't dump Harry over one mistake. The trick, Harry thought, was to find Kato, plead his case and then wheedle his way back into Kato's good graces. Never mind that a humid day had led to a night of heavy rain. Harry darted from dripping eave to dripping eave on his way to the music hall.

The Folies was shut, front doors and back. Harry went around to the bright marquees of the Rokku and, drenched by the rain, ran from movie house to movie house, squandering money on tickets and breathlessly running up and down aisles in search of Kato. There was no sight of him there or in the food stalls along the street, and when the movie marquees went dark, the entire Rokku plunged into black. Harry would have tried finding Oharu, but he realized that he didn't know where she lived. Off the Rokku, the entire city was snuffing lamps and drawing windows shut. The last street vendors retreated with the clatter of clogs on stone, the last red lanterns of the taverns died. At midnight anyone caught on the street without a good excuse would be taken to a police box. Uncle Orin would be summoned, there would be a scene. Yet Harry would not give up. He was sure that Kato had not gone home because the artist had brought a sketchpad to the music hall.

Gone where? Harry splashed to the brothels Kato favored, peeking in doors for the sight of his clogs or umbrella, but Kato had disappeared. Harry's clothes were a wet second skin. He trudged across the Asakusa temple and through the garden to the relative shelter of the temple gate. Looking up at the lantern of the gate, he remembered views of the same giant lantern in a series of Kato's prints, with the same row of souvenir shops leading to the same broad avenue. *A View from the Green House*, the prints had said. Usually that sort of picture included a veranda with courtesans or geishas. These didn't. Harry couldn't think of a brothel that had exactly such a view. For lack of any other idea, he set off to find what house did.

He moved in the shadows, watching for rickshaws or the shuttered lanterns of police until he reached a two-story house that seemed shut tight. It was sheathed in copper tiles green as dragon scales and Chinese eaves curled like tails. A shimmer of water over tiles gave the house the illusion of shifting life. On either side, an umbrella store and a bicycle repair shop appeared to cringe at the proximity of such a fearsome neighbor. The upper windows were closed to the rain. On the front doors and gate were padlocks the size of horseshoes, and the front window was locked and covered by bamboo grown wild in pots. Harry sank as far into the doorway as he could get, soaked and defeated. Resting his head against the door, he heard the faintest possible plucking of a shamisen, like the idle sound of overflowing water. No one simply passing by would have noticed.

Harry threw his clogs over the gate. Using the gate's copper bosses for handholds, he scaled the top and went after, landing on a cushion of moss. The house was larger than it had appeared from the street, with a side garden not of flowers and trees but of large stones set among raked pebbles. In a brief illumination of lightning, Harry saw the garden as it was meant to be contemplated, as small islands in a sea of perfect waves. The pebbles chattered in the rain. Harry was so wet the downpour no longer made any difference to him.

In August, Tokyo yearned for breezes. The outer screens of a long veranda were removed, and inner screens that were nothing more than frames of paper were left half open to the night air. In the front room, Kato sat in a kimono and beret, sketchpad on his knees, working by the overhead light of a paper lantern. At first Harry thought that Kato saw him, too, before he realized that between the artist's concentration and the lantern's muted glow, anything in the garden was virtually invisible. A brilliantly quick artist, Kato drew fluid contours and penciled notes in the margin for color and shade. The interior dividers seemed to be open so that Kato's eye could run the entire length of the house, although what Kato saw Harry couldn't.

Careful to stay on the moss that trimmed the stones, Harry moved past the front room to the second. The veranda was hardwood polished to a black sheen. A chain led rainwater from the roof to the ground. Although the screens of the second room were dark and shut, it was where the sound of the shamisen emanated from. Harry admired how Kato had arranged matters, the artist with a bare minimum of light, an unseen musician in a middle room creating ambience and then, at a distance, the artist's model bathed in light.

Not quite bathed. The screens were wide open to the garden, and Harry saw inside the third room a shallow light of candles around a canopy of mosquito netting draped from the ceiling. Outside a corner of the netting lay a bowl, a fan and a mosquito coil with wispy smoke. The netting was a gauzy green shadow. Within it, Harry could see two heads and the glint of a gold kimono. He was sure they couldn't see him.

At a word from Kato, the figures began to shift. One climbed behind the other, and Harry heard breathing mix with the notes of the shamisen. The canopy shifted like a skirt from side to side. While the netting moved, a slim hand pulled up the green mesh on Harry's side, and Oharu looked out. She was on all fours, her kimono bunched between her shoulders and her hips. One moon-white breast spilled out. The kimono was a peacock pattern, green on gold with an undone purple sash. Harry could imagine Kato jotting down the colors, indicating inks. In her sleeve, Oharu found a pack of cigarettes and matches. The other figure stuck his head out; it was the gap-toothed comedian, the amusing violinist. She lit a cigarette even while he pushed into her. The bowl was an ashtray. Veins bulged on the comedian's neck as his face reddened and his eyes squeezed shut. Oharu showed no emotion beyond mild impatience and irritation.

The forehead above her rounded brows stayed porcelain-smooth. Kato said something. Oharu stretched out on her side and loosened her kimono more to show her legs and black stripe of pubic hair and the man behind her still plugged in, grinding his dark balls between her thighs, his fingers on her throat.

Harry stumbled back onto the pebbles. Oharu looked up at the sound as a bolt of lightning wandered from the main storm and exploded overhead, revealing everything in the garden—rocks, rake lines, Harry with his hand across his mouth—in the white of a photographer's bulb.

Harry ran. He clambered over the gate and landed with knees pumping. He wasn't so much aware of his route as of houses and shops flying by. A policeman shouted, but Harry easily outstripped him, racing through a narrow alley and around the reek of a night-soil wagon. Over a wall, scattering cats, pounding through the overflow of gutters until he turned the corner to a street of one-story wooden houses that seemed to sink in the rain. In the middle of the block were the bleak accommodations he shared with his uncle. He rushed in the front door and threw himself on a mat. The house was essentially a single room. A kitchen area with a stone sink and gas stove was tucked in back with a water closet and a narrow bath. Orin Niles was out, which was a mercy. Usually Harry cursed the lack of ventilation, but now he wanted the room warm and dark, and he hung on to the sweet smell of the tatami.

When he started shivering, he stripped down to his wet shirt and underpants and curled up between two quilts. His uncle's space was a narrow mattress on the other side. Orin could be found in bed most days, drying out. If he was out this late, the drought was over and he'd spend the night at a sailors' bar in Yokohama, sitting in a haze of laudanum and rye. The housekeeper lived apart with her own family. Harry was alone.

His domain: the mats, the rats that lived in the tiles of the roof, a shelf of schoolbooks, a stack of baseball cards, a cigar box with playing cards and dice, a beetle named Oishi in a bamboo cage, his parents' print of the child Christ confounding Pharisees, his print of Japanese warships sinking the Russian fleet, his money wrapped in oilcloth and hidden under floorboards. He turned his back on his earthly possessions and laid his face toward the wall.

"Harry? Harry, are you in there?"

There was a scratch at the door. It opened, letting in a moment of air and the sound of rain on macadam, and slid shut again.

"This place is almost impossible to find. You forgot your clogs."

"Leave them," Harry muttered and pulled his quilt tighter. He didn't need to see Oharu in the dark, taking in his shabby port in a storm, condescending to her little errand. He hated her. He'd left his clogs in the garden of the green house. He hated his clogs, too.

"I'm sorry, Harry. It was just sex."

Exactly what the Folies manager had said about Gen. Everyone mouthed the same hypocrisy. He didn't dignify her with a reply.

"Do you want me to go, Harry?"

Silence was good enough. That had to be clear to the stupidest person in the world. He hadn't heard her slip off her shoes or fold an umbrella, so she obviously wasn't sincere.

"It was just for money, Harry, it didn't mean anything. I am very sorry."

There was one drip in particular that Harry heard right on the other side of the wall, a steady tapping on the ground outside. Oharu stirred. At any second Harry expected to hear the door slap shut behind her.

"You're still wet." Oharu felt his hair. "You must be soaked."

"It meant enough."

"You're right, Harry, it did. I am so sorry. But you're shivering." Her hand slid down to his neck. "You're wet all the way through."

"How could you do it?"

"I'm getting by, Harry. Doing what a modern girl has to do. You have to take those wet clothes off. We have to dry you."

"No." The last thing Harry was going to do was undress in front of her.

"You're sure?"

"Yes."

"Then we'll warm you."

Harry still had his face to the wall. He heard silk slip over skin, and then he felt Oharu crawl under the quilt with him. She was so warm it was like being by a fire.

"So cold and uncomfortable, Harry. You're sure you don't want to get dry?"

"I'm sure."

She cupped herself around him, her hips against his, her breasts against his back, her breath on his neck.

"It gives me gooseflesh. Feel my skin, Harry."

She took his hand and ran it lightly up and down her leg. She had muscular dancer's legs.

"Like a goose, right, Harry?"

Harry's damp back had made her breasts stiffen. He felt himself grow hard and held his breath.

"That's all I am, a goose, a silly girl. Can you forgive me?"

He let his hand spread on her leg as if he were touching a temple column of cool marble. He was angry with her. At the same time, he was afraid that if he turned toward her, she would disappear.

"I want to give you something, Harry. It's not worth anything, don't fool yourself, but it's all I have to give." She slid her hand down his stomach. "I think you're ready for it."

Harry swallowed because a mere second touch might set him off. He was no longer chilled at all, he burned like a coal. She turned him toward her and the small blue eye of the lamp and pulled his head down to her breast. The tip stiffened more in his mouth. She lifted herself and led his hand between her legs.

"Softer, even softer, even softer."

He felt the crispness of the hair there and the heat unfolding at his fingertips.

"You're going to be a good lover, Harry. You're going to care."

She smiled proudly, the best smile he'd had in his life. Oharu led him in. It was for Harry the closest to heaven he'd ever been, and he'd barely touched bottom when he came and clung to Oharu like a boy on a raft. When his heart stopped pounding, he looked up and saw she was still smiling.

"That was a little fast," Harry said.

"No, for a first time that was perfect. My Harry, my wild boy, what will we do with you?"

"I don't know."

Harry did know that his knowledge of the world had just doubled, as if the moon shone not as brightly as the sun but as fully in a softer way, as if he could see his body by her light. She changed the nature and purpose of skin, of hands, of mouth. The scent of Oharu stayed on him like salt on a swimmer. Many things made more sense now than they had ten minutes before. An equal number of things no longer made any sense at all. For example, he was already hard again.

"I should be going," Oharu said.

"Don't go," said Harry.

Oharu smoothed his hair from his forehead. Between her own rounded eyebrows lay one wrinkle of concern, and she studied his face as if coming to a fateful conclusion. She had him sit up and peeled off the rest of his damp clothes. She showed him how to kiss Japanese-style with the tip of the tongue, and French-style, with an open mouth. On his own inspiration, he slid behind her to kiss the nape of her neck, the soft weight of her breasts, their softer aureoles, while she took his hand as she had before. This time where his hand went his mouth followed. He felt a moment of hesitation in her before she lifted herself to him and caressed his head. A groan came from deep inside her, and Harry lifted his eyes in time to see her put a cloth between her teeth. As her eyes rolled back and her hips moved against him, Harry thought, this is for real, this time she means it, I did this for her. She raked him up onto her, and as he entered, he heard an electric crack of lightning that rolled down his spine and limbs and nailed him deep, deep inside her.

Followed by a profound sleep with Harry folded around Oharu as if they were riding with their eyes closed slowly through the rain, the heart's rhythm like a black horse. A faint electric haze lay in all directions. They rode through high grass soughing in the wind.

•　•　•

"OH MY GOD, he's with a whore!"

Harry sat up, blinded by lights. He saw Oharu cover herself with her arms.

"My son is with a whore!" Harriet Niles said again.

Roger Niles grabbed Oharu by the hair and shook her. "Who are you?"

"She's a friend," Harry said.

On her knees, Oharu tried to gather her dress. She said, "So sorry, so sorry."

"She can speak for herself," Roger Niles said.

"That's all the English she knows. She doesn't speak English, and you don't speak Japanese."

Harry didn't see his father's slap coming. It bowled him to the wall with his ears ringing, but at least it got him out of the direct glare of the lanterns and he could see his parents in their wet capes, umbrellas and galoshes. Behind them hovered his uncle Orin in a drowned hat, luggage still in hand, disaster in his eyes. Obviously he had met Harry's parents at the train station, and this was their homecoming. Harry lying with Oharu. Orin, in loco parentis, did seem chagrined.

"What is a whore doing in our house?" Harriet asked.

"That's rather self-evident, dear," Roger said. He pulled Oharu up by her hair and thrust her toward the door. "Get out."

Oharu bowed. "So sorry."

"If she says that one more time, I'm going to scream," Harriet said.

"It's raining," Harry said.

"So it is, Harry," his father said. "So your whore might have to run down the street naked and get her bottom wet."

"The neighbors," Harriet said.

"Get dressed." Roger threw Oharu's clothes at her. She looked small and humiliated to Harry, her eyes darting this way and that as she dressed in disarray. Roger turned on Harry. "As for you, do you know why the surprise visit? Because we have been informed by the mission board that you have been sending your uncle Orin to China to make money off the currency exchange. We come here to spread the word of God, and you have found every conceivable way to spread corruption. It's like having a viper for a son."

"I'm sorry," Harry told Oharu in Japanese. "It's not your fault. Thank you for everything. Thank Kato, too."

Roger Niles put his whole weight into a roundhouse slap. Harry took half a step back. He'd received as bad from the school drillmaster.

"I'm talking to you," Roger said. "My mission here is over. You have destroyed it. You have broken your mother's heart, you have abused our trust, and I see not one sign of repentance."

"Good-bye," Harry told Oharu.

"God damn it." Roger undid his belt. "Turn around."

"Go to hell," said Harry.

Roger Niles gathered both ends of the belt in his hand as a whip and laid into Harry. A white welt edged in red curled from his ribs to his neck. Harry gasped but otherwise said nothing. Oharu ran as soon as she was in her shoes. Staggering from fury and frustration, Roger raised the cry, "All the way to Japan around the world for this. Like whipping a stone." He whipped until Harry was crisscrossed with welts, until Harriet and even the derelict Orin hung on to Roger's arm and consoled him as family must have once consoled the father of the prodigal son.

THE NILES FAMILY left two days later on a Colombian freighter bound from Yokohama to Panama and a connection to the States. To keep Harry's condition secret, they stayed almost entirely in their cabin, and as no one in the family spoke Spanish, it wasn't until they saw American newspapers in the Canal Zone that they read about the earthquake in Japan. While the Nileses had been at sea, 120,000 Japanese had died in Tokyo in three days of shaking and fire. Except for the Imperial Hotel and Tokyo Station, hardly a building was left standing. The updraft of the fire was so intense it lifted people high into the air, where they burst into flame. American observers said it was the end of Tokyo as a modern city and that it would take the Japanese fifty years to recover.

Over the next few years, Harry wrote everyone in Tokyo he could think of. Finally Gen answered as a project for high school, where he was studying English. All the old gang, the five samurai, had miraculously survived, most by crowding into the Asakusa temple grounds as the fire swirled around them. Kato, however, had died while retrieving paintings; his building collapsed on his last trip in. The little dancer Chizuko was killed by rioters who took her for Korean; mobs who blamed Koreans for everything blamed them for the fires and killed a thousand for revenge. She had looked vaguely Korean, Gen added. Oharu had simply disappeared. A lot of people disappeared.

16

A S HARRY DROVE, he learned on the radio that the evening English lesson had been replaced by German.

Ist Hans in seinem Wanderjahr?

Ja, Hans ist in seinem Wanderjahr. Er ist in Paris.

Harry wondered where that madcap Hans would turn up next. Moscow? London? Where would Harry be? At ten thousand feet on the Hong Kong Clipper, a flying boat en route to Manila, Midway, Honolulu and America, Home of the Free, the Chrysler Airflow, the platinum blonde. He'd give Alice Beechum an inside tour of the movie studio, introduce her to her favorite stars, take in Tijuana and Santa Anita.

The radio said, "And now that popular tune 'Neighborhood Association.' " After a space of a few seconds, a lively voice began, *"A knock on the door from friendly neighbors saying, 'Watch out for foreign spies!' "*

Well, that was catchy, too, Harry thought.

When Harry was a kid, he found it odd that his parents and other missionary adults had trouble speaking Japanese. Some missionaries were sent home with what was called "Japan head," an overloading of the brain. The problem, Harry came to understand, was that Japanese did not translate into English or vice versa. Basic words had no equivalents or meant different things. What was warm and expansive in English was presumptuous in Japanese. What was respectful in Japanese was craven in English. To Americans, a whore was a whore unless she was willing to be rescued; to the Japanese, a girl sold by her family to a brothel was a model daughter. Japanese said yes when they meant no because other Japanese knew when yes meant no. Americans cursed and vilified an endless number of fuckers, assholes, bastards, bootlickers, et cetera, et cetera. With shading and intonation, Japanese made one word, "Fool!" express them all. Harry learned this naturally. Now he was about to unlearn, simplify, drop his Japanese side and be 100 percent red-white-and-blue American. He had wired $85,000 to New York the day before Japan froze American assets. If that didn't make him American, what the hell did?

Not yet, though. On the banks of the Tama River, south of the palace, stood the villas of patriots who had done well by the war. There Harry arrived with his donation for the shrine of National Purity, ten thousand yen in a furoshiki cloth bag. Tetsu and Taro were already waiting at the gate. What more fitting entourage for modern Japan, Harry thought, than a sumo in a formal black Japanese jacket and a yakuza sweaty with tattoo fever? Actually, both looked uneasy as Harry approached.

Taro's shoulders filled the gateway. Inside, a pathway climbed through a garden of evergreens to a large house ablaze with lights. A second path lit by stone lanterns ran even farther to a torii gate, a barracks and dojo and, finally, enveloped in a gauzy light, a ring of ancient pines that was the shrine itself.

"Ready?" Harry asked. "I'm here to pay my respects to Saburo-san."

Taro didn't move. "Sorry, Saburo's not here."

Harry could see Saburo with a circle of devotees, enjoying a cigarette in the living room of the house. There were groups of men inside and outside the house, which wasn't unusual for a man with Saburo's following. He'd started off as a moneyless Japanese patriot in Manchuria seven years before but had had the prescience to hook up with an energetic army officer named Tojo. By the time Tojo and Saburo were done, the army and National Purity comanaged railroads, cotton mills, coal and iron mines throughout Manchuria in the name of imperial harmony. Tojo became a general and prime minister. Saburo returned to Tokyo and established academies, charities and shrines dedicated to his Society of National Purity.

"What are you talking about?" Harry said.

"He's not here, Harry," Tetsu said. He looked sick and miserable.

"I just need Saburo's ear for a second."

"I'm sorry, Harry," Taro said.

It would have been discourteous for Harry to point out the visible Saburo. Anyway, Harry was at a rare loss for words. He had invited his own friends along, and now they were blocking his way.

"Tetsu, did you talk to Saburo about the donation?"

"I mentioned it. He said it was unnecessary."

"I still want to talk to him. I could see one of his assistants."

Taro said, "It's late, Harry. Everything is pretty much closed up."

Harry saw people bustling all over the grounds. "We talked about this. All I want is to leave this generous donation so someone will call the Foreign Office and free the exit papers for the bride of a German ally. A one-minute phone call."

"That would be difficult," Tetsu said, meaning no.

"Let me go to the shrine."

"Very difficult," Taro said, meaning absolutely no.

"Then suppose I try Saburo-san tomorrow."

Tetsu said, "I don't know, Harry, he may be gone for days."

Taro folded his arms. Nothing but a truck could have dislodged him.

"Then I hope he has a good trip," Harry said. "Please tell Saburo-san that I stopped by."

"We'll do that," said Taro.

"Sorry, Harry," Tetsu said. "Really."

"I guess things are changing. Get that fever looked at."

"Thanks," Tetsu said.

Harry fumed all the way back to his car. Snubbed, as if Saburo hadn't sold favors for years. Being turned away by friends, however, that brought acid to the craw. It was downright comical; he'd asked them to come, and they'd told him to go. So that's what friends were for: betrayal. The hell with them. In two more days, Harry would be gone and Japan would be a speck in the Pacific Ocean. As for Willie and Iris, well, Harry had tried.

He felt better by the time he reached Asakusa and parked the car. The theaters were bright with moviegoers wandering from *Die Deutsche Wehrmacht* to *The Texas Rangers*. Customers lined up at food stalls, the curious filled the peep shows and the side streets were strings of red lanterns and cozy bonhomie, the same as any weekend night. It would be odd, Harry decided, if he didn't make an appearance at his own club, although he braced himself for an evening under the scrutiny of the Record Girl. Tonight he would tell Michiko that he was going. She must know, she had to have figured it out weeks ago. No doubt there were snakes who stood taller than Harry Niles, but to run out on her with no warning was too low even for him. He just had to make sure she didn't get her hands on the gun.

However, the Happy Paris was dark. The sign should have been bright, buzzing red. On a Saturday night, Harry expected to see a neon Eiffel Tower beckoning the thirsty of all races and creeds. He paid Tetsu good money not to be harassed, although he didn't know what to expect from Tetsu anymore. Harry took a cautionary pause in the shadow of a doorway and watched a bicycle go by with a swaying stack of noodle boxes, followed by sailors, a chestnut vendor's cart, businessmen who passed in high spirits and returned disappointed a few seconds later, complaining about jungle-music establishments that closed with no apologies or explanation.

Harry crossed the street. The club's neon sign was not damaged, as far as he could see, simply off. He unlocked the door and found the Happy Paris empty. No customers, no Kondo to mix drinks, no waitresses to serve them. Harry went to the small galley behind the bar and found fresh cold cuts wrapped in butcher paper resting in the icebox, so someone had taken deliveries earlier in the day. Kondo the bartender was so reliable it was hard to believe he'd abandon his post: he loved his Happy Paris uniform so much he wanted to be buried in it. Harry turned the lights on, off, on. Off. What was the point of opening alone?

Michiko came to mind. Had she heard about the plane already?

Considering her temper, he was surprised only that she didn't burn the place down. He ran his hand over the smooth shoulders of the jukebox, looking for support, for his Record Girl, his black-widow spider. Harry pulled down the ladder stairs behind the bar and went up to his apartment. Nothing there was touched. His clothes and hers were still neatly laid in drawers, there were no bodies on the floor or notes in blood. He looked out the window and noticed that the willow house directly across was open for business, its polished gate ajar to a discreet candle glow. A willow suggested something yielding and feminine, the sort of tree that knelt by water to admire its own reflection.

Harry returned to the Happy Paris and slipped into the narrow kitchen. Kondo used the cool space under the floorboards for pickling eggplant, ginger, melon. Harry shifted loose boards, moved pickle jars aside and pulled out a loosely buried cookie tin. Just enough light made its way from the street to see a picture of Tara on the lid. Framed by white plantation columns, Scarlett O'Hara wore a bustle skirt as big as a parachute. Harry lifted the lid. Inside the tin were separate envelopes of cash: $10,000 American, $5,000 in yen and even $1,000 in Chinese yuan. Traveling money. He added the pistol to the money, set the tin on the damp ground and replaced the boards. Things were moving so fast now that he felt light-headed as he stood.

It was just him and the jukebox now. He selected "Any Old Time" and set the volume low. The intro was smooth, melodious, going nowhere in particular until Billie Holiday shyly chimed in, *"Any old time you're blue, you have our love to chase away the blues."* As if Michiko were with him, Harry took a solo turn around the record player. For some reason he was put in mind of Kato's copy of the Moulin Rouge, the redheaded cancan dancer. Too bad they never had dancing at the Happy Paris, Harry thought, only the immobile, inscrutable Record Girl. The front door was open a crack, and figures on the street flickered by. Harry decided he needed something not so sad. Who needed love if they had wings? How many hours till takeoff? Thirty-six? Harry punched three, six. Behind glass the automatic arm lifted Shaw off the turntable and put on "Sing, Sing, Sing," which Harry regarded as four minutes of pure inspiration, starting with Krupa's native drums, then joined by a growl of brass and, diving boldly in, Goodman on clarinet. Because of Krupa, "Sing, Sing, Sing" had a manic force that usually made Harry think of Tarzan, conga lines, war canoes. Tonight was different. He imagined tanks rolling over trenches and flamethrowers lighting huts. A horn soloed and a temple turned to a poppy-red ball of fire. Krupa took over and machine guns chattered. Harry didn't know how long he had listened before he stopped the record and noticed that a geisha stood at the front door, her matte-white face cocked to one side.

"Niles-san?" she asked in a high voice.

"Yes."

"Please." The geisha bowed and motioned Harry to follow her. She was small, a shimmer of silk in the dark.

"Now?"

She stayed bowed. "Yes, please."

Harry saw that she was trying to direct him to the willow house. "Who is there?"

"A friend, please."

She showed no sign of straightening up, a social pressure that was like a soft nutcracker. Although a geisha party was the last thing Harry was in the mood for, people did not snub geishas in public. Also, this was not a smart time for a gaijin to offend anybody. Even if it was to make excuses, Harry had no choice but to go.

"Okay."

"Thank you, thank you so much."

While they crossed the street, the girl chirped about what excellent Japanese he spoke, about such pleasant weather for December. She was vaguely familiar to Harry. He'd seen geisha go in and out of the willow house for the past two years. The problem was that the whole geisha presentation was a mask. Their faces were masks of white greasepaint under elaborate, top-heavy wigs with hairpins and tiny bells. They were wrapped in volumes of kimono and minced unnaturally in high wedge sandals. Every gesture and every note were pieces of acting, a doll-like combination of the innocent and erotic.

Inside the willow-house gate, a walkway lit by stone lanterns led to a slatted door with saucers of salt on either side. Harry left his shoes in a foyer that was discreetly dim and followed the geisha down a hallway lit by standing lanterns. Usually an older man or a lady of the house welcomed a visitor to make sure of the privacy of the parties within. Harry saw no one, heard no one, although on either side were the screens of different rooms. At this hour on a Saturday night, each room should have been ringing with idiot hilarity. There was a parabola to geisha parties: first, the soulful plucking of the shamisen; second, sake-fueled parlor games; third, maudlin singing; fourth, collapse. The girl made not a sound, just a beeline to the end of the corridor where the best room was, as far from the street as possible. As the geisha bustled ahead, he had a good view of the seasonal blue of her kimono and the tinkling bells in her hair and the way the red inner collar revealed the nape of the neck. Every once in a while she would glance back, a painted simper on her red double-bow lips. It was like following a puppet until they reached the end of the hall, where she stumbled ever so slightly, and Harry saw the three pinpoint moles on her neck and felt the electrical charge of recognizing Michiko while his legs carried him forward.

She slid open the screen to the last room. In the middle sat Ishigami in a white kimono at a low table of lacquered black. The colonel was darker than Harry remembered, flesh drawn taut around the skull, skin raw from a campaign in bitter weather, hair close-cropped and flecked with gray. The curve of an unsheathed sword lay across the table. Michiko gently pushed Harry to his knees.

Ishigami's eyes lit on Harry. He said, "You owe me five heads."

17

THE SWORD LAY edge out, a sinuous temper line running from the tip of the blade to a long grip of braided silk. Harry wondered if it was the same sword he had seen employed in Nanking or in the demonstration of swordsmanship so many years before.

"I should have recognized you in China," Ishigami said. "Even if you were only a boy the first time I saw you, there is only one like you."

"Well, that can be a good thing or a bad thing."

"Not good for you. You were easy to find."

Harry hoped to hear someone else in the house, but Ishigami seemed to have paid for the absence of the owners. He could afford to; he drew a colonel's pay and a stipend from the imperial household, and what did he have to spend it on in China? Harry had to give him credit, a lot of aristocrats devoted their time to tennis or whisking tea. Instead, Ishigami had been fighting in the never-ending China Incident for four years, five? A hero as indefatigable as that deserved an evening in an elegant willow house. The room's single window was a latticed ring, the lights a pair of paper globes, the only decoration a painted screen of carp with gilded scales. The sword was within reach of either man, but the colonel was poised, a wolf over a bone. He wore a shorter sword tucked into his sash. Harry remembered the gun across the street. If he ran for it, Ishigami would slice him down before he was halfway down the hall.

Although Ishigami demanded total concentration, Harry couldn't keep his eyes off Michiko. With all her shuffling and tittering, the Record Girl did an unsettlingly good imitation of a geisha. He really didn't know all of Michiko's background; part had always been a mystery. Now he saw clues. A geisha's face was painted white, her eyebrows and the outer corners of the eyes extended with red and black lines. Michiko also had the slightest shade of cherry blossom across her eyes and cheeks, and a hint of blue around the temples and the line of her jaw, the added color of a maiko, a younger apprentice geisha. So many bells tinkling from the wig and the incessant giggling were other earmarks of a maiko. She must have been both a young Commie and a geisha-in-training, an interesting combination. She made the whole outfit light up like a neon sign.

"Five heads?" Harry asked.

"Five. That was the number you cheated me of in Nanking."

"It was just a bet."

"It was a humiliation. I have thought about Nanking many times." Ishigami took a deep breath of tightly controlled emotion. There was an exhausted, even emaciated quality to the colonel, yet he still gave an impression of great strength. If the Grim Reaper wore a kimono, he would be Ishigami. This was not the smooth exit from Tokyo Harry had planned. "Do you know I am a hero? Two Orders of the Golden Kite, fifth and second class."

Congratulations, you stupid fuck. Harry thought. He tried to catch Michiko's eye and wondered, What are you doing?

Ishigami went on. "Five years in China and the only dishonorable moment was Nanking."

As Harry remembered, a hundred thousand or more Chinese had been slaughtered in Nanking. He was curious—which dishonorable moment was the colonel thinking about? "War is war. Things happen."

"This was not war, this was a demonstration."

"Oh, that? At the city wall? That looked like an execution to me. I remember ten Chinese: a clerk, a pair of chubby businessmen, a man in pajamas, a coolie, a kid."

"You remember it well."

"It made an impression."

Ishigami never took his eyes off Harry. "It was meant to. There was resistance, an attack on Japanese soldiers. We lost one. I was demonstrating to our men that for every one we lost, the other side would lose ten. It didn't matter whether the ones we executed were exactly the guilty parties, it was a matter of morale."

"Of course." Harry knew how important it was for the Japanese soldier to nourish his fighting spirit.

"That is why your interference was so unforgivable. One moment you and your German friend arrived at the demonstration, and the next you were wagering with the imperial army, offering ten yen to each man, muddying their pride with greed."

"As I recall, the troops seemed pretty interested."

"They were just soldiers, ten yen was a lot to them. Then the sly part: to offer money not only to me, a lieutenant, but the same amount to my aide, a mere corporal, just for washing the blade. Insult upon insult."

"Just feeling things out. It's like any game. You find the chump."

Michiko said in breathless geisha fashion, "Harry treats everything like a game of cards. Nothing is serious."

"You succeeded," Ishigami told Harry. "My aide was too shy to say no, but he felt so much shame over your wager that he could not carry out his function." Ishigami seemed to look directly through Harry. His eyes sparkled, and tears fell down his cheeks. It was as unlikely as seeing a stone weep. "Such a simple boy. I lost my temper." His voice became husky. "I would like to hear you apologize. I have waited years to hear you apologize."

Harry remembered that a soft answer turned away wrath. He knelt and placed his hands on the floor in a deep kowtow. "I am very sorry about your aide-de-camp and sincerely regret if he suffered as a consequence."

"I have waited four years to hear that." Ishigami lifted the sword from a sitting position like a man on horseback, and Harry wondered just how high his head would jump. If ever there was a man meant for an instrument, it was Ishigami and a sword; together they divided the living and the dead. Harry touched his forehead to the mat and stole a look at Michiko. Her expression was so cold and distant that she gave Harry the sweats. But Harry had the colonel down as a scrupulous scorekeeper. He had said Harry owed him *five* heads, and Harry figured the only way to achieve proper payback was if Ishigami saved him for last. Cut off Harry's first and the debt was as good as canceled at the start. Ishigami relaxed. His rage faded into something like a smile. He set his sword down by his side and said, "I like games, too." He added in an expansive tone to Michiko, "Sake!"

Michiko came out from behind the screen with a tray of ceramic sake jars and cups and fan-shaped bowls of ginkgo nuts. "All that arguing must make you thirsty, no?"

"Starved," Ishigami said.

"That's better." Michiko knelt to pour.

"Kampai!" The three raised their cups and drank. The sake was hot and aromatic. At once Michiko refilled the men's cups. Ishigami refilled hers. He seemed relaxed, even pleased, as if Harry had passed a test for cowardice and depravity.

"Your name again?" the colonel asked Michiko.

"Michiko," she got out between titters.

"Nice." Ishigami leaned across the table. "Do you mind if I call you Harry?"

"Go ahead."

"Thank you, Harry. You can call me Ryu. I must say, between you and me, I am happy to find such an attractive geisha as Michiko."

"She's very dynamic."

"Just one geisha for the two of us. Michiko must be very popular."

"She has many sides," Harry said.

"Drink up!" Michiko said.

"Banzai!" Ishigami led the charge and personally reloaded Harry's cup. "You understand, Harry, I admire the fact that you do not flinch at the sight of a sword. That will come in handy."

"Thank you." Harry refilled Ishigami's cup in turn.

Ishigami became more confidential. "Isn't it curious how one person can make an impression in such a short time? One insult can change a life. In Nanking, from the time you drove up with your German friend to the time you drove away with my Chinese, how long do you think that took, five minutes? No more than ten. But I have thought about you every day since. I assumed for years you must have returned to America. Imagine my surprise to hear you hadn't left at all. People in propaganda want me to tour the islands and sell war bonds. No, I came back for you."

"I'm flattered."

The room had become warm. Harry felt the sake insinuate itself through his veins. He became aware how Ishigami's hands rested, fingers curved and clawlike. If Harry were to send some beast out to terrorize the countryside, Ishigami would be it. Samurais had evolved into soft men in Western suits, but Ishigami was a throwback, the real thing. Harry didn't need a gun, he needed a machine gun.

Michiko filled their cups again and went around the screen for a portable record player with a crank that she churned. The notes of a shamisen plinked out of the machine while Michiko posed with a closed fan pressed against her cheek. Harry couldn't believe it. It was her Record Girl routine gone Oriental. She was still as ceramic in her pink tones and white, demure in winter-blue silk, producing her own faint music from the chains of bells and chimes that hung from her hair and stirred with every breath. There was no more artificial creation than a geisha, yet as art, a geisha did possess enormous appeal, half human, half loose-sleeved butterfly. As Michiko shifted, her collar revealed the nape of her neck, painted in a white W to suggest the outline of a woman's sex. It was a geisha's badge.

The gramophone generated a scratchy song about a courtesan who had to buy a present for a lover on a rainy day. Michiko flinched from a threatening sky, tucked her fan into the loose sleeve of her kimono, opened an imaginary umbrella and not so much danced as enacted a series of movements and poses that mimicked a lovesick girl skipping around puddles, gracefully one moment and comically the next, and very different from the Record Girl who vamped in the Happy Paris to

Fish gotta swim, birds gotta fly. Harry's life was on the line, but he was agape at Michiko when she finished.

"Isn't she good?" Ishigami beamed like an impresario.

"She is unbelievable."

"We agree, excellent."

Michiko took the record player behind the screen and returned with bowls of crisply fried fishlings and flowers of red ginger. The food didn't signify the saving presence of someone else in the willow house; fare for geisha parties generally came from restaurants. Was this a geisha party? Harry wondered. A murderer snacks with his victim, what sort of social event was that? Say it was a card game, Harry reminded himself. What did he know about the other player? A bastard son of a royal prince, right-wing fanatic, graduate of the military academy, Berlin attaché and a commander who had survived five years on the China front. In other words, intelligent, sophisticated and as brave as he was mad. He saw Ishigami sizing him up the same way, perhaps coming to a different conclusion. Harry had caught him off guard in Nanking. That wasn't going to happen again.

Ishigami spoke while he ate. "Five heads, Harry. You choose the first four."

"I choose?"

"Why not? It's been so long since I've been in Tokyo, I hardly know anyone anymore."

"You used to cut down Chinese left and right. Why change now?"

"In China I had no choice. There were too many. It just went on, like fighting the sea. That's why the Japanese fighting spirit is so important. That's what makes us different. You wouldn't understand. You're a gambler, all you understand is odds and numbers."

"Because numbers are real. Spirit is a fantasy."

Ishigami peeked up from his bowl. "What odds would you give yourself right now?"

"I see your point."

"Yes. So, you choose. Friends, enemies, people on the street, it doesn't matter to me, and, I suspect, it doesn't matter to you."

Michiko said in an offhand way, "Maybe there is someone he cares about, maybe there's a girl?"

"Didn't you have a friend named Gen?" Ishigami asked.

Harry said, "I'm not going to choose anyone. I'm not going to do your work for you."

"Lazybones," Michiko said.

"We'll do it this way," Ishigami said. "We'll go out in the street. The first four people you look at, I'll kill."

"Innocent Japanese?"

"No one is innocent. Are my men guilty? They're dying."

"Gladly, for the emperor, I know." That was always the propaganda.

"No, as a matter of fact, hardly ever. Asking for their mother, yes. A trench of bloody boys apologizing to their mother and father, yes. I thought it would be different. I thought there would be purity and nobility in struggle. But China is the same as here, a giant black market with businessmen corrupting army commanders for spoils and war matériel. We take a town and lose ten, twenty, a hundred soldiers, and men just like you, Harry, show up like worms within the hour."

Which answered a question Harry hadn't directly posed before: how was it that a heroic officer related to the imperial family was only a colonel after so many years in the field? Ishigami was a butcher, but plenty of butchers had flourished during the so-called China Incident. He was a fanatic, but fanatics had thrived. Was it his high moral code, his reluctance to batten off the slops of war, that had stalled his military career?

"I tried to tell the emperor," Ishigami said. Such an intimate mention of his name brought a bow from Michiko. The Record Girl would have laughed.

"And?" Harry asked.

"I wanted to inform him of how affairs really stood in China. One of the old housekeepers let me in. I found the emperor surrounded by aides and maps, and I was excited that he was concerning himself about the affairs in China. Then I saw that almost all the aides were from the navy, and none of the maps were of China. Just islands. I never had a chance to say a word."

"What islands?"

"What could it possibly matter to you?" He motioned to Michiko. "Bring me the box."

Michiko shuffled behind the screen on her knees and returned with a white box tied in a white cloth, a scaled-down version of the box for a soldier's ashes. Harry had seen only one like it, in a museum. It was a head box, designed to carry a singular trophy.

"I had this made to order today," Ishigami said. He raised the box and gave Harry an appraising look. "I think it will fit."

"On the map, was there a fleet track? From the west or north?"

"Questions like that could have you arrested as a spy."

"How could that possibly matter if my head is in a box?"

Ishigami set down the box and brushed its lid with his hand. "Harry, you never stop, do you?"

"I'll bet you." Harry refilled Ishigami's cup.

"You'll bet me again? Once I have your head, I'll have your money, too."

"Forget the head. I have another thousand yen nearby. A simple wager of a thousand yen."

"What sort of bet is that? I could say anything."

"I trust you. I'll bet the maps showed a chain of islands with a fleet launching station in the northwest and a central island with a southern harbor."

Michiko sighed musically and said, "But there's no bet, Harry. I know where that money is, in the Happy Paris under the floorboards. So, there's nothing to bet with, is there?"

Ishigami let out his breath. But he had held it, Harry thought. It sounded like Pearl to him.

"Are you a spy?" Ishigami asked.

Michiko laughed and hiccuped. "I am sorry. It's just so funny. Harry a spy? Who would trust Harry?"

Ishigami said, "I remember a boy who used to deliver woodblock prints to me. To see him, you would think he was an American lost in Tokyo, but he wasn't lost at all. You knew too much, Harry, even then. Where do you keep all that information?"

Harry avoided the obvious answer. He drained his cup and held it out. "Thanks, I will have more."

Ishigami wavered, his hand halfway between the jar and the sword. He seemed to shift in and out of focus, and Harry felt it wasn't just the effect of the sake. There was something damaged and smudged about the colonel, like a photograph taken into battle too many times. Harry read a mood that was dangerously variable: exhausted, energized, amiable, mad. Talking to Ishigami was like walking in the dark while trapdoors opened and closed on all sides. Michiko busied herself slicing ginger with a small knife until the colonel snapped out of his reverie and they were back on friendly terms, then she refilled the cups. Pouring sake was a geisha's primary concern.

"How long have you really known the colonel?" Harry asked her.

"One day," Michiko said. "Sometimes one day is enough, sometimes a year is too long."

"I wanted to take care of you in your own club," Ishigami said. He smiled as if appreciating an earthy joke. "But she wants to take over the establishment when you're dead, and it's not good to start with a bloody floor, so she convinced me she could bring you here."

"Such an ambitious girl. I never knew," said Harry.

"Oh, Harry, there's so much you don't know." Michiko hid her laugh behind her hand again.

Harry remembered how Kato had said that geisha covered their laugh to hide their teeth, which were bound to look yellow next to their white face paint, although Harry would have been happy to see any sign of the Michiko he thought he'd known.

They played jan-ken-pon—two-fingered scissors cut paper, open paper wrapped rock, fisted rock broke scissors—and the loser drank. It was a favorite geisha party game, and Harry and Ishigami drank twice as much as Michiko. With too much sake in him, Harry found himself staring at this new, illuminated woman. He couldn't help but think of her hidden self, the softer whiteness of her skin, the tiny moles at the base of her neck, the way her spine sank into the swell of her ass. Between cups of sake, he thought he could almost taste her mouth.

This painted outer self didn't so much disguise the Michiko he'd known as split her into two versions.

"Rock breaks scissors!" Michiko clapped for herself and poured Harry another cup.

"If you want the Happy Paris, you can have it. You don't have to kill me for it."

"Don't be a sore loser," Michiko said.

"Drink up," Ishigami said.

"Why are you doing this?" Harry asked Michiko.

She smiled as she refilled his cup. "Because you were leaving, Harry."

"I would have left you everything."

"But I didn't want to be given, Harry, I wanted to take." She laughed as if explaining something simple to a child. "If I take it, it's mine. If you give it, it's always yours. That's at the heart of the Marxist struggle."

"She's a Red, you knew that?" Harry asked Ishigami.

"Asia is the same way," Ishigami said. "We can't wait for the white man to give us what's ours. We have to take it. One, two . . ."

"Three." Michiko squealed with delight as she threw paper to Ishigami's fist. "You drink."

"It's a shell game, the way she plays," Harry said. He caught a glance from her that told him she could have beaten him at any game he chose. Who had he been living with the past two years? In his vanity, he had supposed she'd cared for him in at least a possessive mother-serpent sort of way. He had never spent more time with anyone and never been so wrong. It hurt a man's self-confidence. The way only the pads of her lips were painted gave her a smile within a smile, as if she had one for Harry and another for Ishigami.

"Who did your makeup?" Harry asked. Even the most experienced geisha needed help with all the powders—vermillion, gold and pale blue—and brushes—wide and flat-handled for base glue and paint, sable brushes for the eyebrows—and the wig, a sculpted mass of human hair. Especially for painting the intimate design on the nape of the neck. Simply putting on a kimono, with all its hidden strings and

tightly wrapped obi, demanded the hands of someone else. "Is someone else here?"

"No."

"Somebody helped."

Michiko ducked Harry's eyes while Ishigami lit a Lucky. Harry
finally noticed flecks of white on the tips of the colonel's fingers, the
same way paint used to stick to Kato's hands no matter how hard he
washed. This time Ishigami was the artist. Information came in vivid
images: Ishigami applying white primer to Michiko's skin, brushing
red powder on her cheeks, binding her hair with strips of gauze and
setting the crown of her wig. Which were skills learned only through
long practice. Ishigami blew aside smoke and offered Harry a gaze that
held a whole catalog of images. Of tracers spraying the night sky. Of an
officer's tent sagging under pillows of snow. Inside, the tent was lit by
a kerosene lamp, and an aide with narrow shoulders and a long gentle
face held still as he was painted, his eyelids outlined in black, his lips
budded red. The officer fixed a wig on the boy with strings and gum,
brushed the bells in the hair to make them sing. Well, Harry thought,
gender had always been a slippery item in Japan. The first geisha had
been men, and sex between samurai had been virtually Greek.

Ishigami became confidential. "You must be brutally honest to
achieve beauty. The eye that seemed bewitching can become as stupid
as a cow's. The chin that was handsome becomes heavy, the feet and
hands too large, the neck too crooked. You must erase the flaws. You
lengthen the eye, shade the chin, train the hands and feet. An effect of
the moment, but that's all you need."

Harry remembered the first time he had dressed Michiko in her
Record Girl suit of top hat, sequined jacket and long black stockings.
And the underkimono of red silk she slept in, was that her idea or his?
Meanwhile he said, "What I hear is, there's lead in the paint. People
who paint geishas sooner or later go insane."

"It has that effect." Ishigami's voice tailed off, and his gaze dropped
to the head box, which smelled of freshly cut and sanded wood. The
mood was changing again, losing a little effervescence. They were sliding back into China, Harry thought, back to Nanking, as if his life were

217

on a tether tied to one spot. He even had a brief picture of Ishigami carrying out the execution as before, this time aided by Michiko, who looked likely to start off as Butterfly and end as Salome.

"The emperor," Harry prompted Ishigami, "when you saw him, did he say anything?"

"The emperor asked the aides how long a Pacific war would take. They said three months. He reminded them that the army had told him four years ago that a war in China would take three months. The problem is, we have won decisive battle after decisive battle, and nothing is decided. There are just more Chinese. Now we would lose too much face to leave. It would be better to lose to anyone other than China."

"There's always the option of sanity, declaring yourself winners and coming home."

"It would be defeat. From then on, the hands of America and England would be around our neck. They could cut off our oil anytime, and we would be beggars. Better a truly decisive stroke than slow strangulation, don't you agree?"

Everything seemed to be coming back to the sword shining by Ishigami's side.

"How does the emperor feel?"

"The army will decide for the emperor's sake."

How will they do that, Harry started to ask, when Ishigami held up his hand for silence. Harry heard nothing to begin with, then a door shutting at the front of the hallway.

"These fucking shoes and laces, every time I go in a fucking house. Off and on, off and on. Harry! Harry, are you in there? Why isn't the Happy Paris open? Is there a mama-san in the house? Harry? Anybody home?"

"An American correspondent named DeGeorge," Michiko whispered to Ishigami.

DeGeorge sounded drunk, as if lurching into the sides of the corridor with every step. Harry could picture the man's red nose and dirty gray suit. Go away, he thought.

"Harry Niles is here," Ishigami said loudly. He smiled at his own English. "Come see Harry."

"Where?" DeGeorge's voice shouted. "I filed a story on your little speech. The censor killed it. What are you, hiding? Playing cards?"

"Come see Harry," Ishigami said.

From the sound of it, DeGeorge slid open each door as he progressed up the hall, stumbling around in stocking feet. "Jesus, you hired the whole place? Having a private party, are we?" The heavy steps paused at the closed door behind Harry, who could almost feel the bulk of DeGeorge leaning into the shoji. "This must be the place."

Harry turned and said, "Run! Get out of here!"

"Knockee-knockee."

The door slid open. Al DeGeorge pushed through a leer that changed to a quizzical expression as Ishigami stepped over the table with sword cocked and sliced the correspondent of *The Christian Science Monitor* diagonally from his shoulder to his hip. Holding himself together with his hands, DeGeorge tried to go in reverse. Ishigami followed, poking him with the tip of the sword as if steering a pig into a sty to a room with more space to swing. DeGeorge was out of sight, but Harry heard him, a reporter to the last, ask a plaintive "Why?"

The answer was a sound like scissors closing, weight dropping in a heap and something rolling underfoot. Harry endured a sensation like falling from a window and not yet hitting the ground. Michiko maintained perfect geisha poise.

Ishigami returned, stepping fastidiously around the bloody mat at the threshold and sliding the door shut.

He said, "That's one."

18

THERE WAS AN ETIQUETTE to geisha parties: no groping, no show of money, no sake once rice was served, although the rules were often violated by wartime profiteers who knew no better. Ishigami was a gentleman of the old school, who fueled on nothing but high-octane sake. Screw the rice. Anyway, who was sleepy? Not Ishigami, who sat in a white kimono spotted with blood and tended his sword with an oily rag.

Ishigami seemed to swell and fill the room. Perhaps because every sense of Harry's was sensitized, Ishigami was magnified, every pore of his hatchet face, the blue cap of his cropped hair, the black wires of his brows and lashes, the dark mirrors of his eyes, not to mention the smell of salty sweat tinged by background accents of incense and blood. Harry noticed the checkmarks of fragmentation grenades on the colonel's scalp, a notched ear, the way his neck swelled like a fore-arm when he leaned back. He studied how Ishigami's hands curled around the handle of the sword the way a baseball glove would fit around a ball. Harry had to wonder whether Ishigami had soaked his hands and sword in neat's-foot oil for a better grip. He noted the white kimono, which suggested a sense of ceremony and dedication to a task. He also noticed how little air was in the room, as if he and Ishigami had labored to the thin atmosphere of a mountain peak.

The problem was that Ishigami was smart, moral and psychotic, the worst possible combination. He couldn't be gulled, bought or reasoned with. The last option was to kill him, and Harry couldn't imagine accomplishing that without the gun he had just buried under the floorboards across the street. There was Ishigami's own sword, but the colonel was just waiting for Harry to try.

Meanwhile, there were other plates to keep spinning. For example, the DC-3 being readied in its hangar at Haneda Field. DC-3s were built on license by Nakajima Aircraft, which also built excellent bombers. A crew would work around the clock to make sure the plane shone like a silver spoon on Monday. Harry anticipated speeches at the foot of the ramp from the Foreign Ministry and Nippon Air, appropriate remarks from passengers about the glowing future of the Asian Co-Prosperity Sphere, bouquets, bon voyages, bows all around. Thirty-six hours from now. None of this would include him if he were involved in a homicide, let alone if he were dead.

The other fly in the soup, so to speak, was Hawaii. Harry thought he had helped discourage any adventure in that direction with the phony oil-tank farm. Now, however, Ishigami said he had found the emperor perusing sea charts and maps. A sea chart was for locating a point in the ocean. A map was for finding Pearl Harbor and Battleship Row. Maybe His Majesty was being consulted, but he had about as much influence as the Indian on the hood of a Pontiac. It seemed impossible for the Japanese fleet to get close enough to attack Pearl, but after all, Yamamoto was the man who broke the bank at Monte Carlo. And his fleet was missing. However, if Harry had to bet, he'd say a raid on Pearl was no more than fifty-fifty, and not until he had winged his way back to California, assuming he survived the night.

He pictured the fatally surprised DeGeorge while Michiko laughed and chattered on. Lady Macbeth could learn from Michiko, Harry thought. No craven "Out, damned spot!" from this girl. With her long-sleeved kimono, elaborate wig and her face flattened by matte white, the geisha Michiko was a dangerous two-dimensional version of herself. Over time, the getup actually looked less bizarre and more like Michiko's true face. He couldn't believe he had slept with this woman, known her literally inside out, taught her the difference between an upbeat and down. At least he had never said "I love you," he'd never been that big a fool. Between Ishigami and Michiko, Harry felt as if he had wandered into a samurai drama.

And the sword? Harry had once attempted counterfeiting swords. In fact, his first impulse when he got his hands on a welding torch was to attach an ordinary blade to a tang signed by a famous swordsmith, so he had an eye. Ishigami's long sword had the unusual length, smoky temper line and elegant sweep of a Bizen. All Harry could see of the short sword tucked into the colonel's kimono sash was a worn leather handle. Well, it was good to see these old beauties used instead of being hung on a wall. Think of a sword that had been chopping heads for four hundred years. It took your breath away.

Michiko clapped her hands. "Let's do some haiku. I'll go first."

Haiku, that should pick up the party. Harry thought it had lost its festive air.

Michiko poured more sake, sat back on her heels and began:

> *"The world was born when the*
> *Goddess Izanami*
> *Spoke the first word."*

"That's it?" Harry asked.

"That's it. Five syllables, seven syllables, five. Haiku."

In spite of themselves, Harry and Ishigami shared a glance of amusement.

"That's not it," Harry said. "There's much more to haiku."

Ishigami agreed. "Haiku contains a word that evokes the season. You use the word 'winter,' or you suggest it with 'icicles,' or 'spring' or 'cherry blossoms.' Your poem doesn't have either."

Michiko shrugged in a pretty way. "Because in the beginning there were no seasons."

"More importantly," Ishigami said, "you have the story wrong. When the goddess Izanami and the god Izanagi came down from heaven to create the islands of Japan, yes, Izanami spoke first, saying, 'What a nice man you are.' But Izanagi was offended, because a man should speak first, so nothing was created. Then Izanagi spoke, saying,

'What a beautiful lady you are,' and only then did they create the islands of Japan."

Michiko pouted. "Like any man. It's obvious he never would have said a word if she hadn't gone first. And then he takes the credit."

"That is why women should never be allowed to write poetry," Ishigami told Harry. "They want the first word and the last."

She laughed, and the bells in her hair rang softly. She told Ishigami, "Now you go."

"Harry?" Ishigami offered to wait.

"No, please." Harry hated to break up the flirtation between Michiko and the colonel. There were moments when he felt as if Ishigami and Michiko were enjoying a picnic on his grave.

Ishigami thought for a moment. "This is a favorite of mine."

"This will be very good," Michiko said.

"Can't wait," said Harry.

Ishigami stopped oiling the sword.

> *"They call this flower white peony*
> *Yes, but*
> *A little red."*

Michiko clapped, eyes bright. "The petals are like that. It makes me think of a white kimono edged in red."

"Harry, you seem to know something about haiku. What does it make you think of?" Ishigami asked.

"Round shoulders and blood." What else? Like florists said in the States, "Say it with flowers."

"Yes." Ishigami picked out a fresh cloth to clean the blade. "You and I, Harry, we seem to be on the same wavelength."

"Women just don't understand."

"England has poetry, Shakespeare and Donne. Is there poetry in America?"

"It's different."

"I would think so. It takes history to be distilled into poetry."

"No, there's poetry everywhere you go."

"Such as?"
"Such as:

> *"His face was smooth*
> *And cool as ice*
> *And oh! Louise!*
> *He smelled*
> *So nice*
> *Burma-Shave."*

Harry even remembered seeing the ad outside Palm Springs. He had been driving an ingenue to have her nose bobbed, hair dyed and teeth aligned. The girl sobbed the whole ride. She'd planned to be a nun, for God's sake. In Palm Springs, Harry put her on a bus bound for Iowa City, called the producer and said she skipped. One week later, she was back at the studio begging and worse for a second chance, and Harry had to drive her down all over again. That was when he decided to get out of L.A. Now, admittedly, he was reviewing his life choices. Palm Springs was pretty nice in December.

"Or," Harry said:

> *"The answer to*
> *A maiden's prayer*
> *Is not a chin*
> *Of stubby hair*
> *Burma-Shave."*

"Commercial haiku," Ishigami said. "Now that is American."

"Whatever makes the cash register ring," said Harry. Such an amiable conversation, he thought, if only he ignored the blood on Ishigami's kimono. It was typical of the colonel that he'd spared his uniform. Thinking about the uniform, Harry asked, "You're in the Third Regiment? The Tokyo regiment, is that what you're in?"

"A good regiment. Kyushu boys are known for recklessness, and Osaka boys aren't quite reckless enough. Tokyo boys are just right."

"To Tokyo boys." Harry raised his cup.

"Tokyo boys!"

"Tokyo!"

For a party that was essentially an execution, this was pretty good, Harry thought. Except his legs ached. Since he was used to sitting on his heels, he realized that the only thing his legs could have ached from was fear. From the waist down, he was scared to death. Ishigami wore a look of satisfaction. Once, when Harry was sick in bed as a boy, he had watched a cat play with a mouse for hours, holding it by its tail, flipping it in the air, gnawing gently. Harry had feverish dreams about the mouse for days. He added that picture to his memory of the Chinese prisoners in Nanking. It would be nice to be rescued. For once Harry even missed Shozo and Go. The Thought Police had been watching him for days, and now they were—dare he say it?—thoughtlessly gone. Doing what? Didn't matter. Harry had squirmed out of tight spots all his life, and he would get out of this one. There were ways. For example: when in doubt, flatter.

"What would you have told the emperor if you had been able to see him alone?" he asked.

"I would have told him about parasites like you."

"Besides me, what else?"

"That his troops were ready to carry out any mission and overcome any enemy, but that our real enemy on the mainland was not China but Russia, who is happy to see us waste our blood against the Chinese. I would have said we are no longer at war with any aim but to assure obscene profits for Mitsubishi, Mitsui and Datsun as we buy their tanks and guns. I would have told him that the army with the purest ideals in the world has become an opium broker. I would have said that I no longer recognize the army I have served in for twenty years. I no longer recognize myself."

That wasn't what Harry had expected. Insight and feelings, they always stun us coming from another human being, Harry thought. Especially from a murderer.

"You're against the war?"

"No, but I am for a war with honor."

"Against both the Bolsheviks and the capitalists?"

"Yes."

"Against the workers and the owners? At what point does this touch on reality?"

"Japanese reality is different."

Harry had heard that the moon was different in Japan, the cherry trees were different, the seasons were different, the mountains were different, the rice was different. Add them all up and he supposed that reality itself was different. Japanese swords were different.

"Okay."

"Japanese are different because they live for an ideal, for the veneration of the emperor. Without the ideal, we do not deserve an empire. The idea that Izanami and Izanagi came down from heaven is ridiculous, of course. That the emperor is a living god is a myth. But it is a transformative myth that makes every Japanese godlike. It is an ideal, an ambition that lifts us to heaven."

"Too much ambition. There's a war memorial at Kyoto of forty thousand Korean ears. Has to look like chopped squid. You have to be really ambitious to collect forty thousand ears."

"It's a start."

"It's the cult of the sword. Yamato spirit. The need of attack."

"Always attack, that's true."

Harry was aware of being a little drunk, but he also felt he was on to something. "Ten Japanese against one enemy, attack. One Japanese against ten enemies, attack."

"The element of surprise is decisive."

"Always close combat."

"The closer the better," Ishigami agreed.

"Bayonet work."

"A man with a sword is worth ten rifles. War is spiritual. What is your ideal, Harry?"

"Decent odds and an honest game, I ask nothing more. What would you say my chances are of cutting cards to an ace ten times in a row? If I do it, you let me go, and I'll even dispose of the body in the other room. You have a brilliant military record and a great future ahead of you. Don't throw them both away for vengeance on some lowlife like me. Remember your obligations. The army needs you in China. The emperor needs you in China. Ten cards. That's fate."

Ishigami touched his sword. "This is fate."

"So serious, you two. Like a pair of monks." Michiko frowned at them. "We should sing silly songs. Anyone serious is too sober."

Harry wished he could see some drunkenness or inattention on Ishigami's part, but the colonel seemed to burn off alcohol like a spirit lamp. He also seemed willing to indulge Michiko. Geisha had that talent.

"Well, what shall we sing?" Ishigami asked.

Michiko said, "I have just the song. And to make it interesting, as Harry often says, there will be a little wager. Whoever fails to sing the chorus in one breath must drink his sake in one swallow."

"What if we don't know the song?" Harry asked.

"Oh, you will know it," she said. "But I will go first to make it easy for you."

She sat up straighter and began,

"This is the song of the frog
I can hear the sound of it . . ."

With even the first words, memory flooded back. This was one of the first songs learned by all Japanese children. Harry remembered being in kindergarten, seated next to the open window on a rainy day, picking at the elbow of his sweater and looking wistfully out at a canal while the entire classroom sang in a round,

"Croak . . . croak . . . croak . . . croak.
Croakcroakcroakcroakcroakcroakcroakcroakcroakcroak."

Michiko finished like a cat with cream on its whiskers, and Ishigami picked up the song. Did they sing this childish round at the Peers' School, too? Harry wondered. At the most exclusive school on earth, set on the imperial palace grounds, had the young Ishigami's eyes wandered to the moat? Apparently so, because he sang with gusto, imparting animation to the call of the frog:

"Croakcroakcroakcroakcroakcroakcroakcroakcroakcroak."

It was funny, it was undeniably silly. It was a geisha party with a macabre hilarity built out of Michiko's laughs, Ishigami's baritone frog, the sheer innocence of the song, the unsheathed sword on the table and the invisible DeGeorge in the next room.

"Your turn, Harry," Michiko said.

Harry cleared his throat. He wasn't going to wait any longer, because sooner or later Ishigami was going to kill him, either in the house or in the street. He would come up one "croak" short, lift his cup and throw his hot sake in Ishigami's eyes. He figured the odds of snatching the sword first were about even. Of prevailing with the long sword against Ishigami's short sword—realistically, factoring in skill—about four to one against. Not the best odds. Like a game of Fifty-two Pickup, it was going to be messy. Ishigami liked attack, surprise, close work? Harry would try to give it to him. The question was what Michiko would do.

Harry had a tenor that he roughed up when he sang along with Fats or Louie, but it fit nicely to a child's tune. *"I hear the song of the frog . . ."* He reminded himself to stay relaxed; Ishigami would sense a tensing of the shoulders.

"Croakcroakcroakcroakcroakcroakcroakcroakcroak."

"That was only nine croaks," Michiko said.

"Ten," Harry protested.

"Nine. You lose," said Ishigami.

"I counted ten," Harry said.

"Nine!" Both Michiko and Ishigami shouted Harry down.

"Drink up, that's your penalty," Michiko said, but when she went to fill his cup, the sake flask was empty. "A second."

"Cold sake is fine," Harry said.

"No, no, it's not such good sake, it's better hot."

Ishigami gathered his sword. "Maybe Harry and I should go now. We will see who we meet in the street."

"No," Michiko insisted. "Harry has to pay. I have the sake on a hot plate. It will be ready in a minute." She returned to the table and smiled like a doll. "That was fun. We should sing some more. Please?"

"Very well," Ishigami said.

"Sure," said Harry.

From her knees, Michiko sang a ditty about a virgin learning "The Forty-eight Positions," suggesting with her fingers the more complicated ones. She acted a scene between a beauty and a flea. It was all puerile and inane. What was most maddening to Harry was how attractive Michiko was. He noticed where perspiration had eroded the white paint behind her ear. No one ever touched a geisha's face, that would be like smearing a painting, but he felt the impulse to pull her mouth down to his and taste the red bud of her lip. Geisha wore nothing underneath the kimono. Harry wanted to slip his hand through the folds of her ice-blue kimono and raise his hand between the two columns of her legs to listen to the sound of the bells in her hair.

She told Ishigami, "Now you sing."

"My voice is too poor."

"No, we heard you before. Besides, you are a hero, you shouldn't be afraid. Something humorous."

Ishigami paused and then erupted into *"Camptown ladies sing this song, doo-dah, doo-dah, Camptown racetrack five miles long, oh! doo-dah day . . ."* The Japanese loved Stephen Foster. Harry didn't understand why, but they had made Foster Japanese.

Ishigami finished red-faced and pleased. Harry clapped dutifully. "Sake ready?"

"Sing," Michiko said. "Something humorous. No jazz."

Harry could smell the sake on the hot plate.

"Sing," Ishigami said.

Harry shrugged. What came to him was his mother's favorite song, one she used to sing over Harry like a desperate wish, a mournful tune that brought out the last hints of the Southern Baptist in his voice. *"Amazing grace, how sweet the sound that saved a wretch like me . . . "*

He let the song slowly unroll, as if carrying a body through the cemetery gates. *"I once was lost . . . "* Michiko looked at him through her
geisha mask, rosebud lips tentatively open. *"Was blind . . . "* For a
moment he was in church, the congregation standing and singing
with hymnals open, all except his mother, who knew each hymn by
heart. She leaned forward to send a smile down the pew to Harry. *"But
now I see."*

Harry repeated the song in Japanese, and when he was done, he
needed the sake badly, but Michiko only stared at him. Ishigami
regarded him intently.

"That was a good song," Ishigami said. "That is how I feel. There
comes a time when you feel you are carrying all the dead, all the soldiers who have followed you. They weigh so you can barely place one
step in front of the other, and you see ahead of you an endless road of
more bodies. I don't know why I tell you, except that you surprise
me." He reflected for a moment. "It's good to say things aloud. When I
was young, my mother and I would go to the beach at Kamakura, and
she would tell me to find a seashell to tell my problems to. Not only
problems but ambitions, the foremost being to serve the emperor. And
desires."

"And then?" Harry asked because Ishigami didn't sound quite
done.

"Then my mother said to crush the shell so that no one else would
hear."

"Makes sense."

"You know," the colonel said, "at this moment I feel that I can tell
you anything."

This did not bode well, thought Harry.

"Your sake." Michiko set the flask in front of Harry. "Time for you
to pay your penalty."

The flask was scalding to the touch. All the better.

"Harry? Harry, are you in there?" A voice came from the front of
the willow house. "It's Willie."

Willie Staub, doing his best to call softly. Harry heard the awkward
scuffling of a gaijin removing his shoes. Ishigami took the sword from
the table and motioned Harry to stay seated.

"Harry?" Willie called. "DeGeorge said he was coming here to find you. Are you there?"

"It's late," a woman told Willie.

Iris, Harry thought. Although the hall was dimly lit and the screen to the room was shut. If they got to the end of the hall, however, they'd see the blood or feel it underfoot.

"Harry? DeGeorge?"

Feet padded closer. Even seated, Ishigami achieved perfect balance. He wouldn't wait, Harry thought. As soon as Ishigami saw a shadow on the sliding screen, he would rise and, in the same motion, slice through the paper, step through and finish both.

"Harry, please, are you there?" Willie asked.

"There's no one," Iris said.

"The house would be locked if no one were here."

"It's a geisha house," she said. "They may be . . . you know."

"DeGeorge said he would be here, inside or out. I just want to ask someone."

Heads two and three delivered right to Ishigami. So much for the sweet Nazi and his Oriental bride. Harry opened his mouth to warn them, and the tip of Ishigami's sword was at his neck, like a thumb checking a pulse.

"Answer your friends," Ishigami whispered. "Call them here."

Harry remembered the drills in the schoolyard, being beaten with wooden staves. That wasn't the real thing. The real thing was like being skewered like a martini olive on a toothpick. The Chinaman who shit his pants in Nanking? Harry felt for him now.

"Call them." Ishigami prodded Harry.

Willie and Iris opened shoji screens as they came. "Amazing Grace," what a hell of a dirge to remember. Back in church. But then Harry saw Ishigami's eyes twist backward as Michiko knelt behind the colonel, wrapped one hand around his forehead and, with the other, laid a chopping knife, the one she had cut ginger with, against the colonel's throat.

Harry smiled. Ishigami smiled. Michiko smiled.

Harry thought Japan really was different.

Willie's voice was fainter, farther down the hall. "We had to look."

"We looked enough." Iris was sounding like a wife. "We'll come back tomorrow."

"I just worry about DeGeorge."

Don't worry about DeGeorge, Harry thought. There was a second stumbling into shoes, discreet sounds of retreat along the path and the backfire of a car starting while the three in the back room sat like a family tied in an intimate dispute, waiting for the complete departure of intruders. Harry was still pinned to the sliding screen. At the same time, Ishigami was snug in Michiko's grip, and Harry knew how fierce that could be. The situation reminded Harry of the church parable about people with short arms and long spoons who couldn't feed themselves, only others, but with swords and a different moral: he needed a gun.

Some of Michiko's lipstick rubbed off on the colonel's ear as she said, "Please be so kind as to put down your sword."

Ishigami said, "If nothing else, we have clarified relations between you and Harry. You lied. That's all right, I thought you had."

She lifted his chin with the knife. Philosophically enough, Ishigami laid the sword on the floor, and Harry slid it to the far wall, then relieved Ishigami of his short sword, a beauty of nearly black steel, and did the same with it. Even without his swords, Ishigami didn't appear disarmed enough. He was checked by Michiko's knife but only slightly.

Michiko said, "Run, Harry. Go."

"That's right," Ishigami said. "Run."

All Harry could think of was the gun under the floorboards across the street. No one could hold Ishigami with a knife or sword; that was like trying to hold him down with a paper clip.

"Give me the knife," Harry said to Michiko.

"No, Harry. Go!"

"I'll go," said Ishigami.

With a deep inhale, he slowly rose, lifting Michiko to tiptoe. As she lost her balance, he shifted toward her and then out of her grip. Harry moved to block the way to the door. Instead, Ishigami ran at the side wall and burst through panels of wood and paper. One moment there was a wall, and then a garden Buddha looking in. Too late, Harry remembered the swords. A fist punched through the back wall, gathered the swords and disappeared. Harry folded the gilded screen as the tip of a sword appeared at the top of the last remaining wall and sliced the paper open. As Ishigami stepped through the flaps, Harry launched the screen, wisely not at the colonel's head but at his feet.

Without bothering with shoes, Harry and Michiko raced into the street. The Happy Paris was dark, the jukebox a moon among tables. Michiko locked the door while Harry got on his knees in the kitchen and slapped aside loose floorboards to root through pickle jars for the gun. "Camptown Races," what a stupid song. A police investigation would really nix his travel plans. Was there room under the floorboards for DeGeorge? A jar slipped from Harry's hands and broke. Bits of glass and brine swam around his knees as he dug out the cookie tin. Money spilled as he pried up the lid, found the Nambu, cocked a round into the breech and aimed at the door, at shutters, back to the door as if they were paper for Ishigami to step through.

19

ARRY WATCHED the street from his apartment while Michiko knelt by a mirror and candle to wipe her white face off. She had set the wig aside, and her own short hair was wrapped in gauze, exposing her ear, pink as a shell. Harry remembered Oharu awash in creams and tissues backstage at the Folies. As a kid he'd liked the way performers stripped themselves of one character and painted on another, one deception followed by the next. He wasn't so sure how he felt about it now. Harry was always Harry Niles, blood washed off his knees, shaved now and dressed in a fresh suit, but essentially Harry, while Michiko was revealed in layers.

Harry asked, "Did you know what the colonel wanted?"

"He said he wanted to surprise you."

"Surprise me? You didn't know he wanted to kill me?"

"I thought there was a chance. I think a lot of people would kill you if they had the chance." She said it flatly, as if stating a fact.

"Did he say where he was staying?"

"At the willow house. He's rich. He rented the whole house for a week."

"So he could be there, he could be anywhere."

They had pulled up and tied the ladder stairs from the club, although Harry could still imagine the colonel climbing up a gutter or down from the roof, maybe squeezing through a tap. Harry had thought that lighting the Eiffel Tower might attract a late-night customer or two and provide some security in numbers. A stone knocked out the sign; it shorted amid a rain of glass. Harry had tried the phone; the line was dead. All he had was the gun, but with daylight he could go for the car.

There was, of course, the option of sending up enough hue and cry to draw the police. Except that it was no option at all. Nothing like involvement in a homicide to upset travel plans. Know what a mark is? Harry asked himself. A mark is a guy who can't report a murder. He was a mark.

"Are you going to leave me?" Michiko asked.

Harry didn't have the heart to tell her the truth, and he didn't have the heart to lie. He kept his eyes on the street. "I don't know. I don't know how much future I have in Tokyo. Except for you. I have the feeling I'm not wanted."

"Are you going with *her*?"

"*Her*?" Alice, of course. Harry dropped at least some deceit. "She doesn't have any future here, either. No whites do."

"But you're from Asakusa."

"Yes."

"You'll hate it anywhere else."

"Yes."

Harry didn't ask why Michiko had saved his life. This was no fairweather American girl, he thought, and no sweet all-day-sucker American-style love. Michiko's was more of the pathological jump-into-a-volcano-together type. That didn't change things. When Nippon Air rolled the DC-3 from its hangar, Harry intended to be the first man aboard, and expected to have Alice Beechum in the seat beside him.

"You do a good imitation of a geisha." Harry couldn't help himself. "Did you consider the possibility that we both might lose our heads?"

"No."

"You like being trapped here?"

"No. Yes."

Figure that out, Harry thought. Since whiteface covered Michiko halfway to her shoulders, she dropped the kimono to her waist. She looked divided, warm breasts in contrast to a plaster face. Ishigami had done an expert job, adding the highlights of Chinese red to her cheeks, subtle shades of green and blue around her eyes. Ishigami, the Renaissance man. Of course, Japanese girls seemed boyish, boys like girls. What did Ishigami crave? Love, of course. Harry had cheated him of that not once but twice.

Across the street, the lantern at the willow house had flickered and gone out. No matter, DeGeorge would draw attention soon enough. In cool weather, two days, maybe three. Ishigami didn't hide his work. Ishigami didn't *care*. After four years of slaughter on the China front, one more truncated body wouldn't make a big impression. All the colonel wanted was four more heads. He had a Zenlike equanimity about his goal. Even with Michiko's knife to his throat, he wore a triumphant expression, as if he had finally solved the question of her true allegiance. Harry had figured out the answer at the same moment. Well, it was a matter of gratitude, wasn't it? Harry had taken this skinny kid, this Red on the run, a geisha of all things, planted her by a jukebox and called her the Record Girl. Made her a hit. Well, you could do anything with Michiko. She was like chopsticks. With someone that smooth and slim, the limbs were almost interchangeable. Variable. Inexhaustible. An American girl would have cried, "Save me, Harry, save me!" Michiko had said, "Go." So, the matter of loyalty was settled. At the same time, that was no real obligation on him. If she wanted him to survive, so did he. Harry appreciated what she had done, but he couldn't drive from his mind the image of Ishigami painting her. She still hadn't taken off the whiteface, as if it afforded protection.

Harry spied motion near a streetlamp, but it was a cat with tail intact, flown like a flag. In any other neighborhood, a snoop might have reported strange noises to the police. Not Asakusa, where the late-night carousing of drunks, whores and theatergoers was the norm. And when a detective did investigate the willow house, what would he see? Swordsmanship. A single slash on the bias that had opened DeGeorge from his breastbone to his bowels, and one clean stroke for his head. The detective would also see the telltale sideways spray of blood produced when an executioner flicked his blade to clean it. The idea that anyone but a Japanese could have carried out an execution so *beautifully* would be met with astonishment.

One down and four to go. But perhaps the game had changed from mere numbers, Harry thought. Maybe there was added value in a head Ishigami thought Harry cared about. Just as the colonel had cared for his aide-de-camp in Nanking. Would Ishigami settle on tit for tat, ear for an ear, head for a head? Or would he embellish? There were things a man could do to another man's woman. They certainly did them in China. Maybe he already had.

"You and Ishigami were together all day. What did you do?"

"We talked."

"You talked. You had tea, coffee, a couple of drinks?"

"We talked about my family."

"Talked about family?"

She told Harry how her father failed twice, lost his shop in the Depression, grew rice only to be ruined by drought and, under threat of starvation for the entire family, sold his daughters one by one to the brothels and geisha houses of Osaka. One reason there were so many angry young soldiers in the army was because they had seen their sisters sold. Ishigami had appreciated that. Michiko added that she hadn't only run away from the geisha house. She was proud to have robbed it first.

Harry was struck by how little he had known. How could he reconcile a fugitive geisha with the Record Girl from the Happy Paris? There had been hints of a certain internal tension. Living with her hadn't been like keeping a canary. One night she had thrown a priceless bottle of Black Label at him. Another night she'd broken a Dorsey record and threatened to slice her wrists or his. Granted, in both cases he had just sauntered home from an evening with Alice Beechum; in both cases he and Michiko ended up in bed. He remembered every vertebra in her spine, the way her hair hung around her face, the ten little daggers at her fingertips. Lie down with cats and rise with scratches.

"You were with Ishigami how long? Five hours? Six? All you did was talk about family and then he painted you up like a geisha? The two of you did nothing else?"

"The two of us?"

"That's what I said."

Her voice went even flatter. "I wanted to save your life."

A man couldn't balk at the hurdles, Harry thought. He had to plunge forward. "What did the two of you do? What did that entail?"

"What do you mean?"

"You know what I mean. He did the geisha makeup. What else did he do?"

"Are you angry because I let Ishigami touch me?"

"Is that all he did? That satisfied him, just a touch?"

A silence stretched like a conversation in itself. Michiko stared at the whiteface in the mirror.

Harry said, "It doesn't matter, but I just want to know what happened. You entertained the colonel. You kept him busy. You convinced him there was nothing between you and me. How did you do that?"

"If it doesn't matter, it doesn't matter."

"But it does matter. It must have been pretty good."

"It didn't matter. I'm back."

She rose and handed him a cloth so that he could wipe the nape of her neck and erase the white sexual W. Harry as good as saw Ishigami's fingerprints all over her, her neck a scene of intimacy he found himself afraid to touch. He hadn't escaped Ishigami. Ishigami was in the room with them.

"Did he pay?" he heard himself ask.

"Harry." She pulled up the kimono and sank to his feet, and he was amazed by how small she looked, a puddle of silk.

"Was it good?"

A few more questions, Harry thought, and she would disappear completely. Out the window he noticed the cat run from the street-lamp, chased by a shadow that developed into a black Datsun with the lights off.

THREE IN THE MORNING was the Thought Police's favorite hour for hauling people in, a time when defenses were down and thoughts

239

tended to be in sleepy disarray, so when Sergeant Shozo and Corporal Go pounded on the door, they were surprised to see Harry answer it dressed.

The police gave the apartment the once-over, but they were in a rush to haul him off, not conduct a lengthy search. Harry suggested following the policemen in his own car, but the sergeant said it wasn't necessary. He moved to the back with Harry, who was free to figure out where they were headed. If they couldn't catch him asleep, they could play another game that police around the world enjoyed, the ride with no clear destination in the dead of night. Harry's mind was still on Michiko. While the policemen had stumbled up the stairs, she had slipped down the ladder to the club. Harry had told her to stay with the doors locked until daylight and go to Haruko's to wait for his call. He had given her the gun. Michiko with a gun. That was a scary picture.

"Did your ears tickle?" Go hiked himself to see Harry in the rearview mirror.

"No, they weren't tickling."

"Because we were talking about you. Right, Sergeant? Talking about Harry Niles?"

Shozo said, "The life you've led, Harry. The best of both worlds."

The sergeant had heard about Michiko. She might have disappeared, but Shozo and Go had found her dresses and kimonos and sequined jacket in the apartment. " 'Michiko Funabashi, the famous Record Girl, the woman with icy reserve,' " Shozo read from a notebook with the aid of a penlight. " 'The woman with icy reserve.' She is your paramour?"

"She works in the café below my apartment. Sometimes she stays at my place when the weather's foul."

Shozo shook his head with wonder. " 'When the weather's foul.' Harry, you never disappoint. But the Record Girl was away tonight?"

"As it turned out."

Harry thought that if being rousted was meant to frighten him, it wasn't working. To him, Japanese police were Keystone Kops, with their work done for them. The yakuza maintained a rough sort of law and order and kept their hands off civilians, who in turn kept one another under constant surveillance. This was an entire population that loved to turn in bicycle thieves. The Japanese were so law-abiding by nature that crime was generally accompanied by a complete psychological breakdown. Japanese murderers loved to confess.

Harry knew what would happen if he led Shozo to the willow house and showed him Al DeGeorge. A foreign correspondent executed samurai-style? That said "army" or "patriot," and that meant "Don't touch." Harry could name Ishigami, and it still wouldn't matter. The police would not rush to arrest a war hero who was related to the imperial family. They would interview the owners of the willow house, geishas and Ishigami's fellow officers for months before they even dared, obliquely and with many bows, approach the colonel himself. And if in the end the army decided Ishigami was a homicidal maniac, they would send him back to China, where his talents had an outlet.

However, the gaijin who accused a war hero of murder, who spread such subversive propaganda and disturbed social harmony, would find that things could happen very quickly, beginning with immediate detention and isolation. Harry would be lucky to see the surface of the earth again, let alone the last plane out of Tokyo.

"Why are you up?" Harry asked. The sergeant and corporal were rumpled, as if they'd passed a sleepless night of their own.

"Hoping to catch you by surprise," Shozo said. "I admit it, it's hard to catch an insomniac by surprise."

"What does the newspaper say?" Harry noticed one sticking out of the sergeant's briefcase.

Shozo opened it. "The morning edition. It says that in Singapore, the British have called off picnics and tennis parties. Doesn't that seem to you to be a provocation?"

"Putting tennis on a war footing?"

"Yes."

"Cricket, maybe." It probably wasn't a great idea to wander in the jungle with a picnic hamper. The car kept heading north. Harry had expected them to take him downtown if they had questions. This was the opposite direction.

"Another article says that American battleships are too big to pass through the Panama Canal. Is that true?"

"I wouldn't know. Sergeant, I'm flattered by the wide scope of knowledge you think I possess. Does your newspaper say anything about the talks in Washington?"

"Going well. Roosevelt is backing down."

"Sounds like peace in our time."

The object was to get in sync with events, Harry thought. Go with the flow, avoid the rocks. Ishigami was one, Michiko was another. Harry focused on the prize. It sounded like the flight was still on.

Shozo confided, "When I can't sleep, I do jigsaw puzzles. I once had a five-hundred-piece puzzle of the Grand Canyon in America. It took me a week, but I so looked forward to seeing the complete sweep of this natural wonder. When I was done, however, I was missing a piece right in the center of the puzzle. The effect was ruined. I have to confess, I did something childish. In a fit of frustration, I threw the puzzle out the window, literally out the window and into the canal. I still remember seeing the pieces float away."

"Sounds like you were steaming," Harry said.

"I was livid. Then, two days later, I stepped on a mat and felt something underneath. It was the missing piece, the five-hundredth piece. It showed a man standing at the canyon rim and looking out, only now he looked out at nothing. The entire picture would have been complete if I had only waited. It was at a price, but I learned something, to be patient and not let go of anything. Sooner or later I will see how everything fits."

The headlights projected a film of the city, the street becoming a road with billboards and vacant lots, rice paddies and vegetable plots. The glint of railroad tracks whipped by. Shirts with outstretched arms loomed on drying rods. People said the Japanese treated paper with reverence, that nothing on paper was ever thrown away, but this was where Tokyo's litter blew. Paper skated on the ground, collected against trees, kited in the air ahead of the car. Go aimed toward two tall smokestacks planted among black conifers, and Harry finally knew where he was being taken. Today was Sunday. Most people would head for a day at the movies, neighborhood fairs, family graves. He was headed to Sugamo Prison.

THE PRISONER PROCESSING area had the white tiles, clothes bins and wooden tubs of a public bathhouse. Posters listed rules (NO SPEAKING, NO SIGNALING, NO DISRESPECT) and illustrated the difference between lice and crabs. Harry took it in with the bright attitude of a member of a blue-ribbon committee investigating penal conditions, even when two guards in Sam Browne belts relieved him of his belt, tie and shoelaces, and even though he knew that at any moment he might be stripped, scrubbed and inspected. He understood that it was never more important than when in a correction facility to maintain the air of a visitor. Besides, complaining was something done outside Sugamo. Inside, a man could be held for months, sometimes years, while his case was investigated for *suspicion* of crime. The one way an inmate could force a trial date was by confessing his guilt, and only then could he see a lawyer.

Shozo and Go quick-marched Harry down a steel corridor. The middle was open to the floors above and below, with a grille to prevent anyone from cheating the law by jumping to his death. Sugamo seemed designed to transmit and magnify the sound of misery, and though the week had been relatively warm for December, Harry heard the coughs and spitting of tuberculosis, endemic in jails, and reminded himself that he had the protection of Gen and the very top of the Imperial Navy. He had to act like that. When a con man lost confidence, he was dead.

"With all due respect, Sergeant, what is this all about?"

"The truth."

"Okay, what do you want to know?"

"Tell me about the Magic Show."

"I don't know what you're talking about."

"See, Harry, that's what I mean."

"All foreign correspondents are spies!" Go shoved Harry, who stumbled in his loose shoes as an inmate with a cone-shaped wicker basket over his head was led past. The basket was a dunce cap designed to prevent prisoners from seeing one another. Some spent years in Sugamo never seeing more than an inch ahead when they were out of their cells. A hall sign recommended, CULTIVATE YOUR SPIRITUAL NATURE. Well, this was the place.

Cell 74 was a steel box six feet by twelve, with a sink and toilet and, instead of a window, frosted glass set in iron. All the space was taken up, however, by a man who was tied feet and hands over a wooden bench. His shirt was pulled up to his neck, his pants down to his knees, and his naked back and skinny buttocks were chopped meat. At the sight of Go, he began to shake. The corporal, delighted, picked up a stout cane of bamboo split to chew as it made contact, and slapped it down on the prisoner's thighs. The man went rigid and screamed through strings of saliva, not loudly; his throat was too hoarse. Go squatted at his ear and shouted, "Death to all spies!"

"This is a spy?" Harry asked Shozo.

"Don't you recognize him?"

Not at first. Not with all the blood and vomit, the prisoner's head upside down and his sparse hair wet, but when his eyes picked up Harry and widened with outrage, Harry remembered Kawamura, the fusty Long Beach Oil accountant.

"You . . . you . . ." Kawamura choked.

"He recognizes you, Harry," Shozo said. "We've been talking to Kawamura about the discrepancies in the Long Beach ledger, all that oil that never came to Japan."

"He's a dupe, I said so at Yokohama. He's not responsible."

"That's very American of you to say, but you know better. Individually, Kawamura might not be responsible, but a Japanese takes on more responsibility than that. If one man steals in a company, the entire office is held accountable, and his whole family is shamed. Perhaps the American manager of Long Beach Oil altered the company books by himself before leaving Japan, but Kawamura is also responsible for not detecting those alterations."

Go tied on a rubber apron. "All gaijin are enemies of Japan!"

"He sure knows that tune," Harry said.

"His favorite song," Shozo agreed.

"You've been talking to Kawamura all night?"

"Yes, and it's interesting how many times your name came up."

"I don't know Kawamura, I never met him before yesterday."

"Have you ever been caned?"

"No."

Shozo waited for more before saying, "Any other American brought to Sugamo would demand to call his embassy. Why don't you?"

"I respect Japanese authority. I don't see any need to call my embassy."

"Not yet?"

"No."

"You're not their favorite American, are you?"

"Because I'm a friend of Japan."

"Kawamura says he also respects Japanese authority. He says he accepts responsibility for whatever the American manager at Long Beach did before leaving Japan. But the more we talk, the more certain Kawamura is that the manager did not alter the books. Although you might expect the opposite, the more we beat Kawamura, the more he says that someone else must have altered the books afterward."

"He's a loyal employee, that's understandable."

"Kawamura says he had trouble unlocking the shed for us yesterday, because the lock had been forced open. He could end this painful interrogation anytime by simply admitting the manager's guilt. We would give him medical care. Instead, he forces us to continue."

"Death to spies!" Go said.

The cane whistled down on Kawamura, the bamboo spitting blood. The accountant seized up, mouth agape, eyes trying to escape their sockets.

Shozo asked, "What do you think, Harry? Do you think the Long Beach ledgers were altered by the manager before he went home to America, or by someone else at a later date?"

"How would I know?"

"Is there anything you can tell me that would relieve the suffering of this poor man?"

"I wish I could."

Kawamura twisted back toward Harry to glare. Go put Harry in mind of how chefs cut up fish alive. The man enjoyed his work.

"Tell me about the Magic Show," Shozo said.

"I just have no idea what you're talking about."

"You altered the Long Beach books, Harry."

"No."

"How many books have you altered?"

"What do you mean?"

"The ledgers from Petromar and Manzanita Oil. Did you change those, too?"

There was no point in acting dumb about the oil-company names, Shozo obviously knew too much. Harry felt as if the prison were sinking into the earth and taking him with it.

"I've been helping the navy. I'm a friend of the navy the same way I'm a friend of Japan."

"Helping to examine the books of American oil importers?"

"That's it."

"Setting a thief to catch a thief?"

"Let's say a skeptical eye."

"A thief who counterfeited official papers in Nanking to release Chinese agitators from Japanese authority. A gambler, an extortionist, a moneylender. Who do you think I'm going to believe, you or Kawamura?"

"Me."

"You must be very good at cards, Harry. You don't even blink, although I know everything about you."

Bullshit, Harry thought. Shozo had played Nanking like a man showing two queens, as if that proved he had a lady in the hole. Well, fuck you, to use an expression of the late Al DeGeorge. If Shozo *knew* instead of suspected, Harry would be on the rack in Kawamura's place. Not that Shozo had to prove anything. Although Harry had navy connections, it was true anywhere in the world that possession was nine tenths of the law. Equally disturbing, it was also becoming clear that Shozo had his own connections in the navy. How else could he have come up with Petromar and Manzanita?

Harry said, "I looked at the books of certain oil importers at the request of the Japanese navy. The navy seemed to think that I was helpful."

"More than helpful. You discovered much more than anyone expected."

"I wouldn't know."

"Then I can tell you. You discovered hundreds of thousands of barrels of oil diverted from Japan to Hawaii, and no one else discovered any. And you alone know where that oil went."

"I wish I did."

Go flexed his wrists like a batter ready to hit the ball out of the park, shifted his weight from side to side and whipped the cane down. Taken by surprise, Kawamura lost the air in his lungs and turned blue.

"You cheated," Harry told the corporal. "You didn't ask him a question, you just hit him. You're supposed to ask a question first."

Go shrugged as if the omission were negligible.

"Ask next time," Harry said. "Give him a chance."

"Relax, Harry. Harry Niles, humanitarian," Shozo said. He offered Harry a Japanese-made Cherry, a cigarette of sweepings, which Harry accepted to stay on a polite footing. "Men have been looking for those secret oil tanks in Hawaii that you talked about. They can't find them."

"Because the tanks probably don't exist. I don't think they exist. I met a drunk at a bar in Shanghai who said he helped put in some tanks in Oahu. I think he was lying, but I had to report it. Now you know as much as anyone else."

"It's important to know about those tanks."

"I doubt they exist."

"But they would be a wise precaution for the American navy?"

"I suppose."

Kawamura passed out, hair pasted to his face.

Shozo said, "We wouldn't worry about those tanks except for your report. Why should the Japanese navy take the word of a gaijin?"

"I'm not the enemy. There's no war yet." Harry caught a smirk on Go's face. "Look, your navy asked me to do a job and I did, although I was not paid and my efforts on behalf of Japan were not appreciated by other Americans."

"It's confusing. The five-hundredth piece of the puzzle is still missing. Why would you concoct a story about missing oil or secret tanks in Hawaii? What is in it for Harry Niles?" Shozo paused to watch Go twist his chubby fingers into Kawamura's hair and force his head into a pail of water. The accountant came up blubbering. "My suspicion," Shozo said, "is that we have the wrong Harry Niles."

"How is that?" Harry asked.

"When we went into your apartment, do you know what struck me? I thought, Harry's home is more Japanese than mine. It's true. My wife and I have two rooms, and one is entirely Western. We have the usual middle-class pretensions, a Western table, tasseled lamps. A piano. Except for your gramophone and records, your rooms are entirely Japanese. A simple shrine, a hanging scroll of Fuji, straw mats. A low table of fine lacquer. A typewriter but also a brush and inkstone. A tea set. A vase with a single flower. I said to myself, This is the real Harry. There is the Harry who lives for money and the Harry who takes time to see a soldier off to the front. On the outside is the vulgar American, but inside is someone else. The American would never stand up to the Japanese army in Nanking, but the someone inside would."

"There were plenty of Americans who rescued people in Nanking."

"But they were priests and ministers. Is that what you are, a religious man? I don't think so. You know the expression 'Every man has three hearts'? One he shows the world, one he shows his friends and one he shows no one else at all. I think that's the case with you. I think that deep within you is an honorable part that is Japanese. That's the part of you that so dislikes being responsible for the beating of another man."

"Sergeant Shozo, it sounds as if there is part of you that doesn't like to do the beating."

"Harry, you're too sly, too sly. But I do believe in the value of confession. My work is done only when a criminal sincerely analyzes and confesses his crimes. I have something for you. Remember how we talked on the boat about the truth, how it wasn't even worth taking the confession of a gaijin because it would be so insincere. Can I treat you like a Japanese, Harry, treat you honorably? Do I dare do that?"

From his briefcase, Shozo brought a school composition book, to which he added his own uncapped Waterman pen, the present from his wife. The stiff cover of the book read "The Statement of Harry Niles." Harry opened it. The pages were blank except for ruled vertical lines and the smell of schooldays. "Can you be honest, Harry? How many company ledgers did you alter?"

Harry knew what Shozo meant. Kawamura had been treated like a Japanese, and look at him. Hamburger. But Harry understood the sincerity of the option, and it took him a second to say, "Not any."

"Are there any secret oil tanks in Hawaii?

"I have no idea."

"Or did you just make them up to cause confusion?"

"What confusion?"

Shozo sighed as if a prized student had failed.

Go was infuriated for the sergeant's sake. "You should be ashamed! An opportunity like that? To be treated right?"

"Back off," Harry said. He'd had it with Corporal Go. "What confusion?" he asked Shozo. Although he was half in the maw of Sugamo Prison, this new element had his attention. Uncertainty, yes, but why confusion?

"Just a word," said Shozo.

"A very particular word." Harry tried to get around Go to the sergeant. "Who wants to know?"

"You don't ask the questions. We ask the questions," Go said and broke the cane across Harry's back.

My mistake, Harry thought. Never provoke police, especially in jail. And never let violence get started. The pain radiated through Harry's body from kidney level, and he slid down the wall to his knees.

"Are you all right, Harry?" Shozo stooped to ask.

"Sure." It was a fluid situation, that much was clear. So far as Harry was concerned, Shozo's push for a confession proved he didn't have enough for an arrest. However, the Thought Police were capable of anything when antagonized. Harry had just pressed too hard.

"No hard feelings. No warning, sorry." Go grinned with his upper teeth.

"Now, while you can, Harry, write your statement."

"Can't." He couldn't even stand.

"Then tell me about the tanks."

"Don't know."

"The Magic Show."

"No."

"Lady Beechum. We know she's a spy."

A bugle call and the clamor of a bell were followed by a general coughing, a rustle of bodies on thin mats, a sickly chorus of hundreds in a mausoleum above and below. Time to contemplate a person's spiritual nature, Harry thought. Time to call the bluff.

"I'm ready to go."

Shozo helped Harry up. "Would you like some water? Tea? Last chance, Harry." Shozo had the expression of a fireman removing a ladder from someone who refused to leave a burning building.

"No. May I go?"

"Of course."

Shozo called a guard to return Harry to the processing area. On the way out, he passed a trustee in a patched kimono pasting rules up in the hall:

NO SPEAKING BETWEEN PRISONERS IS ALLOWED. NO SIGNALING BETWEEN PRISONERS IS ALLOWED. NO DISRESPECT TO WARDS OR GUARDS IS ALLOWED. NO REMOVAL OR DAMAGE OF THE CELL LIGHT IS ALLOWED. NO BLOCKING OR COVERING OF THE DOOR SIGHT IS ALLOWED. RISING IS AT 0600, IN- SPECTION AT 0630, EXERCISE AT 0900, LUNCH AT 1100, DINNER AT 1600, SLEEP AT 1900. HAIRCUTS TWICE A MONTH. SPECIAL ITEMS WILL BE AVAILABLE AT THE COMMISSARY. COMMENTS SHOULD BE DI- RECTED ONLY TO THE PRISON GOVERNOR.

This time the rules were in English.

• • •

HARRY FOUND a train platform half a mile from the prison on a road between potato fields. Scarecrows whirled their arms at the rising sun, and Harry found cheer in the fact that his shirt wasn't sticking to his back, which meant he had only a welt, not broken skin, a good sign, although the very fact that he construed a lack of blood a good sign was, he admitted, a bad sign indeed. He sucked on a cigarette to ease the pain and read the schedule plaque. There wasn't much service on a Sunday. And prospects for the rest of the week? He felt the sun stretch his shadow back toward the high walls and chimneys of the prison.

Palm Springs, Palm Springs, Palm Springs, he repeated like a mantra. Alice, Alice, Alice. Sometimes a man sensed a deal falling apart. The blow with the cane was a bad sign through and through. He hadn't been taken so unawares since school, when Gen once caught him with a wooden sword before Harry had his padding on. Someone in the navy had to be sniping at Gen for Shozo to know so much about oil. Worse than the hit, though, was remembering what he'd done to Michiko. She'd laid herself down to save his life, and he'd reacted like a saint stoning a slut.

A crow trudged up the road and shared a glance with Harry, one wiseguy to another. There was nothing he could do. On Sunday morning there was no traffic, not even a truck to bum a ride with.

The worst sign of all was what had earned Harry the welt on his back.

Confusion.

Harry's whole story about secret oil tanks on Oahu was meant to cause uncertainty; that was the point of the fabrication. Uncertainty was a paralyzed state where cooler heads could prevail. Confusion was active, committed, a labeling of targets. Confusion was planes in the air.

20

THE TRAIN WAS a narrow-gauge local that rattled across the hard crust of winter fields, and Harry rode standing up rather than let his back touch a seat. Other riders carried dusty sacks of root vegetables. Beer bottles and dead cigars rolled at his feet. He had never had such good posture, or such a watchful eye from fellow passengers, and when the train reached Ueno Station in Tokyo at nine o'clock and emptied at a platform with a sign that said CELEBRATE ANTI-SPY WEEK!, Harry felt as if a spotlight had followed him from the prison.

Outside the station, he slipped into a phone booth to call the waitress Haruko. Ueno Station was a building on a Mussolini scale, but its phone booths were intimate stalls that crammed the caller against a mouthpiece.

"Michiko isn't here," Haruko said.

"I told her to go to your place and wait there."

"She came all dressed up like a geisha, changed into my best dress and left."

The day was bright enough for men emerging from the station to pull down their hats, and Harry felt himself sinking back into welcome anonymity.

"Where to?"

"She was upset," Haruko said.

"Did she say where she was going?"

"Just that she was going to find you."

"All she had to do was wait at your place."

Haruko was so silent that Harry thought the line had gone dead until she said, "Michiko didn't think so."

"What did she think?"

"You're leaving her. She's sure of it."

"No one can leave. The whole country is closed."

"Except for Houdini."

"What do you mean?"

"That's what Michiko calls you. The escape artist."

From the vantage point of the booth, Harry became aware of a six-wheeled army staff car with soldiers on the running boards, at the park entrance across the avenue from the station. Two army Datsuns stopped in the middle of the traffic. They were full-size sedans, not the "baby cars" Datsun sold to the public, and each car was stuffed with soldiers.

"Harry?"

"I'm sorry, Haruko, you'll have to remind me, what was your best dress?"

"White with a sailor collar and blue buttons down the side. And a white cap and a little blue bag. She just swept in and took them. Then she borrowed some money."

"I'll pay you back."

In a different tone, Haruko said. "She has a gun."

"I know."

The staff car rolled into the park, and a moment later the two army sedans followed.

"Should I come in to work tonight? Will the Happy Paris be open?"

"No, I think the Happy Paris will be closed."

"How long?"

"For a while. If you see Michiko, tell her to meet me at the ballroom."

Harry hung up. He made one more brief phone call, went back into the station and descended steps to an underpass of newsstands, food shops, a shoe shine and pharmacy where Harry picked up a germ mask, a ready-made disguise that he slipped on his face. As he emerged at the park, a backfire led his eye to the gleam of a rear bumper just disappearing behind pines.

Harry set off running. He knew Ueno Park by heart from having carried the art box when Kato sketched the beggars and prostitutes who inhabited the grounds at night. A Sunday-morning crowd was different, and on such a warm December day, people filled the paths, art lovers headed to the museum, families to the zoo. Even so, the cars pushed through and drew away from Harry until he was left breathless at the edge of an undulating field that stretched maybe a hundred yards to a black border of bare cherry trees.

He didn't know why he'd tried to follow the cars, it was a little like following a swarm of wasps. Perhaps because they shouldn't have been on the footpaths. Perhaps because Shozo had used the word "confusion." Harry was confused himself, and there was a side of his nature that hated to be in the dark. Now, gasping for breath, taking in the wide field, digging out a cigarette, he decided that not being in the know was okay, too. That was why a man should spend time around nature, for perspective. In one day he would be bound for California with a Lady by his side. His back stung, but he could breathe, hence no broken ribs, and smoking dulled the pain. Only surface injuries, and Asakusa was definitely walkable from here. Just a little dizzy. The episode at the prison had gone badly. Then there was Ishigami. It was crazy to be angry at someone who was trying to kill you, personal affront was beside the point, but the picture of the colonel with Michiko lit a flame under Harry's brainpan. He wasn't a man given to self-torture, but for some reason he could see Ishigami touch her, expertly apply the paint, lift the collar from her shoulders. In his mind Harry watched her eyes and examined her expression for signs of pleasure. He could stare at the blue sky over Ueno Park and witness the entire scene, the *amour* of the colonel and the Record Girl. Harry was hiding from Ishigami. The question now was whether to hide from her. Pretty funny. She was dangerous enough with a knife, let alone a gun. Did he want her at the ballroom so he could find her or avoid her? Perhaps she was asking the same question. The world was tilting like a pinball machine. East met West, and foreign correspondents lost their heads. Harry felt for DeGeorge, for the faithful accountant Kawamura being caned in a Sugamo cell, but if Harry's story about oil tanks in Hawaii had caused confusion, it was too late to explain or confess. Things were in motion.

He found he had walked out onto the familiar earth of the park's great lawn, in the spring the scene of the debauch called cherry-blossom viewing. Kato and Oharu used to bring a quilt, champagne, sake and a ukulele and drink and sing while blossoms fell, and Harry served as their page. Was there ever a California beach as merry as that? He doubted it.

December was a patchwork month. Kids in threadbare sweaters ran down the field's long incline to launch kites and gliders. Paper octopi and dragons dipped and swooped above a ring of autumn maples, and the breeze carried the smoke of chestnuts and coals. By a bridle path that ringed the field, a group of newspaper reporters and photographers stood with a pretty little girl of about five, wearing a red kimono and holding golden mums. Sundays were always slow news days. He considered letting the reporters in on the headless Al DeGeorge, that would be a scoop.

An army scout car moved along the bridle path and came to a stop fifty yards shy of the newsmen. The car was an open two-seater with a driver and, facing backward, a soldier with a film camera. Bell & Howell, it looked like to Harry. For a minute nothing happened besides the twisting of kites overhead. That was the movie business, as Harry knew full well, hurry up and wait, but curiosity lured him closer.

A horse and rider emerged from the cherry trees onto the path. The horse was a tall gray. The rider was in tweed from hat to boots, and although Harry had seen his joyless little face, mustache and round glasses at the Yasukuni Shrine the day before, it still took him a moment to realize the rider was General Tojo. With the world in the balance, the prime minister was taking a leisurely Sunday ride through Ueno Park in a wholesome tweed and a hat with a pheasant feather plopped on his shaved skull. Tojo was prime minister and war minister in one, and usually when he rode, it was in uniform at the Roppongi barrack grounds, where flags flew, drums beat and cheers of "Banzai!" resounded from a thousand troops. If Harry were to criticize, he would have said that Tojo was a little stiff in the seat, lacking the John Wayne slouch. An open Packard with three women under a plaid blanket crawled onto the path behind him. Harry recognized Mrs. Tojo; she was famous for promoting the patriotic value of big families, having produced seven children herself. Today she made an unhappy brood hen, a daughter on each side, her stare fixed on the back of her husband's bobbing head. Finally a six-wheeled staff car with bodyguards standing on the running boards appeared. Up ahead, the cameraman in the scout car bowed, motioned with his hand, bowed again. Assembled, the entire parade crept forward, and the photographers on the side of the path snapped away as if Tojo were leading a steeplechase. He rode bolt upright, reins in his left hand, right hand free to draw a sword he wasn't wearing, not with a hacking jacket. Harry had never seen General Tojo out of uniform before; had anyone besides the missus? Tweed suggested a fishing pole or a spot of tea. Maybe Alice or the Mad Hatter would show up, Harry thought. The reporters practically prostrated themselves as Tojo approached; the photographers apologized while they took pictures to be on time for the evening edition. A cowboy would have reared his horse. Tojo reined the gray to a stop and sat, motionless, bright certitude shining from his glasses. The staff car of bodyguards hung back, out of the frame, while the girl in the red kimono, exquisite, a little doll, handed up the golden mums. Tojo seemed distracted for a second by the sight of Harry, as if one brushstroke in a masterpiece were wrong, but lost him among flashing bulbs and older people rushing forward to add their bows and small boys to salute. Franklin Roosevelt would have answered with a jaunty grin or Churchill with a V. For Tojo, expression was utterly superfluous; the bouquet could have been ragweed for all he seemed to care. He returned the flowers so they could be presented to his wife, who raised a tepid smile from her blanket. Then the caravan got into gear again, making a slow circuit of the bridle path. The general hadn't smiled, not once, but what Harry had spied behind the glasses was worse, and that was triumph.

• • •

ROY HOOPER was singing "Rock of Ages" in the back row of church when Harry showed up. Things were bad enough for Methodists; American wives and children had been sent home, while Japanese members of the congregation dwindled week by week until only a handful came to Sunday service. Hooper's father had preached in this same modest church with its mahogany pews, pedal organ, plaque with hymnal numbers. Hooper himself had chosen the Foreign Service, but still he resented the fact that the cross now shared wall space with a portrait of the emperor in a Shinto robe, the Son of Heaven ensconced in the house of the Lord.

Hooper also resented a finger jabbing him in the back.

"Hoop, we've got to talk."

Hooper whispered, "Harry, what are you doing here? We're in the middle of the service. Whatever it is can wait."

"It can't wait." Harry poked him again.

"I'm not going."

"I'll have a cigarette while I wait."

"Jesus." Hooper led the way out. As soon as they reached the street, he turned on Harry. "What is the matter with you? Other people go to church on Sunday. Remember that? Do you ever think of anyone but yourself?"

"Keep walking." Harry had pulled his germ mask off, and he thought some of the passengers waiting at a trolley shelter looked more interested in the church than in the next ride. Otherwise, the street held the stillness of shuttered shops. The only store open sold candies and toys, taking advantage of kids being home. A top skittered out the door into the light.

"Cigarette?"

"I'm quitting."

"Good for you. Filthy habit."

"The first cigarette I had was at the age of twelve, with you."

"Fun times."

"No, they weren't fun, they were stupid."

"You're just saying that because you always got caught."

"Not all of us are born thieves."

"Nip?" Harry showed his flask.

"No, I didn't leave church in the middle of a service to have a drink."

"Pretty sparse attendance."

"You noticed. Well, there's been a little intimidation. The authorities demand that the church support the war."

"Which one?"

Harry turned the corner and led Hooper by a row of child-size statues with toys and flowers at their feet. Christians relegated the souls of unbaptized babies to limbo; the Japanese made room and welcomed all. In a corner of the cemetery was a red and gold one-room temple where Harry bought a joss stick. The rest of the plot was a jumble of headstones, stakes and blowsy roses. The stakes had special Sanskrit names given the dead; the more money paid, the longer the name. Harry suspected that when Charon ferried souls across the river Styx, he sold tickets for first class or steerage. At the bottom of one stake was Kato's name. Harry lit the joss stick and set it in a glass on a shelf of the stone. Into another cup he poured an offering of Scotch.

He offered the flask to Hooper. "You're sure?"

"What the hell."

"Yeah, I'm afraid so."

Harry added a cigarette on the shelf for Kato, and Hooper had one, too. It was peaceful in the cemetery, among the stones and wilting flowers.

Hooper said, "I hear you're on the plane. I can think of a few thousand people more deserving than you. Why you?"

"I earned it."

"I bet. And if I brought you a mother whose small children were waiting for her in Shanghai, what would you say?"

"I'd say bring your violin. Anyway, it's not that sort of flight, it's back and forth, just to show the imperial flag."

"Are you coming back, Harry?"

Harry said nothing.

Hooper laughed weakly. "At least you don't lie about it, I suppose that's something."

"The Lord hates a lying tongue. How did you know about the plane?"

"You're not the only one in Tokyo with contacts."

"You're the only one at the embassy with contacts."

"The American embassy is staffed with keenly intelligent men."

"Right, starting with the ambassador, only he can't speak a word of Japanese and he's deaf as a post. Where is he now?"

"As a matter of fact, I think he's golfing. He's a very decent man, and he's made friends with the top people."

"The top people don't run this country, the army does. The man has never met ninety-nine percent of the Japanese. He couldn't communicate with them if he did. If a beautiful woman took his hand and slipped it in her pants and said, 'Give it to me, Mr. Ambassador, give it to me good,' he wouldn't know what to say."

Hooper developed hiccups. Harry shared the flask again.

"Thank you. The ambassador doesn't learn Japanese because—"

"Because he's got you."

"Because he's afraid of making a mistake that would damage the dignity of the United States. How would it be if, say, an ambassador from China came to the States and said, 'No tickee, no washee'?"

"That's the level of competence you expect the ambassador to reach?"

"No. But face is important."

"Not anymore. Something's up."

The hiccups vanished. Hooper looked around. "Harry, I can't give you intelligence information."

"You've got it backward. I'm giving you." Harry plucked a rose and put the petals, like dabs of paint, on Kato's stone.

Hooper said, "You're a tainted source."

"Any good source is tainted. This is not a pact with the devil, do you want the information or not?"

"Harry, I don't know. I'm not even supposed to be seen with you."

"Have I ever lied to you, ever?"

"You're such a cynic."

"Exactly, that's what you call a guy who tells you the truth."

Hooper smiled with resignation. "Okay, Harry, then I'll tell you. The Japanese Combined Fleet disappeared a week ago. It's exercising radio silence, which is the same as sounding a fire alarm, so far as I'm concerned. It could be just to rattle us. I don't think so, they don't have enough oil for that kind of bluff. They're going to the Dutch Indies, I'm sure. That's where the oil is. They'll also probably strike in Malaysia and Singapore. Even the Philippines. It's a matter of days at the most. You'll get out by the skin of your teeth."

"That's the plan." Harry looked at his watch. Where he really wanted to be was the ballroom, to keep tabs on Michiko and lay low.

"You have something to add?"

"Hawaii."

Hooper raised his eyebrows. His bow tie went up and down. "You're serious? Impossible. They'd never reach it without being seen, and then they'd be hung out to dry."

"That's where they're going. If you were going to fight a hundred-foot snake and you had one shot, would you go for the tail or the head? They're after Hawaii—the fleet, the planes and the oil tanks—and then they'll rule the Pacific. They're going to gamble big, Hoop, they don't have a choice."

"Oil tanks, too?"

"Especially."

"When is this attack going to take place?"

"Very soon."

"Just 'soon'? You didn't see a written order?"

"No."

"Where does this information come from?"

From urgent questioning with a bamboo rod about cooked books, not the kind of source the embassy would recognize. "From me."

"From you? From Harry Niles?"

It was one of those moments, Harry thought, when your life was put on the scale and the needle didn't budge.

"I'm the best source you ever met, Hoop. The Russians have sources, but Americans don't, because our embassy is a club of Christian gentlemen who don't snoop. I do."

"You make that sound like a virtue."

"In my trade, yes. And no one knows the Japanese like me."

"That's the problem. Very well, on what exactly is your information based?"

Harry didn't want to go into the details of nonexistent oil tanks, and he didn't have time for a debate. "Hawaii, that's it. Tell the ambassador."

"I told you, he's golfing."

"Warn Pearl, at least. They ought to be on alert, put some planes up, look around."

"They *are* on alert. Besides, it's Saturday there. It's the navy's Christmas-party day, and Hawaii is not going to go to battle stations because someone in Tokyo has secret information he won't divulge. I'm sorry, Harry, it's just not credible. Maybe you mean well, maybe you feel a patriotic twinge, maybe you're just playing us for suckers, which is what you usually do. Anyway, no one is going to attack Hawaii. It's too far from here, and it's too well defended."

"When is the ambassador coming back?"

"He'll be golfing most of the day, so there's no point even trying to get him at the embassy. I tell you what, if you don't take that plane, I'll get a group of fellows together later in the week, somewhere outside the embassy, and we'll kick around your ideas, how's that? It can even be a kind of rehabilitation for you. A start, anyway."

"You know those monkeys who hear no evil, see no evil, speak no evil? You could be a fourth monkey covering your ass."

"I give up. I don't know what you're up to, some inscrutable scheme to turn a tragic situation into a buck, but I'm washing my hands of you, Harry."

"People always say that. Wait." Harry clapped a couple of times and bowed to Kato's stone. He straightened up. Most of the stones in the cemetery weren't carved, just selected for their dignity. "You know why we got along, Hoop?"

"I always hate that nickname."

"Know why, more than the obvious reasons that you secretly liked breaking the rules and I needed a lookout? Because we both liked

Japan. It was like a mysterious club no other Americans could join. We knew what was going on and no one else did, not our parents, not our teachers, not our preachers. We understood Japan."

"That's over now."

"I don't think so. No matter how hard you try, I think you still have a mustard seed of intelligence. You asked when this attack was going to take place. Did I see a written order? No, but I did see Tojo in the park this morning."

That got Hooper's attention. "Really? What was he doing?"

"He was riding. He was riding horseback in tweed and breeches and a sporty hat, followed by the missus and daughters in a convertible. The tweeds are important because, as we know, General Tojo is never seen out of uniform, and he never, ever takes a day off from running the busy empire. Today of all days, he took the time to ride around Ueno Park with his lovely family and be presented flowers by a little girl. There were photographers. The embassies all take each edition of every paper. Everyone can go to sleep tonight with a picture of a new, peace-loving Tojo under their pillow. Now you tell me when they're going to attack."

"Tweeds? Gosh, I wish I'd seen that."

"So?"

Hooper rocked back and forth. Finally he said, "I can't do it. Signal Hawaii on a hunch?"

"It's not a hunch. You *know*."

"All on your say-so, Harry. I'll check the evening paper and see if Tojo's in it."

"And you'll still sit on the pot. Or pray."

Hooper flushed as if Harry had slapped him. In fact, Harry felt a band of pain across his back from bending to the joss stick and thought, Well, I've made my pitch to save the world and failed. It was stupid to even try. Now he thought about aspirin, Michiko and Ishigami, in that order. A gang of kids ran along the cemetery with their arms out like planes. A breeze pushed first one petal and then another off Kato's stone to Hooper's feet. Harry didn't move, and Hooper became aware that although he was with Harry, he could as well have been alone. Before he headed out the gate, he said, "I'll pray for you, too, Harry."

"Do that, Hoop."

AFTER HOOPER LEFT, Harry found a café to use the restroom, which was a cabinet behind a sliding door. He leaned to one side to feel, inside his shirt, a welt raised like a snake across his back. When he pissed, the toilet bowl turned pink. That wasn't good, either.

21

AGAWA'S PAWNSHOP was open on Sunday because December was a busy time, when people needed cash for winter house-cleaning and the big blowout at New Year's. They didn't like banks; banks transferred mysterious papers around, sign here, sign there. At a pawnshop a person's goods were safe, redeemable within three months, and shelves were filled with bright stacks of women's kimonos, toolboxes, movie cameras, tap shoes, ice skates, a golf bag and clubs. A glass case displayed ivory netsuke, a comb and brush set of mother-of-pearl, earrings of black pearl and golden filigree, every-thing a little chipped, a little shabby, and over it all reigned thin, dys-peptic Agawa at the counter with an abacus, ashtray and pack of Golden Bats.

"That story about Noah's ark. That was pretty cute," Agawa said when he saw Harry at the door.

"I knew you were good with numbers. You, saying you couldn't play cards with Jiro's ashes there?"

"Well, I find it distracting to play next to a dead man."

"You're not so far from there yourself. We'll just prop you up at the ballroom and deal you a hand."

"I'd probably still win." The picture obviously appealed to Agawa.

His shoulders shook to indicate that he was laughing. "And I suppose you scratched together some dust for Jiro's box?"

"We found something appropriate."

Agawa looked around his shop, at pawned saws and patched umbrellas hanging from the beams, slightly dingy scrolls hanging on the walls, like a personal museum assembled by a man who never dusted. "Want anything here, Harry? Ski poles, telescope, carving of a bear with a salmon in his mouth?"

"No."

"Good." Agawa shouted for an assistant who crept in to mind the shop while he led Harry out the back and across a dirt yard populated by hens to a two-story cement tower that looked like the keep of a medieval castle. The tower door was a bank-vault door with a combination lock, and the upper window had iron bars and coffered shutters faced in iron plate. Drop cloths covered everything on the ground floor, although Harry caught a luminous hint of porcelains and the dark stare of a samurai helmet. These weren't the pawned baubles of the working class, these were treasures of major debt. He followed Agawa up a ladder to the floor above, where the pawnbroker maneuvered a strongbox toward the crosshatched light of the window. Every movement of Agawa's had been quick and agitated, but in unblocking the box he became nearly reverent, lifting the lid from the rich, swarming glow of gold bars.

The bars were cosseted in red velvet and stacked according to size. Indian tael bars were about the size of calling cards. Chinese "biscuit" bars were six ounces and carried the impression HONG KONG GOLD & SILVER EXCHANGE. Strings of Chinese doughnut coins Harry didn't bother with. Selling or buying gold was illegal, but there was a rough black-market price both he and Agawa knew: five hundred yen per tael bar, and two thousand yen per Hong Kong biscuit. Biscuits made the pockets sag. Harry laid down three thousand for six tael bars that would be his currency from Hong Kong to America.

"How much for the golf clubs?" Harry nodded back toward the shop. "Keeping in mind that the army's taking over all the courses and there's no place to play."

"A hundred."

"Twenty."

"Fifty."

"Forty."

"Done." Agawa spread the bills like playing cards to count them. "Always good to do business with you. Very professional. As long as you let me count the money, not you. Just joking. You know the first time I saw you, Harry, you were running errands for the girls backstage at the Folies. I was interested in a dancer named Oharu, remember her? I wasn't so old. I was married, but I was still interested. But I could never get her away from that artist. I think she posed for him. Now, there's a job, painting someone like Oharu. Anyway, I heard that the artist was going to an exhibition out of town, and at once I got over to the Folies in time to catch Oharu and ask her to meet me after the show. She said she had a date. I got the drift, I didn't have a chance, not with her. I went out and tried to drown my sorrows in drink. Then I went to the movies. I don't think I ever looked at the screen, because three rows ahead of me was Oharu with you. You were her date. A boy, not even Japanese. I fought a powerful impulse to strangle you. I could feel my fingers closing around your throat. I could feel your breath rattle. You were so friendly with her, so easygoing. I wanted to beat your head against the steps and crush it under my heel." Agawa rocked with excitement and slowly settled back. "I didn't, of course. I controlled myself and left the movie theater. I went to a red lantern and got drunk again and calmed down. Although, I have to say, when the earthquake hit soon after and I heard that Oharu didn't survive, my first reaction was Good, I hope the little gaijin died, too. I didn't know you had already gone home."

Harry carefully wrapped the bars in velvet so they wouldn't click together. He looked up. "I guess those were the good old days."

"History. Like Noah's ark. That what you need now, Harry. Noah's ark."

HARRY BOUGHT A newspaper and met Goro at a Ginza pastry shop where the reformed pickpocket was squinting through a display case, trying to decide between napoleon or eclair, meringue or tarte citron.

Everyone had expected Goro to become a yakuza like Tetsu. He had the supple fingers of a born dip, but he also had the exquisite mole of an actor. Goro distracted shopgirls while Tetsu lifted the goods, and the two boys were successful thieves until they wandered into a stationery store they had robbed before. The owner at once recognized the mole. She chased Tetsu, locked the door before Goro could escape and could have turned him in to the police. However, she was a widow only ten years older than he, and the more he wept, the more she sympathized. Within a month they married. Goro took her family name as his and never had to steal again, though he still flirted with salesgirls. To get him out of the shop, his wife found him a position at the government printing office, where all he had to do was sort stationery to different ministries. That was still all he did ten years later, except for card games at the ballroom and occasional business with Harry.

"You're fogging the glass," Harry said.

"It's hard to choose between the meringue and the eclair, each has its merits."

"Then one of each."

"Excellent. Harry, that's why we're still friends."

Goro had his sweets with coffee, Harry had tea and they took a booth under a mural of cancan dancers kicking on the Champs-Élysées. Harry had met the wife once, and she had used the word "chic" in every other sentence. Goro had padded at her side, to all appearances a well-dressed consort, a neutered cat.

Harry opened the newspaper to the movie times. "I was thinking of taking in an early show. Want to come? You can pick."

A tael bar sat in the paper's crease. As Goro pointed to a theater, he incidentally palmed the bar. A moment later he rested his hand in his jacket pocket and let the bar slide down, every move natural and unhurried.

Goro read, "*Stanley and Livingstone,* what's that about?"

"Missionary gets lost. Nothing new there."

"I'm supposed to meet the wife for lunch. She's very Western, strong-willed. She has me on a diet."

"I can see."

"A wonderful woman."

"Absolutely." Harry watched Goro stuff his face. "Marriage suits you."

"She watches every move." Goro's tongue searched the corners of his mouth for crumbs, and only after could he bother with chat. "Are you in trouble, Harry?"

"Me? Furthest from it."

"This request was a little unusual."

"Was it scary at your end?" Harry asked. "Did you have to get into some offices? Get past a guard? Was it fun?"

Goro permitted himself a grunt of satisfaction. He drank the dregs of his coffee and sat for a moment with his eyes closed, breathing deeply the scent of cream and powdered sugar before rising from the table. "The wife."

Harry left a minute later. He waited until he got to his car to unfold the newspaper to an envelope that Goro had slipped in so smoothly that even Harry hadn't noticed. The envelope was government issue, with a twine closure he unwound to draw out two sheets of paper that were blank except for the letterhead of the Department of the Military Police, Defense Section, Ministry of War. A third piece of paper as fine as tissue bore the red imprint of a ministry stamp. The government printing office was also responsible for rubber stamps. A forged document wasn't quite as good for Willie and Iris as a call from Saburo, which would have swept all objections aside. However, it was heartening to see that a son of Asakusa like Goro still had, despite all efforts at reformation, an itch that had to be scratched.

Harry felt better, more the captain of his fate. He didn't have to go to the ballroom right away. Knowing what he did about Hawaii was like standing by a burning fuse and doing nothing. It was just too . . . annoying. He didn't have to go through Hooper, he could go direct.

Michiko would have to wait. He knew she had made it to Haruko's long enough to swipe a dress and she had a gun. At the ballroom card game, she would be protected by the yakuza. Harry couldn't wait to get his hands around Tetsu's throat for the rebuff at Saburo's gate, but Tetsu wouldn't let anyone harm a woman at his game. She was safe.

• • •

WEST TOKYO petered out into dry fields, sun-warped wooden houses and small children with bare bottoms who waved as Harry drove by. If the Japanese fleet really was headed to Hawaii, he felt he had to do something. He wasn't a patriot, but the con he had run on Gen and the navy about phony oil tanks on Oahu was the shell game of a lifetime, his masterpiece, and he refused to see it come to such a miserable end. He refused to lose.

When he thought about Iris, he wondered if he really had helped her. Assuming that the *Orinoco* made it through the blockade, racist Germany was going to be no bed of roses for a Chinese bride. That was the problem with good deeds, they rarely stood up to scrutiny. Besides, mixed marriages always seemed to bring grief. He could just imagine Michiko meeting California girls, like a panther among tabbies. When he did tell her that he was leaving, he had to remember to take the gun away from her first. His back began to throb again, and he chewed aspirin as he drove.

Ten miles out, he reached an oasis ringed by pines that separated the manicured fairways of a golf course from the muck of fallow paddy fields. Everything about the rice paddies suggested a desperate, crowded, exhausting struggle for life, and next to them the course hovered like a green and spacious heaven. The entrance to this paradise was a clubhouse reminiscent of a Spanish hacienda and a circular driveway with limousines and idle bodyguards.

Harry had caddied in Florida, enough to pick up the rudiments of the game, which enabled him to make occasional money teaching golf in Japan. Japanese golf was different from American in that it was tacitly understood before a match began which player, for reasons of respect, should win. Harry wasn't crazy about golf as a game, but it was a gold-plated entrée to Japanese business. Harry could sell the Queen Mary over eighteen holes. He wasn't a member of the club, but he had steered enough players to it to be welcome. To look the part, he shouldered the bag of clubs he'd bought at the pawnshop.

Members came and went through a reception area of Mexican tiles and mission wood. Notices on the reception counter advised that all guests had to be signed in, only golf shoes were allowed on the links, only regular shoes in the clubhouse and, as a patriotic sacrifice, players were limited to two balls per round. One of the first shortages caused by the American embargo was golf balls; some enterprising boys would be out by the water hazards, selling balls they had dredged out. The reception area opened to a sitting room of leather chairs and trophies and a fireplace stoked like a furnace. For Harry, it had never hurt to be seen at the club. Golf was a Japanese version of America, played in plus fours and tam-o'-shanters, celebrated on the nineteenth hole with a round bought by the highest score. Now, however, anything as American as golf was unpatriotic, and the club was virtually empty.

A horseplayer Harry knew was behind the reception desk. He wore a blazer with the club insignia on the breast pocket.

"Harry, what can I do for you?"

"I was supposed to meet the American ambassador here. I wondered whether he checked in."

"An hour ago. You were going to play golf with the ambassador?"

"He asked if I could. Said to find him on the golf course if I missed the tee time."

"Sorry, Harry, he's got a foursome. You know the rules, four's the limit."

"Is the sensei here?"

"The teacher is at the shop. But I'm not supposed to let you past the desk unless a member invites you."

"Since when?"

The receptionist shrugged apologetically.

"That's too bad, because the fact is, I have a deal on golf balls."

"That's different. You'll find the teacher at the shop."

"I know the way."

Harry walked through to the mournful shadows of the bar. The members present were mainly in import-export, and since the embargo, they had all day to drink. Harry worked his way out to a flagstone patio that overlooked the course. In a shop that stood separate from the clubhouse, the pro was demonstrating a putter. Customers were rare, and the pro was thoroughly occupied.

The course might be virtually abandoned, but it was beautiful, famous for fast greens of Korai grass and water hazards that were ponds paved in lily pads. The holes were framed by dark pine and autumn maples, all the colors of a blaze, as if a man with a torch had run around and lit the grounds. On the first tee, facing a relatively short dogleg right, were players Harry didn't recognize, all four in knickers, the uniform of golf, and taking some very bad swings. In Japan, golf was performed with almost religious intensity of effort, never mind that the breeze from off the course carried a rice-paddy tang of rotting cuttlefish and human waste. No one else was even waiting to tee off.

The question was how far out on the course the ambassador was. Past the first pin, Harry could just see a foursome approaching the tee of the second hole.

Harry stepped back inside the bar to borrow a pair of binoculars hanging by the door. He focused on the second tee and a commanding figure with the look of an American eagle—dark brows and mustache and silvery hair—who towered over the other players. Unmistakably the ambassador. He was at the second hole with sixteen to go and would be out on the course at least four more hours. Harry couldn't wait four hours. Michiko wouldn't wait four more hours at the ball-room, safe or not. He'd wasted enough time getting this far.

He replaced the binoculars. Maybe a dozen members sat by the window in the bar but couldn't look out without blinking into the sun. The party on the first tee hit the last of four brutal hacks and started down the fairway with their caddies. Harry waited until they were a hundred yards along and strolled after them with his bag as if he had every right, no questions asked.

He stayed out of their line of vision until he reached the trees and a groundskeeper's path that wound through them. Fallen leaves released a scent like cinnamon with every step. The second hole was a straightaway pinched by sand traps, a test of the player's ability to hit low and use the roll rather than loft the ball into the vagaries of the wind. Behind the pin was a service road that ran outside the wind-break of pines back to the clubhouse driveway. If he could just get the ambassador alone and talk to him, he could walk the road back to his car and no one would be the wiser.

The ambassador's foursome was moving up on the fairway of the second hole when Harry caught sight of them. The ambassador puffed on a pipe, a Gulliver in tow, while his hosts spoke loudly in English to make up for his deafness and lack of Japanese. Harry always described the American ambassador as hopeless. The truth was, Harry didn't think the ambassador was a stupid man so much as stultified by good manners and the absence of curiosity, happier to swim in a swimming pool than in the sea, the sort who, in fact, wouldn't have lasted one year as a missionary. His information was secondhand from other diplomats. His Japanese contacts were financiers and industrialists known for their moderate views and fading influence. None of the players had yet noticed Harry, but he recognized one who was bareheaded and as dark as a caddy, the old pirate Yoshitaki of Yoshitaki Lines.

Harry ducked through the trees. He wasn't sure what he could say in a few minutes that would persuade the ambassador to cable Washington or Hawaii. He couldn't explain about an oil-tank scam or the nuances of the word "confusion" or of Tojo riding in the park. Probably lie, keep it simple, just claim that sources in the navy said the war was on.

Because the ambassador had boomed his drive, he hit his second shot last. Harry hoped it would land on the right side of the fairway. The ambassador did better than that: he sliced a ball that flew viciously into the maples and kicked out to the rough not more than fifty yards from Harry. While the others lined up approaches to the green, the ambassador searched the grass. He wore a maroon sweater, plus fours and the trance of a man lost in a game. He found the ball, set his pipe down on the grass and considered his clubs with his back to Harry, who was close enough, with a quick dash, to pick his pocket.

"Mr. Ambassador!" Harry said. He wanted to get this over with fast.

The ambassador selected a six iron and took a practice swing. The caddy was a skinny boy in a huge cloth cap. He noticed Harry, but gaijin were known to act in bizarre ways. Popping out of the woods could be one of them.

Harry stepped within ten yards. "Mr. Ambassador, we have to talk about Hawaii. There's about to be an attack, Mr. Ambassador, are you aware of that?"

The ambassador got comfortable over the ball. A lot of big men stiffened over the ball, but the ambassador seemed smooth and poised, discounting the slice into the trees. He stepped back for a practice swing and set up over the ball again.

"Mr. Ambassador!" Harry edged closer yet.

"It's my theory," Yoshitaki said, "that a deaf man's concentration is a great advantage on the golf range." He had returned so quietly along the trees that Harry hadn't heard him. Harry felt a little trumped.

The ambassador unleashed a smooth swing and a sharp "click" as the club struck the ball, which sailed low and true toward the pin.

"About Hawaii," Harry tried again.

The ambassador focused on the bounce and roll of his shot as it split the bunkers. Yoshitaki looked in the opposite direction. Harry turned to see the following players and caddies transform to bodyguards and hustle toward him as they ditched their bags. Now Harry understood why they were such atrocious golfers.

"Mr. Ambassador." The man was close enough to touch.

The ambassador's shot had reached the green, from the excited reaction of the players ahead. He retrieved his pipe, produced a contented puff and, without a backward glance, strode toward the flag.

"How is that beetle of yours?" Yoshitaki asked Harry. "Still letting him out for walks?"

"When he needs the air."

"Today is the day. This will be the last Sunday like this we will see for a good while, don't you think?"

"As a matter of fact, I do." Harry watched the ambassador cross the undulations of the fairway. "He heard me."

Yoshitaki said, "No, not if it was the wrong thing to hear or the wrong messenger, he didn't hear a word. He's a friend. I'll make sure he gets home safely. Was it important, what you wanted to tell him?"

"I can't even remember what it was."

"Good. Don't become complicated now. It's not everyone who can lead a life of total selfishness. You should stick with that."

Well, a man that deaf was a wonder, Harry thought. He could have shouted at the top of his lungs, but the moment had passed. Maybe the moment had never existed, Harry thought, any more than he existed to the embassy. It also occurred to him that he could be wrong, that he had failed only in sending the ambassador on a wild goose chase. Who the hell was Harry Niles to announce when war would start?

The bodyguards arrived and surrounded Harry. They didn't seize him, threaten him or even show exasperation, only circled Harry and separated him from his golf bag.

"Don't worry about the plane," Yoshitaki said. "It won't leave without you. Good-bye, Harry Niles."

The bodyguards waited until Yoshitaki's foursome holed out, then headed for the service road behind the green, a phalanx with Harry at the center. Harry had once witnessed a similar technique at a bullfight in Tijuana when a bull gored a matador and took possession of the ring. They got the bull out by sending in a herd of steers that surrounded him, trotted him once around and led him peacefully out the gate.

DRIVING BACK to town, Harry had to laugh at the picture of a con man saving the world. *So through the night rode Paul Revere; And so through the night went his cry of alarm / To every Middlesex village and farm . . .* It would help, he thought, if people would listen or could even hear. No more heroics. The main thing was, he hadn't blown his seat on the plane.

Harry noticed how the sun danced over dry rice stalks sticking up from mud like black stitches on a cloth of gold, a sight he realized he might never see again. Amber waves of grain, not fields of rice. This time tomorrow he'd be airborne. There were things he'd miss: the whistle of a blind masseuse in the early morning, the shimmer of banners the length of a street, the way koi rose to the surface when a shadow passed. The way the tailor's wife had laughed at her own distress so as not to bother him, which struck Harry as the most dignity he'd ever seen, but a dignity he saw in Japan all the time.

And delicacy, the way Yoshitaki's men walked him off the course in the most nonviolent bum's rush possible. There was style in that, a gentle art.

It was midafternoon when Harry got to Asakusa. Walking through Sunday crowds pushing to this movie or that shrine, treating themselves to red-bean buns or candy rabbits, he felt a million miles away from the artificial world of the golf course. Asakusa was still sane, even if the rest of the world was not. On one side a newsstand featured samurai photos, on the other side Shirley Temple. A music-hall billboard offered both patriotic songs and South Seas ukuleles. That was what Harry considered a healthy balance.

The front of the ballroom was locked, unusual on Sunday, when Tetsu sometimes had as many as four games going. Harry went around to the oversize doors in back, where theater flats and props were delivered for storage, the nominal use of the ballroom now. He couldn't wait to get his hands on Tetsu. No one answered Harry's call, but the doors eased open.

"Tetsu? Michiko?"

Since he had never entered through the rear, he didn't know where the light switches were, and he followed the flame of his cigarette lighter around a maze of backdrop flats, prop chests, costume trunks. The Happy Paris had been shut the night before, and now the ballroom? Like parts of his life going dark.

"Michiko?"

There was no return glimmer or whisper, no card game or tango on a gramophone, let alone a welcome. Although Harry was late for Michiko, he decided to act the aggrieved party because she wasn't waiting for him with sake and food. His back was burning, and he hadn't had food or sympathy for a day. He remembered when he used to come to the ballroom with Oharu, how they had sat in the balcony and watched reflections from a mirror ball spin around the floor, over the men with their rolls of tickets and women lined up like pack animals along a velvet rope. The painful couples they made, stepping on each other's feet to the quickstep, fox-trot, waltz. Oharu, the real dancer, would giggle and shush Harry at the same time. The way the reflections spun, he would feel he was rising to the sky. It was interesting how much more disorienting pitch black could be. He kept walking into nowhere across the ballroom floor.

"Tetsu! Where are you?"

His voice circled.

"Michiko!"

He finally saw something. A realization filtered through him that the floor had become slippery and that a warm, cloying scent hung in the air. Harry slowed like a man approaching an abyss. He gave his breath a moment to catch up before the last few steps.

In the wavering light before him, a woman in a white dress with a blue sailor collar slumped at a card table. She didn't have a head. Not on her, but her arms stretched across the table to a white wooden box the right size.

22

H E SET THE lighter on the table like a candle. Her hands were waxy, heavy in death. She wore Haruko's dress, white with blue trim, now flecked with brown around the collar. She looked lonely. Harry supposed that anyone being executed felt alone, but the victims he'd seen in Nanking at least died in a war where death was the norm. To be killed like this, trapped by a man with a sword while a peaceful city lay outside, was to be particularly deserted. Her forearm was cool but soft, perhaps two hours dead. About the time Harry had arrived at the golf course, Ishigami must have arrived at the ballroom, where Harry had told Michiko to wait. He couldn't have set her up better if he'd tried.

"No—"

Was he talking to her? This was a little late, he thought. What he was going to say was that he was just trying to help Willie and then alert the right people about nothing less than a war. It didn't matter, because the right people weren't interested. He certainly hadn't helped her. Harry didn't see his gun, so that hadn't helped her, either.

"It's not—"

He couldn't imagine her dead. There was nothing sweet or pleasing about her, not the candy-box kind of love Americans sang about. He couldn't imagine her dead because she was so difficult, she was the burning fuse, the spark and imminent explosion in his life. Where Michiko died, there should be a smoldering crater in the earth, a volcanic upheaval, at least the smell of gunpowder, instead of a sense that the air was awash in droplets of ruby red. He could almost feel the mist settle on his cheek. Ishigami had painted her once, now twice. Still, it wasn't right, dull submission wasn't Michiko's style. With the world about to roll down the drain, it probably made no difference to examine an individual death, but Harry, having been a bust where the world was concerned, needed to know what had happened.

There should have been more blood. Blood should have flooded the table and the floor around it if she'd been killed where she sat. There was relatively little. Maybe this was coldhearted of him, but he could deal with details better than the whole picture, a little like Sergeant Shozo's jigsaw puzzle, except that Harry refused to see the piece in the center or touch the wooden box, not yet. Before the lighter's flame died, he looked up and found its dim reflection in the mirror ball hanging above, and another glint from a brass post of the velvet rope. Now he knew where he was.

In the dark, Harry climbed to the cockpit over the door and threw on the house lights: whites, cells, spots and mirror ball all at once. The ballroom leaped out of the dark. Michiko and table gained color, focus, dimension. The size of the ballroom, the gilded ceiling and balcony tier made her smaller, braver, a child prodigy playing to an empty house. The parquet shone except for two tracks from the table to the swing door of the women's restroom.

The ballroom management had kept the restroom's size and amenities to a minimum to discourage dancers from loitering. The light was out; why bother changing it after the dancing had stopped? A broken window on an airshaft admitted as much dust as light to two sinks with a cracked mirror and two Western toilets without seats that sat in a floor of hexagonal tiles. Blood pooled around a central drain that was stopped with clotted hair. Harry edged around the blood, searching the ceiling and walls for a bullet hole and the floor for a loose button, anything dropped. Just going tacky, the blood bore the imprints of her knees and toes and a man's shoes, relatively large, a red negative of where she knelt and where he stood.

Harry retreated to the dance floor.

"Tetsu!"

Tetsu was not in his office. Harry found cases of cigarettes, packs of cards, dumbbells, tattoo books, but no sign of blood or disarray. Harry returned to the bathroom door. Had Ishigami surprised Michiko in the bathroom? Had she put the gun down out of reach? Had she meekly sunk to her knees? Did she see the head box? Of course, Ishigami was the man who had peered deeply into her and found the geisha. In some ways, he might know her more intimately than Harry.

Then he set her up. He moved her with her toes dragging to a table in the middle of the ballroom floor and sat her in a chair. There he stretched her arms across the table as if setting the head box down or respectfully offering a gift. Then he locked the front door, which made no sense unless he wanted only Harry to find her. Harry had told her to wait at the ballroom. He was the one man sure to try every door.

Harry pictured it. Wood wasn't paper, and Ishigami couldn't punch through the restroom wall, but he could slip through the door, and in such poor light Michiko might not immediately see who he was. It still wasn't right. Nobody who ever made love with Michiko came away unscathed. There'd be a shot or some of Ishigami's blood. Overhead, the mirror ball hung like a ghostly daytime moon. Harry remembered her in her sequined jacket. There'd be *something*.

He approached the table again, circling as he neared, trying to chase the shakes out of his knees. Bullets were different. Once they left a gun they became, to some degree, middlemen between the killer and the victim. There was distance, if only an inch, and at long distance a sniper's objectivity. A sword, however, never left the hand and was never less than personal. Harry remembered being the butt of bayonet practice at school and how passionately the drill sergeant sprayed spit as he urged students to plunge their bamboo poles through Harry's wicker armor. How smooth, in comparison, Ishigami was. An artist. Americans wondered how samurai could fight in loose-sleeved kimonos, not understanding how the robes accentuated the sweep and thrust of the sword, and how the final plunge of steel through silk wrapped agony in beauty. Harry thought all this as if each idea were armor protecting him from the simple reality of a headless girl sitting like a sack of potatoes in a chair.

Death changed people, but that much?

Harry tentatively raised the lid of the box. The wood was white wisteria sanded to a sheen that emphasized the glossy black of the hair inside, cut short. He dug his fingers in and lifted. Since the head faced away he first saw damp, matted hair and two wounds down to the skull that must have preceded the final slice. A broad neck. Small ears with thick lobes. He turned the head around to face Haruko. Her eyes were slitted, mouth parted, forehead creased by a frown. It was an expression she might wear if a friend had suddenly accosted her with a a trick question, something she didn't have the answer for and was still figuring out.

Haruko in her own dress. That explained a lot. After telling Harry on the phone that Michiko had taken the dress, Haruko must have gone after it and found Michiko, and the two must have come to the ballroom together. Why Michiko didn't wait and Haruko did, Harry couldn't understand, although it explained why Haruko was taken so completely by surprise. In the murk of the restroom, with no gun and no warning, how could she defend herself from Ishigami?

A reverberation pounded at the back door and died. Harry fought the impulse to run. Where to? The door opened for a man dressed in shadow who moved through the scenery racks, emerged onto the ballroom parquet and peeled his goggles back. It was Gen in a leather coat and helmet. He slowed as he approached the table.

"Harry, what did you do?"

"Nothing."

"It doesn't look like nothing. Who is that?" Gen nodded toward the head in Harry's hands.

"Haruko."

"The waitress from your club?"

"Yes."

Harry had a ringing in his ears that he couldn't place as either alarm or relief. He put the head into the box as gently as he could and replaced the lid.

"Any witnesses, Harry?"

"I don't know, I wasn't here."

"Okay." Gen followed the trail to the restroom and edged in, careful to stay out of the blood. He emerged breathing hard and shaking his head. "You've done it now, Harry."

"It was Ishigami. If you'd gotten him out of town when I asked, this wouldn't have happened."

Gen made a show of looking right and left. "I don't see Ishigami. What I see is you and Haruko."

"If I did it, where's the sword?"

"You tell me. Did you kill her?"

"No, I swear."

"On what, Harry? What would you swear on?"

"I didn't do it. Simple as that."

"Nothing is simple with you." Gen looked at Harry coldly. "Did anyone see you come in? Tetsu? Anyone?"

"No."

Gen started twice to say something and finally softened. "Come on."

THE SUN HAD SET while Harry was in the ballroom. He and Gen rode the motorbike the long way around to Asakusa Park. They joined a circle under a streetlamp watching a storyteller with a box of illustrated slides depicting the feats of the Golden Bat, the same show they had watched as kids. Around them the crowd was in constant motion, from food stalls to fortune-tellers, sandal and kimono shops, stands selling toys, masks, souvenirs. Some people flowed out to the movie-theater row while others restlessly wandered back to the precincts of the temple like a sea that didn't know which way to go. Harry didn't know where else to look for Michiko. Would she go to the apartment, the one place where Ishigami was sure to look? Every time Harry thought about her, the ringing in his ears returned like a deafening alarm. He kept moving, hoping to find Tetsu or someone else who might have seen her. In the slide box, the Golden Bat killed an ogre.

MARTIN CRUZ SMITH

Harry wiped his hands with his handkerchief. Gen had tucked his motorcycle cap under his arm, but he still drew admiring glances as if he'd parachuted in.

Gen said, "I should be handing you to the police. What happened at the ballroom?"

"I don't know, but it was Ishigami."

"You're sure?"

Harry pushed through the crowd. "I asked you to get him out of town, and you didn't."

"You also said he was after you. Why would he kill Haruko? Did they even know each other?"

"I doubt it."

"It was a sudden homicidal impulse?"

"Maybe. And he carried a head box, like a Boy Scout. 'Be Prepared.'"

"Harry, if Ishigami and Haruko didn't have a relationship, then someone else was involved."

"I don't know."

"You're holding back. I promise, no matter how bad it is, I'll help, but you have to help me, too. Did you have a fight with Michiko over Haruko?"

"No."

"The fact is, Harry, you have a reputation for women, and Michiko has a reputation for a temper."

"Leave Michiko out of this."

"Okay, okay. Did anyone see you at the ballroom?"

"I don't think so."

"That's good. Where were you?"

"At the golf course."

"With . . . ?"

"Actually, I was talking to the ambassador."

"The American ambassador? That's great."

"Not really. He didn't hear me."

Gen laughed. "Really? Did he see you?"

"No."

Gen wore a smile that suggested he was enjoying a stick of Wrigley's. "That's one hell of an alibi. That's rich. Anyone else?"

"Yoshitaki."

"Of Yoshitaki Lines? Forget it, he has lawyers. He never talks to the police about anything. What did you want to talk to the ambassador about?"

"I ran into my old friend Hooper. He said the ambassador wanted to talk to me. It turned out he didn't."

"I wonder what it was about."

"We'll never know."

The pillowy glow of paper lanterns led to the temple steps. Inside but visible, a row of monks with shaved heads chanted to the beat of a hanging drum. Sweating from steady effort, they repeated sutras over and over like oars pulling through deep water, while a younger monk shook brass cylinders containing fortunes to be sold. Fortunes were sold everywhere, in the forms of paper lilies that opened in water, paper letters with invisible ink, dream papers to take to bed. And prayers, too, with the purchase of candles, joss sticks or the toss of a coin through a temple grate. From the top step, Harry watched smoke billow from the joss sticks set in a great bronze urn. More than ever, people needed a prayer or hope for a son or brother just called to duty. They paid no mind to Gen or Harry.

Gen said, "How are you going to find Michiko in this mob?"

"I'm not going to sit still while Ishigami hunts her down."

"Why would he? You said he was after you."

"He's gotten ambitious."

"So you *have* seen him. What happened?"

Harry had never told Gen about the Chinese prisoners in Nanking, and he did not intend to get into the subject of DeGeorge. Haruko was bad enough.

"Ishigami came to my place last night and saw Michiko with me."

"He's after you but didn't touch you?"

"Remember Sergeant Shozo and Corporal Go? They came by to ask some questions and scared Ishigami off."

"Last night? What time?"

"Three in the morning."

"For questions?"

"Oil-tank questions, Hawaii questions." Harry caught the shift to impassivity on Gen's face. The American breeziness always could be dropped like a mask. "They're talking to someone in Naval Operations. Someone on your end is leaking like a sieve."

"What did you tell them?"

"Nothing."

"Good. Nothing about the Magic Show? Nothing about the C in C?"

"No."

"Terrific. Look, Harry, the navy will protect you, but you've got to be honest. First, you're lying about China. Colonel Ishigami isn't going to chase you around Tokyo over a couple of cars you appropriated years ago in Nanking. Something else happened there. Second, you're lying about last night. The colonel has a sense of honor. He wouldn't harm a woman unless she had betrayed him in a personal way. How could Michiko or Haruko do that if they didn't know him? Why would he hurt either one? Sometimes I think you lie like other people whistle. Do you know why I came by the ballroom? I was looking for you. Sergeant Shozo did you the favor of calling me to say you were one inch away from a prison cell. I vouched for you and went all over town to warn you, and what do I see when I find you?"

"It wasn't pretty."

"You used to be a lot slicker. I hate to say it, but you've lost your touch."

"Yeah, I agree."

Harry could see half of the temple and the park, the world where he and Gen had once run wild. And Taro, Jiro, Tetsu, even Hajime. The stalls and souvenir stands were designed for boys with deft hands and quick feet. Escape routes had led around the pond, behind the Buddhas, in back of the shrine and out to the movie crowds on the Rokku.

"Once a con man, always a con man," Gen said.

"I guess so."

"So I'll just ask you to be honest about one thing. One thing, and we'll let the rest slide."

"What's that?"

"Did you fix the Long Beach books? The changes in the oil ledger, did Long Beach make them or did you?"

"Me? I only looked at those books because the navy asked me to."

"Maybe you did more than that. Maybe you altered the numbers for Long Beach Oil, Manzanita and Petromar. Did you, Harry?"

"I'm looking over there." Harry started down the steps toward the torii gate at the other end of the temple grounds. "I'm searching for a killer and you're talking about oil?"

"Because oil is more important. Tell me about the oil tanks in Hawaii. Are they real or not?"

"I don't know. I told you about the loudmouth in Shanghai—"

"I know the story. The bar, the whores, the drunk who boasted about the tanks. I know the story back and forth. So I'm going to ask you if you made it up. It will be between the two of us, just tell me the truth."

"It's like I told you. Do secret tanks actually exist? I doubt it."

"You know that once the possibility is planted, doubts don't matter."

"I only passed on what I heard. What you make of it is up to you."

"What we make of it can be very big, Harry."

Harry understood Gen's predicament. He was the poor Asakusa boy made good, the C in C's protégé, the hero of the Magic Show. He had brought the rumor of the Hawaiian tanks to the attention of Naval Operations. If there were a strike on Pearl, Operations would want to know exactly what to hit. Gen's career was on the line. All the same, Harry said, "That's up to you. I'm looking for Michiko."

Gen stayed at his shoulder. "Did you make up everything? Are the tanks a con?"

"I have no idea. What does it matter? What's so urgent about Hawaii?"

Gen said nothing, but the two men came to a stop. This was the point in a game where you turned up the cards, Harry thought. He said, "Is it too late to tell your friends in Naval Operations to turn the ships around?"

"You don't know what you're talking about."

"It's happening, isn't it? I saw Tojo taking an innocent ride in the park today, and I knew then it was a matter of hours. You know why I've done so well at cards over the years? The Japanese are lousy bluffers. They have too much honor, too much face. I don't have either, so I've always had the odds on my side. You understand odds?"

Gen looked like a fighter rattled by a combination. "I've heard this before."

"But you haven't understood. Odds are the long run. In the short run, you may sink the American fleet, burn all the oil, send Hawaii under the sea. But you won't win, because the other side will just produce more fleets, more oil and more islands if it needs to." Harry started down the steps again. "I can't believe someone as smart as Yamamoto went along with this."

"The C in C does as he is ordered."

"Doesn't matter. You may win the battle, but in the long run, you can't win the war. The odds are too high."

"That's what you want."

"No, that's not at all what I want."

"Japan defeated is what you want."

"No." Harry stayed one step ahead.

"You have always been against a greater Japan."

"I'll show you what I'm against. I'll demonstrate." At the bottom of the steps, Harry bought out a vendor's stack of dream papers, the cheap prints of seven clownish gods meant to be placed under one's pillow on New Year's to inspire good luck. Harry carried them to the smoking urn, crumpled the papers and tossed them in among the joss sticks. People stepped back, horrified. Harry went on balling up the sheets and throwing them in until the urn was full. "These are paper houses, this is what Japanese people live in. Have you ever seen the effect of incendiary bullets on paper houses? This is what it looks like."

Harry's lighter was good for one more flame. He touched it to a paper, which opened as it burned and touched off all the surrounding papers. They bloomed until the entire urn filled with a floating plasma of orange flames and the blue smoke of joss sticks. For a few seconds, the paper burned brilliantly and cast a light that Harry saw reflected in the eyes of the crowd; then it turned black and twisted on the sand amid the bare glowing wires of the sticks.

Harry said, "That's what I'm against. A Tokyo like that."

The space around him grew. Not all the people were strangers; some vendors had known Harry for years. No matter, all were shamed and offended. Everyone stared at the gaijin and made room only because courtesy prevented them from beating him.

Gen said, "Harry, I know about the plane tomorrow. If you want to be on it, tell me about the tanks. If you want to get out, tell me."

"I don't know."

Harry turned and made his way through the crowd. The pariah's privilege, he thought, was that people let you pass.

THE HAPPY PARIS was only a few blocks away. The club felt cocked like a mousetrap. Harry expected Ishigami to step behind him at any moment. He took a deep breath before turning on the lights.

Michiko wasn't in the club or upstairs in the apartment. There was no note or indication of where she had gone or how she expected to connect with him. Maybe she didn't intend to at all, Harry thought. Why stand next to a target on a firing range? If she took a powder, good for her. If she was smart, she'd go the far end of the island, and if he was smart, he'd be on the plane, so everything evened out. Harry realized that from the moment he stepped into the ballroom, he hadn't even thought about the plane until Gen mentioned it. He hadn't thought about Alice at all.

He dug out a potato stored under the galley floorboards, cut it in two and left a cross-section wrapped in a towel to dry while he typed on the stationery that Goro had delivered. A Japanese typewriter was a special misery, a scroll that rotated over a tray of hundreds of characters that had to be picked up and linked one by one, but over the years Harry had become adept at the creation of documents. While he wrote an official approval of Iris's politics from the War Ministry—that clean bill of health under the ministry letterhead that would allow her to accompany Willie on the *Orinoco*—he played some Ellington, getting up to punch in the numbers for "Mood Indigo."

What kept coming to mind were Haruko's head and vacant eyes. Most awful, however, was his relief when he saw she wasn't Michiko. Harry hadn't thought she was, not once he'd glimpsed her wrists, but he hadn't dared hope. To hope for anything that much was unlike Harry. *You ain't been blue, no, no, no / You ain't been blue / Till you've had that mood indigo.* Haruko had blue beat. Michiko was smart to lay low. Anyone who could be both the Record Girl and a geisha had a gift for survival.

A PLAIN LETTER wasn't enough. Just as important was a chop, an officer's stamp. Harry applied the stamp impression Goro had given him to the round heel of the potato, and the extra-fine paper almost melted, leaving a clear impression in red. With his smallest, sharpest knife, Harry cut away the surface in between, just as Kato had taught him to carve a woodblock. He wet a red inkstone and made a practice impression. Trimmed the excess and stamped the letter. In China he'd done fifty illegal documents a day. There were artists and there were artists.

23

BEECHUM HAD ORGANIZED a party for British expats and embassy couples in the lobby of the Imperial Hotel, the men in black tie and the women in gowns that looked like window drapes. As Harry walked in, Beechum was saying, "We all know what Sundays are like on the ramparts of the British Empire. I am happy to report to you that our fighting men in Singapore are undismayed by certain wild rumors. And not just the men." He watched Alice as she saw Harry arrive, and his baldness took on a purple hue. Harry had shaved and changed clothes to look like a proper friend of Imperial Hotel guests, not someone who juggled heads. "Not only the men," Beechum continued. "Although the Foreign Office has advised them to evacuate and head for home, every British and Commonwealth wife has loyally decided to stick it out. I propose a toast to their calm and fortitude, if you would all raise a glass."

Of gin, with gin courage to follow, Harry thought. After a stop at the reception desk, he rang Willie Staub on the house phone.

"Sorry, Willie, it's no go. I couldn't reach the right people."

"Harry, the *Orinoco* leaves tonight. I must be on it, the embassy says I cannot stay. What will become of Iris? Did you forget about us?"

"I tried, Willie. Things just didn't work out."

"Did Mr. DeGeorge find you?"

"No. Hey, come on down and we'll have a drink before you go."

"I can't leave Iris."

"I feel I let you down. I'd just like to say good luck."

A muffled, emotional conversation on the other end, and then "Just for a second."

Harry took a seat on the opposite end of the lobby, but there was no escaping Beechum's voice as it boomed around the atrium. Alice had described it as the sort of voice that unwittingly set off avalanches in the Alps. The hotel staff had taken a half-step back into invisibility, making Harry the sole audience for the Brits even at a distance. Harry asked for a Scotch, and when he raised it, the ice chattered from the shaking of his hand. Every time he thought of Haruko, he wiped his palm on his pant leg. When he thought of Michiko, he half stood to go. Alice misinterpreted and gave him a warning glance that said to stay clear.

Beechum said, "For those concerned about the safety of our troops in Singapore, I would like to relay the message I received just today from the British commander in chief. He is nearly done perfecting the defenses of the colony, and despite privations, his men confidently soldier on." What privations? Harry wondered. Singapore was paradise. Cheap gin, beautiful women, decent cigarettes. The tent pole of the British Empire was that a corporal from a Manchester brickyard could live like a king in Singapore, Hong Kong, Delhi. "It's important that we stand shoulder-to-shoulder with our officers and men everywhere and most of all in Singapore. Today is Sunday, and as many of you know, there are Sunday traditions in British Singapore. One is Sunday curry and the other is Sunday sing-along. We may not have the curry, but it would send a message in many ways if we sang along with those wonderful men and women."

A woman with a parrot hat sat at the piano and played an enthusiastic "Ta-Da." Alice was sipping a martini so slowly that Harry could feel her lips. What he saw on other faces was a special emotion, an empire in fear of eviction.

"Harry?"

Willie had come down to the lobby with Iris, who was damp around the eyes and apologetic for even asking Harry to help them.

She was in a rumpled cheongsam embroidered with flowers and looked like a crushed bouquet. Willie, too, no longer resembled the confident managing director of China Deutsche-Fon, or even the tourist who had arrived in Tokyo days before. He was desperate, wrung out.

"It's tough," said Harry. "Didn't you have some other people working on this?"

"A clerk at the embassy. You were the only person I knew here."

"It was a pass of some sort?"

"A letter to the German embassy about Iris's political background. You don't remember?"

"I remember now. Willie, that other Scotch is for you."

"You drank yours already?"

"I'll have another. Iris, I want you to know that whatever I can do to make Tokyo more endurable, just ask. Someplace to stay, a bank, a maid? Would you like a drink?"

"No, thank you."

Willie sat back in wonder. "Now I know what DeGeorge meant. I don't even recognize you, Harry."

"Speaking of DeGeorge, have you seen him around?" Harry signaled for more Scotch. Beechum's party launched into "It's a Long Way to Tipperary." It sounded long to Harry.

The waiter's tray carried not only the Scotch but also a manila envelope with Willie's name on it. Willie drew out an envelope with a string closure, and from that a letter.

"It's all in Japanese. What does it say?" Willie seemed to trust the waiter more.

The waiter held the letter by the corners. "If I may, this letter is not to you."

"Oh."

"No, it is to your embassy. It reads, 'This office is pleased to state that Mrs. Iris Staub, a Chinese national, has been found to be a person of good character. She is free to travel with her husband, Wilhelm Staub, a German national.' It's signed by a general of the military police."

"Is it official?"

"It bears the letterhead of the Ministry of War and has the general's stamp."

Willie took the letter back and showed Iris. "It came."

Harry said, "Congratulations. Now you have something to drink to."

"The embassy said it was hopeless. You did nothing?"

"Nothing at all. Kampai!"

As they drank, Harry felt a visual sweep. He didn't recall Beechum's eyes being quite so red, and he had to wonder how much the man knew about the next day's flight. Had Alice mentioned that she wasn't coming back? Harry assumed that, as a rule, women didn't tell husbands much.

Willie studied the letter again. "It's so short."

"The shorter, the better."

"What is 'shorter, the better'? That would be rare." Colonel Meisinger had come out of one of the gloomy hallways the Imperial had so many of. He was strapped into Gestapo black, and when he bowed to Iris, it was like watching a toad pirouette. "Don't you agree?"

Willie said, "Colonel, I have good news, permission for Iris to leave with me. It's wonderful."

Meisinger snatched the letter from Willie. He opened his mouth with amusement. "I will say this in English so your wife understands. This paper, whatever it says, is hardly enough. It has to be in German. We're Germans. Also police and educational records and an examination of her family, all in German."

"Not enough?" Willie asked.

"I just said. I'm sure your wife will find suitable arrangements here." Meisinger cocked his head toward the sing-along. "Wonderful spirit. I'll contact whoever sent this letter and explain things to him."

"Harry?" Iris asked.

Meisinger said, "Yes, Mr. Niles, are you acquainted with the immigration policies of the Third Reich?"

"No, sorry."

"He can't help you," Meisinger explained to Iris.

"Join us, Colonel?" Harry said, ignoring Willie's discouragement.

"One drink," Meisinger settled into the chair next to Iris. "I regret the situation, but it will be resolved, I'm sure. I will take a personal interest."

"You're enjoying Japan?" Harry asked.

"I would enjoy it more if the Japanese would do more than chase Chinese bandits. And do more about the Jews."

"You want the Jews to leave?" Willie asked.

"No, I want them sent back where we can get our hands on them. Harry, you seem to understand the Japanese, why are they so blind to the Jewish problem?"

"They've hardly ever seen Jews. Even the anti-Semites haven't seen any Jews."

"It's a matter of education?"

"And talking to the right people."

"Ah, yes, always the case." Meisinger's drink arrived. He tipped his bulk to raise his glass. "Heil Hitler."

"Cheers," said Harry.

"And who would the right people be?" Meisinger asked.

"Anyone but General Tanaka."

"Who is he?"

Harry tapped Willie's letter. He laughed, and Meisinger joined in.

"I'm sure we can smooth his feathers," Meisinger said. "It's hardly more than a note."

"That's a sign." Harry took his time offering cigarettes. He hummed along with the song. The singing was terrible, but for camaraderie it was hard to beat the Brits. If the piano were a sinking ship, they'd probably still be singing: *What's the use of worrying? It never was worthwhile.* It occurred to Harry that if the Japanese were attacking Hawaii, they would attack Singapore at the same time. Alice Beechum was the only person he knew with the intelligence and means to warn Singapore and Pearl.

"A sign of what?" Meisinger finally bit.

"Rank. The higher you are, the less you have to say. Tanaka is at the very top. A letter this brief is polite, but it's an order. You asked for a check on Iris, and this is your answer."

"But it's inadequate. We need much more and in German."

"You're in Japan."

"I will call this Tanaka and explain."

"A call might settle it, but not from you. It would have to be from someone of equal rank to Tanaka, a German general."

"The only general at the embassy is Ambassador Ott."

"Then the ambassador. It looks like Tanaka sent this letter today, Sunday, which is unusual and suggests someone important got to him. That would involve losing face all around. General Tanaka would certainly be very insulted. The army would be offended, too. So, I think you're right, you should have the ambassador call as soon as possible."

"Because of this note? Over Oriental rank and face?"

Harry produced a helpless shrug. "It's Japan."

"This is preposterous." Meisinger sank into his chair.

"Is the ambassador busy?"

"On a Sunday evening, Ambassador Ott has recitals of classical music for a few friends. He does not like to be disturbed. I myself have other things to do besides sit and eat cookies with a group of professional dilettantes."

"You may want to talk to him before the general does. Anyway, I'm sure you'll come up with a solution."

Meisinger picked up the letter again, as if he'd suddenly learned Japanese. "This stamp is Tanaka's?"

"Yes, it's considered an extension of the general himself. Very important."

The colonel let the letter drop to the table. "Well, Staub, it seems that you have influential friends."

"It does," Willie said.

"So, perhaps this is a matter of 'when in Rome' . . . We certainly don't want to offend our hosts, especially the army, when we are trying to encourage them to cooperate with us. I have no personal objections to Frau Staub joining you. We will even skip the usual procedures. So, everybody's happy."

Meisinger pasted on a magnanimous expression; what had just been a vital sticking point was now casually swept away. When the colonel took his leave, Willie and Iris reacted as if a shark had swum around them and moved on.

Harry said, "You'd better go. What you can't pack in five minutes, leave. Just get to the ship."

"You knew he was going to let us go?" Willie asked.

"He had to. The man was such an embarrassment in Warsaw that the Gestapo sent him here. If he fouled up in Tokyo, his next stop was the South Pole."

"When the waiter read the letter, he never mentioned General Tanaka by name, yet you knew it."

"It's not a talent I advertise, but I can read upside down. Willie, the *Orinoco* leaves from Yokohama, and it's just going to slip into the dark. Go."

"Thank you, Harry," Iris said.

"Don't thank me. You know why else the colonel let you go? He thinks that while he may not be able to stop Iris from boarding the ship, she won't get past the Gestapo on the other end because of German race laws. That's after you've run fifteen hundred miles of blockade, so don't thank me, please. If you put in at any neutral ports, say, Lisbon, you might want to let the ship go on without you."

"We can't avoid the war. We have to take part."

"You're an ant on a dance floor, that's how you'll take part." Harry laid on the letter what looked like two golden calling cards. Tael bars. "Lisbon is a beautiful city."

"What's that?"

"It's something everybody needs."

"I couldn't." Willie pushed the bars toward Harry.

"Willie, we lied and bribed to save people in China. Do you think you're any better than they were? What do you think, Iris?"

She said, "Maybe it's a loan."

"Definitely a loan," said Harry, who thanked God for women, or else the world would be full of proud men sitting on their thumbs. "I know you'd do the same for me."

"I am sorry for what I said before." Willie squeezed Harry's hand. "Do you have your way out?"

"A smart man always knows where the exit is."

"You have an exit here?"

"All over." Harry pulled free. "Don't play cards with anyone, ever.

If you meet anyone who reminds you of me in the least, run the other way. Go."

As Willie and Iris moved toward the elevator, Harry thought they were just another version of lovers giddily leaping into flames. Sometimes he felt he was the only realist he knew. At the other end of the lobby, Beechum's party was reaching its own climax of indomitable good cheer, *"There'll always be an England / And England shall be free / If England means as much to you / As England means to me."* No doubt the same words could be heard, Harry thought, in Singapore, Hong Kong and Sydney, wherever Britons shouldered the white man's burden of ungrateful wogs. The chorus repeated until sentimental tears ran down warm cheeks. Harry wondered how to find Michiko and where to hide from Ishigami. Now that he thought about it, he had needed the gold for himself. And, besides the plane, what exit?

ESPECIALLY AT NIGHT, the hotel looked like an Aztec temple with potted shrubs. As host, Beechum lingered in the driveway by the reflecting pool, making his good-byes of the evening while Alice waited in a car. Harry slid into the dark of the seat behind her.

"Willie and Iris seemed happy when they left," Alice said.

"I don't know why. Dodging destroyers to get to Germany is not, to me, a rational decision."

"Harry, if you were a paragon of reason, you would not be in Beechum's car nuzzling his wife."

"But that's not why I'm here."

"No?" Alice laughed. "My God, what on earth for, then?"

"The Japanese are raiding Pearl Harbor. I think they'll attack Singapore at the same time, probably Hong Kong, too."

"When?"

"Within a day or two."

Alice twisted the rearview mirror to see Harry. "This is not your area of expertise, is it?"

"No. By the way, did you see any photos in the evening papers?"

"Prime Minister Tojo riding in the park."

"In tweeds."

"Jodhpurs."

"Almost British."

"Some people at the embassy thought it was a good thing."

"Did you believe it?" asked Harry.

"No, nor in the tooth fairy. I can't think of anything more ominous."

A man ran over to the car to tell Alice that Beechum would be only a minute longer. Harry raised his head when the man was gone. "I hear that the emperor has been studying charts of the Hawaiian Islands."

"This is all highly circumstantial." Her eyes fixed him via the mirror. "A Japanese attack may be overdue, but there's something else, Harry, to make you so sure."

"There's been a little pressure on me to verify the missing oil."

"Not your phony oil?"

"Suddenly it's an issue. Targets, maybe."

"How much pressure? Anything physical?"

"Just a touch, but they're beating an accountant half to death at Sugamo Prison."

"Harry, you must get on that plane tomorrow."

"My thought, too."

Alice was quiet for a moment. "Do you imagine if I thought anyone would heed our warning of an attack, that I would abandon my post? It's too late for warnings, Harry. There are no brakes on the bus and no ears on the driver. This crash is going to happen."

"We can try."

"I'm not a spy, I'm just someone good at puzzles. If I suddenly had information, I'd have to name the source. Unfortunately, your reputation precedes you. No one will listen to you or me. It's time for us to leave. Oddly enough, you're becoming a better person. First Willie, now this."

"As soon as we get to California, I'll con some old lady out of her life savings, redress the balance." Harry noticed that Beechum had moved out of sight.

"You're going to do this, Harry? You will be on the plane?"

"Cross my heart."

"You've said farewell to Butterfly?" Alice asked.

"Michiko? Not quite."

"I can't believe this. I am vying with a geisha for the affections of a gambler."

Harry would have said that Michiko wasn't a geisha, except now he was no longer sure. "First I have to find her."

"You've lost her?"

"It's complicated."

"I have no doubt. Harry, you don't have to tell her. If she knows you, she'll understand soon enough that you've skipped out. Don't go back to the club. All you need to do is get to the plane. Isn't that what you've been telling me, to just get on the plane?"

"That's what I said. We catch the Clipper from Hong Kong, and from there the world's our oyster. A bungalow at the Beverly Hills, breakfast under an avocado tree."

"So you are choosing me? I am the lucky girl? I wish I could think of something that was sacred to you to swear by."

"I'm choosing California and you, it's a package deal."

"I forgot, you're not a romantic."

"Are you?"

"No. Of course not. We're just a pair of black sheep."

He placed a kiss on her neck and opened his door. Before he slipped out, he said, "You know what white sheep have? No imagination."

HARRY HAD LEFT the Datsun across the street. The more he thought about it, the more he knew that Alice was right. The last thing he should do was look for Michiko. The smartest thing would be to stay out of Asakusa. Just lie low.

As he slid behind the wheel, he smelled the sweet scent of bay rum.

Things were black for a moment, then Harry discovered himself lying on the street and looking up at Beechum, who straddled Harry and pressed the edge of a cricket bat across his neck. Tears dripped from Beechum's face, gone a chalky red.

"Stay away from my wife," Beechum was saying. "Hands off my wife."

Bigger things at play than adultery, Harry would have said if he could. Diplomatic deafness. The emperor's new maps.

"Or I'll kill you," Beechum sobbed.

What was it DeGeorge said? Harry thought. "Get in line."

Which earned him another swing of the bat.

His next conscious moment, Harry was on the sidewalk, unable to do more than raise his head and scan for Beechum, who was gone. An unusual amount of car traffic rolled by on the other side of the car, in the direction of government ministries. Harry concentrated on throwing up. There were dues in adultery. This was one of them.

Harry next found himself on his feet, rocking like a rocking chair and throwing up on the rear fender of his car. He had a knob the size of a golf ball behind his right ear and a tendency to lurch to one side with every step. Two old women with street brooms giggled with embarrassment while he retrieved his hat and reshaped it.

"Too much to drink, maybe," one of the ladies suggested.

"One too many. I apologize for worrying you."

"You should walk," the first lady said. "Drink less, walk more."

WALK? The idea appalled Harry, but he drove only as far as Tokyo Station before the smell of Beechum's bay rum made him start to retch again and he decided that a long nocturnal stroll was just what he needed to reset his inner ear and stop veering to the side. He had fourteen hours to go before the plane, and as Alice had suggested, the smart thing would be to avoid Asakusa altogether, not to mention Ishigami and the Thought Police. It would have been nice to find Michiko, but he had to consider his own neck first. So, what the doctor ordered was a long, therapeutic walk. For an insomniac, a piece of cake.

Cars were gathering at ministry offices, but this late, the plaza between the palace and Tokyo Station was quiet, the palace bridges patrolled by a few guards with white-socked rifles. It was wonderful how, on the eve of war, the emperor's tranquility was maintained. Either the palace was a sinkhole in the middle of reality, or the rest of the world was the emperor's dream. It almost made a man tiptoe as he went by.

Foreigners who walked the city alone at night were suspect, but under streetlamps, with his face shadowed by his hat, the gaijin in Harry disappeared. The cool air refreshed him. As he went by the station, he took on a shorter, busier stride. Mastered his direction, swung a cigarette vigorously with every step, and policemen automatically nodded as he went by. One of the necessaries of being a hustler was resilience. He'd piss a little pinker was all. Harry was tempted to pass the night playing cards, but he knew that he wasn't quite up to a serious game. Also, the less he hit his regular haunts, the better, even if he could practically feel the cards being laid down in Asakusa, hear the snap of the pasteboard, see the tiers of smoke above the table. No one was playing at the ballroom, of course. Haruko had that table to herself.

The advantage of a great city was its labyrinth of streets and alleys. Especially at night, when drab housefronts turned to the fanciful silhouettes of Chinese eaves and ghostly shirts hung on rods to dry. The discreet murmur of geishas issued from a willow house, a flash like brilliant tropical birds in the dark. Even the meanest alley might have a shrine, candles and coins set before a pair of stone fox gods with eyes of green glass. Foxes could change into women, it was well known, so any encounter with a fox at night had an element of danger for a man.

East of the palace was a warren of bookstores and print shops. Harry remembered an evening as warm and humid as a bathhouse, the height of Tokyo's unbearable summer, when Kato had dragged Oharu and Harry to a printer there to pick up a surprise edition of a book entitled *Fifty Views of Fuji*. It was just a sketchbook, with a print run of one. The pictures had been quickly but deftly done. In each, Mount Fuji's white skirt hung in the distance, but in the foreground were Asakusa's narrow alleys, temple festivals and music halls, with Harry either stealing an orange, picking a pocket or smoking at a backstage door, a complete catalog of juvenile delinquency and petty crime. Harry was speechless; if the emperor had awarded him the Order of the Golden Kite, he could not have been more overcome.

Better yet, as they left the printer, Oharu noticed a cart selling balls of shaved ice in paper cones. Three syrups were offered: strawberry, melon and lemon. "Hurry, before it all melts," Oharu said, and it was true, a lake spread from the drain hole of the cart. Kato flavored his ice with brandy from a flask. Harry chose lemon. Oharu took both strawberry and melon.

The lemon ice was tart and fresh. The problem was that it melted so instantly and the cone soaked through so quickly that Harry had to finish his ice in a race. Oharu, with two cones of ice, wasn't fast enough. Red stripes of strawberry ran down one forearm and orange melon down the other. She wiped her hands with a handkerchief, but that left her arms sticky, and she seemed in such distress that what Harry did seemed natural. He took her arm and licked the syrup off, first the sweet strawberry and then the subtler track of the melon, mixed with the salt of her skin.

"We're going to spoil the boy," Kato said. "He'll never be able to go home now."

Harry realized that, moving for hours as mechanically as a sleep-walker, he had returned to familiar ground. The tea merchant, the willow house, the communal pump. He was on his own block, a black space suspended between corner lamps. It was hard to believe that, only two nights before, the Happy Paris had overflowed with customers drinking, boasting, admiring the Record Girl.

The club was shuttered and locked, but he heard the murmur of a saxophone. As Harry unlocked the door, the music stopped. He entered and locked the door behind him. The club was dark except for a moonbeam glow around the jukebox, the lowest setting of the light, where Michiko stood with a gun.

"I'm back," said Harry.

Michiko stared as if he were an apparition. "Where were you?"

"Looking for you."

"Not soon enough. Were you busy, Harry?"

"A lot of places to look."

"And women to see?"

"Here and there." Trying to stop a war, but Michiko always personalized things, Harry thought.

She turned the gun around and offered it to him. "Why don't you just kill me, Harry?"

"No, thanks. I can see the headline, 'Tragic End of Woman with Gaijin.'"

" 'Lovers End Life Together.' "

" 'Together'? After I kill you, I'm honor-bound to kill myself? My honor doesn't stretch that far. To be honest, I'd cheat."

"Okay." She turned the gun around and aimed at him. "I waited at the ballroom, then I waited here."

"Did you see Ishigami?"

"No, but I heard him."

"Heard what?" Harry didn't like the way she put it.

Michiko brought the words out slowly, as if from a hole she didn't dare look into. "Haruko came for her stupid dress and hat. So we changed. I was in Tetsu's office when someone else came. When I went out, Haruko was dead."

"Where was Tetsu? Where was everyone else?"

"He had tattoo fever. He chased everyone out and went home. He said I could wait."

"Why were you in his office?"

"I didn't want anyone to see me. I was ashamed."

"Why?"

"Haruko said that you were going to China with an Englishwoman. She said you weren't coming back. Is that true?" She turned the gun toward herself, and he saw that the safety was off. He hated emotional blackmail. At the same time, he admired her nerve, the way she coolly placed the barrel to her temple.

"No, I said good-bye to my English friend and her husband. They were very good about it."

"You're lying."

"Maybe, but I'm back."

"You'll be gone tomorrow, so what does it matter?"

Harry punched in "Mood Indigo." "You like this one? Ellington uses a baritone sax instead of a tenor to carry the lead. Did I ever tell you that before?"

"Every time."

"Well, it's a classy touch. I saw him at the Starlight in L.A., the whole band in white jackets. Duke was in tails."

"Don't do it," she said when Harry reached for her.

"What have I got to lose?" He laid her cheek on his shoulder. She resisted for a moment, but they really fit together, he thought. A person couldn't shoot herself and dance at the same time. They didn't dance so much as drift. The great thing about "Mood Indigo" was that a couple couldn't dance too slowly.

"How many times did you play this song tonight?" he asked.

"Ten times? Twenty?"

"You must really like it."

She said, "Not anymore."

The turntable clicked to a stop. An arm rotated the record to the vertical and let it roll against a soft bumper of felt. For a moment she stayed in his arms.

Harry heard a clicking noise from the shutters. They were metal, padlocked from the outside against burglars, effectively blinding and trapping Harry and Michiko within. There was no light outside since the neon sign had been broken. It was a Sunday night, a working day tomorrow, the weekend over, time for women to rest their heads on wooden pillows and for the police to knee up to office heaters. No one abroad but goblins, cats and insomniacs. Harry threw on the club's interior lights and located the source of the sound, a sword tip that vigorously probed one shutter slat and then the next like a tongue. What had he expected? It was just what Alice warned him about. So far, the shutters were holding.

"Are you staying?" Michiko asked.

"How can I get out?"

"No, are you *staying*?"

Staying? Harry had never asked himself the question in exactly that way.

"I wouldn't leave you. Couldn't leave you."

With those words, Harry pictured the plane, his getaway, the Air Nippon DC-3 in its hangar at Haneda Field. It shone in the dark. Then it disappeared.

24

H ARRY AND MICHIKO retreated to the apartment. Even there, every sound was Ishigami. A drunk stumbled in the dark against the club and was Ishigami breaking through the shutters. A cat padded across the roof and was Ishigami prying off the tiles.

Harry assumed that Willie and Iris had weighed anchor. Alice would be packing for Hong Kong. She might be surprised to be traveling alone, but she didn't need Harry, all she'd needed was a head start. Once she was away from him, she'd see what a narrow escape she'd had. He hadn't meant to mislead her. Alice was light and sanity. Michiko exercised a much stronger call, the dark where a rib was taken. Being attacked by Beechum didn't dissuade Harry. With a cricket bat? No, it was a matter of Harry acknowledging that the Nippon Air DC-3 had been a delusion, a fantasy. In the end, he had no choice. There was simply Michiko, all else paled. Even this situation, being trapped with Michiko, now seemed strangely inevitable. He had watched Kabuki all his life and finally had a role. *Exit, pursued by samurai.* Only there was no exit.

Harry fed the beetle paper-thin slices of cucumber—with pets came responsibilities—and asked Michiko for the details of what happened at the ballroom. She said she had gone there from Haruko's as Harry asked. Tetsu, sick with tattoo fever, had closed down the ballroom and gone home. Michiko waited alone in semidark for an hour before Haruko arrived, determined to reclaim her favorite outfit. What Haruko offered in exchange was her second-best dress and information about Harry and the plane to China. They traded in the women's lounge. Haruko was still there when Michiko, too disgraced to face anyone, slipped into Tetsu's office at the sound of someone at the ball-room door. Whoever it was, they were quick, in shoes or boots rather than clogs or sandals. Michiko heard no conversation, only a chair dragged across the floor and footsteps that retreated as swiftly as they had come. When Michiko emerged, she found Haruko propped up at the table with the box. Like a mouse and a hawk, she said, it was that fast.

Harry asked, "Didn't it strike you that, wearing a dress and hat she had just taken back from you, with her hair styled like yours, Haruko looked like you?"

"You thought it was me? You were worried?"

"Well, with their head in a box, a lot of people look alike."

Mist started to drain from the street. A woman with a lantern and a roll of kindling on her back bowed deeply to a shadow in the willow-house gate. The lantern briefly lit Ishigami's eyes, his field uniform and cap, his sword worn blade up. Harry considered a shot but knew that with his powers of marksmanship, he was more likely to hit a cat than Ishigami. The pipes and chimes of other morning peddlers were approaching. If the colonel was going to attack in the dark, time was running out. Under the circumstances, Harry found Michiko's faith touching. She sat on her heels, a magician's assistant waiting for a trick.

"Happy?" he asked, because in a curious way, she seemed to be.

"Yes."

"Why? Right now, being with me is not like winning a lottery. Tell me, Michiko, because I've always wondered, how much English do you understand?"

"Why should I understand English? We're in Japan."

"How much of the songs on the jukebox do you understand?"

She shrugged.

Harry suspected that had always been part of the appeal of the Record Girl, her vamping to lyrics that were a mystery to her.

"For example," Harry said, "the songs about love."

She nodded.

"You only mouth them," he said.

"I think most people only mouth them, American or Japanese."

"But you and I have never actually said it to each other, have we? 'I love you,' we've never said."

"Americans say, Japanese do."

"Ah, and love is different in Japan."

"Yes, and you're here." She caught Harry's glance out the window. "Is the colonel still there?"

"He's not going anywhere. He's after us."

"After you. He already cut my head off."

An electronic squawk startled Harry. He remembered the loudspeaker hanging on the lamppost at the corner. The pipes and bells of vendors ceased as they listened to the navy anthem pouring from the speaker.

The music quit, followed by a voice. The voice was humble and excited. The voice flowed through the gray winter morning and multiplied from street to street and house to house. Harry turned on the radio and the voice filled his room: "We repeat to you this urgent news. Imperial General Headquarters announced this morning, December eighth, that the Imperial Army and Navy have begun hostilities against American and British forces in the Pacific at dawn today."

Harry read his watch by the light of the radio dial. Six-thirty. "Forces in the Pacific"? What did that mean, Harry wondered. Pearl Harbor? The Philippines? Singapore? Hong Kong? But could the Japanese navy have caught Pearl napping? It seemed impossible, except for the mundane human fact that the U.S. Navy held its Christmas parties on December 6. Across the dateline, it was still December 7, a day for sleeping in at Pearl.

"Will this mean war?" Michiko asked.

"It is war. We're in it now," said Harry.

Alice Beechum would not be flying out on Air Nippon. Air Nippon was going nowhere; the flight to Hong Kong was as much a ruse as Tojo's ride in the park. The radio repeated, "The Imperial General Staff announced this morning . . ." This time the announcement was followed not with the dumb astonishment of a waking population but with spontaneous clapping and cries of "Banzai!" in the street. People opened their windows to share the excitement. As the sky lightened, vendors, the lame and burdened, bowed to one another, standing taller as they straightened up. Schoolchildren erupted from their homes to cheer as if Japan's warplanes were passing directly overhead.

"He's gone." Harry realized that Ishigami had dematerialized during the announcement. The gateway was empty.

Michiko joined Harry at the window. "Where to?"

"I don't know, but it's going to get a little crowded here. After the declaration the police will round up Americans. Probably already started."

"What will happen?"

"They'll hold us in cells for a while and then exchange us. I'm not exactly Abe Lincoln or Andy Hardy, but I am an American citizen."

"You aren't like other Americans. The police will kill you."

"I have connections."

"That's why."

"The embassy will have a list for repatriation. I'll be on it."

"You must go to the embassy and be sure."

"I've never asked for their protection." He had always been proud of his independence.

Michiko said, "If you wait here, you're dead."

She'd put her finger on it. War was God's way of overturning the card game. Even Harry was outraged.

"Maybe the war will be over quickly," she said.

"After an attack like this? It had to be a surprise to work, and if it was a surprise, it will be a fight to the death."

"Why are you on the Americans' side?"

Harry watched a boy run by with an open umbrella of oiled paper and lacquered spokes. The boy spun the umbrella so that warplanes painted on the paper chased one another. It was a handsome umbrella, much like the planes themselves.

"Because they'll win."

EACH RADIO REPORT began with the opening bars of the "Warship March," and with every account, Tokyo seemed to rise farther above sea level. Sun flags festooned streetcars, framed shopwindows, waved in hands. The air turned intoxicating. Eyes grew brighter and faces flushed with pride as loudspeakers broadcast news of an astonishing raid on Hawaii and the sinking of the entire American Battleship Row, as if history's menacing giant had been slain with a single righteous blow. Paced by a military beat that poured from the radio, the entire city seemed in motion, becoming the new center of the world.

Harry left the apartment first, in case the colonel was still lurking. He wore a dark suit and fedora with a germ mask over his face, like any midlevel salaryman afflicted with a head cold but duty-bound to go to work. Michiko emerged minutes later in a beret, knitted cashmere coat and bright red lips, like a smart little sailboat challenging a squall. Her pace was quick enough so that by the time he reached the subway station, Michiko was only twenty feet behind. The throngs were themselves some protection—there was a giddy milling among the turnstiles. Just in case Ishigami did appear, Harry had tucked a boning knife wrapped in cloth into his waistband. Michiko carried the gun in a handbag, ready to plug a colonel of the Imperial Army in the middle of a station. Altogether, Harry thought, one hell of a girl. Loudspeakers advised all troops to return to their regiments, though Harry believed that Ishigami was no longer strictly responding to orders. The clumsy blows on Haruko, for example, suggested a deterioration of the colonel's usually immaculate style. On the other hand, Michiko's likening the suddenness of the attack to a hawk and mouse sounded right.

Although rhythmic clapping broke out on the train, Harry feigned drowsiness on the short ride to Tokyo Station rather than show his eyes. There the entire country seemed to pour out the station doors.

Harry and Michiko were swept along by crowds to the plaza that faced the imperial palace, where thousands silently knelt along the moat. Men removed their hats, women set down their red-stitched scarves and trusted their prayers to a morning wind just as, not too many hours before, in the mid-Pacific, their sons had stood on the decks of aircraft carriers and launched their planes into the wind of the new day. Half of Harry wanted to rail at what a gimmick the emperor was, a nobody for a thousand years, just a mantelpiece curio; the other half had to bow to not only the beauty of the con but its beauty, period, the sweeping rampart of the walls and brocade of golden trees, perfect as both a screen and royal throne under a dome of blue. No imperial figure appeared on the battlements or bridge. No cannonade hastened the drop of a single leaf. Serenity, more than anything, was the mark of a demigod. A troop of Hitler Youth arrived in shorts and caps only to have their "Sieg Heil!" brushed aside. Responding to shadows on the moat, carp rose and tinged the green murk gold, reminding Harry of the tael bars he had wasted.

Harry pointed out the Datsun parked at the south end of the station, but Michiko wanted to walk.

"And be seen." She was definite about that.

MOUNTED POLICE blocked the gate of the American embassy as if they'd trapped the Dillinger gang, which seemed, to Harry, to be going overboard, especially since down the street they'd left the embassy garage unguarded. He situated Michiko at a French café on the corner while he went through the garage door.

He pulled off his mask. The embassy he had known as a boy had been destroyed by earthquake, and a new residency of white stucco and black eaves stood at the top of a long compound landscaped with fountains and arbors like a college campus. However, the activity around them this morning suggested an anthill half kicked in. Attachés and secretaries huffed from building to building under the weight of cartons. All these Americans he had never seen before. Amazing. Moving was never easy, Harry thought, especially under the pressure of a declaration of war, and he was happy to help a clerk pick up folders she had dropped. She said that Roy Hooper was with the ambassador, which Harry took as invitation enough to wander into the official residency. No one seemed to be home. Harry was impressed by the bronzed doors, central hall and grand staircase of polished teak, a ballroom with a movie projector and screen, salon with piano, walnut-paneled smoking room, separate banquet hall empty except for a card table with an unfinished jigsaw puzzle of cowboys and Indians. The ambassador's own desk sat on a Turkish carpet and held a silver-framed photo of Bobby Jones and a portrait of Franklin Roosevelt signed "With admiration and warmest regards to Good Old Joe from Frank." The window looked down on the front driveway, where the ambassador and a pair of aides seemed to be effectively stalling Japanese diplomats in top hats while document destruction went on. No Hooper.

The chancery, down the hill, was the center of mayhem, where staff spilled as many files as they carried down the stairwells. Harry found Hooper's office, a room with woodblock prints of Tokyo. Again no Hooper, but Harry shut the door behind himself.

The office safe was wide open and empty, but what he was after wasn't particularly secret. The desk drawers that opened easily were stuffed with economic analyses and clippings from Japanese magazines and journals. He forced a locked drawer by hammering in a letter opener with his flask and found what he was after, a master list of American citizens residing in Japan: Foreign Service officers and staff, businessmen and agents, teachers and instructors, medical doctors and nurses, missionaries, military on liaison duty, foreign correspondents, American employees of either non-Japanese or Japanese companies, sailors or ships' officers, Japanese wives of Americans, women and children, invalids or anyone requiring medical care, a list for every category, hundreds of names in all. "Harry Niles" was entered vaguely under "Self-employed." A second list was of Americans for whom the embassy would request repatriation or safe internment. It was identical to the master list except for one name crossed out, Harry's.

The smell of smoke insinuated itself into the office. Harry joined the traffic on the stairwell and asked, "Where's Hooper?"

A man negotiating a carton around a corner asked, "Who are you?"

Harry began to tip the carton. "Where?"

"Jesus, fellow. Below, in the code room."

Harry pushed ahead to the basement and followed the smoke to an open door where Hooper directed a bucket brigade. Inside the room, desks had been pushed aside to make space for iron-wire wastebaskets set on metal chairs. Files and codes had been stuffed into the baskets and set on fire, flames wrestling like torches and spewing smoke that collected under the ceiling and snowed black confetti. A nervous circle of diplomats stood ready with their pails.

"Was I right?" Harry asked.

Hooper almost dropped his pail from surprise. "Get out. You're the last person who should be here."

"Was I right about the attack? Did you ever tell the ambassador? I saw him trying to repel boarders. A little late."

"He did everything he could. You have no idea of the efforts he made."

"On the golf course?"

"Look, this is a top-secret area."

"Was. It's a firetrap now." Harry peered in. The staff that wasn't feeding the baskets were dismantling what looked like hooded, over-sized typewriters.

"This is secret material, and you, Harry, are the most notorious collaborator in Japan."

"First, how could I collaborate, when we haven't been at war until today? Second, I warned you about the attack on Pearl."

"That just proves it, in the eyes of some people."

"So you did tell someone."

"I passed it on to the experts."

"Who ignored it."

"Harry, we've been getting ten warnings a day."

"But this was from me. You knew me, Hoop. You knew it was the real deal, and you let it sit."

"Harry, I don't have time to argue."

314

"I don't warn you, I lose. I warn you, I lose. What kind of game is that?"

"It's not a game. We weighed your information with all the rest. We treated you like anyone else."

"Bullshit. I'm not on the list, Hoop. I'm the only American in Japan who's not on the list for repatriation."

"I wouldn't—"

Harry pulled out the list. "From your office."

"That's a preliminary—"

"Don't lie to me. I always tell you, 'The Lord hates a lying tongue.' Don't do it."

"People do feel that you have associated too closely with the Japanese. Maybe even switched allegiance. There are all the scandals and shady activities you've been involved in. The fact is, for a lot of people, you're not the kind of citizen we necessarily want back."

"Suddenly you have standards? George Washington had slaves. Look around, not a slave on me."

"I get it. But, just for your information, I did have your name down on the original list for repatriation."

"Who took it off? The ambassador? The British leaned on you? Was it Beechum?"

"You should have left Beechum's wife alone. It's a small community."

"Beechum, then? How can you let a hairless limey run American-Japanese affairs?"

"That's the funny part. It wasn't the British and it wasn't us. It was the Japanese. I'm sorry. No negotiations, they want you right here."

The smoke thickened and lowered. Pages that floated half aflame were doused with water. Harry took a step back, not from the heat of the wastebasket but from the staggering flush of his own error. The Japanese? The Japanese had taken away first the plane and now the boat. There weren't many other ways off an island.

Hooper asked, "What did you do, Harry? You did something they want to hold you for. How did you know about the attack, really? Because you were absolutely right." As the baskets turned to bonfires, staff threw precautionary dashes of water. Hooper smiled at the scene. "Remember being kids the first time we were here? The fireworks, the fireflies? Lord, we had fun. I always wondered why the Japanese didn't kick you out. Now I wonder why they won't let you go. Got a cigarette?" Harry tapped out a couple and gave one to Hooper, who spit loose tobacco toward the fire and gazed at the flames. "Remember, you once bet me five dollars you could get a fish in and out of a sake bottle without breaking the glass, then you switched the fish with an eel. In and out, slick as butter. The high cost of education, you said." He pulled Harry close enough to whisper. "I used that trick the whole summer. Made fifty dollars. Thought my old man would have a stroke."

In and out like an eel in a bottle? Not a bad trick, Harry thought. He wished he could do it now.

"I'll miss you, Harry," Hooper said.

"See you, Hoop."

Which wasn't likely, both men knew.

Hooper went back to the delicate task of incinerating papers in a closed room, but he got inspired before Harry cleared the door. "The reason they want you is that you screwed them, didn't you? Somehow you screwed them."

HARRY GATHERED MICHIKO at the café, and they walked back toward the car, a stylish couple on a sunny day, ignoring the constant bombardment of military music from loudspeakers.

"So, I'm set," he said. "They figure one month, two at the most, and they'll ship us home on the *President Cleveland*. They'll put me in steerage, but I'll start a card game and make a fortune. Serve them right. What about you? I'll get back here as soon as I can, but you'll want to do something in the meantime."

"During the war?"

"That's right."

"Don't you think it will be over soon?"

"I wouldn't bet on it."

She edged infinitesimally closer, tantamount to touching. "I'll wait."

"But what will you do?"

"That is inconsequential. I'll be here."

They walked for a while.

"Okay."

The street was like Park Avenue, with plane trees and canopies and people with little dogs, so Harry was unprepared for a fracas as the American manager of First National City was hustled out of his apartment house and into a car full of military police in plainclothes. He waved and shouted, "Hey, Harry, stand me a drink now?" The attention of the Kempeitai turned to Harry. Of the different arms of the law a person could be seized by, the Kempeitai were the worst. The officer in charge had a face that was creased down the middle with the sides slightly mismatched.

"Identity papers? American? We're taking in all Americans."

"You may want to radio in my name."

"Why would I bother?"

"You may."

The officer pressed Harry against the marble facing of the building. He riffled through Harry's papers, then again, and took them to the radio operator in the car. It wasn't the big punch you saw coming that hurt you, Harry thought, but the little punch you didn't see. The officer returned and nodded toward the sound of the loudspeaker.

"There'll be more news soon."

"I'm sure there will be."

The officer included Michiko in his study. "You like Japanese women?"

"Yes," said Harry.

"And you like gaijin?"

"Yes," Michiko said.

The officer told Harry, "Get on your knees."

"My knees?"

"That's right."

Before Harry could move, the music in the loudspeakers died.

317

Harry felt the street and all of Tokyo go quiet to take in the vigorous, raspy voice of General Tojo speaking from headquarters. Tojo was one of the Kempeitai's own, and they came to attention for the general's sharp, explosive Japanese. Well, give them credit, Harry thought. Less than a century before, they didn't have a steamship, railroad or rifle to their name. They were a quaint little people who shuffled around in silk robes and sipped tea. "Monkey Island," the Chinese called Japan, because it imitated China. Until the Japanese imitated the Prussian army and Royal Navy, humiliated China and sank the Russian fleet, and, now, with bright Yamato spirit, were taking on both the British and American empires in one go.

"I am resolved," Tojo said, "to dedicate myself, body and soul, to the country, and to set at ease the august mind of our sovereign. And I believe that every one of you, my fellow countrymen, will not care for your life but gladly share in the honor to make of yourself His Majesty's humble shield. The key to victory lies in a 'faith in victory.' For twenty-six hundred years since it was founded, our empire has never known defeat. This record alone is enough to produce a conviction in our ability to crush any enemy no matter how strong."

An announcer followed with more news of annihilating blows delivered to the enemy and victories unprecedented in human history, the Battle of Trafalgar and Little Big Horn rolled up in one, but lacking details of how many battleships, cruisers or aircraft carriers were hit, let alone docks or depots.

The officer had not forgotten Harry. In fact, the speech had fired him with more pugnacity. "Get on your knees! Both get on your knees. You have soiled this sacred day."

Harry said, "Excuse me, the lady—"

"She is not a lady, she is a whore. Your knees!"

"No," Michiko said.

She was calmly going for the gun in her bag when the officer was interrupted and called to his car. He sat for a radio conversation that he contributed nothing to, and a minute later he returned with Harry's papers and half his face red.

"You can go. Take the woman and leave."

Harry said, "Thank you."

The banker laughed. He had been watching the whole scene through an open car door. "It still works, I don't believe it. The Niles luck."

Harry and Michiko did as the Kempeitai officer suggested. Harry's legs operated stiffly, while Michiko was smooth enough for two.

Harry said, "Connected and protected, even now." All the same, he slipped on his germ mask. He didn't feel quite that connected or protected. Shozo and Ishigami had let Harry walk, and now the Kempeitai?

When he was a kid working his way across California, Harry once worked at a slaughterhouse, prodding cattle with a long pole as they went through a chute toward the kill room. He had to keep the steers moving so they wouldn't kick one another, get tangled on fence boards or otherwise make a fuss. Part of his job was to spot any animal that looked particularly diseased and move it into a side chute so that it could be killed separately. That was how Harry felt now. Not connected or protected but shunted aside.

WAR TRANSFORMED THE CITY. Flags grew like flowers. Shopgirls and office boys, lured by the din of loudspeakers, ran after a fire engine bringing a fireman to the station for military service. His engine mates carried poles with long fringes that they twirled like lion heads on pikes to the beat of clappers, while the draftee rode on top, cheeks red from sake and the honor. And the radios sang,

You and I are cherry blossoms,
Having bloomed, we've resolved to die
But we will meet again at Yasukuni,
Blooming on the same treetop.

Harry felt the thinness of his disguise. Michiko, on the other hand, took the low winter light and glowed. The beret lazed against her hair. Her stride made the loose cashmere slide along her legs. Despite the excitement of the fire engine, the clamor of the loudspeakers and the lines at the newspaper stands, people noticed Michiko and gave way. To make sure no one missed who was with her, she took possession of Harry's arm. She seemed so radiant that he hated to point out how dangerous her run-in with the Kempeitai had almost been. Not just dangerous but suicidal.

"I suppose so," she agreed.

"Well, it may be petty of me, but I still want to come out of this war alive."

"Why? If we're together, that's what matters."

"And being alive."

She shrugged as if Harry were dwelling on nonessentials, and it finally occurred to him why she was so happy. Michiko had always admired lovers who sealed their lives together. There might be no romantic volcano or waterfall handy for a dive, but there were so many other means—Ishigami, Shozo, Kempeitai, the gun in her bag—that she was virtually skipping.

25

Harry and Michiko drove around the Ginza, cruising by the addresses of other Americans. Everywhere they saw the black sedans of the Kempeitai and went on circling while the needle in the gas gauge dropped. Once it touched bottom, that would be it, but Harry went on circling because he didn't know where to take Michiko. Anywhere they stopped, there would be Kempeitai, Thought Police or Ishigami. They were all after Harry, not her, but Michiko was twice as brave as he was, and she wouldn't have a chance.

News continued to come over the car radio. Japanese planes had bombed Singapore, inflicting heavy damage. Another wave had caught American bombers on the ground in the Philippines. When Tojo returned on the radio to speak for the emperor—a mortal speaking for Someone too exalted to be heard directly—Harry pulled into the shadow of a railroad viaduct, removed his mask and shared a smoke with Michiko.

"We, by grace of heaven . . . seated on the throne of a line unbroken for ages eternal, enjoin upon ye, our brave and loyal subjects . . ." And the people swallowed it, Harry thought. It was a royal horse pill, but people swallowed it every time, all over the world, from "England expects every man to do his duty" to "The Shores of Tripoli." He found the beetle box in his jacket, released the prisoner from cotton batting and set it on the dash, where it raised its rhino horn and moved stiffly, like a rusty machine. "It has been truly unavoidable and far from our wishes that our empire has been brought to cross swords with the United States and Great Britain," but Japan's enemies had disturbed the peace of East Asia in their "inordinate ambition to dominate the Orient." My country right or wrong, thought Harry. He closed the windshield vent to protect the beetle from its own curiosity. This was no stay-at-home insect, this was a bold explorer. "Our empire, for its existence and self-defense, has no other recourse but to appeal to arms." Natch, thought Harry. Hitler invaded Poland in self-defense. ". . . in our confident expectation . . . that the sources of evil will be speedily eradicated and an enduring peace immutably established, raising and enhancing the glory of the Imperial Way within and without our homeland." The beetle ventured out to the dashboard clock and stood as if surveying its domain while a million shouts of "Banzai!" broke out across the city. Five o'clock; the beetle seemed to point out the time.

"Maybe we should get married," Harry said.

"Why?"

"Things being unsettled as they are, we could retire to a place in the country and live the simple life. You would have children and I would have my beetles. I would walk my beetles around the garden on strings of silk."

"What would you do for a living?"

"Run the village shell game. Drop jazz, pick up the shamisen, mumble around in an old kimono. That's not bad, is it? We'd just sit under the mulberry tree and listen to the silkworms munching on the leaves."

"They're just waiting to pick you up."

"As for the wedding, well, that's pretty simple. Do it country-style and just share a drink." He brought out his silver flask. "Presto, you're married." He continued to pay attention to the beetle, to make sure it didn't slide off the dashboard.

"I'm not going to let them take you," she said.

"Let's stick to the subject, do you want to get married or not? I'm afraid this is a one-time offer."

She looked at the flask. "This is the best you can do?"

"It's the thought that counts."

Michiko took a healthy swallow, and the interior of the Datsun filled with fumes of good Scotch. Harry carefully followed suit, watching in case she decided to pull the gun and execute a honeymoon suicide by surprise. Besides, it would scare the beetle.

"We'll get old and gum away on tofu and tea," he said.

"What about sex?"

"I didn't know you liked sex that much. I take it back, I take it back."

"That has always been good, even when you have been bad."

"May I?" He leaned forward and lightly put his lips on hers. He knew she disliked kissing on the mouth, but all the same, she let him linger for a moment.

"It's been interesting, Harry. It's always been that."

The street had fallen into a shadow that put Harry in mind of two sailors sitting in a lifeboat by a sinking ship, waiting for the great, overturned hull to go under and suck them down with it, this moment or the next.

"Listen." Michiko put her hand up suddenly. "A sound I heard when Haruko died."

Harry heard the usual traffic echoes, the nasty buzz of unseen trams and the squeal of a train crossing the viaduct.

"I didn't catch it."

"Did you feel it?"

"No."

Something, however, had prompted the beetle to raise its head, and the lifting of such a magnificent horn was its undoing. It slid down the dash, legs scratching and scrambling, until it fell into Harry's palm. He let the beetle climb round and round his hands like a treadmill before he handed the insect to Michiko and shifted into first.

Michiko was occupied enough with replacing the beetle in its box for Harry to take away her bag with the gun. She looked up sharply, betrayed.

"Just for a minute," Harry said. As he pulled away from the curb and started toward the train station, the car down the street did the same.

The nearer they drew to the station, the more the sidewalks filled with exuberant draftees, families and well-wishers, newsboys, vendors of war bonds and sun flags, most arriving simply to draw on the proximity of the Son of Heaven. The throng Harry had seen earlier on the plaza between the station and the imperial palace had doubled. Wives had rushed out with their thousand-stitch belts. More than one veteran had put on his old uniform and medals. Well, this was Buckingham Palace and the Vatican rolled up in one, Harry thought. He looked over. In her beret and cashmere coat, Michiko was French enough for Kato. With her ivory face and lidded eyes, better than French. Traffic police tried to maintain lanes for buses and trams, which was like trying to stop the waves of the sea. Michiko could, though. She was brave enough to part the sea. Harry dug out the last tael bars, tucked them in the bag with the gun and reached across to open Michiko's door.

"Out." He stopped the car.

"I won't—"

Harry tossed her bag out the door. As Michiko stepped out to retrieve it, he stepped on the accelerator and left her in the street. A policeman bleated on a whistle, but Harry swung behind an army truck and passed through the main crush. In the mirror, he saw Michiko fall behind a wall of flags.

No one seemed to notice the gaijin driving toward the road along the river. In the general euphoria, people were blind to details. As the workday ended, they swept into the street, most headed to the palace or Hibiya Park but also moving in countercurrents along the river. Cadets waved flags from the roofs of the river buses, the boats competing in cheers. A collegiate type sliding by in a one-man scull hoisted a bottle of champagne. On the sidewalk, shopgirls linked arms to sing, "*Mount Saiko is deep in mist, waves rise on the river. Sounds that travel from afar are waves or soldiers' cries, brightly, brightly, brightly!*" As night came on, Harry became aware of streetlamps staying unlit, the first blackout of the war. A policeman walked along the cars, ordering their headlights off, although it hardly mattered with all the paper lanterns on the sidewalk. Traffic inched. Looking in the rearview mirror, Harry couldn't find any particular car following him, although he *felt* something, as Michiko had said. He didn't doubt he had been followed; he hadn't exactly hidden. If anyone wondered where he was going, so did he, apart from simply gravitating to territory most familiar to him. Which gave him ample opportunity to contemplate the folly of toying with history. History was celebrating all around him. He hadn't changed a thing, except for losing DeGeorge and Haruko their heads. Michiko was angry, which was bad enough, but she was alive and had a gun to defend herself with. Most important, she wouldn't be trying to defend him. That was her weak spot. People called back and forth. Harry rolled down his window to hear that rallies were gathering at Ueno and Asakusa. The radio played "The Battleship March" over and over. Paper lanterns streamed, creating a soft melding of people into one entity, one heart, one Yamato spirit.

Azuma Bridge was a span of candles and lanterns above the starry water. There were spots of rowdiness, but over all spread an awe-filled hush of self-astonishment that, in a single day, they had vaulted to the top of the world. They had dared and they had won. On the radio, announcers made the point again and again that each victory was made possible only by the "virtues of the emperor," but they were all demigods now. Here it was barely the second week in December, and everyone had had their lucky New Year's dream, the wealth of Asia and the Pacific in their hands. As he approached Asakusa Park in traffic that was almost stopped, the Datsun coughed and died. Harry abandoned the car in the middle of the street, sliding the beetle into a jacket pocket and adjusting the knife in his belt. Despite the blackout, the movie marquees were a bank of blinding tungsten lights. A cardboard John Wayne was the first Western face Harry had seen in hours. He debated with himself whether to hide his own face behind the germ mask. "To be or not to be," Hamlet asked. "I yam what I yam," said Popeye. Harry kept it off.

Asakusa Park and the Kannon grounds were a nighttime festival. Lanterns lit the avenue of souvenir stalls leading to the double-roofed temple. Whole families were out for a spontaneous promenade, father followed by wife, trailed by children in descending size. Fortune-teller tents were swamped. Monks, too, did a land-office business with divining rods next to confectioners who fashioned candy cranes and turtles, symbols of long life. Harry drew a few astonished looks, but he was so familiar to so many shopkeepers and regulars that he passed unchallenged. A beam swung against a bell for evening prayer as Harry climbed the temple stairs. From a threshold of red columns came throaty chanting and a haze of joss sticks. Harry remembered reading that during the earthquake that killed Kato and Oharu, a hundred thousand citizens had survived by taking sanctuary at the Kannon and the park. Since then, in crises, it had been the place to come. People crowded around a grate to toss in money, clap their hands and pray. Harry emptied his pockets and said what little he had to say to the few spirits who meant anything to him. His father had written him after Nanking to say he had heard from China missionaries that Harry had helped save lives. Roger Niles wrote that the stories were painful because they were so implausible, no doubt an elaborate fraud. The old man's problem, Harry decided, was that, having confused himself with God, he had to be right without exception. Harry's mother, on the other hand, had great faith in exceptions. She could stand under a tree that he was hiding in and talk as if he were a cherub who happened to be snagged on an upper branch. She deserved a word or two. And Oharu. The expression of surprise painted on her brows. Would she be surprised now? She would lead him to a balcony seat so they could watch together. Kato? Harry had often wondered which work of art Kato had died trying to save. He preferred to think it wasn't one of the French pastiches but a print of Oharu powdering herself at the backstage mirror of the Folies. What had Kato's words been? *I baptize you Japanese.*

"Harry, isn't it fantastic?" Gen stepped next to him at the grate. In a navy coat and cap, he looked like a midshipman in a ticker-tape parade. As the sun had set, the temperature had dropped enough to turn breath to clouds. Gen slapped his hands together to keep them warm; they were gloved, as if he might have to ride away at any second on his motorbike. "What a day! Unbelievable results. Naval Operations is over the moon. I wish I could tell you. What we did today, Harry, was turn the world upside down, nothing less. American control of the Pacific? Gone! British control of Asia? Gone! The white man in Asia? Gone. And oil from the Indies? All we want! Remember how yesterday you were warning me about American bombers over Tokyo? There are no more American bombers, there's hardly an American navy. Admit it, you were wrong. Tokyo will never see an American bomber. We called their bluff, Harry, is what we did."

Harry hadn't seen Gen coming. He looked around. "What are you doing here?"

"Taking a break, first one since yesterday. Naval Operations is crowded, a madhouse, and I needed a shave and a decent cup of coffee. The whole town is crazy, like Times Square on New Year's Eve. It's inspiring. How about you?"

"I've been lucky, too. The Kempeitai started to take me in but made a call and had to let me go."

"Harry, the navy protects its friends. You don't have anything to worry about. Where's Michiko, isn't she along?"

"She ditched me. You know, it turned out that she's some kind of patriotic fanatic. Won't have anything more to do with me. Then there's Haruko."

Gen frowned as if it were unfair how a headless girl could cast a shadow on a glorious day. "Any news there?"

"Not that I know of. I could make a wild guess."

The press of bodies wanting their turn at good fortune pushed Gen and Harry down the steps. As they descended, Gen said, "Troops are being recalled, all leaves are canceled. Ishigami will probably be back in China within a day or two."

"So you think Ishigami did it?" Harry asked.

"Isn't that what you think?"

Harry stopped at the bottom of the stairs for a cigarette. His last pack of Luckies, the end of the line. He shared one with Gen. "Well, I've seen Ishigami at work. The colonel is a real craftsman even under pressure. I saw him take off five heads in a row with only one false swing. Haruko alone suffered two unnecessary cuts. Made me wonder."

"The less we hear about Haruko, the better. You know what I'm looking forward to, Harry? The two of us going back to California

when the war is over. San Francisco. Hollywood. But this time as con-
querors."

"When is that?"

"Soon. The C in C's got it all worked out, a negotiated peace that
leaves the Pacific to us. After all, we won."

A scholar gathered a crowd with an impromptu speech on how the
number eight symbolized Japan: the Eight Views of Japanese places,
the Eight Great Islands that made up Japan, and now the victorious
December Eight. A boy with a popgun startled pigeons. He aimed at
Harry, but the sight of Gen made him post arms and salute. A policeman gave Harry a long scrutiny.

Gen asked, "Is somebody following you?"

"I think so."

"Shozo and Go?"

"I haven't seen them today, but I'm sure I will."

"Have you been back to your place since the news?"

"No."

"Harry, they're probably waiting for you. I've been protecting you,
but what if they take you in and don't call me?"

"You think there's a chance of that?"

"With Thought Police? Are you kidding? I heard that all Americans
except diplomats are being taken to Sugamo Prison. If Shozo and Go
get you back there, they'll throw away the key."

"Well, what's your plan?"

"Get you to a naval base, put you under protective custody until
things get sorted out. If everything goes according to plan, you could
find yourself in a great situation."

"You could put me in charge of Hawaii?"

"The sky's the limit."

Harry blew on his hands. It wasn't this cold in Hawaii. "What's
happening to the British?"

"Same as Americans. The diplomats are going to have to camp out
in the embassy for a while." Gen looked at his watch. "I don't have to
be back at Operations for another hour. Let's just see if Shozo's waiting
for you."

"You'd do that? Go to the club with me?"

"Of course."

As they moved toward the lights of the Rokku, Harry was struck by the deference paid by the crowd to the sight of such a dashing officer, and by how Gen took admiration as his due. The drumming of the temple fell behind, but a separate, deeper drumming kept pace.

"I still can't get over Haruko," Harry said. "Why would Ishigami want to kill her?"

"That's what I asked you when I found you with her."

"And I appreciate that. But why would *anyone* want to kill Haruko? Killing Michiko, that I could understand. Maybe it was a mistake. I have a theory. You know how Haruko imitated Michiko. I can see someone being confused, especially in bad light. Someone goes with certain expectations, hasn't done this sort of thing before and wants to be fast. That might account for the less than accurate swings, too, don't you think? Some people think chopping a head off is like hitting a golf ball. It's not."

Harry shouldered his way through the excitement caused by a newsstand offering postcards of warships. A display of Ginger Rogers photos hit the ground. The drumming grew closer, a bubbling timpani, a reverberation that Harry felt through his bones.

"Another thing," he said. "When a real swordsman uses his sword, he flicks the blood off with a swing that produces a telltale kind of spray that wasn't there with Haruko. Ishigami is sort of fastidious about that."

Gen asked, "Did Michiko see anyone?"

"No, she was gone."

"So what are you saying?"

"I'm just speculating. Whoever it was, what if they were after Michiko and killed the wrong woman? It could be someone who even knew Haruko. If he phoned her or saw her, and if he was a friend, she would have said where Michiko was. She would have even told him how Michiko stole her dress, probably even described it. She did to me."

"She liked to gossip."

"But then, after the call, she got up the nerve to go to the ballroom and get her dress back. No one expected that."

"She was a stupid girl."

"She was crazy about you."

The Rokku marquees, the fanciful swirls and fans and rays of colored lightbulbs, made a cold blaze in the night. Poster samurai hiked their swords. When Harry stopped, the drumming subsided. But a drunk tripped out of a sake stall into the middle of the pavement and collided with a vendor carrying a rack of candlelit paper lanterns. The lanterns caught fire as they rolled around the ground and chased the crowd, laughing, to either side so that Harry had a clear view of Gen's Harley-Davidson idling at a low throb no more than fifty feet behind. Hajime sat on the bike and Ishigami in the sidecar, both in uniform, with the same regimental tab. It dawned on Harry rather late that Hajime had probably served under the colonel in China. Was that a smile on Ishigami's lips or only patience?

Harry was curious. "When did you tell the colonel about you and Hawaii?"

"This morning. Can you imagine me being on the team that planned the raid?"

"Sure, why not?"

"I just wanted one accomplishment, Harry, that was all mine, not handed to me by you or Ishigami. It was top-secret. There was so much pressure from the top to confirm information that only you had."

"Why try to hurt Michiko?"

"She was always in the way. I thought that if she was gone and I was the only one between you and Ishigami that you'd finally tell the truth about the oil tanks. I tried to carry out my assignment, please the colonel and save you, too. Do you understand the problem?"

"That's a balancing act," Harry granted. He stepped on his cigarette. "So now what?"

Gen's tone became more certain. "Now there's no problem."

Ishigami hadn't blinked. It was like being watched by a Buddha. And as the crowd closed in and stamped out the fires, Harry ran. Gen paused a second on his dignity, which allowed Harry to bolt into a movie-house lobby as ornate as a Moorish palace and through the theater doors. On the screen, a Western stagecoach rolled across a black-and-white canyon of wind-sculpted rocks. Harry ran down the aisle and plunged through the emergency door into a back street of noodle shops.

Behind, Gen came out of the emergency door. Harry pulled on his germ mask as he detoured into a pub, through the kitchen frying tofu and a narrow passage encrusted with fish bones to a backyard alley and the window of a prostitute who suggested, "Celebrate our victory. Be the first tonight." Harry caught a glimpse over his shoulder of Gen jumping the garbage of the pub, getting closer. The drumming of the motorcycle swung ahead. The alley ended at a bamboo fence wound in dry vines. Harry climbed the fence and landed in a market of silk flowers and bonsai tied in straw ropes. A geisha started in surprise, leaving a whiff of face powder in the air. Gen soared over the fence. Harry turned through a food market, by trays of squid legs and satiny kelp, spilling a tower of rice tubs in Gen's way. Harry got ahead enough to join the crowd at the shooting range, waiting their turn to fire an air rifle at enemy bombers already repainted from Chinese to American. Gen went by. Harry backtracked through the market and found Hajime waiting alone on the motorcycle. Ishigami was gone. There was no option left for Harry except a fence planted with nails. He tossed the knife over, spread his fingers between the nails and tried to swing himself up and across in one try. Didn't quite, and landed on his back in a house garden with a row of red puncture marks across his shirt. At least there was a kimono drying on a rod. Lose some, win some. Harry pulled on the kimono as he walked through the house past an astonished maid, into another street of noodle shops and cafés with photos on the wall for choosing licensed women. With the power cut, shops made a murky glow, but Gen was a head taller than the crowd, and Harry picked him out from a block away. Harry turned and saw Hajime pull up to the other corner, and the maid came out of the doorway, looking in all directions. Harry tucked himself into a group around a printer's stall doing a brisk business in maps of the Pacific. Because of the maid, Harry couldn't stand still. With a map spread before his face, he took slow, abstracted steps toward Gen, who seemed content to shepherd Harry rather than chase him. Another group of men gathered around a chess club, everyone suddenly a military tactician. As the maid saw Harry, he ducked into the chess club and took the stairs, climbing over games in progress, and came out on a balcony that was a garden of flowerpots. A small, hairy dog came to life and yapped possessively. Harry stepped onto the one-story roof next door, walked across the tiles to a yet higher adjoining roof and caught his breath. Barking drifted below. With streetlamps dark and houses at half power, the city had the brooding glow of a volcano, not one that was subsiding but one about to blow. Harry crossed the roof and found a fire escape that let him down to a black sidewalk. As the counterweight swung the escape back up and out of reach, he heard the motorcycle coast up the street. The door behind Harry was padlocked, but the sash was old. He levered off the hasp with the knife, slipped inside and realized where he was.

He would have known before, but he didn't usually approach via the roof, without streetlamps or in such a hurry. The building itself was dark because the peep show, the Museum of Curiosities, had been closed by the police on suspicion of frivolity. Closed but not emptied. In the shadows Harry saw familiar forms. The Venus de Milo that was billed as an "exotic nude." A stereopticon with views of belly dancers. Best of all, the freaks. The "mermaid" concocted of a flounder's tail, papier-mâché body and horsehair wig. Siamese twins with the gaping jaws of lantern fish. With paste, paper and imagination, an artist could make anything. Harry's stomach didn't feel good. It felt cold. He sank to a sitting position, pulled off the germ mask and lit a cigarette to give himself a different focus than the pain. Between his kidneys and his stomach, he felt like he'd been run over by a thresher. What was this, Plan D or E? He hadn't flown away on a silver plane, hadn't stopped the war, had no more money. There was an old saying, that if after five minutes in a card game you don't know who the mark is, it's you. Harry admitted he didn't even have a clue what the game was anymore. All he knew was that a creature concocted of fish scales and paper was hardly more patchwork than Harry Niles.

"Harry." Gen stood with a gun at the end of the aisle and motioned Harry up. "Leave the knife."

Hajime arrived by Gen's side. "Maybe he has a gun. I'll look."

Harry said, "Hajime, Hajime, Hajime. Was that your idea to drop the gun on me? Pretty stupid."

" 'Sergeant' to you." Hajime hit him on the side of the face and searched him. To Gen, Hajime reported, "No gun."

"Guns aren't Harry's style. Harry trusts in luck."

Harry spat out blood. "I've always been a lucky man."

Gen smiled sadly, humoring the delusional. "Come on, Harry, it will be like old times."

They left the peep show, Harry in the middle with a gun in his back, and turned not out to the street but up the stairs to a door with a sign that read, by the flame of Gen's cigarette lighter, No ENTRANCE. THIS DOOR IS LOCKED AT ALL TIMES. Gen had the key and led the way into a narrow room of vanity mirrors. Dirty slippers were piled by the door, tatty costumes hung from a rack, and although the Folies had been closed for a year, the changing room was still redolent with stale sweat, body powder and perfume. At that table, Oharu had first turned to the young Harry as he fell through the door. At that chair, Kato reigned as artist-king. Little Chizuko undressed behind that screen. The main difference was that the mirrors had been stripped of lightbulbs, and what had been a space full of color and life was a dusty coffin. No music, either. Music had always stolen up from the show. Harry remembered a burst of fanfare, light shining and dancers flying through the door.

"Decadence," Hajime said.

"Fun," Harry said. "It was the best place on earth."

Gen said, "Long gone. Times have changed. Look at today, a Japanese task force goes undetected halfway across the Pacific and catches the American fleet like a row of ducks. Practically without resistance. Catches American planes parked on the ground and wipes them out. The greatest naval victory in the annals of war." While he talked, Gen led Harry out the other door and down a spiral staircase to a backstage maze of ropes, trapdoors and sandbags. Rays of light from the front probed the painted flats of a barbershop, streetcar, battleship cannons, the palms of a tropical island, the playground of boyhood friends. Harry remembered the skits: the doctor routine, the cannibal scene, the bumblebee. And the chorus line's top hats and kicks. The curtains framed a black abyss of orchestra seats. Ishigami was onstage, busy setting tatami mats in the subdued glow of footlights. A chair with a water pitcher, bowl and head box stood to one side. A belt and sword hung off the chair back. Harry couldn't see past the lights. He wouldn't have minded a full house, the Folies orchestra pumping out "Daisy, Daisy" and the chorus line crossing the stage on bikes. He tried to keep his eyes off the head box. Concentrating on Ishigami didn't necessarily help. From the first day Harry had met him, the colonel had stayed essentially the same, the way a knife becomes more itself, both worn and sharp, by use. Harry missed Michiko. She would have evened the odds more than most. However, it was interesting to watch the interaction of the three men, awe for the colonel, adoration for Gen, acceptance for the loathsome Hajime. Harry was with them and not with them. They were going on, and Harry was definitely staying behind. Gen continued, "Despite the longest odds in history, we did it. The greatest gamble of all time, and we did it." Harry was trying to think of some agreeable response when Gen sent him sprawling over the boards. Harry rolled over to find Gen's gun dug into his cheek. Gen's cap had fallen off, and his hair hung wildly down. "And it was worthless, worse than worthless."

"What do you mean?"

Gen talked through his teeth. "We waited all day at Operations for the reports to come in from the task force, Harry. Now the reports are in. Now we know. The attack on Hawaii had three main targets: the battleships, the aircraft carriers and the oil. Those are the three legs of a navy. We sank the battleships. But the carriers were all out on exercises, we didn't see a one. And the oil, Harry, the planes didn't touch a tank. Instead, our planes went into the valleys looking for your secret tanks. Of course, they didn't see any secret oil tanks because the tanks never existed."

"I told you they didn't."

"You knew a hint would do. We couldn't ignore what you said, Harry. It became an obsession. So, by the time the pilots realized there were no secret tanks of oil, their own fuel was low. They all returned to their carriers. All we needed was a single Zero to strafe the tanks sitting in plain view by the docks, and Pearl Harbor would burn until they didn't have a drop of oil, not a drop in the whole Pacific. Instead, the Americans have their carriers and their oil. All they have to do is move some warships, and we will have achieved nothing. All the planning, the risk, the war for nothing."

Harry looked over at Ishigami.

"It's over," the colonel said. "I could have told them. It will take years, but the war is lost."

They were right, Harry thought. In the long term, Pearl Harbor was a Japanese disaster. They'd needed to grab three brass rings in one go-round of the carousel, and they had missed two.

The bitterness of years poured out of Gen. "I knew all your con games, and I still bit. Fictitious oil tanks. Fraudulent ledgers. What a sucker."

Harry said, "I warned you."

Ishigami placed his cap on the chair and drew his long Bizen sword as Gen pulled Harry up to all fours. Hajime sobbed. It was all going too fast, Harry thought. One minute they were kids rushing up the stairs, and the next they were men crawling onstage in the footlights.

"It was to stop the war," Harry told the colonel. He tried it on Gen. "It was to keep the war from starting."

"I believe you," Ishigami said.

Gen weighted down Harry's back. Suddenly the punctures in his stomach felt like mere pinpricks. Hajime aimed a gun at Harry in case he moved. Ishigami's boots creaked as they took an executioner's stance.

"A thousand yen says you need just one swing," Harry said, because the last thing Harry needed now was two.

"Remember that song 'Amazing Grace'?" Ishigami asked. "That was a good song. Fill your mind with that."

Instead, Harry sensed every hair on his head stand. He rocked to the pumping of his heart, an engine trying to wrest itself off its moorings. His head, his hands, his legs, every organ wanted to divest itself of any association with a target named Harry. He heard the colonel's explosive grunt and the furious whisper of the blade and sudden impact.

Harry opened his eyes to find his head still on his shoulders. Gen's wasn't. It had rolled almost off the apron of the stage. His body, in its long leather coat and gloves, poured blood that drained, with the rake of the stage, into the pit. Ishigami flicked blood from the blade, retrieved the head and delicately washed it in the bowl. Harry couldn't find at first the proper word for Gen's expression. Melancholy, perhaps. A son of Asakusa born with nothing but beauty, a poor boy who had to bet his all, time and again, to advance, a prey for wrong companions. Ishigami closed Gen's eyes, smoothed his hair and toweled his face, kissed his cheek and set him in the head box.

"Why him?" Harry asked.

"After such an error in judgment? Such dishonor? An officer has no choice."

"People think it was a great victory."

"People will learn otherwise. Who could live with that?"

Ishigami wiped his sword until the blade showed its distinctive swirling line of black and white. Hajime dropped to his knees and removed his cap. Vile little Hajime closed his eyes.

"Wait!" Harry said.

Ishigami raised his sword, took three sideways steps and sliced off Hajime's head. Hajime's eyeglasses shot into the orchestra pit while his body slumped, one arm cradling his head, the gun loose.

"Jesus," Harry said.

The colonel flicked the sword, spraying the floor. This was a new medium of art, Harry thought; there was blood everywhere. He didn't dare move.

"Credit where credit is due," Ishigami said.

"I'm not a spy."

"You're not a spy, you're only Harry Niles, and that is dangerous enough. Oil? That's your weapon."

"A lot of modern things run on oil. Gasoline, lubricants, aviator fuel."

"Please, you remind me of your commercial poetry. Burma Shave."

"Exactly."

"See, you are never what you seem to be. I remember the first time I met you, you were just a boy. I thought you were like a trained monkey. At Nanking, years later, I took you for a profiteer, a cheat. You cheated me of five heads. Six, actually."

Including the aide-de-camp, Harry thought. He said nothing. A conversation with Ishigami was like sharing a high wire with a lunatic; the slightest misstep would be fatal.

"It wasn't until the willow house that I began to see what you really were. Now I am put in mind of the 'Forty-seven Ronin,' the samurai who hid behind a mask of gambling and drink. That's what you are, a true ronin. That's the secret."

"What secret?"

"I told you at the willow house what my mother said about telling a secret to a seashell?"

"And then crushing it?" Harry could picture the young illegitimate Ishigami standing on a beach, getting this wisdom from a woman who could never name the man she slept with. For some reason, Harry also thought of his father at the stern of the ship that carried the Niles family back to the States. His father had found the *Fifty Views of Fuji*, the damning evidence Kato had sketched of Harry's life on the streets of Asakusa, the pilfering, brawling, utter joy. Roger Niles balled up each page and threw them to the gulls that dipped and tilted in the breeze behind the ship.

"Yes. You're not what I expected, Harry."

"Who is?" Well, Harry thought, he could be killed on the floor or on his feet, so he got up. "Now we're done?"

"Almost."

Ishigami gave the sword a final brief inspection before handing it to Harry by its grip of braided leather. The blade trembled in an unfamiliar hand. The colonel sank to his knees. It was like watching a statue climb down from its pedestal.

"Oh, no," Harry said.

"Do me the honor. It would be shameful if I didn't follow my own men." Ishigami unbuttoned the top of his tunic and rolled the collar back, unveiling the contrast between his brown neck and broad white shoulders. "Seppuku is too honorable an end for such failure. Sometimes the sword is more sincere."

"You'd rather lose your head than lose face? What about the war?"

"As a soldier, I never expected to live out the war. The war is over." Ishigami dismissed it like an episode in history already passed. He clasped his hands behind his back and lowered his head, scalp shining through the stubble. "It is less dishonor to be beheaded by a friend. You are the one gaijin who understands."

"Well, the war is young." Harry considered the outstretched neck. "Sorry, I won't do it."

"You'd be doing me a favor."

"I know, but I have to go with the numbers. Three men, their heads lopped off, indicates the help of a fourth. Two men beheaded and a third a suicide by gunshot, that's a believable parlay."

"Harry Niles is still Harry Niles."

"That's right."

"That's your only reason?"

"Part of the reason."

Ishigami raised his head and fixed not on Harry but on the sword a gaze of disappointment. As if a cup of sake had been whisked away.

"Go ahead." Harry picked up Hajime's gun and gave it to Ishigami, who turned the Nambu over and over in his hands, the thought process in action. His eyes reached out for Harry's.

"You owe me five heads."

"And I always will."

Ishigami's hands seemed to make up his mind. He pressed the muzzle to his chest and fired. He swayed, managed a second pull on the trigger and folded over. The sound of the shots rang around the theater, followed by a resonant stillness.

WHEN HARRY STUMBLED OUT, dazed, slightly deafened, he discovered no one could have heard the gun. The street was a rally swept by the contagion of enthusiasm, songs and cheers and the rattle of firecrackers. He had his germ mask on and, except for dried blood on his pants cuffs, looked like any other reveler. The crush was overwhelming and good-natured, faces red from celebration, silk kimonos rubbing against sufu uniforms. The idea of a wartime blackout added novelty, and the lack of streetlamps made the carbide lights of the stalls and the red lanterns of pubs more intense against the dark.

Harry knew that Shozo and Go would pick him up. But as part of the general sweep of gaijin or something more particular? He bet the police would not investigate much. No one wanted to hear at the beginning of a long, arduous war that it was already lost. Knowing what he knew, he almost felt that he stood in a street of ghosts. Faces loomed and bobbed. Bodies pressed against him with a certain insubstantiality, voices hollow as echoes.

Then his hearing cleared and the clamor of the street was overwhelming—the martial delirium of a loudspeaker, the chatter of clogs running after a cascade of lanterns—and in one step Harry was swept along by the bright, irresistible stream.

Martin Cruz Smith is the author of such novels as *Gorky Park*, *Red Square*, *Havana Bay*, and *Rose*. He has won two Hammett Awards and a Golden Dagger Award for his writing. He lives with his family in California.